Other Sean Michael Novels

The Jarheads Series:
Don't Ask, Don't Tell
Personal Leave
Three Day Passes
Tempering
Out of the Closet
On the Sand

Going for the Gold
Making a Splash: A Going for the Gold Novel
Perfect Ten: A Going for the Gold Novel
Personal Best I: A Going for the Gold Novel
Personal Best II: A Going for the Gold Novel

Contemporary
Amnesia • Between Friends
The Broken Road • Catching a Second Wind
Secrets, Skin and Leather
Tripwire • Two Beginnings

Fantasy and Paranormal
Bite • Caged • Chosen • Fantasy's Hand
Need • A Private Hunger
Velvet Glove, Volume I
Where Flows the Water • Windbrothers

Anthologies
Bus Stories and Other Tales
Cowboy Up edited by Rob Knight
Galleons & Gangplanks, editor Rob Knight
Shifting, Volumes I-III, edited by Rob Knight
Torqued Tales, edited by SA Clements

Available at Torquere Press & fine booksellers

On the Sand
By Sean Michael

Torquere Press, Inc.
romance for the rest of us
www.torquerepress.com

This is a work of fiction. Names, characters, places, and incidents either are the product of the author's imagination or are used fictitiously. Any resemblance to actual events, locales, organizations, or persons, living or dead, is entirely coincidental and beyond the intent of either the author or the publisher.

On the Sand
TOP SHELF
An imprint of Torquere Press Publishers
PO Box 2545
Round Rock, TX 78680
Copyright 2007 © by Sean Michael
Cover illustration by A. Squires
Published with permission
ISBN: 978-1-60370-217-1, 1-60370-217-2
www.torquerepress.com

First Torquere Press Printing: December 2007
Printed in the USA

Chapter One

Sun.

Surf.

His rock.

The only thing that would make it better would be another cold beer, but Rig wasn't in the mood to move. Nope. He was in full basking-lizard mode. Well, trying to be. If the wind didn't blow he could forget it was just an incredibly warm day.

He let one foot dangle down into the water, the touch cool and comfortable, almost chilly.

Yep. He was a lucky motherfucking redneck.

A shadow blocked the sun, and something wet and warm slid along his exposed collarbone. "Mmm... sweaty cowboy. My favorite kind."

"Mmm. Blue." His own growly stud, right there. Life was good.

"I've got a thing or two for you." Rock's tongue slid up along his neck, circled the skin just below his ear.

"I. Uh. What?" He got a little side-tracked. Well, more than a little.

"They're kind of the same shape. Both hard. One's hot, the other's cold." Rock nipped his earlobe.

"Hard." Rig liked hard. He tilted his head, encouraging his big, studly ex-marine to keep going.

Those warm lips slid down his neck again and along his shoulder, tongue licking, wetting his skin. "Both hard. Here's the cold one." The bottom end of a beer bottle landed on an exposed strip of his belly, making him jump.

"Fuck!" He hooted, grabbing for the longneck. Oh, fuck yes. Beer.

Beer. Beer. Beer.

Laughing, Rock slid a hand along his hip. "Drink it up and I'll give you the other one."

"Mmm. You're good to me, Blue. Y'all have a good workout?" Rock and Dick had gone out after lunch to do... something at the gym.

Rock grinned. "I showed the kid a thing or two, yeah."

One finger slid under his shirt, up over his nipple, all the way over to his other one, and flicked the little gold ring in it. Every Goddamn nerve in his body went tingly, Rig's cock filling right up, unmistakable, undeniable. And from the shit-eating grin on his Blue's face, Rock knew it. The ring was flicked again, and then Rock's fingers trailed down along his belly.

"Mmm. You're wanting." His cock tried to reach that square, callused hand, just needing the touch. Needing something, even after all this time.

Rock's fingers stilled, staying at a level with his navel, torturing him. "Always. I'm not the only one, either."

Just listen to that husky growl.

"Never the only one." His hips rolled a little, trying to get his prick closer.

"You're supposed to finish up your beer." Rock might have been teasing, but those eyes were eating him up where he lay.

"Uh-huh." Beer. Right. He liked beer.

The cold bottle was taken out of his hand and plonked down somewhere above his head, Rock's grin growing feral as he was grabbed up, carried up to the house, to their little sun-drenched porch, Rock stripping his clothes off.

"Hey." Oh. Good. Time to get serious.

His only reply was a grunt, Rock's mouth closing over his about the same time that big hand wrapped around his prick, just like that.

Blue! He groaned into the kiss, Rock's touch familiar and welcome and right as rain.

His cheek was cupped, Rock tilting his face all the better to devour him, to fill him with the taste of his lover. Rig dove right into it, the kiss just making the day all that much better, that much more perfect. The hand around his prick worked him slowly, Rock not trying to get him off yet, just revving things up, warming him up hotter inside than the sun was warming him outside. Rig let his legs sprawl, hips rocking a bit. God, this was something.

Rock broke their kiss long enough to growl at him. "Take my shorts off, Rig."

"Uh-huh." That was really Dick's job.

Really.

Rock's fingers slid away from his cock.

"Rock." He worked the fly of Rock's shorts open, even as he protested the loss of Rock's touch.

"Just trying to help you get your focus where it needs to be." Rock helped, pushing the offending shorts down as soon as they were undone.

Right. Like his focus was supposed to be anywhere else but... Mmm. Rock was hard, smelled so good.

Preening for a moment, Rock soon settled between his legs and slowly lowered that hard body down onto his. "You like what you see? How about what you feel?"

"Blue, there hasn't been a single solitary fucking day I haven't admired your ass. You and Dick - y'all are the finest men on Earth." No bullshit.

"You know it." He got a happy grin, a hot grin, as Rock rolled their hips together, that thick cock sliding, as fine as you please, along his own.

"Rock..." Fuck, that was still hot. Still. So many fucking years and it was *still* hot. Those too blue to be true eyes started into his, full of heat and want and everything he could ever ask for.

Rig arched up, tongue licking at Rock's lips, eyes caught, sure as shit. Lips parting with a moan, Rock continued to move slowly against him, just enough to keep the heat intense between them. The kiss went deeper and Rig just poured himself into it, not worrying about a single fucking thing but that man, that heat. That pleasure. Rock's weight lowered slowly onto him, those strong muscles keeping Rock from crushing him, and their legs tangled together as they moved a little faster, their cocks rubbing and bumping.

Fuck, this was. Perfect. Fucking amazing. Just what he needed.

"Want you," muttered Rock, hips pulling back, and when they pushed forward again, Rock's cock bumped against his balls and pushed beyond them to slide over his skin.

"Yours." Balls to bones. Every fucking inch of him.

Rock slid two fingers along his lips, and then slid them in between, fucking his mouth with them. "All mine."

He nodded, sucking and licked, humming around those fingers. All Rock's.

"And mine," piped up a voice from above, Dick suddenly there, blocking out the sun, grinning down at them. The kid was almost Rock's size these days, muscled and broad-shouldered.

Rock's rumble made him pull harder, eyes rolling a little as his hips jerked.

"Mmmm... you guys look fucking good. You look good fucking, too." Dick crouched down next to them, fingers sliding over his chest, Rock's. "I brought beer. And lube."

Oh. Oh, smart boy. Lube. Beer. Sex. Uhn.

"Good job. You can slick Rig up while he sucks on my fingers."

Dick laughed and leaned in, mouth meeting Rock's in a kiss that Rig swore steamed. He fucking loved watching his men – his. The way their lips moved, the way Dick just melted, sweet as pie.

Rig nipped Rock's fingertips, wanting his part of that passion, that kiss.

Their lips parted, Rock chuckling. "Someone's wanting."

"Well that's what we're here for, yeah?" Dick grinned and bent to kiss him, tongue dipping into his mouth for a moment, licking his tongue and Rock's fingers together.

That got him to chuckling, teasing Rock and Dick both, so fucking happy inside that it damn near hurt.

Rock's legs spread his, and Dick's fingers teased behind his balls, slick and wet.

His head fell back, throat working a little. "Y'all... y'all are good at that."

"Lots of practice," murmured Rock, nipping at his collarbone.

Dick's fingers pushed into him, two spreading him open.

"Years..." More. Fuck. More. That was fucking sweet.

"Yep." Rock chuckled. "We can't give up now, have to keep practicing."

"Uh-huh." Dick pushed another finger into him, opening him wide.

"Pretty." His knees spread wider, heart pounding in his chest. "Fuck. Fuck."

"Shit, just look at you." Rock shifted and Dick bent, mouthing his balls. It was the easiest thing ever, to just let himself over to his men, just like he always had, always would, God willing.

For a moment Dick pushed his little finger in with the others, and then the warm fingers were gone, Rock settling between his legs again and holding his eyes as the thick head pushed against him.

"Rock." He bore down and Rock pressed in, filling him, just like he needed.

Dick lay down next to them, cock hard and leaking where it pressed up against his upper thigh. His Pretty's fingers slid over his chest, over Rock's touching as Dick laid one kiss after another on him and Rock.

A low, happy hum pulled up from Rock's belly, the muscled body moving over him once again.

It took a second for his brain and his fingers to communicate, but he managed to get his fingers wrapped around Dick's long cock, jacking it in time with the thrusts of Rock's prick inside him. Dick's gasp was sweet and Rock nodded.

"That's it, Rabbit, bring us all together." That low voice growled over him.

"Yeah." Rock's voice made him goosepimple up, body gripping that heavy cock and squeezing tight. A shudder moved through Rock, his Blue moving faster, letting him really feel it.

The sun beat down on them as they all moved together, worked as one. That was his job. Loving his men. His fucking family. "Blue. Soon."

Like it was the cue Rock had been waiting for he sped up, thrusting harder.

It was Dick's hand, though, that slid between him and Rock, wrapping around his prick and tugging as Rock hit his gland over and over.

Oh. Oh, shit. Oh, fuck yeah. Just. Just right. "Fuck!"

He shot hard, ass digging into the sand. Rock kept pushing into him, Dick's hand still moving on him, his men making his orgasm last and last.

"My men." He blinked up, begging a kiss. Rock's mouth closed over his, filling him with his Blue's cry as the thick cock inside him jerked and filled him with the heat of Rock's spunk.

Dick's cock continued to slide through his hand, his Pretty's gasps loud. His thumb rubbed across the tip of Dick's cock, pushing hard, demanding Dick's orgasm.

"Rig!" Dick cried out, cock throbbing in his hand and spraying come over his hand and thigh.

"Mmm." Yeah. Yeah, that's what he needed. Just that.

"Uh-huh." Dick nuzzled into his neck, breath hot as it brushed against him. Rock gave him one last kiss before sliding out and rolling next to lie next to him.

"Did someone say there was more beer?" Rock asked, low voice rumbling with satisfaction.

Dick passed a bottle over.

Oh, fuck he was happy. Bone deep. Maybe deeper.

Chapter Two

Dick loved lying on the beach. He loved the sound of the waves and the feeling of the sun against his skin. He loved having the pups lying around him, Lucy licking his fingers now and then, begging a scratch, which he always gave her.

Of course that usually got Mutt and Trouble going and he'd have to give them all a good loving before they let him settle again.

That was okay though -- it kept him from falling asleep.

He loved lying on the beach, but even more than that he loved spending time with Rock and Rig, so he didn't want to fall asleep waiting for them to get home.

He couldn't have slept through their homecoming -- he wasn't sure what was up, but Rigger was laughing and squeaking, the sounds of running loud in the house. "Dick! Pretty! Help!"

Rig burst out the back door, shirt collar ripped, laughing, eyes dancing. "Hey kid. How're you? Gotta hustle..."

Laughing he leapt up and managed to grab Rig around the waist, both of them nearly going down as the dogs ran excitedly around their legs. He wasn't sure what was up, but he knew he wanted to be a part of it. Rock came barreling out the door, slowing as he saw Rig was caught.

"Oh, shit. Pretty. Lemme go. Come on. Please." Rig tugged, hard as hell against his hip, eyes dancing. "I haven't done a damned thing to you."

"I know -- care to change that?"

"Oh, cheating..." Rig kept moving, keeping him between Rock and his cowboy. "What do you want? It's yours."

He laughed, feeling Rig up. "Why're you running?"

"Well..." Grey eyes flashed at Rock. "Let's just say it involves ice cubes and open flies..."

His jaw dropped as Rock growled. And then he started to laugh. "Was he sleeping?"

"He was *supposed* to be keeping me company on the ride home from the store."

His laugh turned into a yelp as Rock goosed him.

"See? Grumpy! Don't let him get me!" Rigger was laughing hard enough that he couldn't quite catch his breath.

Rock's arms slid around him and Rig, catching him between their bodies. Oh fuck, he loved them, loved the way they felt, the way they smelled, the way they moved and the happy noises Rig was making. He leaned against Rock's strength, both of them holding Rig up.

Those grey eyes shone up at them. "Sexy bastards."

"Prick freezer," accused Rock, making Dick laugh again.

"I don't know, Rock. If it's this big frozen, it's going to be unbelievable hot and hard."

"I got somewhere you can warm it, you old fart." Rig winked at Rock, hands moved to stroke Rock's cheek.

"Who are you calling old?" growled Rock.

"Well... Dick's just a baby..." Oh, Rig was baiting the bear.

Suddenly right between them didn't seem like quite the right place to be. He began to slowly extricate himself.

"Uh-uh. You wanted to play, Pretty."

"That was before I realized you were suicidal."

Rigger grinned, eyes dancing. "No, just playing with my old man."

"There's that word again." Rock's arms tightened, squeezing them both and then lifting them up off the ground.

"Shit! Blue! Be careful!" Rig gasped, shooting Rock a look. "You'll strain something."

"Oh, now I'm old and infirm am I?" Rock dropped them back to the ground and let them go, heading back inside.

Dick sighed and gave Rig a quick kiss.

Rig flushed dark and backed away from him. "I didn't mean to piss you off, Rock. I'm sorry."

Rock didn't turn around, but he did stop. "A man likes to think he still has a little something to impress his lovers with."

Rig snorted. "Oh, come on, Blue. You've had me hunting your ass for twenty years. There's never been a single little thing about you." A soft, sad little sigh sounded. "I was just picking at you, Rocketman. I should learn when to just shut the fuck up. I'm sorry." He got a smile and then Rig headed around the side of the house. "I'm going to get the stuff from the truck and start supper."

He was torn between going to help Rig and staying with Rock.

Used to be an easy decision, but these days Rock was a little more sensitive than he used to be, especially about the age thing.

"If we go in the back way we can have supper started before he brings the first bag in." Rock grunted, but headed in and started banging pots around.

Their cowboy was quiet-quiet when he came in, unloading the bags, helping with the food, setting the table, feeding the dogs. Dick shook his head and smiled, waiting for the inevitable 'oh, I fucked up' move into that cave Rig called an office.

Before he could make it Rock grabbed Rig around the waist and pulled him close. "I can still bench press your skinny ass."

"Yeah." Rig pushed close, face hidden in Rock's throat, arms wrapping around for a hug.

"Dinner can wait, kid," Rock growled. "I'm gonna show you both the Rocketman isn't that old yet."

He nodded, happily turning off the stove and following Rock, who'd hoisted Rig and was headed down to the bedroom.

Rigger was holding on, lips at Rock's ear, whispering low and soft. Looked like things were pretty much back to normal.

Rock dropped Rig on the bed, making Rig bounce. Yep. Normal.

Rig pulled off his t-shirt and reached up for Rock. "'mere. I want."

Dick went over and slid Rock's t-shirt off and then pulled down his jeans, stripping the man for Rig. Rock sure didn't look old. Those grey eyes trailed over Rock's body, Rig biting his bottom and moaning low. Rig sure didn't look at Rock like the big guy was old. He took his own t-shirt off and undid his jeans, settling in the chair by the bed.

He spread his legs and slid his hand along his belly and into his jeans as Rock climbed onto the bed and took Rig's mouth hard. Rig's body disappeared beneath Rock, except for those long arms holding Rock's head.

Rock was moving against Rig, that beautiful ass going up and down, making his cock twitch and porno noises come from his mouth. One leg came up, wrapped around Rock's hip, Rig curling around the big guy. The motions gained a rhythm then, his lovers rocking together.

"Oh... 's good, Blue. Need you." Rig's voice filled the room, husky and low and sweet.

Dick wrapped his hand around his prick as Rock reached up for the lube. They shifted on the bed, giving him a perfect view as two of Rock's slick fingers slid right into Rig's ass. Rig took Rock's fingers in eagerly, riding them with a sure, needy motion. His own hips started to imitate that motion, his moans and groans marking time.

Whatever worry Rock had about getting old couldn't possibly hold up to the way Rigger watched the big man move, the way Rigger begged and needed and offered Rock everything. Rick didn't tease, didn't draw it out, he just slid right in, filling Rig up.

"Oh... fuck, yes." Rig arched, lips open and gasping like it was the first time ever.

Dick moaned, pulling at his cock, not sure he'd be able to just keep watching. Another series of low moans filled the air, then Rig's hand reached out for him, fingers open, searching. He slid out of the chair and took Rig's hand sucking on each finger.

"Pretty... Blue... Oh, fuck. So close." The words were sweet, fucking sweet and wild and thrown into the air as Rig shook. He reached over and wrapped his hand around Rig's prick, thumb sliding across the tip. He wasn't sure whether Rig's cry or the splash of spunk on his fingers came first. Somehow he figured it really didn't matter.

He kissed Rig's palm, smiling as Rock's roar sounded, heralding the big guy's orgasm. Rig's fingers stroked his face, his jaw -- just loving on him, touching him.

"You needing, kid?" Rock asked. He shook his head, hand working his prick, letting the sight of the, the smell of them, Rig's soft touches, push him over.

Rig's hand cupped his jaw, drawing him up onto the bed and into their kiss, into their arms. This is what he'd been waiting for. Lying out on the beach had nothing on lying here with Rig and Rock.

Chapter Three

Rock walked into the kitchen, grumbling as he grabbed a beer, slamming the fridge door closed. "Is that stew?"

Dick nodded, biting back his grin.

"There better not be any fancy vegetables in it."

"Just beef and potatoes and carrots -- just like you like it."

Rock harrumphed and started grumbling again as he left the kitchen. Dick shook his head, let out his grin, though it faded into a sigh. He checked the clock again and went back to scrubbing the counter. Rig was due home any second after a week at a conference on health care in L.A.

Rock took out his frustration at having to wait a moment longer by growling and grumping. He was trying to make time pass faster by scrubbing everything in sight. Besides, the first thing he wanted Rig to do when the man walked through the front door was him and Rock, not the cleaning.

He could hear Rock cursing out the TV as he dumped the dirty water and stored his bucket. Damn, but Rig better show up soon. He washed his hands and grabbed himself a beer of his own, going quietly to the front room to see if it was safe to sit and pretend to watch the television with Rock. Rock was finally settled, pouting at a game of beach volleyball. Dick settled on the other end of the couch without a word, knowing that the only thing that was going to improve Rock's mood was Rig. A week was just too dammed long and next time he was going to insist the gym could do without them and they could go along.

The pups heard Rig's truck pull into the drive before he did, the happy barks one of the most welcome sounds he'd heard all week.

"Well, aren't y'all a sight? Are my men in there? Huh?" Rig's lazy, easy drawl floated in, warm and familiar and sexy and theirs.

He and Rock were up and out of their chairs, no attempts at casual or letting the man in. If Rig didn't have splinters before the next ten minutes were over, it would only be because they weren't going to let him get his clothes off. Rock grabbed Rig and hauled him up against the big, muscled body, mouth diving for a kiss as Dick closed the front door. Then he was pushing in for a share.

Hands wrapped around his head, Rig open and panting for it, just sort of melting between them and rubbing against them with that long skinny body. That whimper came from Rock, but there was a matching one in his own throat.

Rock's arms wrapped around him and Rig, shifting them so that he was behind Rig, all three of them writhing together. He was harder than stone himself, and he figured Rock and Rig had to be, too. It had just been too long since their bodies had been pressed together, too long since their kisses tasted just right. Rig's hips were moving, ratcheting the heat between them higher and hotter. The little gasps and happy moans made him hard as hell; and the smell? Stetson and laundry soap and coffee and something sweet and hot and pure Rig...

"Oh fuck." He whimpered, Rock's hands hot on his ass keeping him moving against Rig's ass. He cried out, shooting hard, filling his jeans like he was eighteen all over again.

Rig pushed a groan into Rock's mouth that was harsh and hungry, pure raw need. He fell to his knees, pushing between them. As soon as Rock realized what he was doing, he was given a bit more room, a very little bit. He got Rock's jeans undone and Rig's pants and grabbed both of their pricks in his hand, bringing the heads to his mouth.

The flavor was pure bliss.

"Pretty! Blue! Oh, please..." Rig's body rippled against him, hips jerking.

He hummed, happy and feeling good and just opened his mouth wide, taking both cocks in and sucking hard. Rig prick slid along Rock's only a few times, before hot, salty spunk sprayed over his tongue, Rig's cry echoing through the house. Fuck, it felt good, that sound, the taste, the way Rock's hips jerked a few more times before he was swallowing again, the way Rock's spunk tasted different when it followed Rig's. He moaned, taking his time to lick them both clean.

"Hey Blue-Eyes. I missed y'all something fierce." The words were husky, whispered and then Rock's mouth was taken in a long, deep kiss.

Rock made another sound that was suspiciously whimper-like and just took the kiss, hand tilting Rig's head. Fuck, they were beautiful together. Always had been. Rock's fingers tangled in Rig's white curls, the look on Rig's face simple and honest and happy.

He nuzzled their groins, the smells as familiar as anything in his life.

The kiss showed no signs of stopping so he started stripping them, working off their pants and underwear and then worked t-shirt and dress shirt open and up and off, hands running over all that glorious skin.

One of Rig's hands slid around his waist, fingers playing the bundle of nerves at his lower back, drawing little patterns and keeping him close. Shivers went up and down his spine and he got himself as naked as they were. "Bed. While we can still all walk and before we're too desperate for more than humping against the wall."

"He's a sharp one, our Dick." The words were whispered against Rock's lips, Rig grinning and happy.

"Except for the having to stop kissing you while we move thing, yeah, he's got it all figured out."

Dick laughed, grabbed their arms and started tugging. "I'm just thinking of your back, Rock."

They made it down the hall in slow stages, leaving time for a long kiss here, a grope there, accentuated with rubbing and snuggling and moaning. By the time they reached the bedroom, they were all hard again.

"Want you to fuck me," Dick told Rig. "While Rock does you."

"Fuck, yes." Rig turned, took his face in those warm, long-fingers hands. "Missed you."

Then he got one of those kisses, Rig leading him to the bed, wanting him. The kiss never broke as they lay down together, him on his back, Rig long and hard against him. There was the sound of the lube snapping open, but it wasn't fingers that pushed against his hole, just the slick, wet tip of Rig's cock sliding in, letting him feel every inch. He moaned and whimpered, spreading his legs, offering himself to his lover.

Rock's hands were hot, sliding slickly over his skin, grabbing his prick and pumping, tweaking his and then Rig's nipples. Rig's head was thrown back, kiss-swollen lips parted. "So fucking sweet..."

He nodded, groaning as Rig's prick settled in deep.

"You're fucking Dick," Rock growled. "And I'm fucking you."

He could see Rock settling behind Rig, knew that fat cock was filling Rig up.

"Oh Pretty... Oh, my Blue..." Hungry and happy -- that cry echoed, gelling between his own moans and Rock's rumble.

"Fuck... oh fuck, move, please." He was begging, hands sliding over Rig's skin, moving back to touch Rock, to wrap around his back and tug.

Rock rumbled again and then moved, setting the rhythm for Rig's movements as well. Rigger leaned forward, kissing hard enough their teeth clicked, want overtaking skill, even after so many years. He lifted his legs up, hooking his heels around Rock's hips. One hand played with Rig's nipple, the other found the ring in Rock's.

Rigger's hand wrapped around his cock, tugging in time with their thrusts, thumb sliding over the slit again and again. "Oh fuck... fuck. Good."

He was practically incoherent, body moving, sensation just flooding him.

Rig's head rested on his shoulder, mouth open and gasping against his skin. "Needed you. So bad. Needed you both."

"Never letting you go without us again," growled Rock, moving faster and harder, making the three of them slam together noisily. He just nodded and came, pleasure sweet and sharp, overwhelming.

Teeth fastened on his shoulder -- not enough to hurt, but enough to mark, enough that he felt it -- as Rigger keened, skinny body convulsing as he was filled with heat. It was more than enough to tip him over and he could see Rock's eyes go dark with pleasure as the big guy roared.

Dick hadn't come so hard in at least a week.

Rig collapsed against him, humming softly, snuggling, arms wrapped around him. "Oh, God. So good."

"Mmmhmm. Missed you," he murmured, stroking Rig's back.

Rock shifted, lying half on half next to Rig.

"Uh-huh." Rig blinked up, eyes dark and shadowed, tired. "'s good to be home."

He nodded and gave Rig a soft kiss as Rock settled a quilt over the three of them, pushing up close behind Rig. "Nap time."

"I need to unload the truck and..." Rig's eyes were closed and the words trailed off, turning to soft purrs and snores as Rock stroked and petting.

"Later," he whispered, placing another kiss on Rig's forehead.

"Much later," growled Rock softly.

Yeah. Like maybe next week sometime.

Chapter Four

"Are you lonesome, tonight, do you miss me tonight." Rock sang along with the radio, barely aware he was doing it until Dick chuckled.

"What?" he asked, growling as he chopped cherry tomatoes into little pieces. And why the fuck they weren't small enough as they were he didn't know, except that Rig liked them all to help out with supper and this gave him something to do without being in the way. He had to admit, he liked it when they were together, even if they were cooking. Well, except when the kid got that shit eating grin of his.

"I just didn't think you liked country music."

"Elvis Presley is not country music."

"We're listening to Y105 Country, so I'd say yes, he is."

"Hey I was alive while the man was still performing -- not fucking country."

Dick just gave him a look and then turned to Rig. "Well?"

Rig looked over at Dick, flour smeared over one cheek. "Elvis is just Elvis, kid, and I like hearing Rock sing, so let it be."

"You hear that kid, he likes it when I sing?"

Dick grinned at him again and came close, sliding up against his hip. He got a soft kiss. "I never said I didn't like it."

Then Dick went back to what he was doing and he picked the song back up as he started in on the tomatoes again. They'd never done anything to him. Well, except he was expected to eat them. He chopped them a little finer.

He stopped singing, knife poised over the cutting board.

"Shit, this is a depressing song. Fucking kid was right -- it's country."

Rig gave him a look. "My kitchen, my radio station."

He raised an eyebrow, hand going out to hit autosearch for the next station up.

Rig reached out and popped his knuckles with the spatula. "Don't make me beat you, Rocketman."

He snorted, attention turning to Rig. "You and what army?"

"Don't need an army, you Neaderthal. I'll just make the kid hold you down."

"Oh, it's like that is it?" He put down his knife, wiping his hands on his jeans. Fuck, he was hard and his skinny-assed Texan was asking for a piece of him.

Rig nodded as he pulled the pork chops out of the skillet and onto a big plate, turning off the oven. "You don't fuck with a man's radio station, you know?"

"And what exactly do you fuck with?" He stalked slowly toward Rig, ready to pounce, waiting for exactly the right moment. Fuck, it had been too long since they played like this.

Rig moved away from the stove, steadfastly ignoring him as he dug some potatoes from the bin and headed toward the sink. "I'd think you'd have figured that out by now, Rock."

Teasing and lazy, that drawl didn't have even a hint of edge.

"Oh, I've got it figured out, Rig. I'm just trying to decide whether or not to show mercy to that sweet ass of yours. Bed or couch are a lot softer than the kitchen floor."

He could see Dick out of the corner of his eye, fucking kid was already naked and just waiting for them to sort out exactly when and where.

"I'm *cooking*, Rock." Rig dropped the potatoes in the sink, muscles tensed, ready to bolt.

One more step and he reached out, hand wrapping around Rig's arm, pulling that lean body around and up tight against his own, mouth covering Rig's before the sweet son of a bitch could even take a breath. Rig's hips were cradled in close and, oh, yeah, his favorite slut was hard for him, cock hot enough to feel through both layers of clothes. Dick moaned and he looked over. The kid was watching them, legs spread, back against the counter, hand sliding up and down that long cock. He nudged Rig to look.

The grey eyes slid down the kid's body, hips jerking against him when Rig hit that long fucking prick. Rig's moan was sweet as all fuck.

"Yeah," he said softly, agreeing. He slid his hands under Rig's t-shirt, pulling it up and off, hands going immediately to the button and zipper of the tight jeans. "The kid wants you. I want you. All you gotta do is tell us what you want, aside from the fucking country music station blaring depressing as shit music at us while we fuck ourselves blind."

"You're not changing the station, Rock." Rig's hands were busy on his clothes, that mouth licking and sucking along his jawline.

"No, I'm not. Dick is."

"He touches that fucking radio, I'll kick his ass, too." Rig was nibbling on his ear now, breath hot and teasing.

"Is that a promise or a threat, cowboy?"

Not that Dick was in any fit shape to change anything -- the kid was well on his way, eyes hot on them, hand working his prick like it was his last time ever.

"'s a threat, Yankee. You forgot what they sounded like?" Rig's hand wrapped around his cock, fingers sliding and teasing, thumb working the nerves right below the head. Oh, Rig wasn't playing fair now -- the only way he could cheat harder was if he dropped to his knees. Before Rig had a chance to do just that, he grabbed Rig's ring between his fingers and tugged.

The good old boy gave a groaning squeak, teeth nipping his earlobe hard. Fuck, but the shudders that rocked that long body were sweet. "Cheating, Blue."

"You started it."

"Fuck!" Dick shouted out and the scent of sex filled the room.

Groaning, he tugged at Rig's ring again.

"Nope. You did. Singing -- love hearing you." Rig's voice was desperate, cock sliding against his hip. Those smart, long fingers were working him hard, just right, just where he liked it.

Rock chuckled and sang low and soft into Rig's ear, whispering for his favorite slut. His Rabbit groaned, melted against him, so fucking easy. It didn't take but another tug to the ring, one hand cupping the tight, little ass before Rig's hand tightened, spunk spraying between them. He repeated the last line of the song, mouth fastening to Rig's as he came, shooting over Rig's hand and belly.

Rig kissed him until his head was swimming, fingers and lips pulling out every fucking wave of pleasure, one after another. He wrapped his arms around Rig, holding him close, rubbing their come-slick bodies together. Another sound pushed into his mouth, one of Rig's arms wrapping around his neck, the other held out for the kid.

Dick's joined them, grinning happily. "You sure you don't want me to finish those potatoes, Rig?"

"Potatoes?" Rig's eyes were stoned, hand sliding down to cup Dick's ass.

Rock chuckled and slid one arm around the kid, keeping the other one locked around Rig. "Forget the fucking potatoes, kid -- we'll order a pizza. Later."

"Mm... much later." Rig pulled Dick into their kiss, lips parted and hungry for something that had nothing to do with cooking or kitchens.

He opened his mouth wide, taking the flavor of them both into him. Yeah, who needed food when you had this?

Rig and Dick took his mouth, single-minded and fuck! Were there two better mouths anywhere? He started to walk backward, with the general idea that they'd be more comfortable in a room with a bed rather than one with knives and forks and other pointy objects.

His lovers followed him without complaint, Rig plastered to his stomach, Dick rubbing against his side. He bumped into the side of the door, but not hard enough to make him break the kiss and kept going down the hall. The living room was closer but the bed was more comfortable. Rig's hand curled behind his head, kept it from hitting the picture on the wall. Dick maneuvered them around the little bookcase. All three of their hands reached for the knob on the bedroom door.

He chuckled into their kiss. "My bedroom. My radio station," he murmured, looking into Rig's eyes.

Rig grinned and nodded, eyes twinkling. "I can handle that, Blue."

Dick just laughed, opening the door and pushing them all through. "Fuck the radio; let's get naked!"

Rock looked at Rig and laughed, landing a smack on the kid's ass. "We already are naked, genius."

"This is why we don't give him a radio station of his own. Poor kid can't even remember if he's dressed or not." Rig was laughing, leaning forward to nuzzle Dick's cheek.

Dick tried to look annoyed, but it wasn't easy with Rig loving on him. "It was figurative."

"Whoa, give the kid a college course or two and he thinks he's Einstein."

"Nope. I'm betting Einstein wasn't hung so well." Rig slid down to his knees, bringing his and the kid's hips closer together. "If he had been, he wouldn't have thought so Goddamned much."

His and Dick's laughter faded as the tips of their cocks rubbed together.

"Fuck, yeah." Rig wrapped his hands around them, flat tongue sliding over both of them. Their Texan shuddered, moaned over their cocks. "Yeah."

"Oh, you fucking slut." Rock growled the words, hips jerking. He wrapped one arm around Dick and grabbed hold of Rig's shoulder with the other one. Fuck he loved Rig's mouth.

Dick just whimpered. Rig nodded, whispering 'yours' against his cock before those lips opened and took both of them in, tongue sliding over them.

"Oh, fuck." He groaned and met Dick's eyes, the kid's glazed, a big, happy goofy smile on his face. Smiling, he leaned forward and took the kid's mouth. Oh, yeah. There was nothing like this. The suction kept his cock snugged right next to Dick's, Rig's head bobbing slower and less smoothly than normal. Rig's hand was wrapped around the base of his cock, pumping in time with that sweet fucking mouth.

"Fuck, Rig, that's good," muttered Dick. Rock growled agreement, words fucking gone, sucked out of his cock by Rig.

Rigger hummed around their cocks, mouth pulling harder, tongue dragging along the underside, sparking sensitive nerves. Dick jerked and gasped and reached for his mouth, kissing him sloppily. They started moving, slow and easy, one pushing in as the other backed away, slick cocks sliding together.

He had to make an effort to brace his knees as his bones turned to jelly. So fucking good. One day this was going to kill him and he couldn't think of a better way to go. Rig was moaning and humming, lips pulling fucking hard, keeping them deep. They moved together with an ease born of familiarity, practice. He could feel the pleasure settling in his balls, in the base of his spine, could feel it sparking high every time he sunk into Rig's mouth.

Rock reached out to stroke through those white-blond curls, his hand meeting Dick's, Rig fucking vibrating around their cocks, tongue sliding over the tip of his prick.

Fucking perfection.

It wasn't going to last, but for a few moments, it was forever. With a groan, he came, shooting into Rig's mouth. Rig was swallowing hard, pulling hard, tugging the kid over with him, the heat of Dick's spunk splashing on his cock. It made him shudder, sent sparks shooting up his spine. Rig panted, spunk sliding from the corners of that amazing fucking mouth.

He wiped it away with his thumb, tilting Rig's face up as he and Dick slid out. "You're something else, Rabbit."

Rig's lips wrapped around his thumb, sucking gently, grey eyes hot.

"Yeah. Something else." He pulled gently, wanting Rig up against him, now.

The thin body pressed close, Rig's lips brushing the underside of his jaw, cock hot as a brand against his hip.

"What do you want, Rig?" He chuckled. "You can set the dial to any station you want."

Rigger whimpered, reaching for them. "Touch me. Please."

He let his hand slide down from Rig's shoulders to his buttocks, finding Dick's hand already there, the two of them pulling Rig tight against him. Soft, hungry groans sounded, Rig's face buried against his throat.

"Bed," he rumbled, nudging Dick that way. They settled on the mattress, Dick pressed up against Rig's back, Rig held close and hot against his chest. He touched Rig everywhere he could reach, stroking the soft, warm skin as he brought their mouths together. Dick was kissing the skin of Rig's neck, finding those spots that made his rabbit shake.

Rig was melted and hot, feeding little needy sounds into his mouth, cock painting his belly.

"Fuck but you're sexy, Rig. You were the sexiest fucking thing I'd ever seen in that bar and you still are."

Dick made a little noise and pressed them closer together. "You two make me so hot."

"Just know what I need." Rig licked at his lips, reaching back for Dick's hand. Dick's hand slipped into Rig's as Rock chased down Rig's tongue. Heat spread over his stomach, Rig just giving it up as their mouths locked together.

If he hadn't just come twice himself, he probably would have come again. As it was his cock twitched. Dick moaned and suddenly there was another mouth in their kiss and he turned just enough to pull Dick's tongue in.

Rig made a soft, happy noise and just relaxed into the kiss. Rock could taste Rig and Dick and himself in their mouths. Fucking A. Who needed fucking tomatoes and potatoes when you could have this? He didn't even care what music was playing either.

As long as the song they sang was their own.

Chapter Five

Dick dragged his ass out of the car and up the stairs, staring at the piles of lumber that someone had stacked beside the workshop. Looked like Rig was really going to build an upstairs rec room. Jesus, the man had too much energy. It was his night to do supper and he'd spent too much time in the library doing research to even to that, much less go to work and then build a whole room.

He wasn't sure about this whole going back to school thing. He thought maybe he was too old to be doing this. Hell, he wasn't sure he hadn't been born too old. What had he been thinking? Going to school, taking fifteen hours. With math. Jesus.

He was good at marine stuff, good at running a gym stuff. The studying was not falling into the good category.

He tossed his bag down by the front door and headed for the kitchen, wondering how grumpy Rock would be if he just made hot dogs.

The smell of syrup and bacon hit him before he got to the kitchen, Brad Paisley's music just blaring, Rig singing along. Oh, someone was home early and in a good mood.

"Hey," he called out, smiling as he hit the kitchen and found Rig boogying to the music, Rock working the frying pan, flipping pancakes. Fuck, they looked good. And they were making supper for him. He was the luckiest ex-marine in the world.

"Hey, Pretty." Rig grinned from the griddle where the bacon and eggs were bubbling away. "I wanted breakfast for supper, figured you wouldn't mind."

"He conscripted me to do my world famous Sunday morning pancakes."

Dick grinned at Rock and rubbed his hand over the muscled back. Weren't they good to him? "Yeah, I don't mind at all."

Rock turned long enough for a quick kiss and then Dick turned to give one to Rig as well. Rig tasted like coffee and maple syrup and Rock, all together. Man, they'd been having a good time. He should've been here for it.

"Thanks," he murmured, setting his hip on the counter between them, hoping there'd be loads more fun to be had. "Is there anything I can do?"

"You want to make orange juice? There's a can of frozen left." Rig went back to whistling, turning the bacon as that tight little ass swayed.

"Sure." He grabbed a pitcher from the cupboard and got the can out of the freezer, swaying along to the music, noting that Rock was doing it, too, muscled ass moving just a little, though he'd lay dollar to doughnuts that the man would deny it.

"The library have what you were looking for?" It was fascinating watching Rig - the man could cook and clean and set the table like a whirling dervish.

"Uh-huh. It was more a matter of narrowing it down from like a bazillion books to two or three. I tried to find some that weren't too textbook-y but it's all pretty heavy reading." Even thinking about it made his head hurt. Ethics. Socrates. Jesus fucking Christ. "Those kids were running circles around me..."

"You'll figure it. You're a smart boy." Rig patted his ass, gave him a sympathetic look.

"I guess."

"Suck it up, kid. You're younger than anyone in this room." He chuckled at Rock's unsympathetic growl.

"Yep. He's got two old men in his hip pocket." Rig swatted Rock's ass. "Give me a break, neither of you are that old." He gave both their asses a swat, and then came back to rub and caress them. Shit, that was nice.

"Mmm." Rig pushed back into his hands, pulling the eggs off the griddle. "Soup's on."

"Yep, these are finished, too. You're just going to have to wait to have your wicked way with us until after the dishes are done." Rock gave him a wink.

They got settled, started eating, poking and laughing and bullshitting like always. Rig was trying to plan an Easter cookout. Rock was doing his best to interfere with the plan. Rig fucking had a million friends, and each and every one of them – from the nurses at the clinic to the guys at the club to the little old couple that lived next door – all of them wanted to be invited to Rig's parties.

That didn't even include the guys from the gym.

The food and his lovers improved his mood greatly and by the time they were done, Dick didn't even mind that he had a shitload of dishes to do -- Rock somehow always managed to use every dish in the place whenever he cooked anything.

"We all home tonight?"

"I am. I'm not on late call for another two weeks."

"We're all home." Rock looked very pleased about that. "And I better not hear that you've got more studying to do."

"I don't. I'm free and clear, too." Grinning, he started to clear up as the sink ran.

"Excellent. Y'all want to play Parcheesi?" Oh, butter wouldn't melt in Rig's mouth.

One of Rock's eyebrows went up. "Is that what we're calling it now, Rig? Because I think we should pick something easier to say."

Rig started laughing, eyes lit up. "Rocketman, you already had a blowjob today. You think you need more?"

"Alexander Jeremy Roberts, you'd better not be saying you're gonna start rationing me." Look at those eyes flare.

Dick bit his bottom lip to keep from laughing.

"Oh, Jim. You know it turns me on when you call me by name..." Oh, man. Rig was gonna get pounced.

Turning off the water, Dick settled his ass against the counter; he had a prime seat for watching said pouncing.

Rock kind of looked like a fish, his mouth open like that. "You... I..."

Rig grinned, eyes just lit up like Christmas. "I think he's broke, Pretty."

He chuckled and nodded. "Yeah. Broke-dick."

"There's nothing wrong with my dick, kid. I'm just trying to decide which of your asses I'm going to kick first."

"Like you can catch me." Shit, Rig was begging for it.

"You're not that fast, Rabbit." That was Rock's version of a warning and damn, if he didn't he move fast when he wanted to. Rig tried to feint, but those huge hands landing on Rig's hips. Oh, fuck. That was hot.

He licked his lips, watching intently. He didn't want to miss a second of this.

"You've been asking for it," growled Rock, tugging Rig in close, up against that hard chest.

"You think so? You going to give it to me?" Rig almost vibrated, the sudden heat in the air making Dick's cock ache as he watched.

"You know it. Right here. Right now." Rock turned them, pushing Rig back onto the table, the syrup bottle and butter dish falling onto the floor.

Dick moaned, spreading his legs a little.

Rig went easy, trusting Rock implicitly, knowing the big man wouldn't let him fall.

Their mouths met, the kiss hot and wet, and Dick pushed his hand into his jeans. This was still one of his favorite things in the world, watching his lovers love each other. Rig's hand curled around Rock's nape, one leg curling around one strong hip. Rock's hips moved, that big body rubbing against Rig as the kisses continued.

Look at that. Look at the way Rock fucking touched Rig. Jesus. It was something else.

Rock turned suddenly, lazer-blue eyes looking right at him. "What are you doing way over there?" he asked, voice all growl and heat.

"Watching the best fucking thing ever."

"Looks better from close-up, kid."

"Mmmhmm." One of Rig's hands reached out, begging for him, just calling for him – like he could resist that.

He tugged off his t-shirt, and then unzipped his pants, shucking them onto the tile as he went over to them. Rock smiled and nodded. "Good man."

"You just need someone to get rid of your clothes."

"Not someone. You." Oh, that growl made his prick jerk.

"Yeah." Rig met his eyes, the look serious, sure, enough to make him weak at the knees.

He nodded, grabbing Rig's hand and squeezing tight. "Wouldn't let anyone else do it."

Their mouths all met, tongues tangling and sliding together and, fuck, it was good. Rig held them together, all three of them. Of course, his hip was pushing into the table, Rig was sliding on the wood.

"We need to move into the living room. Or the bedroom," he suggested, tugging Rock's shirt out of his jeans.

"Shower. We haven't fucked in the shower in days." Rig's words made Rock grin.

"The man wants to get fucked in the shower, the man's gonna get fucked in the shower." Rock planted a hard kiss on Rig and stood, bringing Rig up along with him. Rig wrapped around Rock, letting the big man bear his weight.

They made the trip down the hall with frequent stops for kissing and touching, Dick slowly working off t-shirts and undoing jeans. Familiar as breathing, he'd been doing this for so long, and it still felt so good, so right.

They got to the bathroom and he broke off to start the shower, wriggling his ass as he bent over to turn on the taps. Right on cue, Rig's hands landed on his hips, mouth hot and wet on his lower back, tongue working the nerves and making him scream. He spread his legs, pushing back like the slut he was when it came to these men.

"More," he begged.

Rock's chuckle was deep, sliding right up his back, following the same path, the big hand sliding along his spine.

Rig nibbled and licked, knowing just where to touch him, where to taste him. His fingers wrapped around the edge of the tub, his eyes closing as he began to move into the touches.

The room began to warm, steam filling it. "In the shower, Pretty. Need y'all. So bad."

"Want," he agreed, and stumbled into the shower, Rock's hand steadying him. Rig followed along, hard and lean behind him, cock poking his ass. Oh, he wanted some of that. He just leaned against the blue tiles and spread his legs, pushing his ass back in offer.

"Mmm, he begs so pretty," muttered Rock.

"He does." Rig pressed close, hips rocking. "Jesus, Pretty, you're so fucking fine."

"Oh, fuck. In me. Please, Rig." He bent a little harder and felt Rock's hands spreading his cheeks for Rig.

Rig didn't make him wait too long, slick fingers pushing in once, twice, then it was Rig's cock, those hands getting him to bend into it, take Rig in. The stretch was so good, the heat of Rig's cock filling him. Groaning, he let Rig's hands guide him, pushing back and then rocking forward.

"Just like that. So good." Rig's forehead was on his back, the water pouring around them from that fancy rain showerhead Rock'd given Rig for Christmas. Man, they'd had some fun with that thing.

They moved together for a bit, Rock's hands sliding over his chest, over Rig's. And then Rock settled behind Rig, making Rig jerk. Rig's cock swelled inside him and Rig stopped, just in him up to the hilt. He squeezed around that long prick, tightening and releasing slowly as they waited for Rock to push into Rig.

"Pretty. Pretty, Goddamn." Rig started sucking up a mark, moaning against his skin.

He shuddered. It still thrilled him to the bone to get marked, to wear a dark spot made by one of his lovers, made by both of them. His fingers curled against the tiles and he tightened his body around Rig's prick again. "Please. Come on, Rock."

A grunt and Rock pushing into Rig hard enough to rock all three of them were his answer, one big hand settling over Rig's on his hip as they found themselves a rhythm.

It took them a minute, rocking and shifting and moving until they got it, but they did and damn, it was good. Back and forth, in and out. He lived for this, for all three of them loving, moving together.

"Pretty." Rig was starting to rock, pushing into him, rocking hard, cock brushing his gland over and over.

"Rig. Oh, fuck. Oh." He pushed back. "Right fucking there."

Then Rock's hand wrapped around his prick and he whimpered, his mouth dropping open as he gasped. They came in sequence - one, two, three. All of them groaning and rocking together, all of them smelling of sex.

He melted against the tiles, cheek on the slickness, breathing hard and loving the weight of Rig and Rock against him. One of Rock's hands rested by his head and he turned to kiss Rock's wrist. He could feel Rig's smile against his shoulder, feel Rig stroke his hip.

Dick figured he could handle the coursework if he had this to come home to. Or, if nothing else, he had one hell of an incentive.

Chapter Six

He warmed up the oil and put the soft sheets on the bed. Rig had seen Rock wince at the dinner table, had seen the frown lines in that forehead and the frustration in those blue-blue eyes. Rock worked himself too hard, didn't allow for getting older, and Rig knew that sometimes having a lover twenty years younger wore on him.

There was only one thing to do about it, too.

He stripped down to nothing and went hunting Rock. Rig found his Blue in the front room, flipping channels with that grumpy look on his face. The look changed when Rock caught sight of him. "Well now, what's the occasion?"

"I'm needing my man." He moved closer, letting his need show. "Want to touch you."

Rock purred for him. "I've got what you need. Bed?"

He nodded, cock bobbing, one hand held out. He didn't have to fake this, not at all. "Bed."

Rock got up, that wince back for a fleeting moment before it disappeared beneath a smoldering look as Rock took his hand.

"Mmm..." He teased them both with a soft, light kiss, just breathing into Rock's lips before backing away towards the bedroom.

Eyes hot, Rock followed where he led an almost sub-vocal growl sounding, letting him know his Blue was wanting, too. It gave him goose bumps, made him move faster, made a hot flush start at the base of his spine.

"Sexy motherfucker."

"Yours." He was never going to make it to the oil and the massage.

"I know it and you know it. The bed might need proof." He got a smile from Rock and then he was pushed down onto his back, that hard body following him down.

He arched up under Rock, toes curling as their mouths crashed together, his happy cry filling Rock's lips. Rock moved against him, prick hard and hot through the sweats his Blue wore. He pushed the sweats down, hands curling around Rock's hard ass. So fucking hot. Rock growled for him. Ass pushing back into his hands before Rock thrust against him, sliding their cocks together.

"So fucking hot, Blue. Need you so fucking bad." He raised his chin, tongue sliding along Rock's ear. "Want to ride your cock."

Rock's answer was a growl, his Blue rolling them so that he was on top. "Yes."

He reached for the oil, slicking his hands before running them over Rock's belly and hips, around to circle that heavy prick and pump. "Beautiful fucking stud."

"You know it," growled Rock, muscles rippling, flexing.

He nodded. He did and he fucking adored it. Loved every square inch of his Blue. He let his hands and his lips and his eyes tell Rock all those things, let his sexy lover know. Rock's solid hands slid over his head, along his shoulders and down his arms, that growling purr sounding again.

It made him moan, made him move to take that hard prick and slide it against his hole, lowering himself on heated fucking steel. "Blue..."

"Oh fuck, Rig..." Rock groaned, eyes all but closing, hand coming to rest on his thighs.

"Yeah. Yeah, Blue. So fucking good." He leaned forward, licking and moaning against Rock's lips.

Rock groaned, one hand cupping the back of his neck and pulling him in for a deep kiss. He started moving, riding slow and easy, feeling every inch of that fat cock buried inside him. Rock moved with him, hands and hips guiding his movements, pulling him down onto Rock's cock. Whimpers and moans and low sighs were pushed from him, his cock rubbed against Rock's belly. Rock offered him groans and moans in return, legs spreading, feet digging into the mattress to push up harder into him.

"So fucking good, Blue. Fucking made for your cock."

"It's made for you." Rock's voice was gruff, one of those big hands wrapping around his prick.

"Yes." He met those eyes, nodding. Needing. "Yes, Blue."

Rock purred, hand moving faster, eyes hot. He stopped worrying about anything but them, together, loving and fucking and moving and needing. Over and over again, Rock pushed up into him, their bodies joined intimately.

"Soon." He licked Rock's lips. "Soon, Blue."

Rock nodded, tongue tangling with his. "Come for me, Rabbit. Wanna feel you on my cock."

He moaned, body rippling, sinking into those blue-blue beautiful fucking eyes and shooting, ass clenching around his Blue. Rock roared for him, hips jerking as heat filled him. Rock's chest was hot and perfect, the sound of that steady heart more familiar than breathing.

Strong arms wrapped around him, Rock purring, stroking his back.

"So good, Blue." He stroked Rock's belly, cuddling. "Needed that."

"Anytime, Rabbit."

Rig smiled, nuzzling. "Gonna let me rub your back? I warmed the oil up."

Rock chuckled. "I thought you were warming me up."

He was given a hard kiss and then Rock turned onto his belly with a soft groan. He cleaned up a little, then oiled his hands, straddling that fine ass and starting to work those beautiful muscles.

Rock groaned, muscles rippling beneath his hands.

"Mmm... feel so good to me." He massaged deep, working out one knot after another. Rock grunted, melting into the mattress. Oh, yeah. There you go. Let me give you what you need.

The groans and moans slowly faded into long, deep breaths. He kept going until his hands were sore, then pulled the covers over his sleeping lover. Every so often, he did something just right.

Chapter Seven

"No, I do not have Alzheimer's, ma'am, I just got busy and I forgot."

Rock glared at the phone. "I have already apologized for missing the appointment. I have told you to send the missed appointment bill to me; that's just going to have to be enough."

"Well I suppose you want to reschedule. Again."

"No, ma'am, I don't have my appointment book here. I'll call later." Rock put down the phone with a growl. Stupid receptionist. Alzheimer's. As if.

He'd just forgotten about it until he was in the middle of his workout and by then... well he was in the middle of his workout and would have had to shower and whatnot and by then he would have been late anyway, so he'd just blown the check up off. It was only a check-up and Rig didn't know, no harm, no foul.

"I've got your calendar right here, jackass. Call her back." Rig was leaning against the doorframe, eyes dead-on serious.

Fuck.

"She's doing call outs; I'll call in the morning." He straightened his shoulders and headed past Rig to the kitchen for a beer, giving Rig a smile as he went by him. Never let him see you sweat. And it was just a fucking check up.

"It's important, Rock. Linda in the office just lost her husband to cancer because he's... he was a stubborn cuss and wouldn't go in for his checkup." Rig followed him, grabbing a beer of his own.

"I know it's important. I'll go. It's not like I forgot on purpose. Besides, it's not like I don't have you checking my prostate on a regular basis."

"I know. I know." Rig nodded, gave him a sympathetic look. "Call tomorrow and make an appointment on a day I'm not on call. I'll go with."

He snorted. "You just want to make sure I show up."

Rig nodded. "Yep. Not losing you, Jim. Not for anything."

"I'm not going anywhere, Rig." He grabbed hold of Rig around the arm and pulled him in close. "Not going anywhere."

Rig pushed close, his hold almost panicked. "Good. Good."

"Hey, take it easy now. I'm in fucking amazing shape, Rig." He pet Rig's back awkwardly.

Rig took a deep breath, gave him a chuckle, a nod. "I know. I'm just old and sentimental. You want chicken or pork chops for dinner?"

"You're offering me meat? I'll take the chops. With mashed potatoes." He gave Rig the eyes, the ones every dammed pup they had used to get their way with his Rabbit.

Rig grinned, hand sliding down his belly and petting. "Green beans or salad? You peel potatoes; I'll make a peach cobbler..."

He made a face and went for salad -- the lesser of two evils and Rig had some dressings that actually gave it some flavor besides grass. "Salad. We got ice cream to go with the cobbler?"

"We do. Homemade. Liz sent it home with me yesterday."

He bit back his sigh. Homemade. Fucking low-fat, no-sugar, no fucking taste, Goddamned natural ice cream. Still it was better than greens.

Rig arched an eyebrow. "She made it as a birthday gift for you, picky. I bet there's cream and sugar and maybe even no fruit."

"I didn't say a thing." And how come Rig could read his mind, but he couldn't read Rig's?

"You didn't have to. I know you." Smug bastard.

"Yeah? What am I thinking now?"

"You're thinking I'm too big for my britches and you want to fuck me through the floor."

"Damn you're good." He tugged Rig in close again. "You deserve a reward for that."

"The amazing psychic slut?" Rig wrapped those long arms around his neck.

"You think we could sell it on Jerry Springer?" He slid his hands down to grab that fine, fine ass.

"I'm way too fucking classy for that. Montel Williams, minimum." Oh, yeah. There was that look, hot and wanting and warm.

"Too bad for them I'm not sharing." He growled and took Rig's mouth, kissing hard. Rig moaned, one leg hooking around his hip, holding on tight, lips opening right up as they kissed. That was his slut. Time passed, but this never changed.

He massaged that sweet ass, tongue working Rig's mouth, fucking it. Rig pushed into the kiss, one long taste after another, hands sliding over his body. He purred, just rumbling as he started to pull Rig's clothes off.

"Mmm... horny bastard." Rig was humming, rubbing. Slut.

He snorted. "Takes on to know one."

Rig laughed, nodding. "Fuck, yeah. Know what I need, Blue."

"Me." He growled and pushed Rig up against a wall, fingers finding the ringed nipple and tugging at the metal.

"Oh... Fuck. Fuck, yes. Please." Rig nodded, hips rubbing against him.

He twisted the ring, mouth on Rig's as his other hand dug for Rig's cock. Rig groaned, eyes wide, needy, still wanting him. After all this time, he still had it.

With a growl, he dropped to his knees, holding Rig's eyes as he opened the tight jeans. Rig's mouth was open, tongue sliding along the swollen upper lip. "Oh, Blue..."

"I've got what you need." He slid his hand over Rig's prick as it pushed out of his open jeans. "Smell good, Rabbit."

"You've always been who I needed. Oh. Want you."

He purred, taking the head of Rig's cock into his mouth and sucking hard. Rig lifted up onto his toes, hands sliding over his cheeks, petting. He just kept sucking, planning to make his Rabbit scream. Rig kept watching him, moaning, eyes hot and fastened on him like he was a fucking god. He took more of Rig in, bobbing on Rig's cock, giving back as good as he always, always got from his Rabbit.

"Oh! Oh, Blue! Gonna... Oh..." Rig cried out, hips moving faster and faster. Yeah, yeah, Rig, give it to me. He kept sucking, hands on that tight ass, encouraging the movements. Rig cried out, jerking, cock pulsing as spunk filled his mouth.

He slowly pulled off Rig's prick, leaning back to look up into his Rabbit's face, licking his lips.

Rig's hands trailed over his face, petting. "Oh. Blue. Damn."

Oh yeah, he was still a stud.

He turned his face and nipped playfully at Rig's fingers. Rig whimpered -- fucking whimpered -- for him, grey eyes warm and happy. Hell, for that look he didn't even need to come himself.

"Come to bed, Blue. Want to return the favor. I'll take you out for supper after."

It was his turn to purr and he stood, taking Rig's mouth. "It's a deal."

"Good." Rig rubbed, pressing close. "Mmm... my Blue."

"Yeah, Rig. Yours."

And if it made his Rabbit happy, he'd go to the fucking doctor's every day.

Chapter Eight

The phone rang, waking Rock from his half-doze on the deck.

It rang again and he took a mouthful from his beer bottle, making a face when it proved to be warm. Damn, he'd been napping awhile. Another ring had him grunting, and he hauled himself out of his chair, muttering. He knew he wasn't the only one home. "'lo?"

"Hey Rock. How are you doing, old man?"

"Sissy. Good, I'm good. How're things in Texas?" He strode through the house, looking for Rig to hand off the phone before she could really get going.

He found his target in the office and he shoved the phone at Rig after a quick "Here's your brother."

Rig took the phone, blinking for a second. Shit, he hadn't been the only one napping. The room was a damn mess, too – weirdly enough – Rig's paperwork and files and shit everywhere. His plan to thump back down the hall and grab another beer on his way to his chair on the deck was forestalled, and he settled into the couch, watching Rig talk to his sister instead. He'd figured Rig was just being stubborn about answering the house phone while he was working on paperwork and shit, not napping.

Rig pulled two bottles of water out of the tiny fridge under his desk, handing one over to him along with a tired-assed smile. He accepted it with a grunt, wishing he'd fobbed Sissy off now instead of making Rig take the call -- the man worked too fucking hard.

His Rabbit drank a few sips of his own water, then put the bottle down, wandering. "No, Sissy. Not this year. Dick's taking a few classes. I'm real busy working and working on the extra room and just life. Honest. Tell the girls we'll come out in the fall maybe."

"Tell her if she doesn't stop hassling you every week we'll stop taking her calls." Damn it, Rig needed a vacation. Maybe he could call someone to work on the upstairs, just help Rig out a little on the QT.

Rig grinned over, looking down at his lap, wanting to sit. "Rock says he's sorry y'all can't make it, but things are busy as hell."

He smiled back and patted his legs, spreading them a little.

That skinny ass settled close, Rig curling right in, relaxing against him. "Mmhmm. I hear you. Kiss the babies for me."

He slid his hands around Rig's back, rubbing, fingers digging in a little on Rig's shoulders, wondering idly if Sissy would actually go kiss the kids and tell them it was from Rig.

"Mmm. Huh? Yeah. Sure. Whatever. Bye Sissy. Love you." The phone clicked off, fell to the floor with a clunk.

"That was short." He was impressed -- she usually kept Rig on the phone for ages.

"I'm tired and she's all strident and shit. Wants me to volunteer to take the girls for two weeks."

"Fuck that shit. We barely survived that the last time." Ever since Charlene had died, Sissy'd been trying to get Rig more and more involved – her way of getting free beaches and babysitting. He shuddered and worked on Rig's shoulders some more.

"Mmhmm. And Dick'd have a stroke." Come on, Rabbit, loosen up.

He leaned in and licked at Rig's throat. "Two strokes."

"Mmm... Two..." Rig tilted his head, letting him have all that skin. Groaning, he wrapped his lips over Rig's vein and sucked hard, his hand sliding down to grab Rig's ass and tug him closer.

"Gonna... gonna leave a hickey." Yeah. Yeah, he was. His mark. His Rabbit. He kept sucking, hands rolling Rig, sliding their cocks together. Mmm. Rig wasn't hard, wasn't even close, but it felt fine, just rubbing and touching and feeling.

He checked out the mark he'd let and decided it wasn't big enough. So he liked it, traced it with his tongue and then wrapped his lips back around the area. Fuck, Rig tasted good.

"Blue..." Rig's cock jerked, starting to fill up for him. "More."

"Mmm... you like that? You want more?" He nipped at Rig's Adam's apple.

"Yeah. Yeah, Rock. Want." Mmm. That felt good, felt right. He slid one hand back up along Rig's spine to cup his head, tilt it. Then he took that mouth, tongue sweeping in. Rig groaned into his lips, hands holding him close, his rabbit just diving in.

Rock sank into the kiss, tasting Rig's mouth, tasting the heat and need that was always there, just below the surface. It was fucking good.

"Blue." Those eyes just fucking begged for him, fucking needed him.

"Right fucking here -- and I've got what you need." He had it in spades. He pulled Rig tight against him, grinding their crotches together.

"Yeah." Rig nodded, spread right out for him. Tugging at the bottom of Rig's t-shirt, he pulled it out of the tight jeans and slowly worked it up and off, fingers dragging over the warm skin.

That little gold ring caught his attention, his fingers, Rig's moan as he tugged it enough to make his cock throb. He bent Rig back, his rabbit's back arching, trust that he wouldn't drop Rig automatic. Leaning in, he took that ring into his mouth, tugging it, playing with it.

He loved those sounds, the way Rig jerked and arched for him. He kept one hand planted in the middle of Rig's back, the other slid down along Rig's belly, teasing and playing and touching.

"Don't stop." His hand slid into Rig's waistband, toward that heavy cock.

"Have I ever?" he asked, fingers skating across the tip of Rig's prick before wrapping around it, the heat of it burning against his palm.

"No. Thank god. Never." Rig's smile was all for him, made him feel like a god.

He grinned right back, moving his hand along heat. "You wanna come before I fuck you?"

"You think I'm too old to come twice."

He snorted. "You feeling my age, Rig?" He jacked a little harder, letting is fingers drag along Rig's prick.

"Uh. I. What?"

Chuckling, he bent back to Rig's nipple. He'd show Rig who wasn't old.

"Mmm." He could smell Rig - male and sorta warm and musky with a hint of cologne. That little bit of flesh went tight, wrinkling around the metal ring.

Rock tugged Rig a little closer, got that ass sitting on his prick as he jacked Rig. Oh yeah, now he could rub off as he did this. They started slow and easy, Rig relaxing, rolling up against him, head thrown back.

He stopped long enough to pop open the button on Rig's pants and tug down the zipper, giving him more room to work that sweet cock. The near-white curls over Rig's cock just hid the black ink, Rig's prick curved up, the tip leaving wet kisses on Rig's flat belly. He could smell Rig, too, the heat, the sex, the pure maleness of him.

Groaning, he bit at the unringed nipple, gnawing on Rig's flesh. Each nibble got him a whimper, a groan, a deep noise. Hell, yeah, he knew how to make his rabbit sing. He worked that prick hard, thumb sliding across the tip, playing with it.

Rig just bucked and rubbed, giving it right up for him, cock leaking.

"Come on now, show me what you've got." He growled against Rig's skin.

"Fuck, yeah." Rig nodded and shot, the scent of his rabbit strong and sudden.

He groaned, rubbing up against Rig's ass, his hand slowing but not stopping, drawing out Rig's pleasure.

"Yeah. Yeah, Blue. Just like that."

"Yeah, I know what you like." He chuckled suddenly. "And it usually involves more naked."

Rig stopped a little, grinning at him, the look a little wild. "Well, that's Dick's job."

Rock put back his head and laughed. "Well he's at the damn library again, so I guess we're going to have to figure it out without him."

"Man, I'll give it a try..." Rig's fingers started working his belt open.

Rock was still laughing as he worked on tugging Rig's jeans down. The man was going to have to move though, unless he tore them... He wrapped his hands around the sides and gave Rig a measuring look -- his cowboy could get ornery when it came to having his clothes torn. Of course, they must be old ones, they were too damned big to be Rig's.

He went ahead and tore them off, the denim trying to resist him. There wasn't much that could stop him from getting to Rig's ass though, and these jeans were no exception, and he tore them with a grunt.

"Bastard." Uh-huh. That was him. Bastard through and through.

"Yep." He grinned and nipped at Rig's lower lip. "They needed to go so I could get to this." He wrapped his hands around Rig's ass, fingers sliding along that hot little crack.

Rig snorted at him, but one leg hooked over his hip, spreading that tight little ass wide.

He teased Rig's hole, fingers passing over it again and again, making no attempt to press in. "Come on, Rabbit. I'm still mostly dressed -- let the beast out."

"The beast..." Rig started chuckling, getting his fly open, his jeans pushed down.

Grinning, he winked, letting one finger push into Rig -- just the tip, a little tease for them both.

"Mmm. My beast." Rig got his prick freed, hands wrapping around his shaft.

Groaning, he pushed up into Rig's hand. "You know it."

He reached around under the cushions, sure there had to be some lube there somewhere.

Rig's eyes lit up. "Mmm. Toward the corner. I didn't want it to squish."

"No sit and splat, huh?" Laughing, he stretched and reached over, finding the relatively new tube. "Good man."

"Squishy isn't good for upholstery, Blue Eyes." Why were they talking about furniture? Not only that, but was leather upholstery?

He slicked up two fingers and pushed them unceremoniously into Rig's ass. He'd get his rabbit's mind where it belonged. His, too.

"Rock!" Rig clenched, squeezed around his fingers. "More."

That was better.

He pushed his fingers apart, and slid in a third as he handed over the tube. "I'm getting you ready -- you do me."

"My pleasure," Rig said. It was, he could tell. Rig fucking loved his cock, loved jacking him, touching him. And it felt so fucking good, so fine. He spread his legs wider, and pushed his fingers deeper, hitting Rig's gland. "Rock. Rock, fuck." Rig's head rolled on his shoulders, eyes wide.

"Right there, huh?" He kept pegging it, working Rig until that sweet cock had no choice but to go hard again. He got a nod, a gasp, hands opening and closing on his shoulders. He nodded back and slowly eased his fingers out. "All right, Rig. Show me how you ride."

"Mmm." Rig moved right up - eager and hungry and wanton, sliding up along his thighs. "I'm pretty good at this kind."

"I know. I count on it. Come on now." He wrapped his hands around Rig's ass and helped, spreading those cheeks wide.

"Now." Rig got settled and just sank down, body pulling him in and holding him like they'd never been apart. Hell, yes. Fucking sweet.

His head dropped forward, resting against Rig's as a low, happy moan dragged up out of him. "Ride," he murmured, hands wrapping around Rig's waist and tugging him up.

"Pushy old man." Rig laughed, bouncing on him, that sweet belly tight as a board.

Oh, he could handle being called pushy for that. He helped Rig do it again, and then again, groaning as Rig's body slid on his cock.

"Mmm. You like that." Rig grinned, squeezed and then did it again.

"Fuck, yeah." Rig knew what he liked, how he liked it.

"Faster."

"Uh-huh." The fucking couch started creaking, both of them giving the old thing one hell of a workout.

He rolled his hips, groaning as the amazing sensation of being buried inside Rig's body.

The kiss he got took the top of his head right off, stealing his breath and making him feel like he was a Goddamn kid again. He ran a hand through those little blond curls, losing himself in that kiss, in the next one and the one after that. Then Rig started squeezing him, gripping his cock with every thrust of that tongue. He wrapped his other hand around Rig's prick, tugging, wanting them to go off at the same time.

"Soon." Rig jerked, lips clinging to his.

"Uh-huh." He pressed his thumb into Rig's slit and slammed into his Rabbit's gland at the same time. "Now."

His own orgasm shot through him, and he filled Rig up. Heat poured over his fingers, Rig's muscles rippled around his prick. He shuddered as Rig's prick drew out his pleasure, made it repeat in slow waves. And then it was gone and there was just that relaxed, boneless feeling, Rig's body still holding him in.

"Oh. Blue. Damn." Rig cuddled in, lips on his shoulder, tongue tracing his skin.

"Yeah. Damn." He rubbed his cheek against Rig's head, and then relaxed back against the couch.

He ran his hands up and down Rig's back in slow sweeps.

It didn't take but a minute before Rig was sleeping again, holding onto him, dead to the world.

"You're working too hard," he growled softly.

At the same time, this was an excellent spot for a nap and he had his very own human blanket. Settling a little further into the couch, he closed his eyes and joined Rig in dreamland.

Chapter Nine

Rig sat reading, chopsticks in hand, dipping his tuna roll into some soy, and ignoring Rock with everything he had in him.

It was his night to come up with supper.

And Mrs. Saito had made the sushi fresh.

For them.

Damn it.

And if Rock didn't want to eat it, he didn't have to, but Rig would be damned if he fixed anything else.

The sound of the front door opening and closing was loud and Dick's "Hey honey I'm home" broke the silence.

"Ooo, is that sushi?"

God, he loved that boy.

"Yeah, Pretty. Made fresh. Come eat." He stuck his tongue out at Rock and went back to reading.

"Are there any shellfish ones? Those are my favorite." Dick grabbed his book and gave him a kiss and then gave Rock one before sitting down, all smiles.

"Yep. Crab and lobster." Rig pushed the tray over. "Tuna, too. How was your day?"

"Good. Better now." Dick grinned at him and grabbed a half dozen of the seafood rolls. His Pretty peeled off the outsides and spread the rolls out so that instead of sushi there was a pile of crab and lobster flesh. Without a word, Dick took Rock's clean plate and replaced it with the crab and lobster one and then helped himself to a variety for himself. "How 'bout you, Rig?"

He arched an eyebrow at Dick, but didn't bitch. "Not bad. Busy. Glad it's the weekend."

"Cool." Dick leaned over and opened the utensil drawer, grabbing a fork and passing it to Rock. His Blue looked put out, but took the fork and started eating. "Mrs. Saito's grandson still doing well?"

"He is, yeah." Rig put his book down, nodded. "She says he's starting up a band, can you believe it?"

"Yeah? Cool. I bet she made dessert too, then."

Rock looked a little more interested all of a sudden.

Rig nodded, grinned. "Almond cookies. They're good. She also invited us down to the restaurant, says she put in a karaoke bar."

Dick chuckled and gave him a wink. "Oh, I bet Rock would love that."

Rock grunted and Dick just looked at Blue. "What was that, Rock?"

Rock put another forkful of lobster in his mouth and didn't say a word.

He reached out with his foot, rubbing Dick's calf. "I got the stuff to make cinnamon rolls one morning this week, too."

No reason to not cheer his Blue a little.

"The ones with the icing?" Dick gave him a happy smile.

"Yep. And the pecans."

"Yum."

"Sounds good," grunted Rock.

He nodded and stood, old bones creaking and cracking as he stretched. One day he was going to have to start working out. "Y'all got plans tonight?"

"Yes, we do," said Dick, voice sure. Rock gave him a look. Dick nodded. "We do. Every single one of us is going into that bedroom and fucking our brains out."

His grin was slow, absolutely unstoppable. Yes, loved his men -- the grouchy one, the pretty one, the kid, the rock. Loved them. "We are?"

"We are." Dick nodded firmly.

Rock chuckled, hand going to stroke Dick's cheek. "You're a good kid, Dick. Let's go fuck."

Rig took off down the hall. "Last one in sleeps in the wet spot!"

He knew exactly what was going to happen and sure enough, there came his marines, wrestling like crazy. He was undressed and bouncing in the middle of the bed by the time they hit the door. They landed up breathless and half dressed, tumbling onto the bed.

The wrestling turned to kissing, hard bodies rubbing together. He leaned back against the headboard, pumping his cock slowly and watching, encouraging his prick to fill. Sexy bastards.

Dick pushed Rock over onto his back, kissing him hard, just taking Blue's mouth.

"Mmm..." Yeah. Fucking gorgeous. He moaned, arching into his hand.

The kiss ended and his marines did that silent agreement thing they did and as one turned and pounced him, Dick's mouth covering his, Rock's taking his nipple. He moaned into Dick's mouth, hands holding them both. Oh. Oh, shit. Yeah. Fuck.

Two hot pricks pressed against his legs, four warm hands slid over his skin, two mouths driving him wild. Shit, they were good at that. He shuddered hard, thighs parting.

Rock growled around his titty.

Dick laughed and licked at his lips. "That meant slut."

"Mm-hmm. Yours. His. More." He grinned, lips parting for his Pretty. "Fuck, you taste good."

"Mmm, sushi." Dick chuckled, feeding him that sweet tongue. He snorted and took Dick's mouth, wrapping his lips around the hot tongue and sucking hard. Dick moaned into his mouth, hips humping against him.

Rock's hand slid around his cock, down to his balls and beyond. He shifted, searching for that touch, those fingers, refusing to let Dick's tongue go. Rock's thumb slid along his cock, pinkie finger tickling at his hole.

Whimpering, he grinned against Dick's lips. "Son of a bitch is going to drive me to drinking with his teasing."

Dick chuckled. "You love it."

"You know it." He met those round, bright riverstone eyes, smiling. "I know what I need."

"Sexy and smart."

Rock growled. "Are you two chitter chattering or fucking?"

"Sweet nothings, Rocketman. Counts as foreplay." He winked, grinning up at Dick.

"Foreplay." Rock sounded unimpressed.

"How's this for foreplay." That pinky slipped into him, smooth and deep.

"Oh... More." He nodded, head falling back into the pillows.

Rock chuckled. "Fucking foreplay."

Dick laughed, mouth taking his again, feeding him the happy noises. He reached down for Dick's prick, hand stroking slow and easy, matching those sweet noises that were pouring over him.

"Oh fuck, Rig." Dick pushed into his hand, moaning sweetly.

A second of Rock's fingers slid into him.

"Oh, yeah. Blue, listen to Dick. Fuck Rig." He dove back into the kiss, working that amazing, long fucking cock for all it was worth, hips bucking on Rock's fingers.

"I thought you wanted foreplay," growled Rock, a third fucking thick finger pushing into him.

He spread wide, moaning, taking Rock in, fucking loving it. God, yes. More. It wasn't long before those fingers were leaving him, Rock sliding between his legs. "Enough fucking foreplay."

Slick, warm and hard, Rock's prick filled him up.

"Fucking heaven."

Dick's eyes caught his and they bought smiled, the whispered, "No, fucking Rig," tickling between them.

His Pretty picked up Rock's rhythm, prick sliding through his hand as Rock fucked him. They moved together, groaning and fucking and rocking and, oh, fuck, it was good. So sweet. So fucking right. Dick's hand slid around his cock, completing the circle.

Oh...

He whimpered into Dick's mouth, turning them a little so his Blue could push into the kiss.

Nothing like a little a three way kiss, their tongues, their flavors, their lips all tangled together. Easy and familiar and hot and sexy and good -- Rig didn't know what he'd done to deserve this, but he hoped he'd be doing it forever. Without a word they sped, pushed harder, faster, sending each other soaring.

He didn't know whether he came first, or Dick did, but Rock was right behind them, filling him with heat. The kiss kept going, went from hot and hungry to sated and lazy.

Rig hummed into their mouths, happy and warm. "Could stay here forever, just like this."

"I can live with that," murmured Dick.

"Good," growled Rock, settling next to him.

"We'll break for cinnamon rolls on Sunday."

Rig nodded. "Yeah, Blue. With icing and pecans, just like you like them."

"Good." Rock was soon snoring, arm solid around him, hand on Dick's hip.

His Pretty's hand slid into his, lips nibbling along his skin.

He squeezed Dick's hand, smiling into those eyes. "Yeah. Right here. Forever. Just like this."

"You bet. Forever." Dick kissed him softly and settled, warm and solid.

His marine bookends.

God, but he loved them.

Chapter Ten

Jesus, look at the rain.

Rig stood in the doorframe, washing the storm pound, the waves crashing on the ground. He'd gotten the dogs in and settled, got candles ready. Blankets all on the sofa. He was ready to spend a weekend in the terrible weather with his men. Now he needed said men to get home.

The boys had called when they left the gym, but the weather and the traffic were terrible and it had been over an hour and the temptation to go get them was huge.

He wouldn't do it, but he wanted to.

The dogs suddenly started barking, running to the front door. He followed, watching Rock's truck come crawling slowly down the road.

"Oh, thank God." He grabbed two umbrellas and headed for the porch. The truck finally pulled in, his marines climbing out, Rock swearing a blue streak. He hurried out, tossing Dick one of the umbrellas as he got closer. "Shit, I was worrying on y'all."

His Pretty caught the umbrella and opened it, leaning in to grab their bags. "Yeah, you weren't the only one."

"It's fucking evil out there," growled Rock, crowding under his umbrella with him.

"I have a roast done. Candles lit. Blankets. Two days off and nothing but storms."

"Pie?" Rock asked hopefully.

Dick chuckled and slipped a kiss on his cheek before bending to greet the dogs at the door.

"Brownies. They keep better if we lose the lights." He had towel waiting, tossing them over. "Y'all want beer or Irish coffee?"

Rock's "Beer," and Dick's "Irish coffee," came together and Dick snapped his towel at Rock. "Come on, live a little."

Rig chuckled, shook his head. "There's both. I want whiskey."

Dick finished toweling off first, coming up and wrapping around him from behind. "Hey."

"Hey." He leaned a second. "Glad y'all are home."

Real glad. The storm could rage and rage now.

"Yeah. We know how to beat a storm." Dick's lips slid over his neck, tongue wet and hot on his skin.

The lightning crashed outside, the lights flickering. "God *damn*."

"We got wood in?" Rock asked.

"Not enough. Let me go grab a few more handfuls." He headed out toward the shed, grabbing his hat on the way.

"Go sit down, the kid and I'll do it," growled Rock, his marines following him, the dogs traling along behind.

"I got it." Fuck, it was raining hard.

"We'll all do it." Dick had to shout to be heard over the noise of the surf and rain and wind.

It didn't take them long with all three working, but by the time they were done, they were all completely soaked through, and there was a trail of water through the house.

"Goddamn." He shook the water off his hat, stripped his soaked t-shirt off.

"Keep going," growled Rock. "You've just gotten over that cold -- you don't need to be in soaking clothes." Rock gave him a sharp look and then turned his attention to the fireplace, building it up.

"Shit, it's nasty out there." Dick came over, fingers on the top button of his jeans, playing with it.

"Yeah." He was shaking like a leaf. Shit. He seemed to have lost any extra padding he had, being sick, and the cold just ate at him.

Dick had him stripped down in short order and grabbed a blanket off the couch, wrapping it around his shoulders. "You want that whiskey?" Dick asked against his lips.

"Mmm. I'll get it, Pretty." Oh, better. Honest. Better.

"I'll get it. You sit and admire Rock's fire-building skills." A warm kiss was placed on his lips, and then Dick pushed him down onto the couch. He curled into the blankets, hands sliding on his thighs and sides, trying to warm himself up.

Dick came back before Rock had finished building the fire, clothes gone, three glasses in his hands. "Got one for each of us."

"Good deal." He opened the blanket, welcoming Dick in.

His Pretty sat and curled right into him, body far warmer than his own, for all Dick had been just as soaked through.

"Shit, you're like an icicle!" Dick wrapped both arms around him, hands rubbing over his skin.

"Chilly out there." Dick was like a little furnace. "Hurry up, Rock. You'll freeze."

"Almost done."

Dick's head rested on his shoulder, and his Pretty whistled loudly when Rock finally stood and started stripping down.

"Mmm. Look at that man." The firelight made their marine glow, muscles clearly outlined. Rig went through on after another, mentally touching each one.

"Prime stud," murmured Dick, cock rising in his lap. Rock grinned over, flexed for them.

"Mmm. Rock. 'mere." He leaned back against Dick, held his arms open.

"Come get warm," added Dick.

Rock grinned. "The two of you think you're hot, do you?" He winked and came over, joining them, hot and solid.

"Not me. The kid is, though. Hot as hell."

His pretty was hot as hell against him.

"You're hot, too, Rig. Sex on legs." Dick's mouth slid over his shoulder, the words sliding on his skin.

"Kid's right. Sex on fucking legs."

"It's a talent. Come here, Rocketman. Need you too." The lightning flashed again, the whole house seeming to shake.

"Jesus fuck, that's a nasty storm." Rock pressed close, cock pushing hard against his belly, an answering heat and hardness against his thigh, his Pretty's need just as strong.

"'sposed to be that way for a couple days." He lifted his chin, begging a kiss, looking into those blue, blue eyes.

"Good thing we're all home then." Rock smiled and brought their mouths together, tongue sliding on his lips as Dick's mouth continued to nibble the skin of his shoulder. Home. Home, hell yes. Rig melted - finally relaxed and warm and settled, things back to rights, like they ought to be.

Rock chuckled. "God, you're easy."

"Which makes us lucky," murmured Dick, as those warm fingers slid around to play with his nipples, tugging on the ringed one, pinching the other.

"Just know what I need, huh?" He needed some rest, he couldn't get enough.

"Yeah, Rabbit." Rock smile loomed closer, and then his Blue's lips were on his, the kiss long and slow, matched by the almost gentle rolling of Rock's hips against his.

Oh. Oh, sweet Jesus. This was exactly what he'd been needing, so much that he didn't notice that the lights went out at first. In fact, it was the dogs who alerted him, their barking starting up.

"Hush now, crazy mutts. We've got the fire." Then those lips were on his again, not letting him worry, or even care, about the electricity going out.

Dick stayed busy, too, touching and licking, the two of them keeping him warm as could be. Rig went with it, fingers sliding down Rock's spine, one hand reaching behind to work Dick's cock. His Pretty's breath hitched audibly, followed by a low moan that vibrated against his skin. One of Dick's hands stayed on him, the other moving over Rock.

A crash of thunder sounded, and Rock grunted, deepening their kiss, distracting him from the noise of the storm. Hot. He was hot, now, burning up, starting to moan and beg, whispering into Rock's lips.

"That's right, Rig, you know we've got what you need." Rock's voice simply growled over him, sending shivers of pleasure down his spine, the sound settling right in his balls. Dick's moan echoed his, and the fingers toying with his nipple ring jerked, tugging hard.

Rig cried out, eyes wide. "More. More, y'all. **Please.**"

"You want more?" Dick asked, mouth sliding up along his neck, stopping to nibble on his earlobe. "We'll give it to you. Put you on your hands and knees in front of the fire and fuck you from both ends, give you both our pricks at the same time, feed them into your body again and again and again."

Rock groaned at Dick's words, hips jerking, prick leaving a hot, wet trail as it slid along his belly.

He damned near shot, shaking hard as he nodded, eyes rolled back in his head. "Uh-huh. Uh-huh."

"I think he likes the sound of that." Of course, the thick huskiness in Rock's voice said he liked the sound of it, too. "Been ages since I had that mouth."

Dick laughed softly. "Yeah, not since this morning. Been longer than that since I've felt Rig's ass around me."

"Stop talking about it and do it. I fucking need, Marines." He was on fucking fire.

Oh, their laughter was fine, and at another time he might appreciate it a little more than he did just now. It was accompanied by movement, though, Rock standing and tugging him up against all those muscles. Dick followed quickly behind, rubbing against his ass.

They got the blankets sorted, giving him a good cushion for his knees. Goddamn. Their skin all glowed in the firelight, and he could feel their eyes on him, making him feel beautiful and shit, and then Dick's fingers slid down along his spine, tickling and teasing.

Rock found the lube and tossed it at Dick who settled behind him, between his legs, while that magnificent body moved in front of him.

"My men." He groaned, leaned in to lick the tip of Rock's amazing cock, so thick, so wide. His.

"Fuck, yeah. Love that mouth."

Dick's touches moved over his skin, just touching him for now, as Rock rubbed the thick cock across his lips, one hand cupping his cheek and sliding over it.

"Mmm. Blue." Rig opened, cuddling into Rock's hand, tongue sliding over that shaft.

"Been too long," muttered Rock. It had been only been that morning he'd given his usual wake-up call, but his Blue was right, it had been ages since they'd taken their time at it. He didn't hurry a bit, just licked and nuzzled, nibbling the tip, tongue sliding on the shaft, letting the smell and taste of his Blue fill him up, make him hot and happy, deep down.

All the while, his Pretty was touching him, almost massaging him, shoulders and back, rubbing his spine and squeezing his ass. "So sexy, Rig. You feel so good."

He did. He felt so good for the first time in days. It was hell getting old.

Dick kissed his spine as one slippery finger slid over his hole, up and down along his crease, teasing him, making his ass tense up. Rock was teasing, too, sliding the tip of that fat cock in and out of his mouth. He started moving, taking one in and then the other, muscles loose and easy in the firelight.

"Just look at that," muttered Rock. "So fucking eager for it."

"Yeah, sexy as fuck."

Who was he to argue with that? Eager. Horny. Hungry. Needy. Their slut.

"Our slut." Rock's words echoed his thoughts. "Just the way we like him."

Dick laughed softly, two fingers suddenly pushing in deep.

"Oh!" He grunted around Rock's prick, swallowing hard, all of the sudden.

That had Rock jerking, pushing that thick prick deeper, a low moan rumbling from Rock's chest. Dick did it again, and then again, fingers twisting, searching, and finally finding his sweet spot, nailing it. There. There. Oh, fuck him. Right there. Everything went tight and he twisted, groaning and riding that touch as he sucked, trying to get his men inside him.

Rock kept his cock from going deep, though, hips pulling back, obviously waiting on Dick. Dick was busy taking his time. Two fingers finally became three, pegging him each time they pushed into him.

Soft sounds started pouring out of him, his thighs starting to shake. So good. So fucking hot.

"Hurry the fuck up, Dick." Rock' s growl came with a push of his hips, the fat cock hitting the back of his throat.

"Hush, I'm enjoying myself, him." Dick's fingers slid away, though, that long cock pushing spreading him open.

Yeah. Yeah. He fucking needed. Now. He swallowed hard, pulling at Rock for all it was worth. Rock and Dick's fingers met on his back and twisted together, resting there as the two of them started working together, pushing into him at the same time, filling him over and over.

They found a good rhythm, in and out, over and over, the pressure and pleasure just fine as fuck. Rock and Dick thrust deeper and deeper, like they were trying to reach each other through his body. Those sweet as fuck noises of Dick's filled the air, too, telling him it was good for his Pretty. He didn't have to wonder if it was good for Rock. He could taste it in every drop, every bittersalt sip Rock offered him.

Rock's free hand slid through his curls, over his shoulders, hips moving faster, pushing that fat prick even deeper so that it hit the back of his throat each time.

"Fuck. Good." Each word was a growl.

"Mmmhmm." Good. Fucking. More. He needed.

Dick reached around him, fingers circling his cock and tugging roughly in time with each thrust.

Oh. Oh, he was. Oh. That felt. Rig buried his nose in Rock's pubes, swallowing hard as his ass squeezed Dick's long prick.

"Rig!" Dick went first, crying out and jerking into him, filling him with glorious heat.

He was next and Rock followed behind, all of them hot and happy, all of them getting what they needed.

Dick stayed buried inside him, dropping down to rest over his back while Rock slowly moved in and out of his mouth with slow, shallow strokes, one hand rubbing his cheek. He hummed, cleaning Rock's cock, all of them easing into the blankets.

Rock spooned up behind him, keeping him warm, while Dick faced him, nuzzling into his neck, stroking his side. It was warm and snuggly and good.

"Mmm. Can we just stay right here a minute?" Dinner'd stay warm a bit.

"Don't see why not - nobody's got anywhere to be." Rock's voice vibrated against his back.

"Not 'til tomorrow anyway."

"I have a hunch you aren't going anywhere tomorrow, kid."

"Aw... too bad. No library tomorrow..." Dick grinned at him, and then past him at Rock.

"Nope. Just the three of us and the pups and the storm." Perfect. Just perfect.

Him and his men.

Chapter Eleven

Dick washed the dishes, singing along to the radio and shaking his ass. It was oldies night on Kfox and wasn't it depressing that all his favorite stuff was oldies now? Nah, he was still the baby.

Besides, he was nicely full of chicken shish kabobs done on the grill, wild rice and salad. Rock hadn't even complained once -- not even about the vegetables on the skewers with the meat. They had a three day ahead of him. He chuckled at himself. It was still a three-day when there was a long weekend and it probably always would be, no matter how long ago he'd gotten out of the corps. He kept shimmying, convinced it was making the dishes come cleaner faster.

Long, lean heat pressed up against him, hands sliding around his waist. "Mmm... Pretty. So fine."

He leaned back into Rig's heat, smile getting bigger. "Hey, Rig. Supper was great."

Rig nodded. "Y'all both liked it. I'll have to make it more often." A grin tickled his ear. "Of course, there's a chocolate pie in the fridge as a reward for the big guy eating his veggies."

"Not only ate -- he didn't complain once. Is he feeling all right?"

"I'm just fine," growled Rock.

Dick was pushed against the sink as Rig was pushed against him, Rock's solid hands coming around him, too, holding all three of them together. "I'm on my best behavior."

Rig chuckled, the sound warm and breathy. "Are you being a good, Rocketman?"

"I am. I saw the Chocolate pie in the fridge. When was the last time you made that?" Dick grinned at the words. Rock did love his chocolate pie.

"Mmmm... couple months ago, I think. When Jack and Sarge flew out."

"*Months*," grumped Rock. "So I was good. I was very good. I even ate the gerbil food you were passing off as potatoes."

"Yep. You were very good and the pie's just waiting for you, Blue. Real, honest to God whipped cream and everything."

Rock moaned, the sound making Dick's cock jerk. Oh, fuck, the big guy still had it and he wasn't even moaning over sex but food.

He did the last dish. "Can the chocolate pie wait a bit?"

"Mmm... Someone's wanting." Rig's thumb traced his cock, tongue hot on his neck.

Rock snorted. "You're always wanting, Rig."

Laughing, Dick pushed back with his ass. "I think he meant me."

"See? I'm not the only slut around here..." Rig pushed up against him, rubbing harder.

"Hell no," he moaned, setting his hands on the lip of the sink for leverage and pushing back.

Rock chuckled. "Good thing there's enough Rocketman for both of you."

Rig's laughter joined with his, and he turned, Rig's arms wrapping around his neck, those grey eyes dancing. He wrapped one hand around Rig's head, the other sliding back to cup Rock's as he kissed Rig. Rig opened right up, tongue sliding deep, lapping at his lips. He whimpered, the sensations intensifying as Rock joined the kiss and it was all lips and tongues and just so good. Rig's hands cupped their heads, holding him and Rock close, body rubbing against them both.

"Come on -- if I have to wait for pie, I'm gonna do it in comfort." Rock grabbed their hands and dragged them off to the bedroom. Rig's laughter bounced off the ceiling, the walls, goosing Rock as they went. Rock growled for Rig, strong arming everyone into the bedroom and tossing him and Rig onto the bed.

Fuck, he loved it when Rock got all growly and he-mannish. Mostly because he knew it made Rig hot, but also because it was sexy as hell. Rig rolled on top of him, smiling lips crashing down on his, hips pressing and sliding that hard cock against his belly.

Moaning, he started working off Rig's shirt, smiling into the kiss as he met Rock's hands. Rig wriggled, belly rubbing against him, Rig's hands working open his belt buckle.

Rock chuckled. "Going straight for the gold? That's our slut."

Dick just writhed happily. Rig's hand worked open his fly, fingers wrapping around his prick and tugging it free. He gasped, hips bucking up. "Fuck!"

"That's the idea, kid." Rock's blue eyes grinned down at him from over Rig's shoulder.

"He's so clever, our Pretty."

"I think the word you're looking for is horny," Rock winked down at him and pulled down Rig's jeans and then his own.

"Horny is good, too. I like horny..." Rig was getting distracted, leaving soft, sucking kisses on his skin.

He could do distracted. Hell he could anything Rig and Rock wanted with their hands on him, that mouth sending him flying.

"Fucking sweet..." Rig's lips wrapped around his nipple, tongue sliding in the ring.

He whimpered, hands wrapping around Rig's head, holding him there.

Rig pulled harder, hips rocking that hard prick against his thigh. "Reach me the lube, kid."

He reached up under the pillows, getting the tube and passing it over to Rock.

"I'm gonna do you while you do the kid, Rig."

"Mmm... you have the best plans, Blue." Rig nipped his skin, breath coming faster.

"I just know what I like and what you like." That made him laugh, but the sound was breathless, husky.

"Mmm... fucking. Chocolate pie. Fucking. Blow jobs. Steaks."

Dick laughed harder. "You need to put blow jobs first, Rig."

"Kid's right." Rig chuckled. "Gotta love a good morning suck."

"I do. Every morning."

Rig pinked, those eyes so pleased, grin happy. Dick grinned up at Rig and pulled him in for a kiss, moaning as Rock's hands spread his legs, thick fingers pushing into him. Rig reached down, finger pushing in alongside Rock's, stretching him.

"Oh, fuck." Oh, fuck, it drove him crazy when they did that.

Rig hummed into their kiss, fingers moving together, pushing deep, inside him. He just lay back and let them send him flying, fingers catching his gland and shaking him to his toes.

"We're gonna make him come, Blue." Rig was purring, rubbing, watching him.

"He doesn't need to be hard for you to fuck him."

He just moaned his agreement. Rig nodded, licking at his lips, fingers moving faster, harder. He moaned and wriggled, riding their fingers. Fuck it was good. Too good and it wasn't long before he was crying out, coming like a virgin.

It wasn't a handful of seconds before those fingers were replaced by Rig's heat, Rig's mouth hot and hungry on his own.

He tilted his hips, pulling Rig's cock deeper. Rig groaned into his mouth, hips starting up a sure, steady rhythm. Moaning, he moved with Rig, cock not even going soft. Rock grunted and Dick reached down, holding Rig's ass open for those thick fingers. Rig slowed, stilling to let Rock have him, shuddering above him.

Dick moaned, shivering, needing. He repeated the noise as Rock's fingers slid away and he could feel the fat, hot prick sliding into Rig's body.

"Oh..." Rig's cry was fucking sweet -- all about pleasure and sex and want and pure need.

"Yeah. 's fucking good." He took Rig's mouth, kissed him as Rock settled in deep.

They started rocking, moving together with an ease of long-time loving, of knowing exactly how each other moved and wanted. Rock's hands were on Rig's hips, thumbs touching his arms as he held Rig. They moved together forever, but it still wasn't long enough before his spine was tingling, balls aching as his cock rubbed between his and Rig's bellies.

Rock knew, as Rock always did, and the big guy picked up the pace, moved a little faster, a little harder, pushing them all. Every stroke pushed Rig deep into him, making him shudder as that hard cock slid over his gland. Oh, fuck. He cried out, hands hard on Rig as he came again, squeezing hard around Rig's prick.

"Pretty!" Rig jerked between them, head thrown back as heat filled him.

Rock groaned and thrust harder, making him and Rig shudder through aftershocks and then Rock was coming, too, roaring.

Rig settled down against him, cheek on his shoulder, snuggling. "Damn, we're good."

Rock chuckled and he laughed, but he had to admit Rig was right. After all, they'd convinced Rock to do this instead of eat pie and they hadn't even tried very hard.

Of course, this way? Rock got a happy, snuggly Rig who might just feed it to him, with long kisses between bites.

Damn, Rock was good.

Chapter Twelve

Dick drove into the carport, grinning at the sight of Rig's convertible. Awesome. Rock was working late, and he hadn't been sure if he'd be home alone, or if he'd have company. He was pleased he wouldn't be on his own.

He had a bag full of fried chicken and biscuits and mashed potatoes and a big bottle of Coke, along with bite-sized brownies, and he didn't want to eat alone. There were a lot of things that were better shared. Grinning, he set the bags of food down on the kitchen table and wandered through the house, looking for Rig.

In the end, he found the man on the deck, blueprints scattered all around, lying in the sun with a blanket over him, fast asleep. Just after six and not only was Rig home, but asleep?

Funny, now that Dick thought about it, Rig had still been in bed when he'd gotten up this morning, too. Maybe Rig was coming down with something.

Dick decided to let the man sleep, and he grabbed his books, setting himself up to study out on the deck. Before long, he was absorbed in his Psych 101 studies.

The front door opened and closed, then the back door did, and he looked up, frowning at Rock. Goddamn. It had gotten dark. Late. After nine. And a glance over at Rig proved him to be still asleep. "Hey. There's chicken in the kitchen. Probably cold now."

"You didn't have to wait for me to eat."

"We didn't. Exactly. Rig's sleeping."

One of Rock's eyebrows went up and he went over to the hammock, shaking Rig's shoulder.

Rig groaned, sitting up a little, looking about as grey as could be. "What? What's up?"

"Shit, Rig. You're sick again." Rock growled and manhandled Rig up into his arms. "Get the door, kid."

He hurried over to the door. Damn it, Rig had only just gotten over a bad cold that had just lingered and lingered.

"I'm okay. Just tired. Long day." Rig didn't fight, though. He just leaned in, eyes closing again.

Long day? Rig had been home and already asleep when he'd come in. Dick met Rock's eyes over Rig's head. What could he say?

"I'll make some hot chocolate." He'd spike it, too.

Rock nodded and Rig didn't... do anything. Weird. Too fucking weird.

He grabbed a saucepan and the milk out of the fridge, started making up the hot chocolate as he fretted. They were all working too hard, and, as always, Rig worked the hardest of them all, taking care of his patients, of Rock and him... they needed another holiday. He'd talk to Rock about it, let his lover know when he had time off school.

With the hot chocolate made and a generous splash of whiskey added, he headed for their bedroom.

Rock had stripped Rig down and was heading for the bathroom, Rig's cheeks red and splotchy.

Damn.

Dick made a detour from the bedroom, following them, and then getting the shower started. "Cool or outright cold?"

"Hot. Hot, Pretty. I'm fucking cold."

"You look hot," he pointed out, reaching to press his hand against Rig's forehead. Jesus. He met Rock's unhappy eyes and got the water going, the temperature tepid. Rock just stepped in with Rig, clothes and all, lips tight and unhappy.

"I'll get the thermometer." And if they couldn't get Rig's temperature down with the shower, they'd have to take Rig to the emergency room.

Rig started bitching when the water hit him, complaining that it was too cold, too this, too that. Then Rig started cooling off, the long, skinny-skinny body relaxing. His own sigh of relief was echoed by Rock's, and he put the thermometer down for now. Instead he went and got the bed ready, surprised to find it hadn't been made yet today, the covers all over the place.

Quick as he could, he spread the sheets and blankets back out, then turned them back, fluffed the pillows and made sure the hot chocolate was in reach. Rig didn't get sick often; though that certainly wasn't true of the last couple of months, but he took such good care of him and Rock that Dick always wanted to make sure they returned the favor to their best ability when it was Rig.

He hurried back into the bathroom, grabbing a couple extra towels from the cupboard on his way, worry still nagging at him. Rig was still in Rock's arms, eyes closed, breathing slow and deep. Rock nodded at the taps and Dick got the water turned off, one towel going around Rock's shoulders, the other around Rig.

"Take him," growled Rock, and Dick slid his arms next to Rock's, taking Rig and holding him close. He was still too warm, but not burning up anymore.

Rock stripped out of his sopping wet clothing. Rig didn't fight him, didn't apologize to Rock. It just didn't work. It just wasn't right.

"I'll take him to bed."

Rock nodded, eyebrows together in a frown, expression unhappy. Yeah, he kind of felt the same way.

He tucked Rig into the covers, sitting next to the limp body. "You want some of this hot chocolate?" He should have spiked it with cold medicine.

Rig's eyes opened, head tilted. "Yeah. Yeah, I do. It smells amazing."

He held the cup up to Rig's mouth, helping him take a sip, and he heard Rock come in and stand at the bottom of the bed, watching them.

"You want some, Blue?" Rig was waking up, blinking some. "What time is it?"

"After nine, and no, you drink up. The kid brought chicken if you're hungry." Rock could really growl when he wanted to, the words rumbling and low.

"I'm not hungry." Rig sat up, frowning. "You pissed at me? I just wasn't feeling good..."

"Pissed? What makes you think I'm pissed?"

Dick grinned and leaned in. "I think that's his worried face, but I can see where you'd mistake it for the other."

"I'm okay, Rock. Just tired. Need a vacation, I think."

"Yeah? You volunteering to take time off?"

"Yeah. Yeah, I think I am. I could take a couple weeks."

Rock looked a little dumbfounded and Dick met the blue eyes, shrugged. It wasn't like Rig, but he wasn't about to give up a vacation with the two of them. "I've got a break coming up, and I can afford to take some time off either before or after."

"Just tell me when." Rig took the mug, drank a bit more before putting it aside.

Rock nodded. "That fairly soon, Dick? The gym won't be a problem."

He nodded. "Yeah, in a couple weeks. Would that work?"

"Works for me." Rock sat at the bottom of the bed and started massaging Rig's legs.

"Oh..." Rig groaned, legs looking fucking tiny in Rock's hands. Shit, he hadn't seen Rig this skinny in years.

"Hey, I brought home chicken, you want me to get some? There's biscuits, too." Rig needed some meat on his bones.

"No chicken. I'll take a biscuit."

"No chicken?" Rock's massaging stopped. "When's the last time you ate?"

"I had supper with y'all last night." Dick frowned. No. He and Rock'd had burgers and fries. Rig had sipped at a cup of soup.

"Last fucking night? In case you hadn't noticed, it's a whole fucking day later. Get the man some fucking chicken, kid."

Yeah, Rig needed to eat. No wonder he was sick again.

"I don't. Just the biscuit, Dick, okay? I'm queasy."

"Yeah, okay, I'll be right back." He was going to have to come home a little earlier most nights and make Rig some of his favorites. Hell, they hadn't had chili and cornbread in forever.

Dick sighed and put together three plates, adding some mashed potatoes to Rig's, along with two biscuits and sharing the rest out between himself and Rock. He tossed it all into the microwave to warm back up and then tossed the plates on a tray and carried them back to the bedroom.

Rig was lying across Rock's thighs, eyes closed, breathing slow as Rock rubbed the long back. Dick put the plates on the bed next to Rock and sat with them. He touched Rig's shoulder, and then broke off a bit of biscuit, offering it over.

Rig's lips parted, the bite taken. "Thanks, Pretty."

"How are you feeling?" he asked, handing another biscuit to Rock who stuffed the whole thing in his mouth.

"Tired. Just real tired."

He slid another bite of biscuit between Rig's lips. "We'll all cuddle after you've finished eating, get you some good sleep."

"Yeah. Yeah, sounds like a plan. We could watch a movie."

"Works for me." Rock was barely understandable around the second biscuit that he shoved into his mouth, but Dick nodded in agreement. Rig could fall asleep and they could all pretend he hadn't slept the entire evening away.

"I think that romantic comedy with Hugh Grant came in the mail this morning." Dick ducked Rock's swat.

Rig actually laughed. "I want explosions."

"Right on." Rock nodded and grabbed a piece of chicken, digging in.

Dick offered Rig a spoonful of mashed potatoes and gravy -- he was going to feed the man if it killed him. "I think we've got an ample selection of explosions."

"Cool." Rig ate that bite and then one more before lying back down. "That's enough for now, Pretty."

"You sure?" He'd try again later if Rig managed to stay up. Tomorrow morning he was making sure Rig had breakfast. Even if it meant waking Rig up.

He and Rock finished their supper, chit chatting about the gym, the beach, a party they'd all been invited to next weekend by the new neighbors.

"I think those girls had the hots for you, Rock." He ducked another swat.

"Tell them Rock's taken."

"Oh, I think they'll get the picture when we show up to their barbeque party all together."

"Mmhmm." Rig's fingers brushed Rock's thigh.

"Won't stop 'em from wanting the two of you," Dick said, admiring his lovers. He knew how fucking lucky he was to be a part of them.

"'m an old man. Folks won't want me."

He and Rock snorted in tandem. There was just something about Rig that drew people to him. He nudged Rig in the ribs. "Like three quarter of your patients aren't in love with you."

Rig groaned, pulling away. "Easy, kid."

He blinked and looked over at Rock, whose eyebrow'd gone up. "I'm sorry -- I didn't think I'd poked you that hard."

"It's cool." Rig leaned, kissed his shoulder. "One more sip of chocolate?"

He got himself a proper kiss first, and then leaned over and grabbed the chocolate, which was not quite cold.

"I'll put in the movie." Rock was looking grumpy again, and he cleared their plates into the kitchen. Rock followed him, growling, grumbling, looking unhappy as hell. "He's sick again."

Dick nodded. "Did you see that nudge? I hardly touched him. Do you think he'll talk to one of the other doctors at the clinic? I mean that last cold could have been over way sooner if he'd gone on antibiotics from the start instead of ignoring it."

"He'll talk to one of them," growled Rock, grabbing the chocolate ice cream from the freezer and dishing out three bowls of it.

They grabbed Predator, Terminator and XXX from the DVD stand on their way back to the bedroom.

Rig was in the bathroom, puking. Goddamn it.

He thrust the movies at Rock and hurried over to rub Rig's back, and when his lover was done, he got a cool cloth and wiped it over the back of Rig's neck, his face. He didn't say anything, just offered what comfort he could.

"Sorry. Need to see Sam tomorrow, see if he'll write me a 'scrip."

He gave Rig a genuine smile. "Yeah. Yeah, that sounds like a good idea."

Dick offered over a glass of water for Rig to rinse with.

"You make sure you fill that 'scrip." Rock stood in the doorway, watching them. "Now come on, there's ice cream melting and explosions waiting to happen."

"Fuckin' A." Rig crawled back into the bed, curling up around the pillows.

"Jesus fucking Christ," muttered Rock.

"He's said he'll go to one of the other doctors, now just get in bed and let's watch one of these damned movies and have our ice cream." He was feeling out of sorts himself. Things just weren't right when Rig was sick.

Surprisingly, Rock did as he was told, sitting and tugging Rig up into his lap.

Rig smiled, grabbed him and tugged him close. "I'm okay. I got a bug, Pretty, that's all."

Matching Rig's smile, he settled in with Rig's legs in his lap, Rock's leg sliding over top of his own as he grabbed the remote and started the movie.

And if he spent more time watching his lovers instead of the movie, well he knew this one inside out anyway, and Vin Diesel had nothing on Rock.

Chapter Thirteen

Rock thought long and hard about what kind of vacation they should take.

It couldn't be anywhere wet because he didn't want to tempt yet another bug to come attack Rig. It couldn't be anywhere too far away, Rig was still tired and dragging ass and the last thing he needed was hours and hours of traveling. If they just stayed home, Rig would find shit to do, so that wouldn't work either.

He finally hit on Las Vegas. It was warm and dry. They could gamble, they could eat, they could sightsee and shit, and they could drive out into the desert to say they'd seen that, too. But most of all, they could relax and play in a luxurious hotel room complete with a fucking hot tub.

Not only that, but Rig's upstairs room could be dry-walled and the stairs installed and sealed before they got back.

He booked everything, printed out the relevant information pages and presented them at dinner four days before they were set to go. "Here's where we're staying."

Rig took out his little wire-rimmed glasses, looked over the brochures. "Man, Egyptian pyramid hotel. Fucking cool."

"Room service, hot tubs, all you can eat buffets and all three of us together -- what else could a man ask for?" He'd done pretty fucking good, if he said so himself.

"Oh, they have a mummy exhibit and elevators that go up the side." Rig looked almost tickled.

Dick looked through the brochures. "Hey, you think we can get a tour of the CSI sets? That would be way cool."

Rock shrugged. "We've got two weeks -- I bet you can find all sorts of interesting shit to do if we get tired of lounging and fucking."

"Tired of fucking?" Rig tilted his head. "Us?"

He grinned, nodded. "You never know, there might be a half hour period on day twelve where that happens."

"Nah. Not with us." Rig grinned, winked at him.

He and Dick laughed, the kid looking again. "I'll do some research anyway."

"You're good at that." Rig patted Dick, stood and stretched. The man was looking better after getting some meds and shit, still skinny, but better.

"You got some dessert for us here tonight, Rig? Some chocolate pie?"

"I haven't made any in forever, huh? There's a store-bought one, does that work?"

"It'll do. If you come sit right here and feed me." He patted his lap. Oh, fuck him raw, look at that smile. Rig just beamed and headed for the fridge. Go fucking him.

Rock pushed back from the table, spreading his legs a bit. "Right fucking here." He kept his eyes on that ass as Rig bent to get the pie. The kid moaned, eyes on exactly the same view.

Hot motherfucker. Those long legs ended in that perfect, tiny butt that was made for his cock. His prick pushed hard at his zipper, and he had a moan to match Dick's. He rubbed his thighs, just waiting for Rig to get that pie and come straddle him.

Rig stood, pie plate in hand. "How big a piece?"

He met those grey eyes. "I can take anything you can dish out."

Rig's belly went tight and the tight jeans got tighter, that cock just filling.

"Oh, that sounded like a challenge. Looks like it was accepted, too." Dick grinned from one to the other, licked his lips. Horndog.

Rig didn't bother getting a plate, just brought the whole pie over to the table, eyes fastened to his. "Hey."

"Hey, Cowboy. Have a seat." He wanted that pie. He wanted Rig more.

Rig slid into his lap, legs spreading wide over the top of his thighs. Moaning happily, he slid his hand between Rig's legs, massaging that pretty package.

"Mmm. Blue." Rig pushed right into his touch. "You. You want pie?"

"You know I do." He opened his mouth, just like a bird, his fingers still rubbing against Rig's balls. Dick chuckled and moved his chair closer. Rig stretched, slid his fingers through the pie, slipping the bite into Rock's lips.

Oh, fuck. Yes.

Groaning, he sucked hard, the taste of chocolate and Rig mixing together. His cock throbbed, pushing at his jeans.

Rig arched, ass rocking on his thighs, lips parted. "Oh. Oh, you. You want another. Another bite?"

"Yep. I do. Dick wants some, too."

"Uh-huh." The kid leaned forward, licking the side of his mouth and then looking hopefully at Rig.

"Mmm. I want some Dick..." Rig fed the kid a bite, head falling back on those thin shoulders as Dick sucked.

Rig's fingers left Dick's mouth with a pop, the kid starting up those amazing noises. Yeah, this was the way to eat dessert. Dick got up and pushed the table out of the way, bringing his chair in, knees slipping between his spread legs and bumping Rig's ass.

"Mmm." Rig leaned back, head against Dick's shoulder. "Hey."

Dick licked a line from Rig's neck up to his mouth. "Hey. Dessert's tasting yummy tonight."

Rock chuckled -- it sure was. Sweet and salty. Rig reached out, got another finger full and brought it up.

"Don't mind if I do." He leaned in, catching Rig's gaze as he wrapped his lips around Rig's fingers, sucking strongly.

Those grey eyes went wide, Rig actually bucked up on his thighs.

Oh, someone wanted pretty fucking badly.

He let his teeth graze the tips of Rig's fingers as they slid out of his mouth. Dick's fingers crept around Rig's ribs and started to toy with the buttons of the dress shirt Rig wore on work days.

"More?" He watched Rig swallow, watched that Adam's apple bob in that long, stretched throat.

"Let Dick have another bite and then yeah, I want more." He looked down to where Rig's thighs were stretched over his own, the way that stretched the man's pants tight around his package and up along the thin torso Dick was slowly baring, all the way back up to the needy, grey eyes. "Yeah. Lots more."

"Yeah." Fuck, that was a hot motherfucking smile. Those long fingers dragged through the pie, one bite of whipped cream licked off before they were offered to the kid. Groaning, Dick leaned in and licked at Rig's chocolate coated fingers, tongue lapping, putting on a show. A fucking good show.

Rock rubbed at his own trapped cock, and then Rig's, and then Dick's, making his men moan and shift.

"Hungry men." Rig looked like there wasn't anywhere else he'd rather be, and Rock fucking approved, balls to bones.

"Fucking starving for it." It had been too long since Rig hadn't looked tired to the bone. "My turn again," he added as Dick cleaned the last of the chocolate from between Rig's fingers.

"Mmm. 'kay." Rig got him a bite, heavy on the chocolate and light on the cream, just like he wanted it.

He nibbled at it, and at Rig's fingers indiscriminately, tongue sliding on skin to make sure he had every bit of chocolate. He'd swear he could taste Dick's flavor on them as well, and he sucked hard until there was nothing but Rig there.

"Okay," he growled. "Enough pie. Us now."

"Uh-huh." Dick's agreement was immediate, fingers pulling Rig's shirt off.

Rig grabbed his hand, brought his fingers up to that amazing fucking mouth, lips wrapping around his middle finger and sucking like it was his dick.

"Fuck..." His whole body shuddered at that, cock just throbbing in his jeans. A man could almost come from just that. It was something to watch, Rig working it, just sucking his finger, tongue sliding over his skin, sweet as fuck. Sweet noises came out of Dick and the kid joined Rock on his legs, pressing up close against Rig's ass.

Fuck yeah.

His fucking men. Right there.

Rig pressed close, cock hard and hot, even through both sets of jeans. He grabbed hold of Dick's ass and tugged, rolling the two of them against him. Oh yeah, just like that. He did it again, and on the third one, Rig and Dick moved with him. Good thing the chairs were solid and handmade from their own redneck-with-a-workshop. They kept moving together, Rig giving his finger the best blow job it had ever had. Rig's nipple ring flashed in the light every time he rocked forward, and he leaned in, grabbing it between his teeth and letting Rig's own motions tug it. He felt Rig's cry around his finger, the teeth scraping all along the skin.

Shit, they needed to be a whole lot more naked. He was not coming in his jeans, no matter how good the weight of them on his thighs and against his prick was, no matter how good that sucking on his fingers was or the sound of Rig's cry made his balls tighten up.

Dick's sounds were just surrounding them, adding to the hum going down his spine. "Clothes," he growled, teeth staying firmly attached to that pretty little ring.

He tugged again and Rig's lips popped off his finger. "Blue!"

Rock nodded. "Yeah, right here. Too many clothes."

Oh, the kid's laughter was husky, but Dick's fingers slid down over Rig's abdomen and started working on his button, his fly. About fucking time.

"I can smell you, Rock. Better than dessert."

"You can have me, Rig. Want that mouth. Better than anything."

Dick whimpered, fingers working his jeans open and tugging him out. Rig's mouth found his throat, lips and teeth teasing the skin. Groaning, he pushed his hips up, his cock sliding against Rig's, the bit of a zipper making the heat of Rig's flesh that much better. Dick worked his t-shirt up, Rig's lips leaving his skin for just long enough to get it up over his head.

"Mmm. My marines." Rig's mouth slid down his collarbone, hot as hell.

"You know it." The last word was little more than a cry as Dick's fingers found his own ring and twisted it. Then Rig's mouth joined Dick's fingers, both of them fighting over him. He was the luckiest fucking man on earth.

Dick's free hand wrapped around both their pricks, not really jacking them, just playing, stroking lazily. It was just enough to keep him revved up, keep him feeling high on it. His own fingers found Dick's ring, flicking and tugging on it as his other hand wrapped around Rig's head and held that mouth against his skin. Rig sucked and groaned, tongue flicking his ring, up and down, over and over.

"Christ, Rabbit." He tried to spread his legs wider, his hips bucking all on their own, sending his men up and rolling them back down against him.

He got a nod, Rig sliding that tongue in the ring and fucking it, each push in rubbing his nipple. Oh, fuck, he was gonna blow if Rig kept that up.

The kid suddenly slid off him. Kneeling next to them, Dick opened wide and took the heads of both their cocks into his mouth. Oh, fuck yes.

Rig's eyes went wide, head thrown back. "Fuck!"

He opened his mouth to agree, but fucking shit, all that came out was a low groan, Dick's mouth so fucking tight around the two of them. He dropped a hand down to the kid's head, fingers wrapping in soft hair.

"Pretty. Pretty. Your mouth." Rig's fingers joined his, petting that too-long hair, Rig's cock rubbing against his. Dick hummed around their pricks -- whether response or just enjoyment or just because the kid knew how fucking good it felt, he didn't know. He didn't much care either, he just fucking jerked, the vibrations so good. Rig leaned further back, watching him with heavy-lidded eyes. "Fucking hot. Watching you."

"You, too. Kid, too." He grunted. Fuck, he was gonna blow any minute, especially the way the kid's tongue kept slapping against the tip of his prick as it pushed into that heat.

"Uh. Uh-huh. Dick. Pretty." Rig was gasping, mouth opening and closing for him.

So fucking sexy. All fucking his. Both of them. With that thought, he shot, shooting down Dick's throat, making the kid swallow hard. Rig's cock jerked and throbbed against his, and wasn't that the sexiest thing ever? Both of them tight together, coming inside Dick's mouth. Fuck yes.

He grabbed the back of Rig's neck and brought him in for a kiss, taking a long one as the kid's mouth kept working them. Rig's lips were soft as hell, swollen. Sweet. He kissed Rig for a long time, until Dick's mouth finally came up off their still half-hard pricks.

"Mmm. I do love your chocolate pie, but that was an even better dessert." Look at the face on the kid. Brat.

"I'll make a real one tomorrow." Rig leaned against him.

He grinned, looping an arm around Rig and his other around Dick as the kid leaned against his leg. "I won't say no."

"You didn't say no to the store bought one," Dick pointed out.

"Nope. And look what it got us." It was hard not to sound smug -- he didn't bother trying.

Chapter Fourteen

They gotten into Las Vegas at some ridiculous hour at night and Dick wasn't sure which of them was more tired -- him, Rig or Rock. They'd certainly all collapsed the minute they hit the bedroom. Hell, they hadn't even checked out the room.

He did now, as he came out of the bathroom, bladder much happier than it had been two minutes ago. If the rest of the room was anywhere as cool as the bath, they were set. Hell, the bath was Goddamn big and fancy, complete with a fucking hot tub, right there next to the can. Too fucking cool. The bedroom wasn't filled with bells and whistles, but there was a huge fucking bed, a flat-screen TV, and a view of the Strip. He could so handle that.

Of course the best part of the room was those two fine asses sticking out of the covers on the bed.

Ten whole days of nothing to do but sleep, eat and fuck. And maybe have a little fun at the tables. Maybe.

Grinning, he leapt onto the bed, making it bounce. "Hey, rise and shine, you're missing the best part of the day!"

"You could kill him, Rock. No one would know." Rig didn't open his eyes, but he got a grin.

He chuckled, and danced his fingers down Rig's spine, right into that sweet, hot crack. "You'd know."

"I might do it anyway." Rock cracked an eye open at him. "What the fuck's so special about this part of the day?"

"This is when we start fucking." Duh.

"I thought it was time for room service?" Rig's smile got bigger.

Dick laughed. "It is -- if room service is where I service you here in the room."

"It's too fucking early for puns. Wake me when it's time for my blowjob." Rock rolled over, head firmly buried in his pillow.

"Mmm." Rig's eyes opened at that, one hand sliding over Rock's ass. "So fine."

"You know it," grumbled Rock, ass cheeks tightening, releasing.

Their stud.

"You are, too," he told Rig. his own hand doing some sliding of its own, enjoying the shape of Rig's ass.

"Pshaw." Rig shifted, cheek on the small of Rock's back. "I know the truth."

"Don't make me kick your ass, Rabbit."

Dick nodded, still stroking Rig's skin.

"Uh-huh. 'm scared."

Rock grunted, growled a little, but didn't roll over, working hard to make like he was going to go back to sleep. Like that was going to happen with him and Rig up and wanting.

He bent and licked at Rig's ass. "You don't look scared, Rig."

"Nope. I'm busy loving on this ass." Rig's tongue slid over Rock's butt cheek, teasing.

He echoed the movement, grinning as Rock and Rig's moans came together. Fuck, he loved this. He loved having the time to just enjoy them like this.

"Mmm." Rig stretched out, rubbing against Rock, back against him.

He rubbed his cheek over Rig's ass, and then slid up to lick at Rig's neck, letting his prick nudge and settle between the cheeks of that cowboy butt. Rock moved with them, muscles rippling.

"Mornin' Pretty." Oh, yeah. He got the drawl, that rough, hungry voice. Score.

"Morning," he whispered, tongue finding that spot on Rig's neck. That tight little cowboy ass bucked, Rig's groan muffled against Rock's skin.

Rock's growl urged him on as well. "Whatever you did, do it again."

He let his teeth out this time, rubbing hard against that sensitive skin.

"Pretty!" Rig jerked, belly going tight.

He groaned, licking that same spot, hips moving restlessly, rubbing his prick up and down Rig's crack. God, knew where the damn slick was.

Rig was panting, hands sliding over Rock's skin. "More. Fuck me, more."

"Uh-huh." He slid back down Rig's body, spreading that sweet ass with his thumbs, exposing Rig's little hole where it waited for him. Pushing his face against skin, he breathed Rig in, and then licked, tongue working to open and wet Rig.

"Fuck!" Rig crawled up Rock, cock sliding on the big guy's thigh. Shit, Dick could smell them both, so fucking hot.

He loved making Rig lose it like this, making Rig shout and shake with want. He pushed his tongue deeper, fucked their redneck with it. Rock turned, taking Rig into his arms and started moving, pushing Rig back onto his tongue. Rig was crying out, sounds slipping into Rock's mouth. One of Rock's hands helped him hold Rig's ass open, one finger pushing in along with his tongue.

Fuck.

He shuddered, tongue starting to work Rock's finger as well as Rig's ass. Rig's skin was hot as hell, thigh muscles shaking under his hands. Beautiful man. Dick hummed, eyes closing as he just tasted and breathed it all in. Rig stronger, because he was closer, but Rock's deep, male scent *there*.

"I need. I need more." Rock added another finger and Rig almost sobbed, head thrown back.

Fuck, that was... his cock throbbed, threatening to spill. It amazed him how every day they found a way to blow his mind all over again like he was still an eighteen year old kid seeing things he'd never even dared imagine.

He slid his tongue in and out of Rig, moving faster. And then he couldn't wait any longer and he surged up, pushing right into Rig, right alongside Rock's fingers.

"Oh. Oh, fuck. Yes. Y'all." He couldn't see Rig's face, but he could see Rock, see those blue eyes staring into their cowboy and just eating it up.

He pushed in deeper, Rock's fingers wriggling against his prick, sending everything sparking just a little bit higher. Groaning, he did it again, feeling Rock push against Rig from the other side at the same time, sending him deeper still.

Rig took a kiss from Rock, their mouths crashing together, Rig tight as a fist around his cock. He found a rhythm, Rock's fingers sliding away, reaching around to hold onto his hip and guide his movements. Moaning, he buried his face in Rig's neck, just diving into the sensations.

They all slapped together, the big bed creaking under them.

He shifted a little, kept doing it until he hit the right spot, Rig's sudden cry letting him know exactly when that was. He hit it, again and again, Rig's head snapping back. "More. More, pretty. Please."

So he hit it harder, fingers digging into Rig's hip as he pulled the skinny body back against him. Rock kept shoving back against them, adding that strength to his thrusts.

"Gonna. I..." Rig squeezed tight, ass working his cock.

"Do it, Rig. Come on my cock." So fucking hot - how Rig loved his voice, loved hearing him.

The hottest fucking cowboy he'd even known jerked, crying out, the scent of spunk sudden and strong.

That ass went so tight around his cock it took his breath away for a moment. And then Rig's body started milking him, squeezing rhythmically and his cry matched Rig's as he came hard.

Oh. Oh, damn, that was good. Rig leaned hard into Rock, panting.

Moaning softly, he rubbed his cheek against Rig's shoulder, Rock's fingers sliding over his other cheek, that low groan loving on both of them.

"Mmm. Good morning." Rig grinned, turning to take a kiss.

He smiled back and then gave that kiss, tongue tangling with Rig's, loose and easy and good. The kiss stayed lazy, stayed soft and easy, Rig grinning at him. The man's eyelashes were white this close, pure white and so long. Dick felt his heart thumping in his chest, got lost in that look, in those eyes.

"When you two are finished playing kissy-face, I'm still waiting on that reason to wake up here."

Rig chuckled, eyes rolling. "Bitch, bitch, bitch."

"Nope. I've just got this swelling problem here that shouldn't be ignored."

Dick found himself giggling and he leaned in to whisper in Rig's ear. "We could double team him."

"Mmhmm." Rig slid down, lips heading straight for Rock's balls. He followed, hands staying on Rig as concentrated on the leaking tip, licking and sucking lightly. He could hear Rock, moaning and sighing as Rig took one nut in that amazing Goddamn mouth and starting humming. Flicking his tongue across Rock's slit, he slowly worked his way down the thick flesh, aiming to meet Rig's lips.

Grey eyes stared up at him, happy, lazy, so fucking hot. He moaned around Rock's prick, the big guy's hips jerking, pushing it deeper. Opening his throat the way he'd learned from Rig, he took it all in. Rig found his nipple ring, tugging just a little, just enough to make him moan around Rock's prick. Their lips touched, the vibrations passing through Rock's prick to each other.

"Fuck. You two. Fuck." Oh yeah, they had Rock.

Rig smiled, shaking his head back and forth, just a little, just tugging. He whimpered this time, cock filling back up -- he'd have to be dead to be sucking and rubbing Rig's lips with his own and having that ring tugged and not get hard. And he sure as hell wasn't dead.

Rock shifted, hips moving in little, slow in and outs, just barely fucking his mouth. Rig slid those long fingers into his own mouth, wetting them before sliding them back toward Rock's hole. Oh. Oh, fuck. He sucked harder, started working his mouth along Rock's prick instead of just letting Rock fuck it as he reached up, looking for the matching ring in Rock's nipple.

Dick could feel Rock shudder, feel the tremors in that hard prick as Rig finger-fucked the big guy. He started tugging on Rock's nipple ring, letting each shudder guide him. It wasn't going to be long, he could feel it. He met Rig's eyes, just flying with the pleasure of making Rock need.

There wasn't anything else like this. Nothing. God damn.

Dick started moving his hips without even realizing it, rubbing his own prick half against the sheets, half against Rig. One big hand landed on his head, holding him in place as Rock's hips started jerking, pushing deep into his mouth.

Yeah. Hell, yes. Rig moaned, the sound loud enough that it had to drive Rock crazy.

He put everything he had into sucking, swallowed hard every time Rock's prick hit the back of his throat and then suddenly Rock cried out, spunk pulsing down his throat.

They all slumped, panting together. Rig grinned, licked a drop from his chin. "Mornin'."

Rock just grunted, and Dick laughed. "Yeah. Yeah, good morning."

He stretched out, touching them idly, just enjoying the touch of their skin, and the easy, lazy start. "Man, we're in Vegas. Where to first?"

"Breakfast," growled Rock. "I want one of those all you can eat deals."

Dick nodded. "Yeah. Yeah, breakfast. And the sights."

"Works for me. After a shower." Rig rolled up, skinny naked ass heading toward the bathroom, just swinging.

Dick watched him go, licking his lips as Rock leaned over him, arm sliding to pull him tight against the big body for a moment. He let himself relax back against the muscles, sort of stretching and sliding.

"We shouldn't let him do that alone."

"No, we shouldn't," he agreed. He looked back, meeting Rock's eyes. "Last one there... aw fuck it, let's just go."

Rock rolled them out of bed and they headed after their cowboy.

Chapter Fifteen

There were more nearly naked people in this city than he'd ever seen. Nearly naked people and neon lights. Rig wasn't sure he liked it. It was loud, crowded, everybody was drunk and...

Shit, he was getting old.

They headed over the Strip, the kid laughing at something Rock said, dodging the crowd.

Rock dropped back, arm going around his shoulders for a moment. "You're awfully quiet."

"Yeah? It's just something, taking this all in."

"You having a good time?"

"Yeah. Yeah, it was cooler during the day. Less drunk." Less weird. Less creepy and loud. Less people shoving cards advertising pussy for sale. Less noise.

"You wanna just hit that steak house Flannery told us about and sneak back to the hotel room for some real R and R? The kid won't mind not playing the slots tonight."

Dick had obviously just noticed they'd slowed down, and he darted back toward them, smiling.

"Would you mind? I'm..." Old. Tired. Getting weird. "No, let's go play, man. It's early still."

Dick stopped in front of him, rolling back on his heels. "What's up?"

They were blocking foot traffic, but Rock just stood there arm around his shoulders, not letting them get pushed around. "I'm hungry. For a real steak."

"Cool. I think that place Jim Flannery recommended is around here." Dick craned his neck, looking at the signs on the street corner. "He said they had the best steaks in the country, but I'm guessing he was exaggerating."

"Yeah? I'm a fan." Oh, he could go for a sit, some bread. A potato.

"Oh, there's a cab, let's just grab it instead of getting lost." His Pretty stepped off the curb and hailed the cab down, Rock tugging him over as it pulled up.

"This cool with you, Blue?"

"I wouldn't be doing it if it wasn't."

Rock pushed him into the cab, and Dick told the driver where they were going, grinning back at them from the front seat. "Apparently it's just around the corner."

"Good deal. It's damn warm here, huh? Warmer than home." Well, assuming home was California and not Texas.

Rock chuckled. "Thought you liked it hot, Rig?" The words were casual, but those blue eyes looked over at him, took him in.

"I'm getting used to where we are, huh? Hot men, cooler weather."

Rock preened for him. "You know it."

With that the taxi was pulling up in front of their restaurant, Dick taking care of the fare and bouncing ahead of them. The air conditioning was a relief, as was the quiet atmosphere -- relaxing, welcoming.

He caught himself leaning toward Rock, the smell of meat making him just a little queasy. Man, he needed to eat so that he could feel better. Rock's arm went back around his shoulders for just a moment, steadying him a touch, and then they were being seated at a half-moon booth with a round table. Dick slid in, Rock letting him go next to sit between the two of them.

"Swanky place." He settled in, idly looking at the menu. Jesus, it was dear. Forty dollars for a steak? Momma'd roll over in her grave.

"Steak better be fucking good," was all Rock said.

The waiter showed up with rolls and glasses of water, wanting to know what they'd like to drink. He asked for tea, the guys each got a beer and then they got to the business of looking at menus. By the time the drinks came back, Dick and Rock had decided on shrimp cocktail and fried mushrooms for starters.

Dick's hand rested on his thigh under the table as his Pretty sat back, looking around the place. "You notice how these steak places all kind of look alike? I mean we could be anywhere. Well, except for the slot machines and Keno girls, I guess." Dick nodded toward the back of the place where a bank of one armed bandits lined the wall and those poor tired-looking gals in little bits of nothing.

"Yeah. I guess meat is meat. What all are y'all ordering?"

Rock didn't even have to think about it. "The twenty-ounce porterhouse."

"Now there was a bet I would have won. I'm going to have their fourteen ounce fillet. What about you?" Dick just grinned, bouncing like a youngster.

"I think I just want a salad and a potato. I ate my weight at lunchtime." He really just didn't have the appetite he used to.

"You can't come into a steak place and just have a salad and a potato, Rig." Rock pointed to a peppered beef salad plate. "Don't look at the prices, I've got it covered."

"Oh, I'm not worried about the money." He just. Shit. "Maybe I'll get the little fillet."

Rock looked satisfied at that and Dick nudged him, leaned in a little to whisper, "He's trying to fatten you up."

"Yep. I gotta fit in my jeans." Which he wasn't. Which was a little unnerving.

Dick's hand slid over his thigh, rubbing and squeezing. "You enjoying the trip okay?" The words were still quiet, soft.

"I am. It's a little psycho out there at night, huh? But today I had a ball." So many weird and neat things to see and do. They'd seen the big purple dragon at the Excalibur, watched gals on wires fetch wine in Mandalay Bay, gawked at the glass floweredy ceiling at the Bellagio and watched this fun-as-fuck show with Roman robots in togas at Caesar's Palace. It had rocked.

Dick nodded, relaxing. "All those people -- it is a little weird. My favorite thing today was the King Tut deal. That was really cool."

"I still want to head down to the Bellagio again and really see the fountains. Is it tomorrow we're going to the Grand Canyon?" The Grand Canyon by helicopter. Too fucking cool.

"Yeah, I booked us in at eleven. I know that's the hot part of the day, but we don't have to worry about being up early that way." Rock winked.

Dick snorted. "Like Rig ever sleeps in."

"Yeah, kid, but there's better things for him to be doing first thing in a hotel room with nothing but you and me than worrying about getting us up and out the door for an early helicopter ride." Rock gave him a wink, foot sliding against his leg.

"Always worrying about his wake up call." That made them all laugh, easing the tension he'd been carrying. Man, had he forgotten how to relax that much?

Their appetizers came and Dick was the first to dig in, grabbing a shrimp and offering it to him, riverstone eyes flirting with him. He opened his mouth, ate it. Oh. Sweet, rich. Buttery. That worked.

"Mmm... I bet it tastes ten times as good out of your mouth."

Rock cleared his throat a little. "No getting anyone wanting to kick our asses, kid. We're not at home."

"I know. I know. It's true though, and you know it."

Rock grinned and stole a shrimp from Dick's plate. "I do."

"Y'all are hopeless." Fucking hot, but hopeless. He let them finish the rest of the shrimp, spending his time with a stuffed mushroom. Fuck, that was nice.

They laughed and teased, Rock stealing a mushroom out from under his fork and Dick stealing it right back out from under Rock, popping it in his mouth with a satisfied grin. They looked good, happy. Like his men.

"Did y'all want to go walk down the strip more tonight? There's supposed to be all sorts of shows."

"Yeah, that would be cool." Dick nodded, grabbing a roll out of the basket that had come with their appetizers.

Rock shrugged. "I don't know. I want to make sure we get our money's worth -- we could go back to the room and make sure that jacuzzi works."

"Oh. I could go for that." He could just sit and bubble for an hour or so.

Rock looked pleased, and Dick nodded easily. "I can do hot tub." His pretty grinned wickedly. "Or get done in the hot tub."

"Pretty, you get done in the hot tub at home all the time." In the hot tub, on the beach, on the deck...

Dick's eyes met his, full of wicked heat. "And the appeal still hasn't worn off."

"Sluts," growled Rock. "The pair of you."

"You think? I'm not sure, Rock..." He leaned a second, winking over at Dick.

Rock snorted. "I don't think, I know."

Dick grinned at him. "He counts on it."

"You know it." Rock's hand landed on his thigh, warm and solid.

"Mmm." Now that felt fine. "I do like those hands of yours, Blue Eyes."

"Just wait until we get back to our room. I'll show you my hands."

Oh, listen to the need in that growl. Rig shivered - fucking shivered, for real. Shit, he hadn't done that in a while. "Promise?"

"You fucking know it." Those blue eyes just ate him up, promising him everything.

Rigger sort of just... sat. Jesus.

Jesus.

"You are a fine son of a bitch, I swear to God."

Rock puffed all up. His Blue did like it when he noticed.

"God, the two of you are making me want to say screw the steak, let's go get busy." Dick spoke softly, gaze heavy as he watched them.

"Y'all need to eat." He didn't mind waiting, not at all. The anticipation settled in his belly, hot and solid.

"So do you," Dick said softly as their food came.

Rock grunted what sounded like a cross between an agreement and a happy moan over his steak. He chuckled, cut up his potato as he watched Rock and Dick fall on their steaks like starving men.

They each fed him bites from their plate. "Mine's better than the kid's," teased Rock, and then he was suddenly the judge of a steak-off, more bites fed to him.

He held his hands up, shaking his head, belly aching it was so full. "Enough! Enough!"

"Okay, but mine's the best." Dick popped another piece in his mouth even as Rock shook his head.

"I've got the twenty ounce and I'm going to eat the whole thing -- there's your proof mine's the best."

"Y'all can have mine too. I'm full up." He leaned back, wiping off his mouth.

"We can get a doggie bag -- you'll be hungry later."

"Let's get some desserts to go, too." Dick made hand gestures at their waiter.

He chuckled, shook his head. "We can get dessert at the hotel, not worry about it getting gross."

"You think they'll have that chocolate explosion thing at the hotel?"

"This is Vegas, kid. Whatever you want -- they'll have." Rock handed over his credit card as the waiter came to their table.

Rig finished his beer, chuckled. "Hell, Rock, we've been what Dick's wanted for years."

"That's because I'm the cute one." Oh, look at his Pretty; butter wouldn't melt in that mouth. Of course Rock wasn't buying, and Dick narrowly ducked the smack, laughing.

"Cute. Green. Our sensitive flower." Rigger couldn't hold back his laugh a bit. Shit heads, the both of them.

Rock nearly choked on what was left of his beer. "All right, we'd better get this sensitive flower back to the hotel so we can water him. Is hot water good for flowers?"

Dick shook his head. "I'm not taking a cold shower if that's where you're going."

"Probably wouldn't make a difference anyway." Rock winked and Dick laughed again.

"Not with the heat the two of you put out, it wouldn't."

"Nope, and he'd get us back with cold coffee in the morning." Or worse, ice water in the bed.

"Oh, I could do better than cold coffee in the morning."

"Yeah, but it would take him a day or two to come up with it." It was Rock's turn to duck, his marines just teasing back and forth as they left the restaurant.

"Y'all are something." He ducked to avoid getting his hat hit by the crowd, taking a second to look at all the lights. "Man, it doesn't look real, does it?"

"It's a great big glittery show." Rock put a hand on his arm, maneuvering him around a crowd of people before they turned the corner onto the street their hotel was on. "Has nothing on our beach."

"Oh, hell no. I couldn't live in this place. Not for all the money on earth." Rig leaned a little harder, just for a second.

Rock let him, a low, growling rumble coming from the broad chest. "Let's get out of this crowd."

Dick walked ahead of them, parting the crowd all the way to their hotel. The lobby was just as crowded as the streets and there had to be ten other people squeezed onto the elevator with them.

"Jesus." He growled a little when some drunk asshole bumped his hat. Hard. "Watch it, man."

"Fuck you, asshole. Skinny, loud mouthed prick, worried about his poor baby hat."

Rigger whirled around, temper flaring like somebody'd put a match to paper. "Excuse me? You want to say that to my face, shithead?"

"I said, fuck you, asshole." Short, drunk and stupid shoved him good and hard, a couple of the little gals on the elevator squealing as he took a step back.

His view was suddenly blocked by two angry marines, Rock's hand landing hard against the side of the elevator. "Excuse me," growled Rock. "I think you want to apologize to the man. Or we could rearrange your ugly as shit face for you."

"Who the fuck are you, Gigantor? His fucking security?"

Rig actually grinned, even as pissed as he was. "You know it, you pansy-assed fuckwad, and if you want to fucking take this outside, they'll mangle what I don't tear up."

"Man, do you want to die tonight?" Dick asked. "I'm the most reasonable one of the three of us and even I want to stomp on you. Just say you're sorry and live another day."

"Three to one is cheating."

The elevator door opened and people tumbled out, including the drunk guy, tugged out by one arm, his little girlfriend already screeching at him as the doors slid shut.

"Coward." Rig wrinkled his nose. "Lousy coward."

"We should have pounded him," grunted Rock. "He was too stupid to live."

"Drunk as hell. I'd rather go make out than fight anyway." Dick wrapped an arm around him, adjusting his hat so it sat right on his head.

"I could use a good fight. I haven't had one in... what? Three years, Blue? That little kid at the club."

"Little asshole." Rock growled and shot him a look. "Trying to take what wasn't his." His cock jerked, chin going up, that look doing something for him, bone-deep. "Yeah, you know what I'm talking about." The elevator stopped on their floor and Rock walked out, cock of the block, that back ramrod straight.

"You woke up the bear," murmured Dick.

He nodded, eyes fastened onto Rock's spine. He fucking loved the bear; he found it hot as hell.

"Just look at that man move." Dick made a happy noise and tugged him along.

Rock opened the door and swept a look over the both of them. "I think the hot tub can wait."

He stood, spreading a little. "You do?"

Come on.

Come on, I fucking *need*.

"Bed. Now. Naked."

Dick nodded at Rock's grunted words and hustled him over to the bed, fingers already working the buttons of his shirt. The door closed, the bolt shot home and Rock stalked over to them. He held those blue eyes, sort of shaking with it, the adrenaline rush leaving him shuddering. Dick pushed his shirt off his shoulders and it got caught up on his wrists as Rock's mouth crashed down on his, those big hands holding his face tilted upward.

Please.

Fuck yes.

Rig went up on tiptoe, meeting that need with his own. A low rumble filled his mouth, along with Rock's tongue.

Dick's fingers were quick and nimble, working his jeans open, tugging them down. His prick was given a lick from base to tip. Rig gasped, eyes going wide, chest slapping against Rock's. Oh. Oh, fuck yes. Dick kept on licking and nibbling at him, not really sucking, just playing with his cock.

It almost didn't matter, because Rock wasn't playing. Shit. Rock was in full-on, take no fucking prisoners mode.

Rock pulled out of the kiss long enough to growl. "Dick. Fucking naked. Fucking now."

Then those lips were on his again, sucking the breath right out of him. Rig's eyes rolled and he struggled, tugging at the motherfucking shirt sleeves, trying to get free. Dick worked Rock's jeans off, and tugged the tight t-shirt up over Rock's head, breaking their kiss, making Rock growl again.

"Yours. I fucking need." He did. Now. His Blue. Loving him.

"I've got what you need right here." Rock stepped out of his shoes and jeans, and pushed him back onto the bed. He bounced once and then Rock was on him, pushing him down into the mattress, just stealing his breath. His legs were spread by Rock's knees, Dick's fingers pushing into him, slick and cool. Bearing down, Rig took Dick in, still staring into Rock's eyes. Fuck. Fuck, he loved.

Two fingers quickly became three, Dick stretching him, getting him ready for the fat, hard prick that pushed against his belly, all but branding his skin with Rock's heat. Dick was making his porno noises, moaning and groaning for them. But Rock just made that low, growling rumble, a sound he could feel in his own chest.

"More. More, y'all." Lord, yes. So good.

"You about done down there, Dick?" Rock pushed a finger in alongside Dick's, checking for himself. He gasped, legs spreading wider, muscles shaking some.

"Let me just slick you up, Rock."

Rock grunted, finger-fucking him even as Dick's fingers slid away.

"Mmm. Your hands." He kept kissing, mouth open, so hungry, so wanton.

"Be my cock in a second." God, that growl just got deeper and deeper.

"Made for this, huh? For you." Every fucking inch of him.

"Uh-huh." Rock's finger disappeared, replaced by the amazing heat of that hard cock, Rock pushing into him nice and slow, letting him feel every fucking inch as it slid in. His eyes rolled, body accepting Rock right in like it was meant to be there.

Rock growled again, and started to thrust, just like it should be, nice and steady.

"Blue. Come on." The motions were driving him crazy, each in and out just so fucking slow.

Rock chuckled, those blue eyes twinkling down at him and the thrusts actually slowed.

"Bastard..." He tried to roll up, take more, faster. "Rock. Dick..."

"Want me, too?" Dick asked, fingers sliding in with Rock's prick, one and then another and then another, each having their turn. Fuck. Fuck him. More.

"I. Oh. Oh, y'all." He couldn't fucking *breathe*.

"That's a yes. Slick yourself up." Rock's voice was still all growly, husky.

"Uh-huh." Dick's voice was breathless.

"Kiss me." Something. Please. Both of them covered his lips, tongues pushing into his mouth, sharing it just like their cocks were going to share his ass. Everything in him was shaking, trying to vibrate apart.

Rig held on, fingers digging in, lost in the kisses that just went on and on and on. All the while Rock's prick kept sliding, slow and easy, keeping him on edge.

"Come on now," muttered Rock, breaking the kiss. "Let's do this."

"I. Rock..." He groaned, caught in this.

"Yeah, we got you."

"Where you want me, Rock?" Dick's voice had gone all raspy, those pretty eyes wide and needy.

"Right here in front of me, kid, you just slide right in with me."

Dick shifted, moving to straddle his hips, Rock's fingers guiding the long prick to his hole.

There they were, both of them, staring at him. Jesus. "Easy, huh?"

"Easy as breathing."

"Uh-huh." That and a moan were all that Dick had to say, prick pushing in alongside Rock's, both of them stretching him, filling him. "Oh fuck." Dick's whisper seemed so loud.

Rig stretched, hands reaching up for the headboard, groaning when he just got a board nailed to the wall.

Dick's hand slid along his side, Rock's meaty paw wrapping around his hip. "Nice and slow, Dick."

And that's what they did, Dick pushing forward as Rock pulled back, their groans filling the air. There was only option for him, and Rig took it, shorting out, taking them in and holding them tight. Dick whimpered and Rock groaned, their rhythm stuttering for a moment before they found it again, moving a little faster, pressing into him and it was the biggest thing in the world. He reached down, fingers wrapping around his own cock, tugging slow and easy.

"That's it." Rock moved a little faster, Dick picking up the speed. Their pricks were so hot, working together to blow his mind.

"Blue. Blue, y'all..." He met Dick's eyes, gasping.

Those pretty eyes stared right into his, Dick making one sweet noise after another.

"Faster," growled Rock.

"Uh-huh." His belly clenched, shoulders leaving the mattress. They filled him over and over again, keeping him filled, keeping him flying. He groaned, hand almost burning as he jacked. "Soon. Soon."

"Give it to us," Rock ordered.

His body just went taut, giving it up, pouring his fucking soul out.

"Rig!" Dick cried out, jerking, prick pushing into him as those pretty eyes rolled.

Rock just kept moving, hitting his gland and dragging him through his orgasm. Everything in him just felt so fucking good, just relaxed and tingling and easy.

"Come on, kid, let me feel you around my cock."

Dick jerked, heat filling him in long splashes.

"Yeah. Yeah, that's it. Fuck, the two of you make me need." He reached up, cupped Rock's jaw. "You. You now."

Groaning, Rock turned and nipped the pad of his thumb. A moment later more heat filled him, those blue eyes glazing over.

"Y'all." Fuck, he loved. So much.

Their cocks slid out of him, his marines lying to either side of him, bracketing him and holding him close between them. Dick tilted his face for a kiss, and then Rock did the same.

He held Rock's eyes, blinking nice and slow. Good. So good.

Rock grunted, smiled. "You look like we wore you out."

"Mmhmm. 's good." All good. All right.

"I could nap," muttered Dick, patting his hip, Rock's.

"Uh-huh." For, like, days.

Dick snuggled in close and Rock settled, throwing a leg over both him and his Pretty.

He was comfortable, happy. Settled. Happy vacation to them.

Chapter Sixteen

They spilled out of the helicopter, Dick whooping, pumped from their trip over the Grand Canyon. "Woo! That was fanfuckingtastic!"

Rock laughed. "Yeah, it wasn't bad."

Dick popped him in the arm and grinned at Rig. "What did you think?"

"It was weird, being in a bird again."

"You ever miss it?" They didn't talk about it much. Like as in ever – how Rig gave it up. Flying. Jumping out of birds. All of it. All just taken away one night. Christ.

"Yeah. Yeah, sometimes. I miss..." Rig shrugged, waved one hand. "Come on, y'all. I'm dying of thirst."

"Yeah, I could kill for a beer. Pilot said there was a good place -- a real place a few blocks over from the strip."

Dick grinned. Rock had been comparing notes with the pilot for most of the trip and God knew he didn't want to bring them down.

"Cool." The rental car was waiting, Rig whistling idly, sunglasses on under his gimme cap. He looked good. Too skinny, but relaxed and happy. And so did Rock. Well, relaxed and happy -- there was nothing skinny about Rock.

Looking at them made his prick perk up, but Dick ignored it. "I'll drive," he offered, holding his hands out for the keys. Rock snorted and grinned at him, not handing them over. Rig stretched, tight little cowboy butt shifting, side to side, all backlit by the sun.

Biting back a groan, he looked his fill, shoving his hands in his pockets to disguise the way the front of his jeans bulged. "Never mind, I'll just sit in the back and admire the scenery."

"What're y'all muttering about? Come on." Impatient cowboy.

"I'm sorry, did you not hear me? You're hot." He grinned and gave one of Rig's ass cheeks a nice hard squeeze.

"Mmm." Rig leaned a half a second, then moved away, shaking it.

"You're just encouraging him," murmured Rock. "Keep it up."

Laughing, Dick followed that ass, Rock hitting the button to unlock the car. Rig slid in, legs stretching out, boot heels clicking. Dick climbed into the back as Rock slid into the driver's seat. He popped his head over the front seats, grinning, still bouncing from the helicopter ride, feeling a bit horny.

Rig leaned, kissed his cheek. "So what are your plans for the rest of the day, Dick?"

"I don't know -- I'm pretty easy." In more ways than one.

"When aren't you?" asked Rock, starting up the car and pulling out of the parking lot.

"I'm thinking I want to go nap for a bit, maybe." Rig patted Rock's thigh.

Dick frowned. Rig had been napping an awful lot lately.

"Yeah? You don't want to go swimming or anything? Or maybe they've got a pool table at this bar we're going to."

"Oh, I can nap after pool and beer." He got a grin, a nod. "I'm a fan of a good game of pool."

Rock nodded, checking out the name of the street sign ahead of them. "I can get behind that."

"Cool. We haven't played pool in forever."

"It hasn't been that long, has it?" Rig asked.

"Pretty much."

"Kid's right. it has been forever. Hell we hadn't had a night out before we came on vacation in a month of Sunday's."

"Listen to you. You damn near sound like home." Rig's words were teasing, but the hand that slid up Rock's thigh stopped the grumble.

Rock looked over at Rig. "I *am* home."

Dick grinned, nodding. Oh, yeah. Yeah, they were home. The three of them.

"Yeah. Yeah, Blue. Y'all are home." Rig leaned, lips just brushing Rock's jaw.

Oh, didn't that make Rock puff up and look happy? God, the two of them made him happy. He slid his hands over their shoulders, squeezing. Damn, Rig was tense. Like rock-hard tense. He squeezed Rock's shoulder one more time and then shifted a bit and rubbed both Rig's shoulders, working the tight muscles.

"Oh..." Rig's head fell forward, lips parted. "Don't stop."

"I won't. You okay?"

They were on vacation; Rig should have been relaxed as hell.

"Yeah. I'm fine." The muscles started shaking a little, just slowly relaxing.

He leaned in so just Rig would hear him. "You sure? You're awfully tense."

"Yeah?" He got a kiss, a grin. "I'm fine, honey."

"Yeah, well you can prove it later," he whispered, prick perking up again just at the thought.

"Mmm. To be so young again."

Dick snorted. "You're not old."

"I feel old, some."

"Oh, me and Rock aren't doing our job, then." He kissed Rig's neck, that place he knew would send shivers through Rig's body.

Rig groaned, head falling forward. "We're fixin' to be at a bar, Pretty."

"You think they have a bathroom?" he whispered against Rig's skin.

"We're not fucking in the bar..." Uh-huh. Of course they weren't.

"Hey, Rock, is a blowjob fucking?"

Rock glanced away from the road, one eyebrow going up. "A blowjob's a blowjob."

Dick grinned. "There you go. We won't be fucking in the bar."

God, Rig's laugh was something else. "You know bathrooms are nasty right?"

"I'll put up with nasty for you."

Rock snorted and he whapped the big guy's arm. Rock whapped back and Rig snorted, all of them suddenly laughing and playing, the car zooming down the road. The pilot had been right, the bar was more substance than neon flash, a row of pool tables were at the back.

"I can get us a pitcher while you guys set up a table."

Rig dug some ones out of his pockets - Man, those tight jeans just *weren't*. Skinny asshole. Dick groaned, and met Rock's eyes. He wasn't the only one wanting. Didn't make it much better, but at least he wasn't alone. He went and ordered their beer, leaning against the bar, eyes on his lovers.

Rig was breaking, face shadowed by that cowboy hat. Rock was chuckling, watching Rig, shaking his head.

He nodded his thanks as the pitcher and glasses were served up and he grabbed them, heading for the sexiest pair in the joint. Rock was shooting, Rig propped against the wall, grey eyes warm, watching their marine.

"Who's winning?" He checked out Rock's ass as he asked.

"Rock, of course. Shit, I haven't won a game of pool in years." Rig sounded more resigned than complaining.

"That's because you're not being distracting enough."

"Oh, now. Don't you go blaming this on me..."

"No?" He chuckled, pouring the beer into their glasses. "Well it's not my fault."

"Are you sure? You're damned distracting..."

"Me?" He laughed. When there was Rock to look at? "Only if I pull out the big guns." He rubbed his nipple ring through his t-shirt, eyes on Rig's, just able to see where it was through the t-shirt.

Oh, fuck yeah. Rig's eyes went hot, hungry.

Yeah.

Big guns.

He licked his lips, his own body going tight at that look.

"Hey. We playing pool, or what?" Rock asked.

He voted for what, himself.

"Huh?" Rig blinked, then shook his head. "Sorry, Blue. I got distracted."

Rock chuckled. "The kid cheating again?"

Dick's eyes widened and his mouth dropped open. "Me? I do not cheat or distract!"

"Excuse me, Mr. Nipples?" Mr. Nipples? Wasn't that a chimp?

"Oh, I see what's happening now." Rock came over and tweaked his nipple through his t-shirt, making him gasp. "Behave. No cheating."

"Like you aren't a walking distraction."

Rock didn't take offence at all, just puffed up proudly. Hell, the man had a lot to be proud of. Rig chuckled, went to take a shot, sinking three balls.

Rock frowned. "I thought Dick had distracted you?"

"He had. I only got three." Oh, look at that shit-eating grin.

"And you guys accused *me* of cheating."

"I didn't cheat." Rig looked tickled. "I got lucky."

"Getting lucky." Rock grinned. "I'll show you lucky when we get back to the hotel."

Oh yeah. Now that was lucky.

"Promises, promises." Rig joked and Rock growled, swatting that tight little ass affectionately.

"Now Rock's trying to distract you so you don't sink anymore."

"Would he do that?" Rig wiggled, leaned over to take his shot.

He and Rock spoke at the same time. "Yes."

They were both watching that ass, too, like a pair of dogs panting over a bone. Rig slowed, shifting and sliding, teasing them both.

"Five dollars says he doesn't sink this shot," murmured Rock.

"You're on."

"You're going to lose. He's too busy putting on a show."

"We'll see."

Rig's lips twisted, and then those long, long legs spread. The twelve went in, pretty as you please. Dick crowed and held out his hand, Rock grumbling as he put the fiver in it. "He was distracting us, not himself."

"I live in this body. I have y'all to look at. Why would I be distracted by it?"

"Because you were busy trying to distract us with it and I figured that would be... oh hell." Rock rolled his eyes and shook his head. "Never mind. I just wanted to give the kid five bucks."

Dick laughed and then bit his lip when Rock shot him a look.

Rig chuckled, leaned on the pool table, just smiling at Rock. "You are a fine, fine man, Marine."

Rock puffed up as he always did. The big guy knew he was good-looking, but there was something about the way those grey eyes looked at you that made you know right down to your toes.

"I'd flex for ya, Rig, but I wouldn't want to be accused of cheating when I win."

"Oh, go ahead, flex for me. I've already said you're a better pool player and that'll ease the sting of losing."

Rock didn't need anymore encouragement than that, the muscles of his arms and chest going hard, showing up easily beneath the tight, dark green t-shirt he wore.

Dick's prick, already interested thanks to Rig's butt-wiggling, got even more interested and he groaned. "You know if we're *not* going to get blowjobs in the bathroom, you guys are being really mean." Nothing turned him on like these two. Nothing at all.

Rig was just stock-still, fascinated. "Jesus fuck. I. Damn. Dick, you too."

Those jeans were looking tighter. He wasn't as broad as Rock, or as built, but he wasn't bad and he'd learned everything he knew about flexing for Rig from Rock. Dick stood next to Rock and showed off his guns, and then his abs, eyes sweeping the bar to make sure it was still fairly empty before he tugged up the hem of his t-shirt and really let Rig see his six-pack.

Rig actually whimpered, hand sliding down to barely brush that hard cock. "Fuck me."

"That's the plan," growled Rock, eyes riveted on Rig's hand.

Man, they should have gone back to the hotel -- this wasn't their local club where they knew they were safe going into the bathroom for a little action.

"They say anticipation makes it better," he pointed out. "And we wouldn't want to waste our beer." He wasn't sure who he was trying to convince -- them or himself.

"Uh-huh. Is it still my shot?" Rig wasn't watching anything but them.

"Yep." Rock kept flexing, happily giving Rig a show and there he was, showing off right next to Rock.

The next shot went so wide that it didn't even come close. Rock chuckled and grabbed his cue, took a handful of Rig's ass as he walked by as well.

"Pour me a beer, Pretty." Rig still looked dazed, horny. Please.

He did as he was told, fingers sliding on Rig's as he handed the glass over.

"Thank you." He could smell Rig, smell that Rig needed them. It made him moan and he bit the sound back. Fuck.

Rock managed to sink all his balls, putting the eight ball in the corner pocket. "You wanna break, Dick?"

"Uh. Sure?"

Rock headed over to Rig, standing too close, talking to their redneck, making Rig groan, blush dark. Oh man. Talk about distracting. He took his shot, wincing as the ball went wide, missing totally.

"Try again, Dick." Rig's voice was sandpaper rough, whatever Rock was saying was ratcheting their cowboy into a frenzy.

"Like my focus is getting any better." He did try again though, almost crowing as he managed to sink one of the stripes. He missed the next one, though. "Your go, Rock."

Rock and Rig both groaned, the air between them thick enough to slice.

He traded places with Rock, smiling at Rig as he grabbed his beer and downed it, feeling hot and horny.

He opened his mouth to say something to Rig and Rig hushed him with one finger. "Not a word, Pretty. I know how good you are at that. I'll cream my jeans."

"But-"

"Shh. I'm all riled up."

"I want to go back to the hotel. Rock?"

"I hear you." With military precision and efficiency, Rock proceeded to sink every last solid one after the other before putting the eight ball in the middle pocket. "Fast enough for you?"

"Uh-huh." Rig just vibrated, nodded. "Excellent game. Time to go."

"Yeah. Congrats, Rock. I agree, let's go." He led the way, Rock and Rig right behind him. Maybe him and Rig could get off in the back of the car.

"Who's got the keys?" Rig was a little bowlegged.

"Rock still does. Come sit in the back with me."

Rock grunted, but opened the door for them. "It'll take me five minutes to get us to the hotel. Be quick."

"We're going to be patient." Rig slid in, legs sprawled.

He climbed in after Rig. "We are?"

"Uh... Uh-huh." There was a tiny spot on Rig's jeans.

Dick grinned as Rock climbed in and started the car.

"Okay. I can wait. I can wait to pull down your zipper and tug out your prick. Lick those drops right from the tip..."

"Dick..." Rig's fingers landed on his lips. He let his tongue run across Rig's fingers. He wanted so badly.

"Four minutes," Rock called from the front seat, looking at them in the rear view mirror.

Rig leaned in, tongue sliding in between those fingers, touching his lips. Gasping, he opened wide, tugging one of Rig's fingers in, sucking on it.

"Pretty!" Rig's head slammed back, hips rocking furiously, humping the air. He sucked Rig's finger like it was the man's cock, letting it slide in and out of his mouth, teeth grazing the pad, tongue working the tip. He could feel Rock's gaze on them, heavy even through the mirror.

"Dick. Dick, man. You're gonna make me... I'm not walking through the hotel all nasty..."

"We'll go in the back door," growled Rock. "Fuck, Rig -- I can *smell* you."

He sucked harder, eyes on Rig.

Rig scrambled, free hand jerking his belt open, his fly open and down. That heavy cock pushed right out, red and dark and throbbing. Dick got his own seatbelt undone in record time, bending to suck that hard cock right in.

"Yes!" Rig's hips slammed up, cock filling his lips, spunk splashing on his tongue. He swallowed and swallowed, taking it all in, making sure not to lose a drop. When the pulses had stopped, he licked and lapped at the velvety flesh.

"Pretty..." Rig was still hard, moaning softly, fingers in his hair.

"One minute."

With great reluctance, he pulled of Rig's prick and tucked it back into the tight jeans. "Hold that thought."

"Uh. Uh-huh. Damn, pretty." Rig looked debauched. Utterly debauched.

He grinned, feeling like seven kinds of stud. Feeling even better than he had after getting off that helicopter. Rig's hand cupped his jaw, stroked him.

He nuzzled into the touch and could almost hear Rock roll his eyes. "Come on you two lovebirds. Upstairs where we can do it properly."

"Jealous old man." Rig leaned over the car seat, whispering in Rock's ear, tongue flicking out.

Rock groaned, hand coming up to slide over Rig's head, cupping it. He couldn't hear what Rig was saying, but he could see Rock, see the flush crawling up the big guy's head.

He slid his hand up along Rig's spine, just touching, admiring. Then Rig took Rock's earlobe in his teeth, tugging once, sweet and slow. Jesus.

His moan echoed Rock's.

"Sexy fucker," muttered Rock.

"Yours."

"Yep."

Dick grinned. That was Rock -- Mr. Romance.

He wouldn't change the man for anything.

Rig neither.

Chapter Seventeen

The taxi pulled up in front of their place and Rock groaned as he got out, the salt water in the air smelling good, like home.

He let Rig pay for the taxi and hauled their bags out of the trunk, Dick helping him.

"Good to be home," he muttered as they climbed the stairs, Rig letting them in. It was weird, coming home and not having the dogs pawing and sniffing all over them. They'd get them out of the kennel in the morning, for now, they were just home and that was enough. It was a little stuffy inside, and Dick went around opening up windows.

He grabbed Rig before the man could disappear and try to start washing their laundry or something like notice all the work he'd had done while they were gone. "You have a good vacation?"

"I did. I'm glad to be home. Vegas is something else."

"I keep getting the feeling you would have been happier going somewhere else." He rubbed his lips against Rig's.

"No. No, we had a ball." Rig smiled for him, kissed him, nice and slow.

"We had six, I believe." He grinned against Rig's lips, reached down for that ass. That got him a laugh, just like he'd hoped it would. Excellent.

When their lips parted, Rig noticed the staircase, eyes going wide. "Rock?"

"Yeah?"

"Oh, man. *Look*!" Rig spent a good, long time oohing and aahing over the stairs, over the work – not acting pissed at all, thank god.

"Happy birthday, Rabbit."

"Oh, that rocks, Blue. Fucking rocks."

"You guys hungry?" Dick asked, grabbing the bags and heading down the hall with them. "I can call for pizza or something."

Rock made a face. He'd had enough of restaurant and fast food.

"I'll cook something, Pretty. If I have to, I'll run to the grocery."

"Fuck no. We're all staying put until morning." He could put up with delivery for another day.

"I bet we've got stuff in the freezer," Dick said, heading for the kitchen after leaving their bags in the laundry room

"There's a pan of enchiladas in the deep freeze." Rig stretched, rubbing up against him. "We can warm it up after I thank you for my present."

"So supper is covered. We'll eat later."

Dick wandered back out, grinning at them. "You two gonna come in or just make out in the hallway?"

"We're going to just make out in the hallway." Rig grinned, winked, leaned even harder.

"I can live with that." Rock leaned against the wall, taking Rig's weight.

He got another smile, slow and almost lazy. "You think so, Blue?"

"Fuck, yeah." He rubbed his hand up and down along Rig's ass. Best fucking ass in the whole Goddamned world. Dick wandered over, pressing against Rig, his hands.

"Mmm. Y'all got me." Shit, Rig was hidden between them, arms wrapped around his neck.

Dick's prick was hard, pressing against the back of his hands, rubbing just like he'd been rubbing Rig's ass.

"Yeah, we *got* you. It's good to be home, isn't it?" The kid looked happy.

"Yes. Yes, this is where I belong, y'all." Rig pushed up into a kiss, tongue sliding against his lips.

"You know it." He caught that tongue between his lips and sucked on it, his own tongue sliding along it.

Rig held on, dragging him closer, the kiss going deep. He opened up and let his Rabbit in, one hand sliding beneath Rig's shirt, the other finding Dick's ass, squeezing the kid's cheek. Rig kept feeding him happy little sounds, tongue pushing and playing with his, so they kept kissing, tongues sliding and playing together.

Dick bent to lick and taste at Rig's neck. The kid knew just where to touch, where to lick to make Rig jerk, to make that skinny ass shudder. He could have stood there all night, making out with his men - his fucking men - but there was a couch and a bed and no reason they couldn't get horizontal.

"Bed," he growled. "Wanna fuck you."

"I bet it's right where we left it." Rig grinned for him, looking relaxed as hell.

"We better check."

Dick laughed, pressing up hard against Rig for a moment, lips meeting his. Kid tasted fucking good.

"God, y'all are fine." Yep. And Rig was wanting.

He and Dick kissed a moment longer, showing off a little for their cowboy. Rig's tongue teased along the sides of their mouths, teasing into the kiss. Chuckling, Dick's backed off just enough to let Rig in, and then weren't they all kissing together, three tongues sliding. So fucking good. Rig pushed right in and damn, they were good at this, the three-way kisses going deep.

The bed could wait.

On and on, they kissed, bodies starting to move, rub and rock against each other. Somebody - Rig, he thought - got his fly unzipped, got his prick out and started rubbing.

"Fuck yes." He grunted, the words lost in their kisses, his balls pulling up tight. His own hands held on to two asses, opening and closing. Rig slid down, disappearing from the kiss, manhandling his and Dick's cocks together and licking them with that hot as fuck tongue.

His free hand dropped into Rig's hair, sliding through the curls. Between the kisses and Rig's mouth, he was nearly ready to blow. Taking turns, Rig sucked him, then Dick, one after the other, over and over, looking happy as a fucking lark.

"Fucking love that mouth, Rig."

"Uh-huh." Dick's agreement was breathless and he wrapped his lips around the kid's tongue, sucking it in as his hips jerked, pushing his prick deeper into Rig's mouth. That hot little tongue pushed into his slit, fucking it, just shallowly. His head slammed against the wall, his whole body jerking. One of Dick's hands slid under his t-shirt, all the way up to his nipple, tugging on the ring.

Oh. Oh, shit. They were going to drive him out of his fucking mind. Rig managed to get their cocks together, mouth sinking down, squeezing them together.

Shouting, he let his load go, Dick's cock throbbing against his. His own personal favorite slut drank him down, head bobbing, that tongue moving and moving against him. Dick sank against him, sucking on his neck.

"Fuck, Rig... that was fucking perfect." Just what he'd Goddamned needed.

"Mmm." Rig kissed his abs, lips hot and soft.

Dick headed down him the other way, meeting Rig somewhere around his navel. They kissed, chins bumping his cock, his balls. His hips jerked a little, his hands sliding through almost white curls and shoulder length brown hair.

"Gonna keep me hard," he muttered.

"Good." Rig nuzzled the tip of his cock, humming low.

"Jesus, fuck." He growled. "Bed. Now. Gonna fuck you through the mattress."

"Promises promises." Rig gave him a wild, happy grin. Yeah. Yeah. Someone was glad to be home.

Dick and Rig slid up his body, their mouths meeting in another three-way kiss. He pushed off the wall, started moving them down the hall as they necked. His body knew just where to go, where to take his men. Rig followed, stepping backwards, almost dancing with him and Dick. He had to admit, their own bed looked fucking good, felt right in a way the hotel one hadn't.

That breeze was coming in through the window off the ocean, sharp and bright and salty. That mixed with the smell of the three of them made him groan, made him reach out and tug off Rig's t-shirt, Dick working on three sets of jeans.

"Oh, man. This is what I needed. It was time to be home." Rig pulled his shirt off, tugging hard, the seam creaking. He loved it when Rig needed that hard.

He put his arms up and helped Rig get it off, then together they got rid of Dick's and just like that all three of them were naked.

Standing there for a minute, he let Dick and Rig look their fill, knowing he still had it; they were pretty fucking hot themselves.

Rig stared, reached out, fingers tracing his abs. "Blue."

"This old man still has it."

Dick's fingers slid over his bare ass. "Old man? Where?"

"Must be talking about me, 'cause he's fine." Rig hummed, fingers sliding up to tug his nipple ring.

Groaning, he reached out to return the favor. "You're not old, Rabbit. You're ours."

"Yeah..." Look at that deep, dark blush.

Dick made a soft noise, fingers sliding on both of them. "You're both studs."

Rock chuckled. "Someone's looking to get fucked.'

"Yes, please."

"Mmm. Me too, me too."

Oh yeah, he could do them both. "There's enough of me to go around."

"Always." Rig grabbed hold of his cock, tugged him toward the bed.

"You wanna go first, Rabbit?"

"Y'all both got to come already." Those lips were offered up to him.

"We did. You know we'll take care of you, though."

"Yeah. I wanna suck you while Rock does you." Dick licked his lips. "I can already taste you."

"Oh, sweet fuck. Yes." Rig shuddered, groaned at the kid's words.

"Get that tongue working, Dick, and get him ready for me." He grinned at Dick and lay on the bed, patting his hip. "Rig can make sure I keep it up for him."

"You'll keep it up." There wasn't a fucking ounce of doubt in those grey eyes. Not an ounce.

"I will for the two of you." Until the end of time if he had to.

Rig settled on his hands and knees over him, Dick setting up behind their cowboy.

"What do you need, Blue?" Rig leaned down, lips just brushing over his belly.

"Whatever you want to fucking give me." He slid his hands down along Rig's back, grabbed that perfect ass and spread Rig's cheeks for Dick. That amazing mouth explored his abs, his pecs, fucking adoring him like he was a god or something.

He pushed up into the licks, flexed for Rig, showing off even as he enjoyed the touches.

Dick's tongue slid against the tips of his fingers and he pushed one into Rig, groaning at that heat, at the tickle of Dick's tongue as it pushed in alongside. Rig groaned, breath huffing out against his skin.

"Fucking love your mouth." There wasn't another like it.

"Mmm. My mouth loves fucking." He got a soft laugh, then Rig was sucking and licking at his nipple, pulling and tugging at the ring.

Dick laughed softly, and then really went for it, tongue pushing deep and wriggling around.

"Oh. Oh, fuck. That's... he's *good* at that, man."

"Uh-huh. Blowing your mind -- getting you ready for me."

"Yes. Your cock." Rig nodded, stubbly cheek rubbing on him.

Hips rolling up, he rubbed against Rig. "You about done, Dick?"

A last lick and Dick backed off. "Uh-huh. All ready."

"Yeah. Yeah, Blue. All ready." Rig shifted, their bodies knowing just what to do. Rig's body came down over his prick, those long legs straddling him. Fuck, that tight sheath felt good, felt fucking amazing. Rig, well, he just relaxed, smiled, looked like the fine fucker couldn't be happier.

Dick gave him a quick kiss, lips soft and warm, and then the kid's cheek rested against his belly, mouth starting to work on Rig's prick.

It wasn't furious, it wasn't even blistering hot, but it was pure fucking heaven. He pushed up with his hips, cock going deep inside Rig over and over, while Dick's hair moved against his skin, not quite tickling. Holding Rig's eyes, he reached out and tugged on that little ring in Rig's nipple.

Those grey eyes went wide, dazed, Rig bowing and arching right up into his touch. "Blue."

"Right fucking here." He tugged again, twisting the metal a little.

"Uh... Uh-huh." Rig went tight around him, body just shaking. Dick's head started bobbing madly, and he thrust deep and hard, balls pulling up. "Jesus. Please. Y'all. So good."

"Show us, Rig. Come on now." He tugged hard on that little ring, watching Rig's face.

"Yeah..." Rig's head rolled, lips parting, body rippling around his cock.

"Fuck! Fuck!" He jerked, pushing deep as he could as the movement around his prick pulled him right over the edge, the spunk shooting from him.

Rig groaned as Dick's seed splashed on his thigh, all of them tumbling over.

He relaxed back against the bed, feeling fucking fine, his hands sliding over whatever parts of his lover's he could reach.

Rig cuddled in, humming happily, holding on. Dick shifted up, pressing in from the side and bringing the covers with him. "It's good to be home."

"You got that right, kid."

Rig just nodded, agreeing. Settling down.

Yeah. Home, where they belonged.

Chapter Eighteen

Okay, so he wasn't as young as he used to be. Or as in shape. Or as healthy, hydrated, or or or or...

He shook his head and swung his feet out of the bed. Two days in the hospital bed on IV fluids and twelve hours in the home one was more than enough.

No matter what Blue threatened. Beautiful, pushy asshole.

"Where are you going?" asked Rock from the bedroom door. What had the man been doing, lying in wait, listening for sound of movement?"

"Jesus!" He jumped, gave Rock a look. "Damn, Blue. I need to pee. I need a shower. I need a glass of something cold and wet."

Apparently he needed to gain a couple three pounds back too, but there was no need to discuss that with Rock now, was there?

"We've got a bedpan, the kid'll give you a sponge bath and he's already on his way with a glass of water. Get back in bed."

"You're not serious." He blinked over. There was no fucking way; he could pee standing up.

Rock folded his arms across his chest, looking every inch a three hundred pound muscle bound man intent on not letting him up. "I suppose I could carry you into the bathroom."

"There's nothing wrong with my legs, Blue." To prove it he stood, knees just a little wobbly.

Rock growled and came forward, grabbing him up and carrying him to the bathroom as if he didn't weigh more than a feather.

They passed Dick with his glass of water, his Pretty turning and following them. "Everything all right?"

"Aside from Rig being the most stubborn man alive, just fine," growled Rock.

"I have to pee, is all." He turned to look at Dick, mouthing "help". "As much water as they pushing in me as the fucking hospital, I'm going to have to move into the bathroom."

Rock snorted, but set him down like he was spun glass. "You nearly died of dehydration, Rig. I expected you wouldn't have to pee before next week."

Dick gave him an apologetic look, sort of lounging in the doorway. "It was touch and go for a bit, Rig."

"So I'm a little skinny and a little sicker than I thought. I'm okay now. Honest. Haven't puked in over a day." He peed right quick before Rock changed his mind.

"The doctor said bed rest and bed rest is what you're going to get."

"It won't be that bad," Dick added. "We'll keep you company."

"Bed rest? Dick, he's not serious, is he? How long?"

"Doctor said a week," Rock told him, picking him up again.

"At the most," added Dick.

He wrapped his arms around Rock's neck, cuddling a bit. "A whole week? Did y'all call in for me? I can't be off work a whole week, much less in bed."

"They don't expect you back before Monday," said Dick. His Pretty gave him a wink. "Rock called them."

Oh, God. They were going to think he was dying.

"What day is it... Sunday, right? I'm not so sick as to take a real week off..."

"All right, pack up a bag -- I'm taking you back to the hospital."

"What? No. No, Rock, please." He fucking hated being a patient, hated being woke up and messed with and not being home."

"Then you're taking the week off. And that means if I have to tie you to the bed to keep you here, I will." Rock looked deadly serious.

"We'll keep you company," Dick said again.

"Yeah? Promise? I hate doing nothing." He felt Rock relax against him, knew he'd made the right decision to just give in.

Not that he was officially giving in.

Not yet.

Dick nodded as Rock put him back in bed. "In fact that tying you down thing could be fun."

"No," growled Rock. "He's not up to that."

"Oh, I bet it wouldn't take much for him to up to it." Dick didn't seem in the least bit fazed by Rock's glare.

He grinned at Dick and tugged on Rock's hand, pulling the big guy down to snuggle against. "I didn't try to get sick, Blue. I didn't. Y'all had the same thing I had."

"We didn't wind up in the hospital," growled Rock, but his Blue stretched out and pulled him close, big hand stroking along his hip.

"Yeah. I didn't mean to." He snuggled close, cheek resting on Blue's shoulder. "You just got you a skinny cowboy."

"And I plan to keep him," Rock said, hand holding his hip now in a hard grip.

Dick passed him his water. "I bet you're wanting a shower."

His Pretty looked over at Rock. "Should be okay -- you can carry him there, hold him up?"

Rock shook his head. "Sponge bath until he's not so pale."

"Ooo, that sounds like fun." Dick wagged his eyebrows.

"I'm not all that pale, am I?" He chuckled, sticking his tongue out at Dick, tickled down deep.

"Pale enough." Rock was growling again.

Dick leaned in to give him a soft kiss and whisper. "Enough that I'm siding with Rock on the bed rest thing."

He nodded, one hand petting Rock's belly. "I need to get clean though, I smell like work."

Dick nodded. "I'll go get the stuff for the sponge bath. Maybe Rock'll let you have it in the chair and then we can change the sheets and you can smell clean and fresh in a new bed."

He nodded, slowly working his way into Rock's lap, into Rock's arms. Close enough to feel his Blue all over. Close enough for a soft kiss.

"I'm sorry I scared you. I don't even remember what happened, all I remember was feeling sort of blah, then waking up in the ER."

"You passed out," Rock told him. His Blue was doing a good job at looking grumpy but a second kiss followed the first and it was warm enough.

"Good thing y'all were here. Thank you." The best way to keep Rock from killing him was honest stroking of that ego, sex, and a few days of not pushing his luck.

"You better believe it -- I would have kicked your ass if you'd died."

"Never going to happen. I eat right." He gave his Blue a sheepish grin. "I just need to remember to eat."

"More pizza," Rock told him, giving him a smile before he got another kiss, this one longer.

He stretched out long, wrapping around Rock's body. He stroked Rock's temples, forehead, petting and easing the stress and tension he found there. "You look tired, Blue. Haven't you slept?"

Rock shrugged. "You were in the hospital for a couple of days."

Dick came in with a large bowl of steaming water. "Yeah, but he's out now. Ready to be an octopus, yeah?"

"If I have to be still and rest, between y'all is where I need to be." He nodded. "Where do you want me, Pretty?"

"In the chair -- Rock can change the bed while I wash you."

"I'll carry you over," Rock told him, getting up.

"I can walk, Blue. Really."

"I'll carry you," growled Rock.

He lifted his arms, wrapped them around Rock's neck. Right. No pushing his luck. "Don't hurt your back."

"My back is fine." Rock carried him the few feet over to the chair, Dick waiting silently for them, eyes dancing.

He got settled, then whispered low. "You're not helping, Pretty."

In fact, the kid was having way too much fun.

Dick bent past him to pick up the sponge out of the water. "He hasn't burst a vein yet, has he?"

"No, not yet, and I don't see a single bruise on you, either." Poor thing, dealing with scared Rock was even less fun than dealing with pissed off Rock.

"So I'd say I was helping just fine." Dick gave him a grin and, after soaping up the sponge, started to wash him.

"This is really weird, Dick. I'm not broken. I just got a little dehydrated. I'm hydrated. I promise to eat." He wiggled and shivered, oddly uncomfortable with this, so intimate.

"Just humor him, Rig."

Dick crouched down in front of him, took his hand. "You always hear how doctors make the worst patients."

"I'm not a patient. I've been released." He squeezed Dick's hand. "Are y'all all better? No more puking?"

"We're fine, Rig." Dick leaned up and kissed him. "You took good care of us."

"'s my job." He rested his forehead against Dick's.

Those riverstone eyes gazed at him, Dick's smile soft as he was given another kiss.

"Are you washing or making out over there?" interrupted Rock.

"I can't do both?" Dick asked.

He grinned, licking at Dick's lips. "Which answer's going to get me in the least trouble?"

"We're washing," Dick said and gave him another kiss. "Mouth's almost clean."

He chuckled, relaxing, easing under Dick's hands.

"Just get him clean, kid -- we've got a week to play tonsil hockey."

"And between us all a week since we last played tonsil hockey. Don't tell me you aren't eager, Rock."

"Why do you think I want him washed and back in bed?"

Dick chuckled, sliding the sponge over him quickly. By the time Dick had him cleaned, he was shivering, chilled, tired, more than willing to snuggle back into the covers, into his lovers' arms. His men both stripped down first and then they were on either side of him, making him feel warm and at home.

"Mmm... feels good." He cuddled happily. "We gonna fuck now?"

"I don't think you're up to fucking," growled Rock.

"No." It surprised him to say, but it was the truth. He wasn't. He wasn't up to fucking at all. Cuddling, though? That he could do. "But we could rest."

"Okay." Rock nodded. "Nap."

"I'm okay, Blue."

"We'll talk about it later, Rig. Right now, sleep, or your skinny ass is going back to Mercy."

He nodded. Sleep now. Fuck later. No Mercy.

Right.

Chapter Nineteen

He lost his supper, trying his best to be quiet about it. Shit.

Shit, that was the sixth time this week.

He really needed to grab Dave or Peg or Sammy, have them check him out. This was way weirder than some bug and God knew he wasn't pregnant.

Rig washed his face, brushed his teeth and headed for the shower, hand on his gut. Fuck, he was sore. Tired. Grumpy as hell. Maybe a little on the scared side because damn it, Momma had cancer and...

Well, he wasn't having any of that shit.

"Hey." Dick's head popped around the door. "You're not coming back for dessert?"

"I need a shower, Pretty. Maybe after."

The door opened further and Dick came in. "You want some company?"

"You don't have to. I know you were wanting that cake." He bent to turn the water on, waiting for the steam.

Dick snorted, sounding a whole lot like Rock. "Since when is cake better than naked you?" Dick started stripping. "Besides, the cake'll still be there later."

That made it easy to chuckle, strip off the rest of his clothes and get in the hot water. Dick followed him in, arms wrapping around his middle and tugging him back against the solid body.

"Hey, you." God, Dick felt good. Solid. Strong.

"Mmm... hey." Dick kissed the side of his neck. "You seemed preoccupied at supper."

"Yeah? I'm good." Queasy and sore, but good. "How's things at the gym?"

"Not bad. I feel guilty leaving so much of it up to Rock lately, but my classes are really kicking my ass and the place does sort of run itself. He gets stuck with all the paperwork though." Dick's fingers rubbed over his belly, just touching.

"I can head over once or twice a week, help him out with it." God knew he did enough that he was speedy as all get out. "You liking your classes?"

"Oh, he'd love that." Dick chuckled and hugged him tight. "Though now I'll feel doubly guilty that you're helping out instead of me being able to do it. And yeah. Except for Statistics. I fucking hate Statistics. Feeling is mutual, too."

"No guilt. You need a tutor? We can afford one."

"I don't know. Maybe? I don't know." Dick chuckled. "I just don't want to disappoint you and Rock."

"You won't. Get you a tutor, Pretty. I'll get the tab." Hell, all Dick would need was a little confidence and he'd figure it.

"Yeah?" He got another squeeze. "Thanks, Rig. It means a lot that you think I can do this."

"I know you can. You just need a little hand." He lifted his head, got a kiss. Dick's lips were soft and sure, his Pretty's eyes closing against the water as their lips moved together.

Rig relaxed against Dick, just letting himself float, rest. Dick seemed just as happy to float with him, the strong body supporting him, hands moving idly, gently on his skin. Rig actually dozed off, leaning hard, resting hard. He woke to Dick's hands moving with more intent, slipping and sliding over him, soaping him up as Dick washed him.

"Mmm. Hey. Sorry. Damn, that feels good." Jesus, what was wrong with him?

"You've been working too hard again," Dick murmured. "Ruining all the relaxation of our holiday."

"No, just real tired." Bone-deep.

"You not been sleeping right?" Dick rinsed him down.

"I have." He just wasn't keeping enough down.

Dick turned his face up, looking into his eyes. "Why're you so tired then?"

"I don't know." And that was the God's honest truth.

Dick brought their mouths together, the kiss soft and gentle. "Well let's get you out of the shower and into bed."

"You need your dessert, Pretty. I have laundry." Thank God for Maria and her crew, if he had to do housework, he'd be in trouble.

"I can do the laundry for you, Rig -- you're tired." Dick leaned past him to turn the shower off.

"You're busy." They tumbled out of the shower, leaning on each other.

Dick grabbed two towels, wrapping one around his own shoulders and then drying Rig down. "So? I can throw on some laundry for you, Rig. You're not looking that good, to tell the truth."

"I'm thinking about seeing one of the guys at work, just having them give me a physical."

Dick's hand stilled a moment, and then slowly continued patting him down with the towel. "You feeling that bad, huh?"

"No. No, just being careful. No reason to feel tired if I don't have to..." No reason to worry his boys, if he didn't have to.

"Yeah? Okay." Dick gave him a kiss and grinned. "Come on, let's get you tucked into bed. I'll even go get you a slice of cake, maybe even some ice cream with it."

"Just ice cream, huh?" He kissed Dick's cheek. "Go hang with Rock for a while, keep him company. I'll doze."

"Yeah, okay." Dick's hand squeezed his.

Rig sighed, crawled into bed. Yeah.

Tomorrow.

Tomorrow he'd talk to somebody, get them to run some tests.

Just in case.

Chapter Twenty

He was running the wiring in the spare room, the house weird and quiet with the fuse box turned off. Rig had been working diligently on this room forever. Now it was fixing to be November, and he was reaching done, even if it had taken too long.

The windows were huge, the floor smoothed. The drywall was done, thanks to Rock, and he was ready to prime and paint and have a nice room to watch the winter come in. Maybe put Christmas lights in. He drew the wires down through the ceiling and headed down the ladder to fetch up the ceiling fan, breathing just a little heavy.

"Hey, Rig -- you need some help?" Dick asked, head popping round the door.

"Always." He stretched for a nice, long kiss and then moved to climb the ladder. "Hand me up that ceiling fan, yeah?"

"Okay." He looked down to find Dick grinning up at him. "'Course I might get distracted by the display."

"Flatterer." He stuck his tongue out and winked. He was in ancient, filthy jeans that were damn near falling and one of Rock's oldest sweatshirts, dust in his hair and his tool belt around his waist. Sex on a stick, he wasn't.

"Nope. I just know a good thing when I see one."

Rig blushed and grinned wide. "You make me feel good, Pretty. What do you think? The room's looking damned good, isn't it?"

"Yeah, you've done a real good job." Dick handed him up the fan. "You deserve a reward."

"A reward? I thought Rock deciding to give up bitching at me was my reward." He chuckled and balanced the light fixture, laughter trailing off as he fastened wire together and added insulators.

Dick waited until he was done and then warm hands slid up along his legs. "I was thinking of something a whole lot more physical."

"Mmm... You're a temptation waiting to happen. Hold me steady, I'm going to mount it."

Dick burst out laughing. He rolled his eyes and slid the fan over the mounting hub, screwing in the base.

"I'm sorry," grinned Dick. "You've got to admit it sounded pretty damn suggestive."

"You, Dick-weed, are a jackass. You're mine, and I adore you, but you're a jackass." He chuckled as he finished up. "There we go. Now I can work in here at night."

"We should test it out." Dick's hands slid up his body as he climbed down the ladder.

"Yep. Gotta balance the blades, too." Rig nodded, relaxing back into Dick's hands.

Dick nuzzled at his neck. "You need help balancing your blade, Rig?"

"Mmm..." He tilted his head, humming softly. "You keep that up, Pretty, and I'm going to need, all right."

"Good."

Dick's hand slid across the front of his jeans.

"Just think how it'll be, Dick. Fucking up here while a storm rolls in? Watching the lightning?" He snuggled back, thighs parting.

"Sounds great." Dick rubbed against his ass. "Of course I don't need a storm to fuck you."

"No? You don't think?"

Dick slapped his ass and turned him around, taking his mouth. He chuckled, wrapping his arms around Dick's neck and tugging him closer, lips parting wide. Sexy bastard. Beautiful, dear, sexy bastard. Dick's hands slid along his ass, pulling him close, kissing him deep. He fed Dick a long moan, fingers tangling in the soft-soft hair. "Dick. Pretty. Oh, fuck, you taste good."

"Let's go to bed, Rig. Do this right."

Rig nodded. "Yeah. Okay." He grinned over, kissing the corner of Dick's mouth. "You make me want, Pretty."

"Feeling's mutual, Rig." Dick grinned. "We need a couch in here. Or a bed."

Rig nodded. "A big old cushy sofa. Big enough for three."

"Sounds perfect, but right now? The bedroom. We could even pick Rock up if we swing by the living room."

He had to admire the kid's focus. Rig grabbed Dick's hand and headed for the stairs. "Come on, Pretty. Let's go get our old man and warm the bed sheets."

Chapter Twenty One

Dick sighed and rubbed his eyes. He blinked over at the clock on the oven, surprised at how late it had gotten. And he was only halfway through his chapters. He hated pulling all-nighters. Especially with what he had waiting for him in the bedroom. Still, he was halfway there. Another chapter and he'd make some more coffee.

Hands landed on his shoulders, pushing in deep, working out one ache after another. Oh. Rig. Groaning, he let his head drop and closed his eyes, let Rig's hands make him feel better. Rig never said a word, just touched him. Rubbed him. Loved on him. Inch by inch he relaxed, Rig's hands working magic on him.

The nape of his neck was kissed, so softly, then Rig closed his book, encouraged him to stand.

"I oughta be studying." His heart wasn't in it though, not with Rig right here, making him feel good.

"Mmhmm. Bed, Pretty." Rig walked him back, turning lights out as he went. "Come love on me."

"I can't turn down an offer like that." He smiled, hands tracing Rig's ribs, his sides and abdomen.

"You know it." All the way down the hall, into the bedroom and the whole way he was getting long, slow, lazy kisses. He sank into each one, tongue sliding with Rig's, his heart beat starting to pick up, warmth in his belly.

They had his buttons open, his zipper down by the time they got to the bedroom. He shrugged out of his t-shirt, smiling at Rock, snoring away, arm flung over his eyes. Then his attention was back on Rig, their mouths coming together in a kiss that had a little more heat behind it.

Rig eased him into the bed, never breaking the kiss, tongue sliding against his. He lay back, arms sliding around Rig, loving the weight of Rig on him. One hand was on his cock, moving nice and steady, just right to blow the top of his head off.

"You make me feel so good." It was so easy to forget about his studies and his tiredness with Rig's hands on him.

"It's my job. Relax, Pretty. Let me give this to you." Lips brushed his, slid on his chest.

He could do that. He found Rig's head with his hands, slid his fingers through the almost white curls, heat curling through his body. With the softest touches, tugs, and kisses, Rig just made him fly, made the need grow and throb through him. His body undulated, pushing into the touches, the kisses, working with Rig as the sensations built.

"That's it, Pretty. Come on. Come on for me." Rig kissed him hard, thumb working his cock.

His moans pushed into Rig's mouth as his body jerked, spunk spraying from him.

He was almost asleep as Rig eased him through the aftershocks, tongue sliding down to clean him.

"I need to get up early to finish that book," he murmured, stroking Rig's head, his shoulders,

"Okay. I'll wake you." Rig cuddled in, hand twining with his.

"Cool." He nuzzled, something tickling at him, not letting him drift right off yet. "You good? Less tired?"

"Mmm. I'll be fine, Pretty. Just fine."

"Yeah? Good." He kissed Rig's shoulder and squeezed the hand twined with his, and let go.

He was exactly where he wanted to be and all nighters were for college kids who didn't have lovers to curl up with.

Chapter Twenty Two

He watched as Rig and Dick danced around the new room, making their way slowly from one end of the big windows down to the other and back again. It made a pretty picture with the moon and the waves behind them.

Of course you couldn't make out with pictures.

"That's the fourth song in a row," he told them.

"Mmm?" Rig was cuddled in close, lips sliding over Dick's throat.

"Dancing -- that's the fourth song in a row the two of you have been way over there."

"He wants us to dance closer, Pretty?" Rig rocked, hummed softly.

Dick chuckled and pulled Rig in tighter. "I can do that."

He rolled his eyes. "There's a whole set of horizontal dances you're missing out on."

Rig hummed and started wiggling, drawing them closer, step by step. "You could dance with us..."

"That means getting up," he pointed out reasonably.

"That's bad?" Rig moaned as Dick started working that long throat. Oh, the kid was not playing fair.

"I'm already up," he said, hand on his prick, rubbing. As he watched, his slut licked those sweet, kiss-swollen lips. He grunted, opening his pants and letting his prick push out. Rock took himself in hand, pumping slowly.

Rig moaned. "Mmm... Pretty... Look at our old man. So fucking fine."

Dick moaned softly. "Yeah. Hot."

"It's all yours," he told them, stopping long enough to pull off his t-shirt, sweeten the view and the temptation.

Those grey eyes slid over his body, almost hot enough to feel. They stepped a little closer, Rig rubbing up against Dick's thigh. He pushed off his jeans and spread his legs wide, cupping his balls as he stroked long and slow up along his cock.

"Mmm... Blue..." Rig whimpered and took Dick's lips in a hard, needy kiss, hands burying in Dick's hair.

He growled. No fair. He was getting Rig all hot and bothered and Dick was reaping the rewards. He leaned forward, grunting in triumph as he snagged the belt loop on Dick's jeans and tugged hard, bringing Dick and Rig toward him.

Rig's hand landed on his belly, sliding down to circle his cock. "Mmm... So hot."

He rumbled happily, pushing his hips up, encouraging the touches.

Dick's fingers slid over his chest, tugging at the ring in his nipple and flicking across the unadorned one. He rumbled happily.

"My Blue... Hungry for you." Rig licked his belly, nudging Dick out of the way to get to his cock. Oh yeah, this was what he'd fucking wanted. He spread his legs wider, pushing his prick against Rig's lips.

Dick grinned and mouthed "slut" at him. Rig swallowed him down, lips hot and wet on his cock, pulling hard. He groaned, head falling back. It didn't matter how fucking often Rig sucked him, it was always amazing.

The kid took advantage of his position, kneeling next to him on the couch and licking at his neck. Fucking decadent -- his men licking and sucking and touching his body, making him feel fucking good. He slid his hands over them, touching where he could, groaning, letting them know it was fucking good. Rig was humming, sucking, head bobbing on his prick, tongue fucking the slit. Fuck. Yes.

Dick's fingers were back at his nipples, the kid's sweet mouth pulling a mark up on his neck. It was like Rig and Dick were connected, fire zinging between their mouths. One long finger slid behind his balls, circling his hole before pushing in deep. He roared, shooting his load down Rig's throat. His own personal redneck drank him down, throat working his cock.

He got a long kiss from Dick. Rig started groaning, nuzzling and kissing his belly, his cock, his balls. Loving on him.

Felt good. Felt fucking good.

He could handle this kind of dancing anytime.

Chapter Twenty Three

Paperwork.
The one fucking thing he hated about owning the gym.
Well, hated was a strong word.
Rock looked at the pile of paper still to deal with and took that back. He definitely hated it. And he had to do the kid's fucking share as well lately. Dick going to school was a good thing, but him getting stuck with the paperwork wasn't. Maybe they needed to hire someone to pick up Dick's slack. Only the kid was already feeling so fucking guilty -- he was going to have to talk to Dick, slap him upside the head and tell him to fucking stop it.

Meantime, it was after seven and he was going to be stuck here another couple hours, at least, getting caught up. And he didn't want to call home because Rig was likely sleeping and his cowboy'd been so fucking tired lately.

He couldn't even ask Jilly to go out and get him some supper because the girl was vegetarian or vegan or some shit. Little freak refused to even buy meat for someone else and the last time she'd picked up supper for the staff he'd wound up with a recycled cardboard box of warm salad with fucking tofu on it. Bad enough it was rabbit food, but heated through? Christ.

He'd rather eat the Goddamned paperwork.
The smell of grease and burger and fried shit hit him, made him blink. "Hey, Marine. Reinforcements are here."

Oh, man. Rig. With food. And Coke.

"Oh, fuck. That smells like heaven, Rig." He pushed his paperwork to the side, making space in front of him for the greasy bag of food.

"I thought you'd approve." Rig plopped the bag down, grabbed the pile and a pen. "How's it going?"

"Long fucking day, but it's looking up."

He took a moment to give Rig a once over. Long and skinny, his cowboy looked tired, but fucking good in the chair across his desk.

Then he grabbed the bag and opened it up, groaning as the smell of greasy hamburger and even greasier fries hit his nose. There were two burgers for him. Fries. Two fried pies. Score. Fucking score.

He ate the first burger like a starving man, which he was, and then enjoyed the other one more slowly. "You already eat?" he asked around a mouthful of bun, meat and grease.

"Not hungry yet, man." Rig's head was bent over the papers, pen scribbling away.

He grabbed a handful of fries, licking the salt off his fingers. "You have a late lunch? And you don't have to do that, you know."

"I know. I like to help you out, Blue. You know that." He got a grin, the lines beside Rig's eyes and mouth deep as fuck.

"I know. It's why I keep you around." He winked.

"Yeah, yeah, yeah." Rig snorted, laughed. "I just figure the more I help, the more likely we are to get home together."

"Yeah. I'm a bit backed up here." He nodded at the pile, which already looked a lot fucking shorter. "Dick got a class or a study group meeting?"

"I don't know. I think a study thing. I'm just glad it's not me."

"Been there, done that, huh?" He couldn't fucking imagine it. All those books. Give him a weight machine or a weapon and he knew what he was doing.

"You know it. It's important to him, though."

"Yeah. He's done good -- committed to it." He was proud of the kid, doing something more. He finished the last fry and tossed the bags into his wastebasket. Swish, right in. Two points.

Rig applauded, grinned at him. "Better?"

He grinned and nodded. "Fuck, Rig, I was better the minute you walked in the door with your offering of food and your skills with the paperwork."

Speaking of which... he grabbed half of what was left and started in on it.

Hell, Rig had whaled on it, just leaving him a couple things. Fucking *A*.

He was a fucking lucky man.

It didn't take them more than fifteen minutes to finish everything up and get it all filed or mailed off. "You want to work out or sit in the hot tub or anything?"

"Is there a private room open? I could soak."

"You know there's a private room." He stood and stretched. He could handle a soak with his cowboy.

"Well, I know there *is* one. I didn't know if it was booked." Rig got to his feet, finger sliding over his belly.

He groaned, muscles flexing under Rig's fingers. "It's always open for you, Rig."

"Mmm. Then lead on, Marine. I got old bones that need boiling."

He snorted. "Watch who you're calling old there."

He had ten years on Rig. And some days he felt it, though Rig was fucking good at making him forget it. He put his arm around Rig's shoulders and led him down to the change room.

Christ, Rig was bony. Seriously bony.

He grunted and let his hand slide down along Rig's spine, trying not to let the sound turn into a growl. He could feel every vertebrae, every single one. He did growl this time. "You've been living on coffee again, haven't you?"

"No. No, Blue. I haven't had a cup of coffee in damn near a month."

What the hell? "Why the fuck not?"

"I just haven't. Hasn't been settling." Rig locked the little private door, started stripping off.

He started stripping down himself. With the door locked, they didn't need to worry bathing suits, just the way he liked it.

"Well what are you living on then? Peanuts? You look like a strong wind'll blow you the fuck down."

"I'm fine, Rock." No. No, it didn't look like.

"You're too fucking skinny."

"Quit nagging, Rock. Let's soak."

His eyebrow rose. "I'm not nagging." He climbed into the hot tub though and leaned back, arms open.

Rig smiled, slipping into the water, settling in his arms. "Oh. Better." Way too fucking skinny.

He let it go, though, just wrapped his arms around Rig. "This beats paperwork, hands down."

"Mmmhmm." Rig cuddled in, moaning softly. "You know it, man."

Rock closed his eyes and floated in the bubbles, arms full of his favorite cowboy. Rig's cheek landed on his shoulder, legs floating around him. He stroked his hand along Rig's spine, counting each vertebrae right down to the top of Rig's crack. It wasn't right. It wasn't right at all. "Everything okay?"

"It is now. Damn, you feel good." Rig smiled against his skin, just floating. He grinned, flexed a little, making Rig's head move up and down with the motion of his muscles.

"Mmm. My Blue." Rig's fingers slipped down his belly, stroking and petting him. He groaned, hips pushing a little, encouraging Rig's touch where he most wanted it. Rig murmured, finger slipping down, wrapping around his cock and rubbing, slow and easy.

"Mmm... yeah, just like that." His own hand slid farther down along Rig's crack, rubbing against his hole.

"Yeah. Yeah, Blue." Rig shifted, encouraging his touch, eyelashes teasing his skin.

"You wanting, Rabbit?" He pushed the tip of his finger in, jonesing on the way Rig's body gripped it.

"Uh-huh. Need you." He could hear it, the way Rig needed him. He pushed his finger in the rest of the way, fucked Rig with it.

"Got what you need right here."

"You always have." Rig moaned and spread, hips moving, sliding, riding his touch. He nudged his other finger against Rig's hole, letting his cowboy's own motions pull it in. Curling his fingers, he found Rig's gland.

"Rock." Rig's eyes flew open, belly going tight. "Goddamn, that's hot."

"You sure it's not the water that's hot?" He hit Rig's gland again.

"Uh. Uh-huh." Oh, fuck, that was fine.

He stared into those grey eyes and played Rig's body, fingers stretching and teasing, hitting that little bump over and over.

"Don't stop, hmm? Just want to ride it 'til I shoot."

"Anything you want." He could do this as long as Rig needed him to.

"I want. Shit, I need." Rig exhaled, long and slow, body shaking against him.

"Come on, Rabbit. Give it to me and then I'll give it to you." His cock throbbed; he needed to.

"Kiss me." Those lips lifted, raised to him.

Rock slid his free hand behind Rig's head, holding it as his lips pressed down onto Rig's. His tongue pushed in, devouring Rig's mouth. Rig cried out, hips bucking, ass muscles fluttering around his fingers.

He smiled into the kiss. He was still the stud.

Rig chuckled, eyes happy and laughing. Yeah. Yeah, Rig knew it too.

"You want to ride me?" he asked, fingers still buried, bumping against Rig's gland again. "Or you want to get out and bend over for me?"

"I'll ride, Blue." Rig gasped, legs sliding.

"I thought you might." He nudged Rig's gland again, free hand grabbing that perfect cowboy ass and lifting Rig up.

"You know me." Rig stretched, throat working, lips parted.

"I do." He slid his fingers out of Rig's body, using both hands to slide Rig over his cock, rubbing the head along that sweet crack. Leaning in, he licked at those sweet lips. Rig searched his eyes, just like his cowboy was hunting something, then Rig pushed into the kiss, tongue fucking him, good and hard. Groaning, he sucked on Rig's tongue, and shifted just enough that his prick was pushing into that sweet fucking hole.

He heard Rig's moan, the sound vibrating his lips. Fuck, yeah. Yeah. He lowered Rig slowly, that tight ass taking more and more of his prick in, squeezing him tight. Groaning, he pushed up the last little bit, getting really deep.

"Wish we could stay just like this."

"Nah, you want me to do this." He lifted Rig up, and thrust up as he brought that skinny body back down.

"Oh... Fuck." Rig's head rolled, lips open, parted as the water splashed around them.

"Yeah. Fuck." He met Rig's eyes, grinning at his lover as he repeated the move, bringing that sweet body down hard. Nothing fucking like being buried deep inside Rig.

"More. More, Blue. Now." Demanding asshole.

He loved it. He moved Rig faster, pushed up harder. The water around them splashed against the sides of the hot tub, splashed over it.

When Rig relaxed, gave himself over to the pleasure, he felt it - arms and cock, hell, even inside. That was what he needed. Rig, right here, with him. They kept moving together, letting the water splash, letting everything go but each other. It was fucking good.

"Now this is where we can fucking stay. Right here."

"Yes. Yes, please. Right here." Rig nodded, almost desperate.

"I've got you, Rabbit." He growled the words, and took Rig's mouth in a hard kiss. It blew his fucking mind, that deep, hard, amazing kiss. Just blew his mind.

Groaning, almost disappointed, he shot, the orgasm going through him like lightning. It was fucking good, but over too damned quick. Rig floated for him, holding on, holding tight, the kiss easing some, making him breathless, still.

Hands shifting to wrap around Rig's waist, he just held on, kept his Rabbit close.

"Mmm. Thanks, Blue. Needed this."

"I always have what you need right here."

Rig nodded, swallowed and just held tight.

He slowly stroked Rig's back, floated, the bubbles spraying, the heat making him sleepy.

And that was okay. They could stay right here for awhile.

Chapter Twenty Four

Rig waved goodbye to little Hank and his new baby sister, then headed back into the clinic.

He'd self-medicated. He'd run a couple blood tests. He couldn't figure it. Still, he'd lost thirty pounds and it wasn't looking good on him, not at all, so... He knocked on Sam's door, leaning on the doorframe a bit.

Sam looked up from his desk, little wire-rimmed glasses just barely perched at the end of his long, skinny nose. "Hey, Alex. You done for the day?"

"Yeah. Yeah, I... You busy, man?" Sam was a good guy, knew his shit.

"Just paperwork." It was pushed aside and Sam pointed to the chair in front of his desk. "Have a seat."

"Thanks, man." He shut the door behind him, took a load off. "I got a problem, buddy, and I don't know how to start fixing it."

Sam nodded. "I didn't want to go poking into your business, but you've been looking kind of wiped out lately. Well, for awhile now."

"Yeah. I'm vomiting blood, I'm in a lot of pain, and I've lost damn near thirty two pounds in the last six months. Something's wrong, Sammy, and I can't figure it." There.

There, it was out.

Now maybe he could start fixing it.

"Jesus, Alex, you should have come to me sooner."

"Yeah. I ran some basic blood work, tried the normal stuff - ulcers, hiatal hernia. The works. Help?"

Sam pulled an empty patient folder out of his desk drawer and opened it up, put his name on it. "All right -- you have copies of your blood work?"

"Yeah. Yeah." He handed the sheaf of papers over. "My momma... she just died two Februarys ago, remember. Liver cancer. Just for history's sake."

Just for history.

Please, God. Don't do this to his men.

"Yeah, I remember." Sam took the papers and added them to the folder, glancing at them quickly. "Okay, first things first we're not going to assume the worst, okay? I'm going to take all your symptoms down and we'll make a list of all the things it could possibly be and then just work our way through them until we find it."

He nodded, relaxing back into his chair. Yeah. "Yeah, okay."

Oh. Oh, he could do this.

Chapter Twenty Five

Presents weren't Rock's strong point. Left to his own devices he would invariably wind up purchasing something practical. And there was nothing wrong with buying Rig a new fully loaded tool box or a new set of deck chairs, but it lacked the flair that Dick could manage, so he usually left it to the kid. Every now and then though, he'd see something or an idea would pop into his head and he'd go ahead and buy something frivolous or fun or special. Of course he usually felt like a dork and returned the item, or just sort of flung it at Rig or the kid, depending on who it was for.

The package in the front seat of his truck was a flinger.

A doeskin jacket with fringes and silver and blue beads worked in. It was soft as anything and the perfect size for his favorite cowboy. The chick at the counter had insisted on wrapping it, making a big fucking deal about it and now he was stuck.

Rock picked it up with a sigh and went in. He just didn't do sweet and thoughtful. It wasn't his style. He found Rig in his office. He knocked, package under his arm.

"Come on in. I'm decent!" Rig sounded happy, peaceful in that 'I'm pottering around and fixing to rearrange furniture' way that sparked terror in lesser men.

Of course he didn't have to go in. He could take 'fling the gift' to a whole new level and just leave it by the door.

Yeah, that sounded good. He'd leave Rig the present and go fix himself a sandwich. He put the box on the floor and knocked again before heading to the kitchen.

It didn't take long before Rig's steps sounded, his redneck holding the wrapped box. "Look what I found." Shining grey eyes smiled at him, then Rig interrupted his sandwich-making to take a long kiss. "Hey, Blue."

"Hey. Did you open it?" he asked causally.

"Not yet. Wanted my kiss first." Rig gave him a grin. "I bought new bookshelves for the office and the bedroom, so we could get those boxes out of the garage."

His own personal slut kept chattering, but headed straight for the box. "I figured with Dick's schoolbooks and the paperwork from the office and the gym and... Oh... Oh, Blue!"

Rig pulled the jacket out, eyes just shining.

"You like it?" he asked, voice rough.

Rig slipped it on, fingers sliding over the doeskin. "Oh, damn! I'll be the finest dressed fucking cowboy on the west coast!"

It took about ten or fifteen more seconds of Rig admiring the jacket, then his arms were filled with his Rabbit. "Thank you. It's fucking wonderful."

He grunted, holding Rig close. "It seemed like something you'd like."

"It's perfect -- so soft!" Rig reached up, twining long arms around his neck. "So good to me. However will I thank you..."

He grinned. "I have an idea or two."

"Mmm... yeah? Gonna whisper in my ear?" That long, slim body was snuggled in close, moving against him.

"You need me to tell you?" he teased, hands going to Rig's ass, tugging him in closer.

"Want to make sure I get it right." Rig licked the corner of his mouth, breath sweet.

Rock chuckled. "Well you know how much I love that mouth."

"Mmm... I do." Warm and wicked, a series of little kisses trailed up along his jaw towards his ear. "Gonna fuck my mouth, Blue?"

"If that's what you want," he answered, mouth trying to capture Rig's.

Rig's chuckle tickled his skin. "Want you. Always."

He rumbled happily. "Ditto."

That got him Rig's mouth, full-on and focused, kissing him with that mind-blowing hunger that made him feel ten feet tall. He returned the kiss, returned the focus, body hard and wanting for this man. One of Rig's hands worked his slacks open, fingers wrapping around his cock and pumping slowly. He pulled Rig's tongue into his mouth, sucking as his hands tightened on his Rabbit's ass.

A needy little noise pushed into his lips, Rigger gasping as those fingers tightened around his prick, thumb teasing the head. Another rumble came from him and he pushed his hips into Rig's hand, enjoying the slide of his cock along Rig's skin. Steady and sure he was touched and stroked, kissed and held. Rig knew his body better than he did, knew how to make him want, make him need, make him happy.

Rock spread his legs, finding his balance as he rocked into Rig's hand.

"Blue. So fucking hot." Rig was rubbing against his hip, gasping into his mouth.

"You know it," he murmured, hands on Rig's ass bringing his Rabbit in harder against his muscles.

Rig whimpered, tongue sliding into his lips. "Could do this forever."

He chuckled, feeling loose and hot and hard and just about fucking perfect. "I'm good, but I don't know if I'm quite that good."

"I have faith in you, Blue." Rig smiled at him, looking good and happy, horny and sexy and his.

Purring at that, Rock took Rig's mouth again, owning it. The hand working him tightened, Rig arching into him, crying out. He growled for Rig, holding his Rabbit tighter. Rig jerked against him, thumb sliding over the slit in his cock as those grey eyes went dark and wide. He let himself go, let

Rig's pleasure push him over the edge. He shuddered as he came, spunk splashing over Rig's hand.

His Rabbit was panting, cheek resting on his shoulder. "'s good, Blue."

He stroked Rig's back, fingers sweeping. "Yeah."

Rig brought that too-long, thin hand up, slowly licking it clean, moaning softly. "Well... That was a good thank you for thinking of me. Now, I need to thank you for getting the right size." He got a soft kiss. "And finding one so soft." Another kiss. "And picking my favorite color beads."

"Getting it wrapped."

"Mm-hmm. And the soft part, you know how I love doeskin."

He nodded. "Yeah, you could even thank me three times for that."

"Maybe four. I'm feeling damned thankful."

"How 'bout we head to the bedroom and you can get to work on showing me just how thankful you are."

Rig took his hand, those eyes sparkling, sunlight making the beads on that jacket shine. "Sounds like a plan, Blue."

He nodded. It did.

Presents weren't his strong suit, but every now and then he hit one out of the ballpark.

Chapter Twenty Six

Rig had been losing a lot of sleep, waking up earlier and earlier with the pain ripping through him, making him sweat and shake, teeth clenched against his cries, so he talked to Sammy and got a prescription for something to take when things got unbearable.

He hadn't needed it until one late Friday night when he was exhausted, when the toilet bowl was full of blood and bile. Then he took the pill and took to bed.

He didn't even crack an eyelid at dawn.

Or eight a.m.

In fact it was the shaking that woke him up at nine seventeen.

"Damn it, Rig, don't you make me call the fucking ambulance."

He blinked, shook his head. Fuck, his throat was dry. "What? Blue? What's wrong?"

Rock's face was worried, real worried. "Fuck, Rig -- you tell me. It's after nine and you were out hard."

"Oh." He reached out and pulled Rock close. "I'm okay. Christ. Sammy gave me something to help me sleep, is all. For the nights when I... when I needed them. I'm okay."

"Fuck." Rock leaned heavily against him, face buried in his neck. "I thought you were in a fucking coma. Dick and me went to work out and I came home and you were still in the bed..."

"Fuck, no. Just sleeping hard, Blue." He wrapped around Rock, shaking a little now, Rock's fear scaring him. "I'm okay."

Suddenly Rock was kissing him, mouth hard on his, tongue pushing in as those big hands moved over him. Rock wasn't trying to turn him on, Rock was checking to make sure he was all right. Rig opened wide, hands sliding over the strong shoulders, trying to soothe, trying to ease his Blue with all he had.

A long shudder went through Rock and the kiss got harder, more intense as the touching morphed into hungry need. He held on tight, pulling on Rock's tongue, legs wrapping around the thick thighs.

Rock moved against him, hands hard on his skin, tugging at his nipples, stroking across his belly. Oh. Fuck, he needed that ache to ease. He arched up, moaning, toes curling into the sheets. "Blue. My Blue..."

The big guy spread his legs with insistent knees, two fingers sliding in to stretch him. "Need you," growled Rock.

"'m yours, Blue. Always have me." He looked into those blueblue eyes, pushing down onto those fingers. "Won't leave you here, Jim. I swear it. I won't."

His Blue just growled, fingers sliding away, cock pushing in.

"Yes..." He stretched, reaching up for the headboard to brace himself, to give Blue what he needed. Rock's mouth closed over his again, tongue thrusting as hard as that cock, taking him. The motions were frantic, needy and desperate, bodies slamming together until Rig thought his bones were vibrating.

Harder and harder Rock fucked him, one hand going around his prick and pulling roughly.

"Oh. Oh, fuck. Rock!" He shuddered, eyes rolling as he came, heat spraying between them. Rock roared, coming with him, filling him with heat. As soon as he could move, he wrapped around Rock, holding on, mouth moving over Rock's skin.

"Love you," muttered Rock, hands holding him close, holding him hard.

Rig nodded, snuggling close enough that he couldn't feel his own skin. "My Blue."

Rock grunted, petting, the muscled body slowly relaxing. Soft kisses, gentle touches, low humming encouraged Rock to sink fully onto him, let it go, rest. Rig stroked Rock's nape, lips tracing the strong jaw. He would not leave his Blue. He couldn't. Rock needed him.

A sloppy kiss landed on his neck and a few moments later Rock's snores filled the room.

He held Rock for a long time, belly aching something fierce. Then, when he was sure Blue wouldn't wake up, Rig went to get started on his chores, putting the pills away in the back of the medicine cabinet.

Chapter Twenty Seven

Rock had to admit, Rig's second floor was pretty sweet. The couch was big enough for three to lie on and comfortable as fuck. The view was fucking magnificent. There was even a bar-sized fridge full of beer and a cupboard full of bar nuts and chips.

A nice stereo system rounded out the deal and he'd brought up some AC/DC and was currently playing it at full blast. It made him feel twenty-one again, the music blaring, a bottle of beer in his hand, sun shining in brightly.

Life was fucking good.

Hands fell on his shoulders, thumbs rubbing hard circles, easing knots that Rock didn't even know he had. He groaned, letting his head drop forward.

Dick's hands fell on his knees, slowly sliding up along his thighs. "Hey stud. How's it hanging?"

He grinned. "Pretty dammed good."

Rig's lips traced his ear. "You're looking good, Blue. Happy."

He nodded. "I like the room, Rig. You did good."

"Thanks. It works nice." He could feel Rig's pleasure in that slow drawl, see Dick's approval in that wide smile.

Dick's fingers trailed over to the button on his jeans, teasing it open, fingers dipping in to brush against the tip of his cock. "You hungry?" the kid asked, eyes shinning up at him.

"Always," he growled.

Hands trailed down, Rig plucking his nipples, a soft moan tickling his ear. Dick freed his prick, fingers sliding over it, making him moan. He tilted his head back, searching out Rig's mouth. Rig gave him what he was looking for, tongue sliding deep, tasting him.

Dick's tongue slid along his slit, fingers rolling his balls -- the kid had learned everything he knew about blow-jobs from Rig, making him a master in his own right.

Rig hummed into his lips, hand tilting his head so the kiss could deepen. He groaned into Rig's mouth, hips jerking as Dick's mouth slid around the head of his cock.

"Mmm... " Rig moved around the couch, stripping off the pale t-shirt before snuggling close. Jesus, Rig looked like a… Oh. Oh, that felt fucking good. "Smell good, Blue."

"Taste good, too," murmured Dick, pulling off his cock long enough to say it and then taking him in again, swallowing him slowly down.

Rig chuckled, leaning down to nuzzle his pubes. "Mmm... yeah."

Oh, fuck. One of them down there was guaranteed to get him off in the best possible of ways -- both of them? They were gonna send him to Goddammed fucking Nirvana.

Rig started licking at Dick's lips where they wrapped around his cock, hands cupping his balls.

"Fucking shit!" He growled, hips bucking, hands sliding into blond and brown hair. Dick's head moved up, far enough that Rig took a deep, hard kiss, catching his cock between their hungry mouths. Their moans were echoed by his. They started taking turns, Rig, then Dick, then both together, sucking over the tip.

"Gonna fucking kill me," he growled, hands tightening on their heads.

"Nope, just gonna fuck you." Rig started tongue-fucking his slit.

Rock groaned. Oh yeah, fucking dead. Dick pulled his jeans off and settled back between his legs, nuzzling against his ass. He spread his legs wider, letting the kid at his hole. Together his men drove him higher and higher, tongues and lips working him hard.

He roared as he shot into Rig's mouth, ass clamping down around Dick's tongue. Rig swallowed him right down, then kept licking and nuzzling. Slut.

Dick came up for air, grinning up at him as one of the kid's fingers slid into him. "You gonna let Rig fuck you? Gonna let me watch?"

He growled. Yeah, he could do that. "You wanna give it to your old man, Rig?"

Rig moaned, mouth tightening on his prick, one finger sliding down to join Dick's inside him. He jerked, prick starting to fill again. Kill him fucking dead.

They fucked him together, fingers pushing deep and steady, Rig's mouth refusing to let him relax.

It wasn't long before they had him hard and wanting. "More. Rig. You. Now."

Nodding, Rig moved up between his legs, damn near shaking with it, cock head nudging his hole. "Oh, Blue..."

The kid helped him tilt his hips. "Do it, Rig."

His grade-A slut pushed inside, fucking him slow and steady, cock spreading him wide. He kept his eyes on Rig's, staring into serious, steady grey.

"My Blue." The words weren't even whispered, just breathed for him.

"Yours," he breathed back.

Dick's hand slid between them, wrapping around his prick. Oh fuck. Lightning shot up his spine, his vision narrowing until all he saw was that fucking perfect grey.

Together they brought him higher and higher, the heat building inside him. Then Rig leaned forward, whispering, "Love you" against his lips.

He roared, world gone grey as pleasure overwhelmed him.

Between them, Dick and Rig got him stretched on the couch, Dick behind him, Rig in his arms, a blanket thrown over top.

It didn't get any better than this.

Chapter Twenty Eight

Rock was half dozing, half watching the nature special that was on the TV.

Tiger sex.

He shook his head. He didn't need to see that ever again. He turned off the TV, got up and went searching for Rig. Tigers weren't the only ones who could have sex. Rock followed the honky tonk music to the workshop, where his Rabbit was perched on an old bar stool, singing along, reading glasses perched on the top of his head. Bits and pieces of wood were scattered everywhere, the scent of Rig strong in here.

"What'cha making?" he asked, moving to stand right behind Rig, arms looping around the thin waist.

Rig leaned back into him immediately, kind of cuddling. "Oh, I'm mostly just playing. I'd like a coffee table upstairs that opens up for blankets and stuff, but I wasn't sure if it wouldn't be worth more just to go buy one, so I was making a little mock-up. You know, see if it would be more aggravation than it's worth. How was your show?"

He snorted. "Tigers fucking."

"Oh." Rig arched an eyebrow, wrinkled that long, thin nose. "Ew."

"Yeah, that's what I was thinking. And then I was thinking that there were too many folks having sex who weren't me. So I came to find you."

Rig tilted back, chin lifting, grey eyes meeting his and sparkling. "I love the way your brain works, Rocketman."

He snorted again and gave Rig a wink. "I didn't think it was my brain you loved."

Those eyes warmed, wrinkling at the corners. "I need the whole package, Blue. Always have. Always will."

He rumbled, hands moving over Rig's belly. "Well right now the whole package needs you."

"Mmm... I'm all yours." Rig reached up, stretching under his touch, thighs parting.

"My slut," he murmured, hands sliding down, cupping Rig's cock through his jeans, hands sliding down to stroke over the inside of Rig's thighs.

"Fuck, yes." That long body responded to his touch like Rig was starving for it, prick firming. "That feels good."

"I thought it might." He latched on to Rig's neck, licking at the salty skin as he started to pull Rig off the stool and back toward the couch. Soft little sounds filled the air, Rig following easily, wood and tools and project forgotten. He sprawled out on the couch, pulling Rig down with him.

Rig straddled his lap, arms wrapping around his neck. "Sexy motherfucker."

"You know it." He slid his hands beneath Rig's t-shirt, all but purring at the feeling of warm skin under his fingertips.

"Yeah." Rig leaned into his touches, mouth brushing over his cheeks, his jaw. "Fuck, you taste so good."

"Pheromones. And I think it's got something to do with the stripes -- camouflage works the same, I imagine."

He winked and pulled Rig's shirt right off over his head before going for Rig's belt buckle.

"Mmm... pheromones. That's why you smell good." Rig nipped right under his ear, the feeling sharp and bright. "Love bite."

He laughed and half-roared, flipping them so he was on top.   Rig grinned, pushing close, eyes dancing. "Ooooh! Alpha-male!"

"You know it." Rock leaned down at bit at Rig's neck. "Mine," he growled.

Rig squeaked, hips pushing up against him, rubbing hard. "Oh, shit. Blue."

"Yeah, mine." He licked at the mark he'd left and then left another next to it.

"Yours." The word was a gasp, Rig's head tilting, offering him more skin. He pulled off his own t-shirt and opened his jeans, getting off on Rig's response, getting hard. His teeth scraped along Rig's collarbone.

"H...hungry. Fuck." Fingers wrapped around his head, holding on, Rig working his jeans down with the free hand.

He just kept biting at Rig, teeth and tongue working his Rabbit's skin. He could feel Rig's prick like a fucking brand on his stomach, burning and wet at the tip.

"Oh, God. Blue. Please. Fuck me. I need you." Rig was wild, titties hard and peaked, undulating beneath him, body begging.

"Anything you want." He split Rig's legs, pushing against that sweet hole with his prick, spreading the leaking spunk along Rig's crack. He took a bite of Rig's un-ringed nipple, teeth closing over the little bit of hard flesh. Rig arched and pushed down on his cock, pulling him in and dancing on his prick. The sharp cries were echoing, the scent of fucking and wanting and them together strong. He started to thrust, taking Rig with long, slow movements. It felt so fucking good.

Rig settled into the rhythm, hands hard and grasping on his skin. He moaned and growled, working hard, just taking Rig with everything he was.

Pushing up, Rig bit his earlobe, moaning. "Yours. Oh, fuck. Yours."

"You fucking know it," he growled, wrapping a hand around Rig's prick.

"Always have." Rig jerked, ass squeezing his cock hard, milking him as spunk sprayed over his fingers. He roared, coming hard. Rig was humming, pliant and warm beneath him, completely satisfied. He settled, half on half beside Rig, feeling relaxed and good.

Those fucking tigers had nothing on them.

Chapter Twenty Nine

"Man, those meds you gave me are making me sleep all the fucking time. I can't do this." Rig twirled his watch around his wrist. Fuck, that was scary loose. "Sam, we have to try something else. Can you call me in something? I've got to run to the store tonight."

He turned his chair toward the sunlight, tugging the sweater around him tighter and rubbing Miss Lucy's belly with his toes.

"You sure you want to give up on them so soon, Alex? It's not even been a week, has it?"

"It's been ten days, Sammy. I slept fifteen hours yesterday. The boys are going to notice." Maybe.

"Well maybe it would be a good opportunity for you to tell them what's going on?"

"Yeah. Yeah. How long are you keeping me on this shit?"

"Have you noticed any changes besides the sleeping thing?"

"No. I am still vomiting after every meal. It's not nausea, it just won't stay down." He heard somebody coming down the hall, lowered his voice.

"All right, let me call you in a script for that other one we were looking at -- it shouldn't be as hard on you sleeping-wise."

"Thanks, man. I'll run out and pick it up tonight. Same place as before." Someone was lurking right outside his office door.

"I'll call it in as soon as I get off the phone with you. I still think you need to reconsider not telling your guys."

"Yeah. Yeah, I know. Night, Sam." He hung up the phone, leaned and stretched. He couldn't do it.

Not until he knew it wasn't cancer.

And if it was cancer, then...

Well.

It couldn't be.

He couldn't look into Rock's eyes and say it.

He couldn't.

There was a knock on his door, Dick poking his head in. "Hey."

"Hey Pretty. How goes?" He found Dick a grin.

"Not bad. I've got to go for study group in a few minutes and I just wanted to say hey."

"Busy, busy, busy." School was kicking Dick's ass, but the kid was keeping up. "Keeping up with the other kids?"

Dick shrugged. "I'm doing my best. Haven't failed yet." He got a big smile and Dick came in. "That earns me at least a kiss, right?"

"You know it." He opened his arms up, welcoming Dick over. "It earns you whatever you need, Pretty."

"I'm afraid I don't have time for more than a kiss." Dick settled across his thighs, humming as their lips pressed together. "You look tired -- you been busy at work?"

"Yeah. Life's kicking my ass." His arms wrapped around Dick's waist, fingers stroking the small of his Pretty's back.

"I know the feeling." Dick made a happy little humming noise, leaning in to kiss him again.

"Mmm." Now this was just fine. Just fine. He could spend a good, long amount of time doing this.

Their mouths slid together, one kiss moving into another and another. There was no hurry in it, though, just a nice, easy loving. Dick finally broke away, leaning their foreheads together. "I have to go."

"Okay, Pretty. Have a good evening at class, huh?"

"Study group, and I'll try. Even if I'd rather be here with you and Rock." He got another kiss, this one quick and hard, and then Dick was climbing off his lap and gone just like that.

Rig sighed, rubbed the back of his neck. Well, at least Rock'd be at the gym all evening and he could get himself another nap.

Chapter Thirty

Christ.

Rig brushed his teeth and grabbed a heavy sweater, heading out into the front room. Tests.

Sammy wanted a surgeon to do tests.

In fucking San Diego, of all places.

Christ.

"Hey, y'all. You finished with the Halloween candy yet?"

Rock looked down at the empty bowl and licked the chocolate from his lips. "Um. Yeah."

Dick started chuckling.

Rig grinned, settled in close. "That was Sam. He needs me in San Diego on Monday, so I'll be gone a few days."

See him. See him not lie.

"You're kidding." Rock grumbled, arm going around him. "When are you going? I could probably arrange something at the gym, come with you."

Dick shook his head. "I can't. These courses are still kicking my ass."

"I'm going down Sunday night, be home Wednesday." He leaned in, snuggling hard. "You've got that meeting with the promotional folks Tuesday, Blue."

"Maybe the kid can cover it."

Dick was already shaking his head, though. "Sorry, man. I just can't. We could cancel the promotional folks, I guess..."

"I'll be fine." It was just tests. Once this was over, he'd just tell them everything. All of it.

"I suppose we'll just have to do without you for a few days. Hell, I'm looking forward to the pizza and no hassles about vegetables already." Rock winked, hands holding him where he was.

"Don't make me beat you, man." He grinned, leaned hard and let his eyes close. God, he hurt.

"Oh, kinky..." Rock's fingers moved over him, his Blue so fucking warm.

"Mmhmm. That's me. Kinky." Please, God. Please, don't make me tell them something's wrong. Please don't let it be cancer like Momma had. Please.

Dick put down his books and joined them on the couch, snuggling him up from the other side. "Hey. I think it's time for a study break."

"Yeah? We could have a nap." He wasn't up to fucking. Hell, he wasn't up to anything.

He could feel Dick looking at him, and then his Pretty's hand slid across his belly, head coming to rest on his shoulder. "Yeah? Snuggling and napping is good."

Rock grunted. "I thought we were going to get kinky."

"Yeah, yeah. I'm too old for kinky." Too old. Too sick. Too fucking tired.

"You're not old," growled Rock, arm tightening around him.

"Nobody's old. Overworked and tired," suggested Dick. "But not old."

"Works for me." He petted Rock's belly, humming quietly. "Works for me, y'all."

Please God.

Please.

Chapter Thirty One

It just figured.

Dick had a Sunday where he wasn't stuck in study group and Rig was MIA.

He spent most of the morning catching up on reading, and around noon went to wake up Rock. Maybe he could convince big guy to make him pancakes.

But first he had a blow job to give.

Dropping his clothes, he crawled under the covers and made a bee-line for Rock's hard prick. Thick and full and waiting for him, Rock was ready, warm-smelling and fine. Humming, he licked at that cock, put everything Rig had ever taught him into play. Shit, Rock tasted good, so hot on his tongue.

The heavy thighs shifted, Rock's balls drawing up as the big guy groaned. Oh, yeah. Someone was paying attention. He nuzzled Rock's balls, sliding his lips over them before taking one into his mouth and sucking hard enough Rock could feel it.

"Fuck, yeah." Rock's hand landed on the back of his head, tangling in his hair.

Rolling Rock's balls, he hummed around one, his hands sliding along Rock's beautiful abs. The sheets smelled like them, all three of them, and it made him hard as a rock, made him groan and rub against the sheets. He licked his way up Rock's cock, taking the head into his mouth, the flavor of Rock's precome spreading across his tongue, making him rub harder.

It wasn't going to take long - even though it was Sunday and they had time, they were used to hurrying through morning wake up calls. Especially since he'd been taking over for Rig a lot.

Dick's head bobbed, lips tight around Rock's prick, tongue adding to the sensations. Rock started moaning, pushing up into his lips, starting to fuck his mouth. Yeah, just like that. He sucked harder, his hips working against the sheets. He felt Rock's heavy balls drawing up, going tight under his chin.

Yeah, yeah, come on, Rock, give it to me. His fingers slid to roll over the tight balls, his tongue slapping Rock's slit as it passed. Heat poured into his lips, Rock grunting and jerking for him. Fuck, yeah. He humped the bed hard and fast as he swallowed Rock down, the taste familiar, hot and good.

His balls drew up against his body and he shot across the sheets, his hips still sliding his prick against the mattress.

"Mmm. Hey, kid." Rock groaned, patting his head.

Dick managed to push himself up some before collapsing against Rock, narrowly avoiding the wet spot he'd left on the sheets.

His head landed on Rock's chest and he grinned, kissed the muscled flesh. "Hey."

"You want to go out? Get pancakes before we head to Jeff's to watch the game?"

Going out for pancakes was almost as good as Rock making them, and he wouldn't notice the house being empty by one if they did IHOP or the Waffle Barn. He nodded and pushed himself the rest of the way up to take a kiss, tongue lingering in Rock's mouth for just a moment.

"You're paying, though."

"Oh, man. Blackmail." He swatted Rock's ass, scooting out of range of those hands.

"You know it!" Laughing, he ran to the bathroom, figuring Rock would give him enough time to get the water going.

Just a few more days and it would be showers for three.

Chapter Thirty Two

Rock got home from the gym, growling a little as Dick pulled up right behind him. It was the kid's turn to cook and he was fucking hungry, tired, and not in the mood for more Goddamned take out. They were basically living on the stuff since Rig had gone off on this fucking field trip.

"Sorry," muttered Dick. "But I had to get my paper in. That was the last one. Just exams now."

"What did you bring for supper?"

"Shit. It's not my night is it?"

Rock rolled his eyes and let them in, the place smelling lemony -- the maid must have been in. "I'll order a fucking pizza."

"No, no. I'll do something quick." Dick dumped his stuff by the door and headed for the kitchen as the phone began to ring.

"I'll get it." Rock growled and grabbed the phone, sitting hard in his chair. "What?"

"Uncle Jimmy? I called up to the ICU and he wasn't there… They'd taken him for x-rays. What's up? Did Uncle Alex get worse? He was looking better when I left."

Rock frowned. Rig? Worse? What the fuck? "Deuce? What the hell are you talking about?"

If Rig got hurt on this little medical fucking jaunt and didn't bother to tell him, he was going to kick some cowboy ass. And if Robert didn't cough up information on "Uncle Alex," there was going to be bloodshed – Marines, family, or not.

"I. Uh. Nothing, I guess. I just. I got to see Uncle Alex, got to help him out. I mean. Uh. How's y'all?"

Rock snorted. "Nice try. Now why don't you tell me what the fuck is going on?"

"Shit. I. Man, he hasn't been able to call yet, I bet. He's still real sore and shit, Uncle Jimmy."

Not fucking able to call. Rock sat up straight in his chair, glaring at the dogs, who were milling around, whining a little. "Real sore... I think you'd better start at the beginning, Robert -- just pretend I haven't got a fucking clue what you're talking about."

"Huh? Well, you know how they were gonna do the tests? To see if he had cancer? They got in there and found flaps or something - whatever was making him so fucking sick. So they had to take out part of his stomach and stuff, right then and there. I was gonna call when he was in ICU, but he said he wanted to tell y'all. I just wanted to check on him..."

Jesus fucking Christ.

Cancer.

Tests.

I fucking CU.

His Goddamned Rabbit.

Rock was going to kill him.

"Where," he asked, speaking very slowly, and very calmly, "is it that he is again?"

"UCSD, off Arbor Street. I cancelled his hotel room and brought him his stuff. I'm sorry, Uncle Jimmy, I couldn't stay. I had CQ duty." Jesus, the eternal guilt of the Roberts' clan.

"Don't you worry about that, Deuce. You did the right thing." Rock swallowed, a fist in his gut. "You did the right thing. I'll be seeing you."

"Yeah? You... y'all will come, yeah?"

"You know it." He'd get one of the kids from the gym to come look after the dogs and they could go get their supper from a drive through.

"See you tomorrow."

"Cool. Cool. I'll take y'all to supper or something." Robert cleared his throat, sounding guilty as can be. "He was asking for you, crying and stuff, when he was still under. I had to call, huh?"

That fist was getting tighter. "You did the right thing, Deuce. I'll call you tomorrow."

"Okay. Drive safe. Tell Uncle Richard I'll see him too. Love y'all." The phone went dead, the sound just gone.

Rock just sat there staring at it for he didn't know how long. He was either going to slam it across the room or crush it in his hand.

Dick came out of the kitchen. "Okay, supper's -- Shit, Rock. What's wrong?"

He looked over at Dick, mouth open. He shut it with a snap.

"You're white as a ghost. Was that Rig? What's the matter?"

"That was Robert. Deuce. Calling to check on his Uncle Alex. He just wanted to make sure everything was okay since he left Rig in the fucking hospital."

"What? What happened?"

"Grab an overnight bag while I call someone to feed the fucking dogs. I'll tell you in the car."

They had eight hours. They could plan how they were going to kill Rig for keeping this from them.

Chapter Thirty Three

He hurt.

Fuck, he hurt.

There were tubes in his cock, in his nose, draining out of his fucking belly and pumping shit into his veins and...

And he hurt.

And he needed to go home.

Rig groaned, tossing on the sweat-soaked pillow. God *damn* it. He needed his men. He needed help. "Somebody bring me a phone! I gotta call HOME!"

"Please, Dr. Roberts. You've got to calm down." Another masked nurse stared down at him; he'd been trapped in ICU since the surgery, one infection after another just making things crazy.

"I need to go home, honey. Don't you understand?"

A commotion sounded outside, someone yelling. No, roaring.

"--fucking let me see him RIGHT NOW, I'm going to rip this Goddamned hospital apart room by fucking room until I find him."

"No, I do NOT want to FUCKING CALM DOWN!"

"Jim! Jim! I'm in here! Y'all!" He groaned, head tossing. "ROCK!"

Oh. Oh, fuck. Dizzy.

Shit.

The world went gray and fuzzy, his heart just thrumming in his chest.

Then Rock was there, pushing into the room, fucking growling and furious and about the best thing he'd ever seen. Dick was right behind him, looking worried.

"Oh." He blinked, smiled. Here. They were here.

"You have to scrub up, put on masks. He's very susceptible right now." The nurse grabbed Rock's arm, tugged him over to the foot pedal sink. "You have to. Infections are trying to take him over, guys."

"I want to know what the fuck is going on here." Rock was still growling, still glaring, washing his hands.

"Well, who are you that you deserve to know?"

Dick intervened. "What he means is, could you please tell us how Rig -- Alex -- is doing?"

Rock stopped washing to face her head on, puffing up and looking huge, intimidating. "I'm his fucking partner, that's who."

"They... they're mine. My next of kin. My family." Rig blinked, just staring. His boys.

"Okay. Okay, Dr. Roberts. You need to calm down. Your blood pressure's rising again." The nurse - Nancy? Peggy? Judy? - headed over, checking his tubes.

"'m calm. Rock. I been asking for a phone. Needed y'all."

Their hands were washed and they got their masks on, flanking him, Dick taking his hand and squeezing.

"We're here. You gonna tell me what the fuck is going on?" Rock was still glaring, anger hiding everything else.

"I don't know. They aren't talking. Something. I came in for tests and woke up here with TUBES everywhere and I HURT!" His own fury and terror let itself out now that Rock was here to help, to fix it. To help him.

"Okay, if you're going to agitate him, you'll have to leave." Oh, fuck no.

"No! No, please. Please, y'all."

Rock started growling again, looking like he might pick the little nurse up and snap her right in two. Dick squeezed his hand again, and then let it go, going around the bed and taking the nurse's hand.

"Would it be okay if we stepped out for a minute? You could maybe explain to me what all happened? What we need to do to help Alex recover?" Dick led her out, leaving him alone with Rock.

"Rock. Blue. Help me." He shifted, trying to find a way to touch, to get to his lover.

Rock sat on the edge of the bed, the mattress sinking under his weight. One large hand grabbed hold of his, holding on tight. Those blue eyes stared at him from above the mask, looking right into him. "I'm here. Now."

"Thank God." He let himself relax a little, let himself breathe. "Thank you. I needed... Oh."

He held on tight, blinking as his heart started to slow a little.

Rock's free hand slid through his hair, thumb lingering over his lips. "You should have let me come with you from the start."

"I..." He blinked slow, all of the sudden so Goddamn heavy. Rock and Dick were here. Here. "I was just supposed to have a test. Wanted to tell y'all at home, if the docs were right and it was cancer."

"Cancer. You should have." Rock stopped, the hand holding his squeezing impossibly tight for a second before loosening enough it didn't hurt. "We're here now, Rabbit. Why don't you close your eyes and get some sleep. Dick'll get the low-down from the nurse and find out the fastest way for us to get you out of here."

"You'll stay. Promise you'll stay. I woke up and..." And he'd been alone. Scared. Hurting. "Promise."

"It's gonna take a whole case of C4 going off under my ass to get me to move."

"'kay." He reached out, pressed the morphine button, eyes fluttering as the heat flooded him. "Home. Take me home."

Where he belonged.

Chapter Thirty Four

Dick hated leaving Rig, but he knew that Rock was only going to keep growling at the nurse, and Rig was just going to get more agitated, so he sweet talked her out into the hall to let Rock calm Rig down and vice versa. Besides, one of them needed to get the low-down on Rig's condition.

"So can you tell me what happened? He was just supposed to be here for some tests..." Not that Rig had told them that. He kept that little tidbit from the nurse.

"They went in to search for tumors or ulcerations and the surgeon discovered that Mr. Roberts had Menetrier's disease. It's a condition that causes flaps to grow along the stomach lining. They were quite severe and riddled with lesions, so the surgeon decided to remove them, along with about a quarter of Mr. Roberts' stomach."

"Menetrier's disease?" He'd never heard of it. Good thing he had his laptop with him. "Is the surgery a cure?"

"Basically, yes. Mr. Roberts will need to take anti-ulceratives and there will be some dietary changes, but, assuming we can get these infections to clear up and he gains weight back, he'll feel like a new man. Dr. Simmons said that they had to have been causing pain for years. He's been vomiting blood for more than nine months."

"*Nine* months?" Nine months. Oh God, Rig had been going through this by himself for nine months. He didn't understand why Rig hadn't told them.

The nurse nodded, red curls just bouncing. "I feel sorry for him. That sweet tall boy - his nephew? Said that his mother died of cancer. I imagine he was scared to death."

"Yeah. Yeah, I bet he was." Damn it. He should have known. He should have seen it. "Do you know how soon we can take him home?"

"If the infections clear up? I'd guess a week to ten days. If not?" She shrugged. "It could be much, much longer."

"That long?" Rig was going to go crazy.

"His fever broke today and his incision is clearing at the drain site. I have high hopes for the stubborn guy." She winked, smiled. "Look, I have to make my rounds. Go be quiet and convince him to rest, will you? The sooner he's out of ICU and in a regular room, the better. You know doctors are the worst patients."

"Thank you." He gave her his best smile and then made a beeline back to Rig's bedside.

Rig was sleeping restlessly, frowning, mouth moving. The man looked like hell - grey skinned, bruised. Skinny.

"Jesus."

Rock looked up at him, nodded. "What did the nurse say?"

"It's not cancer." The big body sagged a little and he went over, Rock's arms wrapping around him. "It's not cancer," he whispered.

They stayed like that a moment or two, and then Rock grumbled and he backed off, running his hand through his hair. "What is it then?"

"Menetiray or something. It's a stomach ulcer kind of thing. She said he's been throwing up blood for nine months."

"No fucking way."

"That's what she said."

"I'm going to kill him."

"Let him get better first, 'kay?"

"I can do that."

"Good." He went around to the other side, taking Rig's other hand. "He looks like shit."

"He does. Did they say when we can take him home?"

"At least ten days."

"Fuck."

Rig moaned, shifted, eyes fluttering open and rolling in their sockets. "Rock. Y'all... I need to go home. Y'all leave my boys alone."

"Shh. We're right here, Rig." He patted Rig's hand. "Right here."

Rock leaned in. "Kid's right. You need to sleep. We're not gong anywhere."

"Oh. Oh, I woke up..." Rig blinked and blinked. "I keep dreaming. I keep dreaming I lost y'all..."

"That's probably the morphine." He squeezed Rig's hand again, found a smile. "We're not going anywhere, okay? Me and Rock have you."

"Tell me. Tell me that it's not cancer." Those eyes met his, straight on. "Tell me. I heard you."

"They didn't tell you yet?" That was just cruel. "It's not cancer. You don't have cancer, Rig. You just a special diet and ulcer medicine -- you're going to be just fine. No cancer."

"No cancer." Rig's eyes closed, tears dotting the pale lashes. "Thank God. I. Oh, thank God. I didn't want to have to tell y'all that..."

He leaned in and rubbed their cheeks together, not wanting to hurt anything. "You should have told us, Rig. You didn't need to go through this by yourself."

"Mmm... Didn't want to scare y'all. Oh, Pretty, you smell like home."

"Yeah? It's that soap..." He'd get some later, make sure the nurses used that to wash Rig. Hell, maybe they'd let him and Rock do the sponge bath thing. Rig would like that he'd bet.

"Mmmhmm." Rig dozed off again, almost immediately beginning to dream, to mutter.

"Doesn't seem like very restful sleep." Rock glared down at Rig and Dick rubbed the big guy's arm.

"Why don't you try talking to him some, so he knows we're here."

Rock nodded, began telling Rig about the gym, the drive down, just everyday stuff. Dick sat back and watched, realizing how close they'd come to losing this. It made him shudder. And how could he have not noticed how bad Rig was doing? He shook his head. He'd been so fucking busy. Too busy. There wasn't any reason he couldn't cut his course load by half, or even do just one class a term.

If they let him stay, given he was about to blow off his exams.

It didn't matter, though, none of it did.

This right here, this was all that was important.

Chapter Thirty Five

Rock planted himself next to Rig and refused to be budged. He watched every nurse that came in like a hawk, making sure they washed their hands and wore their masks. He wasn't taking any chances.

He'd sent Dick out for food, coffee, and to find out when the fucking doctor was going to show up and give them the official story -- kid was right, though, the nurses probably had better intel. Rig always had. Always. Goddamn it.

Rig was in and out of it, waking himself up out of nightmares every now and then.

He and Dick tried to keep talking, as it seemed to make their cowboy sleep better, but the man couldn't have had more than a half hour in a row.

Rock checked his watch. They'd been there about five hours -- it wasn't even noon yet. Shit, he hated this. He didn't want to have to do another fucking bedside vigil.

At least it wasn't fucking cancer. Shit, he hadn't even known that was on the table. He glared at Rig -- once his cowboy was better the man had a lot to answer for.

Dick came back in, washing his hands and putting on a new mask. "The doctor's making his rounds -- shouldn't be long before he's back. How's Rig?"

"'Bout the same."

Rig sighed, shifted a little. "'m thirsty."

Shit. They'd cut out the man's stomach. Could they give him a drink? He went for the nurse's button, didn't even hesitate for a second, just pushed it, long and hard. "Getting the nurse, Rig."

"'kay." Rig blinked, eyes bloodshot and confused-looking. "Can I help you?"

He turned to find a new nurse at the door. "Yeah -- he's thirsty. What's he allowed to drink?"

"Let's start with some ice chips and I'll get you some apple juice for him. Little bitty sips - he doesn't have much room in there right now and we'll slowly have to stretch it." The nurse washed her hands, stepped in, checking monitors. "I'm Steph, by the way, I'm the day shift nurse. Fever's down. That's good. If he can keep it up, they'll move him to a regular bed and start introducing a liquid diet."

"I'm Rock and this is Dick. And we have insurance -- he gets a private room." He tried not to growl too loudly -- she was trying to help, she was being nice.

"How soon do you think they'll move him? And is the doctor ever going to show up to look at him?" He turned his glare on Dick who was grinning at him.

"They'll move him as soon as he's stable enough. He's been fighting everything up 'til today. Looks like he's finally relaxing, healing up."

Rig groaned. "Please, y'all. I'm dry as a bone here."

"Dick--" He didn't need to say it, though, the kid already up and headed out the door on a search for ice chips. Rock took Rig's hand, not caring if he was in the nurse's way. "The kid's getting you ice chips. And then the nurse said you could have some apple juice."

"Cool. 's the surgeon coming? Want to come home." Rig stretched, wincing. "Fuck, I'm sore."

"Don't pull the stitches, now. I'm rooting for you to take a walk around this time tomorrow, Mr. Roberts." Steph scribbled some notes, nodded. "Do you like apple juice?"

"Yeah. Yeah. I'd kill for some coffee. You know how long it's been since I could keep coffee down?"

She snorted. "Oh, that's not on the approved list, now. Not at all."

Shit, their cowboy fucking lived on coffee. "Like ever?" Rock asked.

"Well, I wouldn't suggest it, it'll aggravate the stomach lining, but we're talking a couple of weeks here of liquid diet, all high in protein. The nutritionist will come in once he's better."

Rock made a face. Somehow even vegetables sounded better than high protein liquid.

"We're more concerned about seeing the doctor than a nutritionist right now." He liked the way she spoke though, like Rig getting better was a matter of fact.

The door opened again, Dick coming back with a Styrofoam cup. "Success!"

"She'll probably be another few minutes, but she's on the way." Steph smiled, nodded to Dick, patting Rig's leg through the blue blanket that all hospitals seemed to have. "Only a spoon or two every ten minutes, okay? His stomach is swollen and where it was reattached is still very much in the healing phase."

Rock took the cup from Dick. "Go wash up again." Dick's eyebrows rose and he growled. "Do it -- his fever broke and I'm not risking it coming back."

Rig had dozed off again, but as soon as the spoon hit the ice, those eyes opened. "Ice?"

"Yeah, here." He held the spoon to Rig's mouth, two little ice chips on it.

Rig sucked them off, eager for them. "More."

"You should pace yourself." Rock checked his watch as he offered over another spoonful. Ten minutes. Fuck, he bet they'd feel like forever.

Dick finished washing up and came over. "I saw the doctor in the next room over. It shouldn't be long."

"Cool." Rig nodded, panting a little. "Tell him to send me home."

He wanted nothing more than to do just that, but he was pretty sure Rig needed to be in the hospital. The man looked pretty fucking bad. "Let's wait until you can do more than eat a few ice chips before you get winded."

"Bossy, bossy." Rig's hand slid from under the covers, wrapped around his thigh. "Hey."

Oh, someone was feeling better, even if it was just a little. And Rig was gonna learn what bossy was. He smiled. "Hey."

"I. What day is it? I just... Nothing seems real but y'all."

"It's Friday. You've got some weird-assed disease and they cut out half your stomach. But it's not cancer." They'd already told Rig all that, but he figured it was worth repeating."

"Not cancer." He got that smile again. "Oh, you could just say that over and over. I've been... Shit."

"Scared it was for a long fucking time." He growled and glowered.

Dick cleared his throat, hand sliding on Rock's. "It doesn't matter right now. All that matters is that it isn't cancer and Rig's getting better."

He met Dick's eyes and nodded. He could wait for Rig to get better before killing him. It just made him growl every time he thought about it. All that time Rig had kept it from him.

"You didn't know did you?" he asked Dick.

Dick shook his head. "No. No, he didn't tell me either. I knew something was wrong, but I let him fob me off."

"I've been working with the docs, guys. I didn't want to scare y'all." Rig squeezed his leg, lips open. "More ice?"

Rock glanced at his watch and shook his head. "She said ten minutes. And Dick's right -- we'll talk about it later."

"Gentlemen?" A tiny, brown skinned lady with dark, happy eyes and a lab coat wandered in. "Can I ask you to leave so I can examine my patient, please?"

Rock shook his head. "I'm not going anywhere." He'd stand in the corner if that's what she wanted, but he wasn't leaving the room. "And you need to wash your hands."

Dick's eyes widened, but he just stood next to Rig's bed, arms crossed over his chest.

He got a long, slow steady look. Then those dark eyes just lit up, the doctor laughing and clapping. "Well, well. This is a good sign, is it not? Stubborn and ready for our patient to be well, are you?"

"She sounds like a psychotic gnome, Blue."

He bit the side of his cheek, guessing laughing at her was not going to win him, or Rig, any favors. He could do stoic, though. It was his fucking stock in trade. "We'll do whatever it takes to make him better, ma'am."

Dick nodded, coming around the bed to stand beside him; the kid was doing a decent job of keeping a straight face after Rig's comment.

She nodded, heading for the sink. "Dr. Balakrishnan. I did Mr. Roberts' surgery. It went very well, considering the severity of the condition."

"Can you explain about that again, please?" Dick asked. "Ri--Alex here is a doctor, too, well, a P.A., and I couldn't remember enough of what the nurse told me."

Rock was happy to let Dick do the talking, because he heard severity of the condition and just saw red again.

"Of course." She lifted the edge of Rig's blanket, started checking incisions. "Menetrier's disease is extremely rare and we're not sure why certain men contract it. The stomach lining begins to create folds, hampering digestion, causing pain and vomiting, ulcers. We removed about twenty percent of the stomach, including the most drastic folds."

She met Rig's eyes. "I assume you've been seriously limited on the amount of food you could eat?"

Rig nodded.

"And your records indicated severe pain and vomiting with blood?"

Another nod.

"The good news is, even with the removal of tissue, you'll have more room in the pouch once the swelling eases and the pain will soon disappear altogether."

Rock's hands and teeth clenched and he didn't realize he was looming, glowering, until Dick's hand landed on the small of his back, rubbing in slow circles. It let him take one breath and then another, it let him focus on the good news. "So he's going to make a full recovery?"

"There will be some alterations, especially to diet. The biggest concern is his weight. Mr. Roberts is seriously underweight and the unfortunate fact is that, with this surgery, we often see drastic weight loss. If he continues to lose weight, his heart will not be able to support him."

He glared at Rig. How often had he said his cowboy was too skinny?

"How can we help make sure he doesn't lose anymore weight?" Dick asked.

"Constant small meals, at first. His condition limits protein absorption, so he'll need to focus on a high-protein diet. Be very careful with alcohol, caffeine, hard-to-digest foods. You'll have to be very careful with early morning vomiting." She smiled at Rig. "This may ache a bit, but I need to check the drain, deep breath, please."

She did something and Rig's eyes rolled, a pained grunt filling the air.

Only Dick's arm around his shoulders and hand on his arm kept him from going for her. He growled, though. "Don't do that again."

"I'm sorry; it's necessary. If the drain blocks, toxins and infection will build up." The doctor didn't look intimidated at all. "You're looking much better, Mr. Roberts. Keep it up and we'll move you out of ICU in the morning."

"That's great!" Dick beamed. "Oh, hey, is there something you can give him besides the morphine? I think it's giving him nightmares."

"How's your pain? Is it easing?"

Rig shrugged, "Some."

"I can try codeine. We can't give him NSAIDs because it might cause the incision where we attached the stomach back to the esophagus to bleed." She scribbled more notes. "If the pain increases, though, we'll have to go back to the morphine."

"Thanks. He should heal faster if he can sleep, right?"

"We'll be sure to tell you if he's hurting more, though." He wasn't letting Rig hurt a second more than needed. Not now that he knew what the hell was going on.

"Excellent. I'll stop by in the morning. If things are still improving, we'll move you to a more comfortable room."

"I'm thirsty." Rig groaned, grabbed her arm. "Can I have water?"

"Let's stay with ice for a few hours. If that stays down, we'll graduate to sips of juice."

"Ice is better than nothing, yeah?" Dick moved back to the other side of the bed, squeezing Rig's arm. "And Rock 'n I'll keep you distracted."

The doctor scribbled a few more things and disappeared, a nurse coming in after a few minutes, changing out one medicine bag for another. "This is codeine and the injection into the IV is Phenergen. It'll help keep any nausea down."

"I hope you don't mind I asked about the morphine." Dick pushed Rig's hair back. "You've been muttering and moaning and startling yourself awake all morning."

"No. No, Dick. I... I keep dreaming. Dreaming that I lost y'all. Was... Was Deuce here?"

"We're right here, yeah? And yeah, I think Deuce was here right after you had surgery." Dick looked over to him and he nodded.

"Yeah, it's thanks to Robert that we're here."

"He's a good boy." Rig's look was unfocused, blinking slower and slower. "He's got a guy here. Oh, I feel that."

"He does? He didn't mention that." Of course, Deuce had had other things on his mind. Rock reached over and squeezed Rig's hand. "We'll have to meet him, give Deuce a hard time over him." Like Rig's dad would have.

The man would have been real proud to have one of his own join the marines.

"Uh-huh." Rig stared at him, head just bobbing. "Thank you for coming. I needed y'all something awful."

"We'd have been here sooner if we'd known." He and Dick reached for Rig's head together, pushing his hair back, trying to get him to just relax against the pillows. "We're not going anywhere, so just relax, okay?"

"The gym?"

"Did I just tell you to relax or to start worrying about things that aren't yours to worry about?" He'd have to make more permanent arrangements, but they had people who could run the place for them for a few weeks.

"Uh..." Rig's eyes closed, then slowly reopened. "Hey, Blue."

Shit, he hated seeing Rig all out of it like this. He just smiled, though. "Hey. Why don't you go to sleep? We'll be here when you wake up."

"'kay." He got this goofy, easy smile. "You're still two of the finest men I've ever seen."

He puffed up for Rig, flexing a little, even if his heart wasn't as in it as usual. "And we always will be."

"Mmhmm. My men." Rig nodded and fell asleep, just like that, smile still on his face.

He looked over at Dick, who just nodded and went back to watching Rig. Yeah.

The fist in his belly relaxed just a little bit.

Chapter Thirty Six

Rig groaned and stared at the new bed.

Private room.

TV.

Water.

He could do this.

He could.

If this fucking wheelchair was higher.

Rock and Dick had gone out with Deuce and the skinny little boy Deuce was dating. Not ten minutes after the boys left, the nurses said it was time to move.

God damn it.

"Come on, Mr. Roberts. Up on the bed and we'll get you settled." A big square hand landed on his arm.

"I'll do it myself." Maybe.

"Come on, Deb and me, we'll help." Frank was the biggest, roundest, grinning-est bastard he'd ever seen. Rig was going to have Rock kill him.

"No. Y'all go on. I said I'll do it myself!"

"You want to pull out your stitches and get an express elevator back to the ICU? Then you just go ahead and do it yourself, Mr. Roberts." Nurse Debbie crossed her arms and stared at him. "Go ahead. Frank and I won't be taking the rap for it from that big fella who's been guarding your bed though."

Shit. Shit, it was gonna hurt like a stone cold bitch to move now and he was fucking scared to move. Fucking exhausted. "Like I'm scared of him."

She leaned in suddenly, talking quietly enough that Frank couldn't hear. "Look. You're going to tear something open climbing up on that bed. Just let me and Frank do it -- we won't tell a soul."

"It's gonna hurt, honey. I'm not looking forward to this..."

He let them take his arms, though.

"It'll hurt worse if you do it yourself."

He'd bet Rock could have managed to move him without too much trouble or pain.

"Can't we wait for Rock and Dick?"

"You want to sit in that wheelchair 'til they get back?" She rolled her eyes. "Fine. We'll leave you by the bed where you can hit the nurses' button if you change your mind. Doctors really are the worst patients."

"Stop it. Come on, let's do this. I know y'all need the chair. I worked at a hospital for years." He braced himself, gritted his teeth against the pain.

They set the chair beside the bed and Deb and Frank got him standing, Frank more or less lifting him up onto the bed from there.

"There, that wasn't so bad, was it?"

"Right." They got his catheter and drain and IV situated. "When do the tubes come out?"

Deb chuckled as Frank grabbed the wheelchair and headed out. "You're not anywhere near ready to go home yet, Dr. Roberts."

Rig rolled his eyes, closed them as a pang of nausea and pain hit him. He was ready.

He was real ready.

She tutted, pulling the covers up and closing the drapes. A glass with ice chips was set on the table and she made sure he could reach the nurses' button. "You just ring if you need anything, okay?"

"I'll be okay. Thanks, honey." He closed his eyes, heart pounding in his chest, world just spinning.

He'd be okay. He would. It wasn't cancer. Oh, fuck. He hurt. She couldn't have been gone very long when he heard

Rock's voice, the low growls carrying. "I left you my cell number -- you should have called when it was time to move him."

"He managed just fine. He's sore, but he's a big... well, compared to all of you he's tiny, but..."

"I asked to be called when it was time to move him. I knew we shouldn't have left."

Rock's voice got louder as the door opened all the way, his Pretty coming in, wry smile on his face. "Hey, Rig. How're you doing?"

"Hey. I want to go home."

"Yeah, I don't think that's going to happen." Dick sat on the edge of his bed, looking around. "It's not home, but it beats the ICU."

"There are two big chairs for y'all." Although he'd been trying to get them both to get a hotel room...

"Yeah, and a TV. We can watch the game."

Rock strode in. "Are you okay?"

"No." His mouth snapped shut and he blinked. Jesus. "I mean, yeah. Yeah, I'm surviving."

Rock glared. "No, you don't get to do that anymore. No more pretending you're fine when you're not. Do you need more pain medication? To see the doctor?"

"I don't want anymore pain meds." But he hurt.

Dick squeezed his hand and then moved down to the end of the bed so Rock could sit next to him. "You sure? You look paler than you were."

"I." Come on, asshole. Buck up. Buck. Up. "It was just rough, getting from the chair to the bed."

"They should have called me."

"They know how to do their jobs, Rock." Dick pushed the covers off his feet, and started to rub them.

"Oh, fuck." He moaned, toes curling as his feet threatened to cramp. Dick worked the sole, fingers digging in. Rock grunted and turned his hand over, started massaging it.

"Oh. More. God." He just melted, those fingers easing him. Hell, just being touched easing him.

Rock looked just as happy to be touching him, Dick, too. They worked his hand and feet, and up his arm, along his calves.

"Is the scar gonna be bad?" He hadn't seen it yet, really. It seemed to run along his rib, just long enough to tug.

Rock shook his head. "No. It'll fade."

"It'll be sexy," Dick suggested, fingers sliding up along his thigh.

"I don't know if I can do sexy. I feel fucking old." Skinny. Ugly. Tired.

"You're not old." Rock growled at him, those blue eyes watching him.

Dick bent and kissed his ankle. "You'll see. When you're not hurting and sick. We'll remind you how sexy you are."

"Like Rock's not going to kill me." He tried to find a smile. "This didn't turn out like I'd expected."

"You're damn right I'm going to kill you." Rock grunted, found a grin for him. "But if I fuck you to death then we could do the sexy thing at the same time."

He started laughing, then groaned, grabbing his chest. "Oh. Oh, ow. Ow. Push the button on the pain meds, Blue."

Rock leaned over and pushed it for him, before sliding those big strong fingers over his cheek. "I fucking hate that you're hurting."

"Me too. It's better, though. I mean, I can tell. The burn is gone."

That tearing, screaming pain was gone.

Rock's leaned their foreheads together. "You should have told us."

"I couldn't. I needed to know what it was before I scared you."

Rock shook his head. "That won't fly, Rig. They said you were fucking throwing up blood for nine months. Nine, Rig."

He nodded. He had. He'd been scared. "I went to the doctors, Jim. We've been running tests for weeks."

"You've been hurting all by yourself for months. Fuck, you were hurting while we were at Vegas -- no wonder the busy streets seemed to take it out of you." Rock growled. "You fucking shut us out."

Dick just kept stroking his legs, but he could feel his Pretty's eyes watching.

"What was I supposed to say, Rock? Y'all couldn't do anything. I couldn't do anything. Shit, I was trying everything they suggested." He'd thought he was dying.

"I don't know what we could have done, but at least we'd have known."

"Support," murmured Dick. "We could have been there for you."

"Yeah. What Dick said."

"If it was... I mean, if I had..." He met Rock's eyes, dead-on. "If it'd been cancer, I didn't want y'all to have only bad memories."

"If you thought it was cancer nine months ago, why were you only having tests now?" Rock sure could growl.

"We had to go through all the options." Jesus, he was tired. "Ulcers. Stress. Food allergies. Gall stones. Hiatal hernia."

"And Dick and I deserved to know!" Rock stood and stalked around the small room,

"I'm sorry." What else was he supposed to say? Rig just closed his eyes, the pain meds making him dizzy, making it easier to just float away.

Rock came back to the chair next to his bed, sitting in it hard. "Just don't do it again."

He nodded, fingers opening and closing. No. Never again.

Rock's hand slipped back into his, Dick's petting slowing, and stopping, hands warm against his shins.

He held on, not knowing what else to do.

Chapter Thirty Seven

Dick knew Rig was starting to feel better because he was bitching and demanding to go home.

And wanting food.

Today they were introducing a liquid diet. He hoped it was more appetizing than the crap they served in the cafeteria. Breakfast was somehow the hardest meal to get just right.

"You think with the emphasis on protein they'll do you a steak, Rig?"

Rock shuddered. "Liquid steak would suck."

Rig turned green, started gagging. Oh, no. Not again. Every morning for the past three days, Rig's mornings were all about nausea.

"Breathe through your nose," he said quietly. "Deep, calm breaths."

"I. Want. To. Go. Home."

"Yeah, I know." He didn't bother repeating that Rig couldn't, that Rig needed to heal. Rig knew. He sighed and rubbed his eyes, feeling tired and out of sorts.

"I'm sorry. Shit." Rig closed his eyes. "Rock, why don't y'all go have breakfast? Get a hotel room. Fuck."

Rock grunted. "Promised you we weren't leaving you here."

"It's okay, Rig. Hospitals are shitty places to be stuck. You want me to read to you or something?"

"No. I'm good." Rig looked green around the gills, stressed, worried.

"Are you? Is the pain okay?"

"I'm gonna make it." Uh-huh. Right.

"Rig... "

Rock came over and put his hands over his hips. "Take the fucking painkillers, Rig."

"If I keep taking them, they won't let me come home with y'all."

"If you're hurting badly enough that you need them, Rig, then you need to take them."

Dick stroked Rig's forehead. "Why don't I ask about getting you transferred to the hospital near us? We can afford to pay for the ambulance, can't we, Rock?"

Rock grunted. "Maybe. Take the fucking painkillers."

Rig shook his head. "Let me eat something first, y'all. It'll help the nausea."

Dick managed not to grimace. Some of the liquid crap they had Rig eating looked pretty foul.

"All right." He rang the bell for the nurse.

Man, Rock had to stop hovering. Or at least do it without looking quite so... grim.

Rig closed his eyes, just leaned back into the pillows.

The little tinny voice sounded. "Can I help you?'

"Can we get some food in here for Mr. Roberts, please? He's on a special diet."

"He'll get breakfast with everyone else, sir. They're coming."

Rock growled. "Man needs his food in order to take his pain meds. I'm going to go hurry them up."

Dick sighed and stroked Rig's hair back. "Won't be long."

"Y'all don't have to flutter. I'll be fine. You heard the surgeon."

"I'm not fluttering. I'm... caring for you." Not that there was much to do, which was why Rock was so damned growly and glowery -- he wanted to make it all better, but couldn't.

"Yeah. Yeah, Pretty. I hear you." Rig nodded, sighed.

"We want you home just as badly as you want to be there. I think that getting you transferred thing was a good idea. We'd be that much closer and you know all the doctors and nurses there, so it would be easier, right?"

"I think we ought to just have me go home. Helen could help me with anything I needed."

"It's only been four days, Rig, and they were talking two weeks. Plus today's your first day on the liquid diet. You think they'll let you go?"

It would be so nice to get home, look after Rig properly. And hell, Thanksgiving was in a few weeks, they could do the place up nice for Rig.

"I'm not a prisoner, here. I'll give it another day, then I want to go home."

"If you think you're up to it."

"Up to what?" growled Rock, tray of bowls in hand. "Look what I found -- food that doesn't drip into your veins."

"My hero." Rig's face lit up. "Tell me there's something good in them."

"Haven't opened them yet." Rock set the tray down on the swinging table and brought it around so Rig could reach it. He proceeded to open each little bowl.

"Applesauce. Broth. Hey, this looks like chocolate pudding."

"It'll have that protein powder in it, but it sure smells good." Rig tried to sit up, moving so careful. Dick slid his arm around Rig's back, helping tug him up a little, Rock adding a pillow behind his back.

"I think you're going to have to get used to the protein powder." Dick grinned. "We've got some good stuff at the gym. Taste like chocolate shakes, especially if you crush ice into it."

"Maybe I'll add it to my morning coffee." Rig took a bite of the pudding, humming happily. "That's good."

Dick saw Rock bite his tongue, knew the big guy was avoiding reminding Rig that he was off coffee. For life.

Instead, Rock put a finger in the pudding and sucked it clean. "Not bad at all."

Rig's eyes followed Rock's finger and said, "My turn."

Rock didn't play coy -- he knew what Rig wanted. Dick watched, warmth curling in his belly, as Rock dipped his finger in the pudding again and held it up to Rig's mouth, blue eyes shining.

Rig grinned, sucked Rock's finger clean, the most satisfied, happy sound leaving their cowboy.

Groaning, Rock leaned against the bed and dipped his finger into the pudding again. That shine in those blue eyes had taken on a whole lot of want.

"Mmm. If you're going to feed me like this, I'm gonna be hungry a lot."

"I'll do whatever it takes."

Dick grinned. "That's mighty good of you, Rock. Sacrificing for Rig like that."

"You know it." Rock grinned back and Dick chuckled, the weight of it all suddenly lightening a bit.

Rig's smile just lit up the little room, making it brighter than the dozens and dozens of vases with flowers that had started pouring in – from Julie to the clinic to all the guys at the club. Dick leaned against the bed and just watched, that warmth slowly growing in scope, sliding into his balls.

Finger full by finger full, Rock fed Rig the pudding, and Dick was as hard as Rock before the bowl was half empty.

"No more, Blue. That's all I can manage." Still, half a bowl was more than he'd seen Rig eat in forever.

"You sure?" Rock's voice was husky. "A few more and I just might come."

Dick groaned at the words.

"I..." Rig just beamed, eyes lit up like it was Christmas. "One more bite."

"Good man." Rock got his finger covered down to the second knuckle and held it up for Rig. "Make it count, now."

"Uh-huh." Rig's eyes closed, the soft, happy moans and sounds of suction just filling the air.

"Fuck." Rock's free hand dropped to the front of his jeans, rubbing and Dick found himself mimicking the movement. He bit his lip to keep from making any noises, held his breath even.

Rig eased back into the pillows, relaxing, head moving nice and easy, lips swollen around Rock's finger.

"Just like that," muttered Rock, rubbing harder, finger pushing in and out now, fucking Rig's lips.

For the first time in days, Rig looked peaceful. Happy. Settled. That was what sent him over. That and the sound that Rock made as he came, wet staining the front of his jeans beneath his hand.

Rock's finger popped out of Rig's mouth and Rig gave the big guy this amazing, happy smile. Then their cowboy just fell asleep like an exhausted puppy.

"Jesus fuck."

Rock's whisper made him shiver and Dick stepped closer, leaning. Rock's arm came around him and they just stood there together, watching Rig sleep.

Chapter Thirty Eight

They rented a little SUV so Rig could lie down for the drive home. Dick' drove the car back the day before to get the house ready. Rock'd taken it as easy as he could, but Rig was still pale as a ghost by the time he pulled in, Dick out the door and down to the drive in a flash.

"Hey. How's he doing?"

"'Bout how you'd expect. Get the side door, I'll carry him in."

The dogs were barking up a storm, but Rig didn't budge, dozing in and out as he got that fucking skinny-skinny body inside. The doctor'd told him they had to make sure Rig didn't lose so much as a pound, or it was back into the hospital.

There was a day bed in the living room, his chair pushed back behind the couch to make room for it, but he went straight on back to the bedroom. A single bed had been squeezed in between their bed and the window -- one of those Posturepedics that you could raise the top or bottom third as you wanted, complete with swinging tray table. Three and a half weeks they'd kept Rig – and Rock thought if they had to fight one more infection or have one more test where they shoved something down Rig's nose, someone might die.

And it wouldn't be Rig.

"Good work."

Dick shook his head. "This one's on Helen. I called her on the cell on the drive in and she moved heaven and earth to get it here today. It only arrived a couple hours ago. It's perfect though, isn't it?"

"Yep." He set Rig down carefully, and then he and Dick started to take off Rig's clothes.

Rig was drugged to the gills, just barely waking for them. The incision was looking better, except for the new, raw, red place where the drain had been. The dogs had followed them in, and he let them sniff around the bed a little, but as soon as Trouble tried to get up to see, he growled, and Dick took them out, closing the door on them.

Those grey eyes fluttered open, hands sliding over the sheets. "I... We're home?"

Rock caught those hands in his and gave them a squeeze. "Yeah, Rabbit, we're home."

"'kay. Okay. Good." Yeah. Yeah, Rig could relax here. Heal. It was getting better and better, every day. More food, more energy, fewer pain meds.

"You ready to have something to eat?" he asked, squeezing Rig's hands.

"I could make you a shake," Dick suggested. "I've got all the stuff we need for 'em."

"Little one, yeah. I just want a few sips."

"Awesome." Dick beamed and Rig and disappeared down the hall.

"We're going to fatten you up like the Christmas turkey."

"Jeans won't fit then." Rig shifted, frowned a little. "This isn't our bed, Blue."

"We'll buy you new fucking jeans. And no, it's a fancy bed with a remote to make your head or feet go up and down. You'll be more comfortable in it, easier to get in and out of, too to start." Rock nodded toward their king-sized bed. "It's close enough it'll be just like being in our bed."

"Maybe." Rig blinked slow, thumb sliding over his hand.

"It will be." He figured playing stubborn might help keep Rig awake long enough to get that shake into him.

"You think so? I been wanting to snuggle with y'all so bad."

He kissed the top of Rig's head. "Sap," he whispered.

"'m not." Rig chuckled softly, moving closer. "You smell good."

"I smell like the fucking hospital. So do you. It'll be right soon, though. We'll all smell right again soon." Rock hated it when Rig didn't taste right.

"Chocolate shake in honor of your homecoming!" Dick came in, looking happier than he'd seen the kid in days, holding a plastic cup with a thick straw out to Rig.

"Mmm." Rig took it, hands trembling a little from the pain pills, and took a sip. They needed to keep him going with those shakes, keep Rig gaining weight and getting healthy.

"You drink that whole thing and the kid and I'll snuggle you until you fall asleep." He'd bribe Rig with anything he had to.

"I don't know if I can. There's a lot." Rig smiled, took another sip. "It's good, though. Better than the hospital ones."

"That's because I made this one." Dick climbed onto their bed and sat at the edge. "I bet you can finish that no problem."

Rock just sat on the edge of Rig's hospital bed and let Dick work his magic.

"Mmm. Did they say when I could go back to work? I had a couple of patients that were having babies in the spring..."

Rock just stared.

When could he fucking go back to work?

He opened his mouth to growl, but Dick beat him to it. Kid wasn't growling, though. "How about we wait until you can sit up without breaking into a sweat before we worry about when you're going back to work?"

"Picky picky picky." Rig chuckled, though. Actually, laughed a little. "I talked to them and told them definitely not before the New Year and then half-time at first, but that's two months off."

That hit him low and deep, that Rig - *his* Rig - felt bad enough to willingly take two months off.

"I bet you'll be feeling great by New Year's. We'll go out and watch fireworks and shit. We'll have something to celebrate." And by fucking god, if they didn't, he was breaking legs.

Dick nodded, smiled. "Sounds like a plan."

"Mmhmm. And Christmas." Rig started dozing a little, shake half-gone. "A nice simple Christmas here at home."

"Yeah, we already told your brood we were doing that."

Dick lifted Rig's hand and got the straw back in Rig's mouth. "Suck, Rig." Soon as the words were out of his mouth, the kid started chuckling, and Rock grinned.

Rig grinned, took another drink. "Asshole."

Dick just nodded happily. "And cock. And nipples. Fuck. All those great words we couldn't say in the hospital."

"Yep. So good to be home." Rig took another, small sip, then leaned back. "So fucking good."

Leaning in, Dick took a sip of the drink. "Okay, I helped you -- you need to finish the rest."

"Pushy." Rig finished the last bit, groaning softly. "Enough. Really. No more."

"You did great! And you can have another after your nap." Dick took the cup and put it on the bedside table.

Rock grinned. "We'll have you fattened up in no time."

"Uh-huh. Bed. Y'all promised."

Rock nodded. "Let's get everyone naked."

"You sure?" Dick asked.

"If we're home," he growled. "Then we're going to act like it."

"Naked is good." Rig nodded, shifting over toward the main bed. "In our bed?"

He growled a little. "We got you this bed so you'd be more comfortable."

"Yeah. Yeah, and when y'all aren't in bed with me, it will be. I just need y'all holding me for awhile, 'kay?"

"I don't want you ripping your scars open shifting over or anything, so no moving." He held up his hand, knowing Rig wanted to interrupt. "You let me and Dick move you. Hell, I fucking bench press more than you weight right now."

Dick nodded, pushing the covers down to the end of the bed. He watched as Dick gathered Rig up in his arms, lifting him into the middle of the bed.

"Okay, Blue. Okay." Rig nodded, eyes blood-shot, the grey too pale.

Dick laid Rig down on their bed, and Rock had to clench his teeth against the noise that tried to claw its way out of his throat. He started undressing with stiff movements as Dick carefully -- so fucking carefully -- stripped Rig.

"Oh. Oh, our bed." Rig just seemed to melt into the sheets. "Oh, I can start getting better now."

Look at that motherfucking smile.

He crawled up onto his side, almost scared to wrap around Rig like he wanted to -- he didn't want to pull that scar or hurt anything. Rig cuddled right in, though, pushing close with a happy, happy sound. He groaned, arm going across Rig, his hand cupping the bony hip, right it belonged. Dick grabbed the covers and pulled them up, cuddling in on the other side. Rock closed his eyes as their hands twined together, and he breathed through his nose, teeth clenched again.

Rig's lips brushed his jaw, soft, gentle. "I'm home, Jim. I'm gonna be fine."

"I'm holding you to that." He opened his eyes and stared into grey. "I'm fucking holding you to that."

"You do that. I won't leave you. I can't. I take care of y'all."

"You know it." He kissed Rig, hard and quick. "You fucking know it."

"Yeah. Stay here with me, y'all. I just need to feel my men."

"Not going anywhere," murmured Dick.

Rock grunted his agreement and squeezed Rig's hip.

Rig nodded and just fell asleep, that smile still on Rig's face.

"He's gonna be okay," whispered Dick.

Rock nodded. "Yeah. Yeah, he is." He closed his eyes, realizing he was fucking tired. He hadn't slept on a bed since they found out Rig was in the hospital. Three and a half weeks.

"Get some sleep."

He nodded and let himself let go.

Chapter Thirty Nine

Home.

Home home home.

Rig slowly raised up the head of the hospital bed, helping himself up so he could get up. He headed to the bathroom and showered, soaping himself up, washing his hair, carefully cleaning the stitches.

Oh.

Better.

Much better.

He took a bit to get out of the tub, then headed to the kitchen in his towel. There was bound to be clean laundry there. Maybe he could even get a bite or start the guys some supper. And turn the damned TV on. It was quiet when the boys were at the gym.

Oh. He needed to start planning Thanksgiving.

The front door opened as he came down the hall, Rock's eyes finding him and going wide. "What the hell are you doing out of bed?"

"I took a shower. I think I'm hungry. Hey, Blue." He smiled over at the big guy, moving nice and slow.

"Hungry's good. But you wait for me or Dick next time you want to take a shower."

Dick came up behind Rock, saw him and grinned. "Hey! You're up. You're looking good."

"Hey, Pretty. Thanks. I smell better. I want a cup of coffee and an apple or... can I have apples?"

"I'll make you special applesauce." Dick gave him a kiss and preceded him into the kitchen.

"You can have a shake with it," growled Rock. "No coffee."

"I like applesauce. Are we out of coffee, man? Is there something besides chocolate? It won't go with applesauce." He headed for the dryer, hoping for a pair of sweats inside.

"I can make it with apple juice and ice. Maybe a bit of cinnamon to help disguise the flavor of the powder." Dick started pulling stuff out of cupboards and the fridge, putting the food together for him, the protein powder going into the applesauce and the blender.

He was about to bend for the dryer when Rock stopped him. "What are you doing?"

"I'm cold, Blue. I need a pair of sweats." It was November.

"I'll get 'em for you." Rock crouched and pulled out a pair of his sweats, socks, and one of Rock's old sweatshirts, the material worn and soft.

"Mmm." He let Rock help him, holding the broad shoulders as the pants came up. "Oh. Better. How're y'all?"

"Good. I like this home by five deal." Rock went to the fridge and pulled out some steaks. "On the stove or grill 'em on the deck?"

"I like 'em on the grill, Rock." Dick brought him a bowl of applesauce and what looked like an apple juice snow cone.

He took the slushie-smoothie-thing. "We sitting outside, then?"

"You gonna be warm enough?" Rock asked.

"If not, I'll come in." He took a drink of the smoothie, the flavor not great, not coffee, but not bad.

Rock brought out the steaks and his grilling tools, starting up the gas.

Dick followed a few minutes later, dropping a blanket around his shoulders and laying the table with plates, utensils and cups. "Did you get some sleep today, Rig?"

"Yeah. Too much. I didn't do anything but that and shower." He took another sip, then set the drink down, full. He was always full.

"That's good though, right? You need to sleep to heal?" Dick sat next to him and offered him a spoonful of the applesauce.

"Yeah. Yeah, lots of rest. I'm feeling better every day." He took half a bite, then shook his head. "I'm full, Dick. I'll have to wait a minute."

"Okay. It'll keep. Besides, Rock'll have the steaks ready in a minute. And there's leftover mashed potatoes."

He was going to explode. "Don't make me a whole steak, guys. I can't eat but a bite or two."

Rock growled. "You need protein. You need to put on weight."

"I'll eat some, Rock, but there's not much room in there."

"We can take our time eating."

Dick's hand grabbed his, squeezed. "We're just worried and don't want you back in the hospital, you know?"

"You think I want to back in? Shit. I just want to feel normal again." He growled a little, shifted.

Rock growled right back. "Then you've got to eat."

Okay. Enough of this. "How long are you going to be pissed at me, Rock?"

"I'm not pissed at you -- I'm pissed that you're sick."

"Yeah. Me too." At Rock's look, he nodded. "You think I liked it, man? I thought I was going to have to come home and tell y'all I was dying. That's a living hell." That had been worse than the worry, the pain, the puking.

"We would have been there for you. I would have held your fucking hand and rubbed your back and--" Rock's mouth shut closed and he turned back to the grill, turning the steaks.

"I know. I was going to tell y'all, as soon as I had an answer."

"Nine fucking months, Rig. That's not as soon as anything."

Dick squeezed his hand, quiet.

"You trying to tell me that in nine months of puking, damn near fifty pounds of weight loss, you didn't notice?" He could feel the anger start to build, just climbing up his spine. Yeah, he hadn't said anything, but neither had Rock.

Rock whirled slammed his flipper down on the table. "Every single fucking time I mentioned how fucking skinny you'd gotten you laughed it off."

"What the *fuck* was I supposed to do? Tell you that me and the guys at the clinic had tried everything? Sit here and tell you that I don't know why, but I'm starving to death and the fucking paperwork is piling up and Dick's got tests and..."

Oh.

Oh, fuck.

"Dick. Your schooling. Tell me I didn't fuck up your schooling."

"Nothing's fucked up." Dick looked out over the beach. "And yeah, you could have told us. I hate thinking of you going through the last year and us not there to help you."

"See! Even Dick thinks you should have told us." Rock went back to flipping the steaks, turning them over and over again, shoulders bunched tight.

"Yeah. Okay." He stood up, chewing his bottom lip as his stomach turned. He'd fucked things up here and, right now, his head wasn't on straight enough to fix them. "I'm fixin' to go lay down a minute."

"Don't go." Dick looked up at him. "You should have told us, but you didn't and it's done now. We don't need to fight about this. Do we, Rock?"

"I don't want to fight," growled Rock. "I don't."

"I don't either." Rig looked at Rock, dead-on. "I couldn't look at you and tell you I might be dying, Rock. I wasn't going to do that until there wasn't a choice."

"I would have been there for you, Rabbit."

"I know, but God *damn* it, I wanted to know what it was, to give you answers." His heart was just pounding in his chest. "I was so fucking scared, man. I kept remembering Momma at the end."

Rock came around the table and pulled him up against that solid body. "It's my fucking job to be there when you're scared. I stand between you and the Goddamned monsters."

"What am I supposed to do when the monster's inside me, Jim?" He reached out, held on tight. "I couldn't figure out what to do, none of us could, and by the end, I couldn't think anymore."

Rock's arms were like bands, holding him tight, and yet so carefully. "I don't care where the fucking monster is, Rig. I'm not letting you go."

"Good." He let Rock hold him, just let the whole fucking broken and wrong and hurt go and let Rock have it a while. "I need this."

"Could have had it from the fucking start."

"Rock." Dick joined them, holding them both.

He got tickled, shook his head. "You always have to have the last word, don't you?"

Rock puffed up a little. "I do not. I was just saying, was all."

"I hear you. I got it, Rock. I fucked up and I'm sorry. I had good fucking inten..." He sniffed. "Somebody rescue supper."

"I got it." Dick hightailed it over to the grill, making the dogs bark and fuss.

Those muscled arms stayed firmly around him. He looked at Rock, staring. "Hey." Christ, Rock was warm.

Rock grunted, held him a little closer. Finally he just leaned in, cheek on Rock's shoulder, lips on the strong throat. Better. This was better. They stood there for awhile, Rock's chest rising and falling against him, the big hands on his ass, holding him close.

Dick came and went, getting supper out on the table.

He might have dozed a little, but Rig really thought it was more just basking. Just letting Rock hold him.

"Dick's got supper on the table and you need to eat." Rock kissed his forehead. "You manage to get some of it down and we can go watch a movie altogether in bed."

"I could so do that." He inhaled, nodded. "It smells great."

"Nah, that's me." Rock winked, hand squeezing his ass cheek.

"Mmhmm. We could just go snuggle..." He might not be able to suck Rock off yet, but he could jack the man off.

"A few bites first."

Damn, Rock was like a dog with a bone.

"Okay. Yeah." He grabbed his smoothie, took a sip. "Come on, Dickie-boy. Let's have supper."

Dick dished up the steaks, giving him the smallest of the three and a dollop of mashed potatoes. "Seems like we're always either trying to convince you to sleep, or we're feeding you."

"Yeah. I'm sorry." Of course, he was always trying to get Rock to take his vitamins and Dick to... Man, this thinking shit made his head hurt.

"You don't have to apologize for being sick."

"Nope. Just eat, Rig." Rock grinned. "You want me to cut your steak for you?"

"No. I'm not an invalid, asshole." He whacked Rock's hand with his fork.

Hard.

"Ow!" Rock rubbed his hand as Dick laughed.

He cut his steak up, ate a bite of potatoes and a couple bites of applesauce. Christ, he was tired.

Dick took his fork and speared a piece of meat. "You have to actually put it in your mouth to count it as eating."

"Fuck off, Pretty." He winked, grinned, and managed a couple of bites, the flavor making him hum. Nobody did steaks like his Rocketman.

Dick and Rock both beamed at him as he ate. It was like feeding time at the zoo.

"Y'all. Come on. I'm not starving myself, huh? I'm all about getting healthy and feeling better."

"You just want to get to the snuggling," Rock accused, grinning at him.

"Yeah. Yeah, and I want normal life back, you know? I want a cup of coffee. A beer. I want to be able to get it up again!" He was going to have a temper tantrum.

"I want you to be able to get it up again, too," murmured Dick, hand sliding on his thigh.

Rock snorted. "That's a given."

"Well, how fucking long? How long 'til things are right?" His hands were shaking a little, blood pressure through the roof. He dropped his fork, trying to reach for his glass.

"Hey." Dick wrapped around him. "It'll happen when it happens, right? You can't expect things to just snap back into place."

"I know. I just. I'm done. I need to relax a minute." His heart was just racing. They'd told him he'd have that, a little arrhythmia. Nothing to panic over. Nothing.

"Let me take you back to bed." Dick stood and reached for him.

"I don't. Don't. Let me." Shit. Shit. Okay. Fuck. His arms jerked, glasses tumping over.

Rock came around and leaned over him, pressing their foreheads together. Those blue eyes stared into his. "Breathe, Rabbit. Just fucking breathe."

Dick's hand rubbed slowly up and down his back.

Breathe.

Okay. Okay, he could do that.

He did too, in and out, in and out, holding Rock's gaze until the panic stopped.

When he'd caught his breath, Rock smiled and kissed him softly. "Good."

He nodded, squeezing Rock's hand. "Yeah. Sorry. Thank you."

He got another kiss and then Rock stood and picked him up like he was as light as a feather. They headed into the house, Rock taking him back into their room, the lights dim, the bed inviting. He was placed in the center of the bed like he was made of glass, Rock's fingers carefully working off his sweats.

"I miss feeling good." He cuddled back into the pillows, though, the scents of them heady.

"Yeah." Rock just nodded, sliding in next to him, Dick climbing in on the other side.

They sandwiched him between them, petting and soothing.

The sun was fading, and so was he, so he dozed. They could nap, then watch explosions in the dark.

Chapter Forty

Dick knocked on the office door, letting himself in at Rock's grunt.

"Hey." He threw himself into the chair in front of the desk.

"Hey." Rock looked up from the equipment catalogue he'd been poring over. "What's up?"

He decided to just cut right to the chase. "It's Thanksgiving in like two days."

Rock nodded. "I know."

"Rig's gonna want to do it right."

"I thought with him being sick, we'd just get one of those stuffed turkey breasts and shit at the store on Wednesday."

He gave Rock a horrifed look.

"What?" Rock sounded defensive. "Rig's not up to putting on a fucking spread."

"No, but if we don't, he's sure as hell going to try."

"We. As in you and me."

Dick made a show of looking around. "Yes, Rock. We as in you and me."

"I wouldn't know where to even fucking start."

"We start at the store. Come on, let's go shopping. The place'll survive without us for a couple of hours."

"I might have appointments."

Dick shook his head, grinning. "Nope, I checked the board before coming to talk to you. And I've arranged for us both to have Wednesday off so we can do all the cooking."

Rock shook his head. "No way Rig's going to let that happen."

"Sure he is. He can supervise and anytime he tries to do more, you can feed him a shake and put him to bed." Dick had it all planned out.

Rock shook his head again, but he was standing, coming around the desk. "This is crazy. How do we know what to buy?"

"I have my secret weapon." Dick pulled out his cell phone, waving it at Rock.

"Your phone is going to cook us Thanksgiving dinner? I haven't been keeping up with the times."

He smacked Rock and waved at Jenny at the front desk. "We'll be back in a few hours."

She waved back and he led the way to Rock's truck. "More room in the back for stuff."

"We're really going all out, the whole fucking nine yards..." Rock might have been growling and grumbling, but he was climbing into the truck, starting it up. "Grocery store?"

Dick nodded, sliding his phone back in his pocket. They didn't need it quite yet.

He'd made a list of the basics -- the things he knew they'd need and they got those first, filling the cart with a huge turkey, vegetables, sweet potatoes, stuff to make cornbread, a few pre-made pie shells, along with a can of crushed pumpkin, the stuff for chocolate pie and a package of pecans.

"Is this everything?" Rock asked when they pulled up into a quiet aisle and he stopped.

"No. I don't know what we need to go with any of it."

"Well, don't look at me."

Chuckling, he pulled out the phone and called home.

It rang a couple times, then he heard the dogs barking and Rig laughing. "'lo?"

"Hey, Rig. The mutts keeping you amused?"

"Yep. They're playing with the squeaky mouse and trying to distract me from my reading. What's up?" Rig sounded almost perky.

"Say I wanted to make Granny Boulware's pea salad, what would I need?"

Rock mouthed "ah", nodding and grinning.

"Peas and mayo. Onions, celery and cheese. Oh, man, that sounds good. You craving some, Pretty? I could make some for you."

"Yeah, I've been craving that and your seven layer salad -- I thought I could buy the ingredients and then make eyes at you."

"Mmm. Well, buy double all the stuff I told you and add. Uh. Bacon. Olives. Tomatoes. Lettuce. Eggs. You want me to make a list and send it to your phone?"

"That would be awesome." He tried to figure out how to ask about some of the other recipes he was going to need... the pumpkin pie he could use the one on the can, same with the pecan pie, but there was the cheese ball, and the dips Rig made, not to mention the sweet potatoes... "Anything you been craving lately -- just add it to the list, okay?"

"Coffee coffee coffee." Rig chuckled again. "We need to go for Thanksgiving stuff, too, huh? Maybe I should come with you. I'm not cleared to drive yet."

Oh man, he was so busted. Oh, well, it wasn't like Rig wasn't going to figure it out when they got home. "Actually... I'm kind of already at the grocery store and there's a huge turkey in the cart. You want to just walk me through all the bits I've got left?"

"Oh? Oh, Pretty, I didn't expect you to deal with all that..."

"I've got Rock driving the cart, so we're good. I just need to know what to buy for like stuffing and I have sweet potatoes but don't know what's needed to turn it into yummy stuff. So if you can just walk us through the store..."

He got another laugh, then they headed off, Rig supervising, teasing Rock via phone whenever he went on a hunt to keep the big guy interested and not growly. It worked. It wasn't perfect, but it worked and by the time they were done, nobody was pissed.

They stayed on the phone with Rig until they were packing up the truck, and he could hear that Rig was fading. "Okay, we're heading home with our booty. See you in a bit."

"'kay, Pretty. I'm going to get a shower, I think." The phone clicked off.

Oh, man, he hoped Rig was out of the shower by the time they got home -- it made Rock growly when Rig did that on his own.

"You want to drop me at the gym and I'll finish up there?" He had his car, so Rock wouldn't have to come back.

"Yeah, that'll work. You really think we can turn all that shit into a Thanksgiving dinner Rig'll be happy with?"

"Are you kidding? He's going to be tickled pink we're doing it in the first place and will eat it no matter what it tastes like. Well, little tiny bites of it -- we'll have leftovers for weeks."

"Yeah. But it'll be normal and shit. Like before."

He put his hand on Rock's knee. "Yeah. It'll be just like normal."

Or what passed for it these days.

Chapter Forty One

Rock was wearing a fucking apron. He was mixing and stirring and fucking baking. He'd made his own Goddamned chocolate pie, as well as a pumpkin and a pecan.

And it was only mid-afternoon.

He growled a little more, just because.

Truth was, it wasn't awful. Dick was wearing an apron, too, and at least his own wasn't red and pink but a manly black. Or at least it had been when he'd started.

Rig would be up soon and would come out and see what they were up to and he couldn't wait to see the expression on his cowboy's face.

"He's been napping forever," he growled.

"Yeah, but he'll be up longer, too, I'll bet."

He just grunted and banged the pots in the sink, washing them as noisily as possible.

The dogs started barking and Rig's voice sounded. "Good Lord, y'all! You let me sleep a thousand years and..."

Rig just stared, eyes huge.

Rock nudged Dick and winked. "Hey Rig. You finally up?"

"Working on it. 'course I might be dreaming. Look at this!"

"What this?" He grinned. "You never seen a pair of ex-marines cooking before?"

Dick snorted and muttered, "I'm thinking he hasn't," under his breath.

"I have, just not together. Y'all... it smells good!" Rig headed over, hand sliding down his back in greeting. "You've been busy."

"I made chocolate pie." It had been a lot fucking easier than he'd expected. But he'd bet it wouldn't be as good as Rig's.

"Oh?" Rig grinned, leaned into him. "Well, it may just become your job, if it's as good as Momma's was."

"Yours is always best."

Dick grinned "Suck up."

"Nah, that's Rig's job, too." He winked and took a kiss from his own personal cowboy. Rig kissed him back, nice and slow, and his knees went weak. He hadn't felt that in weeks. Weeks. He stared into grey eyes as their lips parted. "Hey."

"You taste good." Rig smiled at him, really smiled, and the terrible pale was fading from his Rabbit's cheeks.

Rock smiled back. "Like chocolate."

"Hey, I want me some of that," Dick said.

"Chocolate?"

Dick laughed. "Yeah, I'll take some of that, too." Dick gave him a quick kiss and then puckered up for Rig.

"Mmmhmm." Dick got the same, warm smile, then Rig kissed the kid, nice and thorough, making sure Dick felt it, balls-deep.

Damn. Watching that was almost as good as feeling it.

The kid looked like he'd been knocked on the head when the kiss ended.

"You taste good too, Pretty. Real good." Rig swayed a little, grinning.

Dick beamed. "You've woken just in time. I need direction on the salads. And Rock needs walking through the sweet potato casserole. I'll get you a shake, too."

"No more shakes." Rig held up his hand. "Not right now. I want something real. Eggs. I want some eggs."

"Oh, I can do that. Don't even need a recipe." Dick grinned. "You want them boiled? Scrambled? Fried?"

"Scrambled. Please. Two." Rig stretched a little, creaking. "Let me get a cup of coffee and I'll help."

"No coffee." Rock wrapped his arm around Rig's waist and led him over to the table. "Sit. We need you to tell us what to do."

"I miss coffee." Rig looked good in his sweater, looked cozy. "Are you listening to me?"

"I'm right here, I can hear you." He helped Rig into his chair and took another kiss. "But coffee's not on your approved list. How about some milk?"

Rig rolled his eyes, pressing their lips together again. "Man, as soon as I can suck that cock of yours, I'm so angling for my coffee."

Rock groaned, his knees going weak at the words. "That's so cheating."

Dick piped up from over at the stove. "Spunk's got protein in it."

"It does." Rig's eyes lit up a little, fingers on his fly. "You going to let me have some?"

He just about died. "You." He swallowed. "You up to it?" Fuck, his prick was going to tear right through his jeans.

"I can stop, if something hurts, huh?" Rig leaned, nice and careful, cheek rubbing along his cock through his jeans. "I think you deserve a reward for making pie."

"Oh, fuck, me too." He curled his fingers into his palms to keep from tearing open his jeans like some fuck-starved kid.

"Uh-huh. I think you both deserve some. You willing to wait for yours 'til this evening, Pretty?" Rig's lips were moving over his fly, that breath hot as hell. Rock didn't care what Dick said, the kid was waiting.

There was a sweet groan from the over by the stove. "I can live all day on the promise."

Those grey eyes flashed up to his. "I want your cock, Blue."

"It's all yours, Rig. Every fucking inch." Rig pushed the apron to one side, worked his fly open. His cock pushed out, just battering at his zipper to get to that mouth.

Dick slid into the chair across the table from Rig. "Wanna watch this."

Rock chuckled, the sound husky and needy even to his own ears. He took the apron right off and then dropped his hands onto Rig's head, fingers stroking through those curls. Rig smiled, then slid that hot, soft tongue all the way up along his prick. Oh. Oh, fuck yes. He made a sound that he was going to call a moan; it just ripped from his throat, his cock jerking hard.

"Oh... Oh, Blue..." Rig groaned, wrapped his lips around Rock's prick and just pulled. Hard. Pulled him right into that perfect motherfucking mouth.

Jesus fuck.

"Rig..." He caught himself before his knees buckled, locking them as his hands tightened in Rig's hair. His Rabbit just went to town, sucking, pulling, working him. "Fuck. Fuck. Rig. Oh." He held his hips still as long as he could, but it was too good and he held Rig's head still, fucked that sweet mouth. Rig hummed, the tip of Rig's tongue slapped the head of Rock's cock with every stroke. "Fuck. Now. Rig. Shit."

He jerked, his orgasm coming out of him, pulled out by that magic mouth. Rig drank him right down, fingers on his balls, stroking them, encouraging each pulse, each shock. Looking down, watching, he thought that was the prettiest sight he'd seen in too damn long. "Fucking good, Rig. So fucking good."

"Mmmhmm." Rig nodded, licked him clean.

Dick sighed, the sound happy.

Rig's forehead rested on his belly, both of them breathing together. He stroked his hand through Rig's hair and just stood there, enjoying the fucking afterglow.

"Mmm. Perfect appetizer." Rig's smile tickled his skin.

"You know it."

"That's my cue, isn't it?" Dick bounced up, adjusted himself in his jeans and went over to the stove.

Rig chuckled. "Sorry, Dick. I wasn't pushing." Those eyes were twinkling.

"I know. But I have to make sure you keep your strength up for my turn."

Rock chuckled and bent to kiss him. Oh, hell. Those lips were supposed to taste like him. Just like that.

He lost himself in it, in the flavor of his own come on Rig's lips, on the heat of Rig's mouth, that tongue sliding along his own. Groaning, he went to his knees, deepening the kiss.

Rig's moan was the finest sound he'd ever heard. He didn't stop kissing until Dick brought over Rig's scrambled eggs. "I suppose I'd better get back to work."

"I'll help. I just want my eggs."

Rig was hungry. It was fucking good to see him chowing down like that.

Rock grinned and put himself away, getting the apron back on. "You're only allowed to supervise. Dick said so."

"Did Dick say I could have coffee?"

"No coffee." Dick grinned. "I'll get you a refill on the milk, though."

Rock grinned and leaned in to whisper. "You know he's been on the Internet. Probably knows more about the disease than your doctor."

"Can't you hide that damn thing?"

"I kind of like that he knows what he does."

Rig ate the egg. All of it. And drank about half of the milk. "Yeah, yeah. I'll sit here and make pea salad, keep y'all out of trouble."

"Yeah, we need you to make sure we don't stuff the turkey with marshmallows or something."

"Oh, ew. No marshmallow stuffing." Rig laughed, swatted his ass. "Bring me the cans of peas."

"Is he allowed to make the pea salad, Dick?"

"If he can do it sitting right where he is."

"I can. Come on. Let me play too."

Rock looked over at Dick. "I think he's having a relapse. He thinks this is playing."

Dick laughed, bringing a big bowl and the rest of the ingredients over to Rig.

"You don't think I'd've made us Thanksgiving dinner for all these years if I hated it, do you?"

"No, I know you like. it. Fucking hard work, though."
"Yep." Rig hummed contentedly, getting right to work.
It was fucking good to see
Grunting happily, he started peeling the sweet potatoes.

Chapter Forty Two

He wasn't sure whether to be tickled or worried that they wouldn't need him anymore. Right. Like his marines would have done this for anyone but him. Rig chuckled and wandered through the kitchen, cleaning a little, trying to talk himself out of making a pot of coffee and having one cup.

Just one.

Nice and early.

Before the boys found out.

Dick came out, utterly naked and yawning. "Oh, there you are." He got a soft smile. "Happy Thanksgiving."

Goddamn it.

"Hey, Pretty. Do you have 'keep Rig from coffee temptation' radar?"

"You were out here for coffee?" Dick laughed, came close enough to nuzzle against him. "You wouldn't have found any, you know."

"Huh?" Oh. Warm. Strong. His Pretty.

"There isn't any in the house." Dick's fingers slid along his spine, slipping up beneath his sweatshirt.

"But you and Rock..." Mmm. That felt nice.

Dick shrugged. "It didn't seem fair, making the place smell like coffee when you couldn't have any."

"Oh... Y'all..." He lifted his chin, begged a kiss. Dick gave it to him, mouth meeting his, the kiss starting soft and growing hard. He groaned, kissing right back. His prick tried to fill, just a bit, which gave him a thrill, because it hadn't in a while.

Dick's porno noises filled his mouth, and his Pretty's cock was having no problems perking right up. Rig reached out, stroking Dick nice and easy. Even if he couldn't get off, Dick could. Dick hadn't gotten that blowjob last night, either. He'd been more tired out by the day than he'd expected. He was given a sweet groan, Dick rocking gently into his touch.

Rig leaned hard, letting Dick support him while he loved on that fine, strong body. Dick fed one sweet noise after another into his mouth, rocking faster, pushing into his hand. His cock rubbed against Dick's thigh, the heat and sensation soothing him, feeling so good.

His sweats were tugged down, Dick groaning as soon as they were skin on skin.

"Oh..." He blinked, swayed. Oh. Oh, he might get it up. Strong fingers grabbed his ass, squeezed. "Dick. Bed?"

He wanted to be able to feel this. Enjoy it. Dick nodded, lifted him and headed down the hall, pressing kisses over his face.

Their pricks rubbed with every step.

So strong.

His men were so strong.

Sexy.

His.

He was set down by the bed, Dick grabbing his hands and tugging him into bed. Rig got settled, Rock's arms wrapping right around him immediately. Dick chuckled and climbed in, rubbing up against him and bringing their mouths back together again.

Oh, sweet. He moved, slow and so careful, his body trying to remember how to do this. Dick's tongue parted his lips, his Pretty not seeming to be in any hurry, just loving on him. Rock's cock rubbed against his ass, filling easily, eagerly, swelling against him.

"You taste so good," murmured Dick, licking at his lips and then pressing into his mouth again.

It was all he could do, to moan and touch, encourage Dick's cock to jerk and throb, leak against him. Dick's fingers slid over him, randomly at first, but then they slid to his nipple, playing with the spot where the ring was supposed to be, just flicking it back and forth.

Oh. Oh, it was tender, still. Just barely aching.

He wanted it back

Dick grinned, the smile curing against his mouth, and then the little bit of flesh was tugged, hard.

"Pretty!" He jerked, gasping loud, eyes wide.

"Oh, I haven't heard that sound in far too long." Dick nipped at his lower lip, fingers moving to his other nipple and rubbing it.

"Don't stop." He moaned as Rock's hand landed on his belly. "More."

Rock groaned, mouth nuzzling into his neck as Dick gave him a quick kiss and started wriggling down, stopping to mouth at both nipples.

"Please." Oh, please. He wanted this back. Needed it. Licking all the way, Dick slowly went down on him, nibbling and nuzzling at his belly, and slowly getting closer and closer to his cock. He shuddered, watching. "I don't know if..."

Looking up at him, Dick liked his navel. "Doesn't matter. Just want to taste you, 'kay?"

"Yeah. Yeah, please, huh?" He'd do anything for it.

Beaming, Dick kissed his belly, and bent, tongue flicking across the tip of his cock. Rig closed his eyes, heart pounding as he just leaned into Rock's heat and felt. Rock's prick rubbed against his ass, nice and slow, and one hand slid over his belly. And Dick's tongue moved on him, licked at him. It was so hot, so good.

He just moved, rocked and felt and soared. "Pretty. Blue. I. So good."

Rock hummed, the sound vibrating along his skin, while Dick nibbled at the tip, and then took the whole head in. Rig might have sobbed, the pleasure just overwhelming. He wasn't even sure he was hard; he was pretty sure it didn't matter. It just felt so fucking good.

Dick licked and kissed and sucked him, loved on him like he was the most precious thing in the world. The familiar rush of orgasm started building in the base of his spine, heat swelling, sliding through him.

Rock's teeth scraped over the sweet spot on his neck, started sucking up a mark.

"Fuck. Yeah. Please." He was going to. Oh. Oh, sweet fuck. "Gonna..."

Dick's head bobbed, suction stronger, hard and insistent. Spunk poured from him, his entire body arching, rejoicing. Rock groaned, Dick crying out around his flesh, swallowing around him. Rig just shuddered, shaking hard. So good.

"That's fucking sweet." Rock's words were growled against his skin, his Blue's hips beginning to rock, pushing that cock along his ass, the small of his back.

"Uh-huh. I needed, so bad."

Dick kissed his way back up, smiling, prick rubbing against his belly. "Missed your taste. So much."

Rig nodded, took a kiss that thanked Dick the best way he knew how. They moved together, pricks sliding against his belly and back, the smell of sex rising up strong around them. Perfect. This was perfect. He reached back, fingers twining with Rock's. Rock squeezed his hand, and nibbled at his earlobe, breath loud and eager.

He could feel them getting closer, knew it wouldn't be long in the way their bodies lost the rhythm.

"Come on. Come on." He wanted to feel them. Smell like them.

Dick cried out first, bucking as heat splashed up his belly, but Rock came right after, coating his back as well.

"My men." Thank God. He hadn't lost this.

"Mmm... Happy Thanksgiving." Rock murmured against his jaw, turning his face for a kiss.

Dick cuddled in. "We've got a lot to be thankful for."

He nodded, opening up to Rock's kiss.

"We've got awhile still before we have to put the turkey in the oven, right?"

"Uh-huh. Thank God." He needed a nap.

Dick's "cool" was almost lost beneath Rock "Thank fucking God."

Chuckling, Dick snuggled in, smiling at him, eyes happy. "Thank you."

"Anytime. And I really mean that."

"Forever."

And he really meant that.

Chapter Forty Three

Dick was feeling a little frazzled. He and Rock usually helped out some, but damn, there was a lot of stuff to pull off at the same time, even with all the prep work they'd done the day before, and Rock was distracting Rig from trying to push himself too much with a little tonsil hockey.

Which was distracting enough for him.

And then the doorbell went. Oh man, that was Deuce and Gary.

"I'll get it." Rig stood, heading for the door, moving easier each and every day.

"You wanna set the table? If we don't get it done now, you know Rig'll do it." And easier as Rig seemed in his skin, Dick had a hunch having visitors was going to take it out of him. Grunting a yes, Rock started setting the table while he got the rolls into the oven.

"Uncle Jimmy! Richard!" Deuce came in, arms filled with a box of beer, chips, dip and random snack food. "I brought stuff and Gary made a cheese tray."

Dick grinned. He still found it amusing when Deuce called Rock Uncle Jimmy; the kid had grown up into a big burly marine and it seemed incongruous. "Did you think we weren't going to lay on a spread for you?"

"I knew, but..." Deuce blushed a little and Rig clapped him on the shoulder.

"But he was raised right and knows you always bring stuff. Hey, Gary, how's it going?"

"Just fine, Mr. Roberts. Thank you. Are you feeling better?"

Rock took the case of beer from Deuce and took a few out to put into the refrigerator. "He's feeling well enough to backseat drive the cooking."

"I was helping. Asshole. And I'm Rig or Alex, please."

"Oh, is that what you call it... And you can call me Rock."

"And I'm Dick." They'd been through all this when they'd first met Gary at the hospital, but they hadn't exactly spent a lot of time with Deuce and Gary.

"I'll try to remember that. Thank you for inviting me to have Thanksgiving with you."

Dick felt for the guy -- it was never easy meeting the in-laws. Of course Rig's family had made him feel like one of them right from the get go.

Deuce just beamed. "Don't worry, Gar. This is a safe place. You feeling better, Uncle Alex?"

"Getting there, son. You know it."

"Is the game on yet?" Dick asked. "We could have the stuff you brought and our munchies and watch the start. I think I've got everything covered here for awhile."

"I'll help you, Dick. Guys, go. Sit." Rig headed toward the sink and Rock growled.

"Deuce could help me, yeah?"

"That sounds like a great idea." Rock grabbed the cheese tray from Gary in one hand, and Rig's arm with the other.

Duece chuckled, shook his head. "Shit, he looks way better, but Ma-maw'd scream, huh?"

"Yeah, she would. I think Rock probably made up for her." He wasn't convinced Rock'd really taken a proper breath yet.

"Why don't you go in and join them, Gary?" He handed over a tray with the cheeseball, ranch dip and a bowl of chips. "Deuce and me'll be out in a bit."

Gary looked a bit like a deer caught in the headlights as he looked over at Deuce.

"Go on, honey. They don't bite." Deuce patted Gary's ass, winked.

"You sure? The big guy's bigger even than you." Gary leaned up to kiss Deuce's cheek and then headed into the front room, tray in hand.

Dick chuckled. "He's cute, even if he is short. Where did you find him?"

"At a VA hospital visit." Deuce looked down, then back up.

Dick frowned. What was it with the Roberts men and not sharing their burdens? He went to the fridge and got them each a cold beer, handing one over to Deuce. "What were you doing at the hospital?"

"Me? My unit goes once a month to visit the patients. You know, be good to other folks." Deuce took the beer, sucked it down.

"Hey, that's cool. So what was Gary doing there?" He put his hip against the counter and drank his more slowly.

"He was in for pneumonia. He, uh, he's got... Well. I mean, he's sorta. Shit."

Dick put his hand on Deuce's shoulder. "Hey. We're family here, right?"

"Yeah. I just. I ain't told nobody, Richard, you know? Not Alex or Jimmy, either." Deuce's lips twisted. "He's got AIDS. And before you say anything, I'm careful and we don't do stuff that's dangerous and stuff."

Dick's hand froze with his bottle halfway to his mouth. Shit. That was pretty heavy.

"So you knew before you got involved with him? Don't you think... I mean didn't..." Shit. He was supposed to be good at this kind of thing.

"Yeah. Yeah, I knew." Deuce shrugged. "I love him. He's a real good man, Uncle Richard. Funny, smart. Fine."

"I know you don't get to choose who you love." And Deuce, being not only Rig's nephew, but Rock's as well, really, wouldn't have turned his back on someone he loved just because the man was sick and it was going to be a hard row to hoe. "You're being really, really careful, though, right? And getting tested regularly?"

"I am. I swear." Deuce nodded. "Don't go tellin' Uncle Alex, though, 'kay? Not until he's better. He'll get all doctory and shit." Jesus, was he ever that young?

"Don't you want to talk to him because he is a doctor? He could help you both." And he wasn't sure if he could keep something like this from Rig.

"Not yet. Not unless Gary wants me to."

Dick sighed. "How bad is it? I mean is he really sick? Taking pills?" The guy hadn't looked sick.

"He takes this cocktail deal, but he could have years and years, man. They're trying new stuff all the time. Don't worry, huh? I'm a marine. I'm good."

"You have anyone to talk to?"

"Yeah. Gary." The empty went into the recycle bin, another longneck snagged. "So? What do you need me to do, man?"

"Well, we need drinks for everyone. And we can bring out more chips. I think everything else is good until the timers go off." He grabbed the stuff to put a shake together for Rig. "Look, if you ever need someone to talk to, or if you want help telling Rig..."

"Thanks, Uncle Richard." He got a sudden, hard hug. "Thanks for not being mad about Alex, too. He plumb scared me, when I saw him."

Dick hugged Deuce back. "No, no, we were really glad you called. It's good you could come for Thanksgiving, too, yeah? Good for Rig to have family around."

"Yeah. Come on. Football!"

"Yeah, football and beer and munchies. Sounds good." He patted Deuce on the shoulder and grabbed some more longnecks out of the fridge, carrying them and Rig's shake into the front room.

Rig was sitting on the floor, head on Rock's thigh, Rock's hand on those curls. Gary was sitting on the old green sectional and staring everywhere but at the two of them.

He passed out the drinks and sat next to Gary. "So who's winning?"

"Redskins. Thank you." Gary relaxed as Deuce sat too. Leaned.

"How come y'all got beer and I got a milkshake?" Rig was pouting mightily.

"Because you're special." If Rig wasn't careful he was going to lean right in and kiss that pout.

"Uh-huh. Right." Rig took a drink, hummed softly. It was pineapple and strawberry with protein powder and Rig liked it, had been drinking them for two days without complaint.

He split his attention between the game, Rig and Rock, and Gary and Deuce. Gary looked at Deuce with stars in his eyes. Well they had that going for them at least. Rig, on the other hand, finished half his shake and started dozing again.

Rock was munching away, he and Deuce putting away the food like there wasn't a huge meal on its way. He grinned, sitting back, enjoying the almost normality of it.

Gary looked over, nodded at Rig. "Is he feeling better?"

"Yeah, he's good. Still too fucking skinny and he needs a lot of sleep, but he's good." He smiled over at Rig and caught Rock's eye, smile widening. Rock gave him a wink and raised his beer bottle.

"So what do you do, Gary?"

"I'm a graphic designer for a little entertainment magazine. Layout, covers, photo manips - that sort of thing."

"That sounds pretty cool -- you like it?"

"I do. I learned in the Navy, believe it or not."

"For real?"

"Yep. Worked for the Armed Forces press. Rob says you're in school and you own a gym?"

Rob. Man did that sound weird, but it made sense. "Yeah, me and Rock own a gym and I've just started taking courses to get a degree in psychology."

Well, he would be starting again in January -- none of his courses were going to count this semester, but they weren't going to count against him either. He'd managed to keep that tidbit from Rig.

"Very cool. Good luck to you. I keep trying to convince Rob to go to school, but he's still into the Marines."

Deuce arched an eyebrow. "I'm not into books, honey."

"There's nothing wrong with the Marines," Dick said.

"That's fucking right." Looked like Rock was paying more attention to them than the game.

"Well, it's not the friendliest place for a queer man." Gary shrugged. "And Rob's smarter than he thinks."

Rig blinked awake. "Nothing wrong with Deuce, y'all."

Dick chuckled. "I don't think anyone's saying there is, Rig."

Rock grunted. "I've been queer my whole fucking life, including the twenty years I served uncle Sam, and I'd do them over again just the same. There isn't a damn thing wrong with being a Marine."

"No, Rocketman. Not a thing. I fucking love marines." Rig stretched, wincing. "Gonna have to move. My butt's sore."

"Got a lap right here with your name on it." Rock patted his thighs.

Gary stared as Rig crawled up, settled right in Rock's lap and cuddled.

Dick chuckled. "I take it you're not out at all?"

"No. No, we... We're very careful."

Deuce chuckled, patted Gary's hand. "Uncle Jimmy and Alex have been together forever."

"They have. And you don't have to be careful here."

"No, not at all." Rig cuddled into Rock with a sigh. Dick grinned as Gary's hand slowly slid over to rest on Deuce's thigh. Then Dallas made a touchdown and suddenly it all didn't matter. They were all hooting and hollering.

Now as long as the turkey wasn't raw or totally dried out, it was going to turn out to be a great Thanksgiving. He glanced over at Rig and Rock. Yeah, even if the turkey did get screwed up it would be great. He sure as fuck had a lot to be thankful for.

Chapter Forty Four

They'd eaten like fucking kings.

The food had been pretty damned good, if he did say so himself. Rig was settled in bed, Dick and Deuce were doing dishes, leaving him alone with Gary.

Rock grinned over at the kid -- shit didn't that make him feel old -- Deuce a fucking Marine and Goddamned dating. "So Gary. You treating my nephew right?"

He figured if Jeremy wasn't around to give anyone Deuce brought home a hard time, he'd have to pick up the slack and do it himself.

"I try, sir. He's a sweet man." Gary wasn't his type, not at all, short and square, too-long black hair and pointed goatee. Still, Deuce liked him.

Sweet. "He's a good man. A marine."

"He is. Not many men would start a relationship with someone in my condition. He never even hesitated."

One of his eyebrows went up. "Your condition?"

"Rob didn't tell you? I thought... Fuck."

"I think maybe *you'd* better tell me." He puffed up some, growled a little.

"Don't pull the family intimidation thing, man. Trust me. I'm not into that." Dark eyes just stared at him. "I've got AIDS."

Rock just stared.

He must have heard wrong.

Gary's cheeks went a deep dark red, but the man didn't look away.

"You start up with someone with a thing like that hanging over your head?"

"I did. If you'll excuse me." Gary stood and just headed for the kitchen, spine stiff as a board.

Fucking hell.

He sat staring at the TV, kind of stunned. How the fuck was he going to tell Rig?

Rock heard the back door open, then shut, then Deuce appeared in the doorway, jacket on. "Don't know what happened during dishes, Uncle Jimmy, but we're heading out. I'll come back by tomorrow."

"No, you sit down a minute, Robert."

"Gary's in the car..." Robert came in, lips tight. "Did y'all have words?"

"He told me he's got AIDS. He told me he started up with you knowing he had AIDS."

"That's right."

Rock crossed his arms. "Then I don't know how he can say he cares for you."

"Well, I don't reckon you have to know. This ain't about you. This is between me and Gary."

"I'm your family, Deuce."

"You are and I love you, Uncle Jimmy, but that don't mean you can speak against Gary." Deuce sighed, hand rubbing over his high and tight.

Rig came wandering in from the hallway, swaying, frowning. "What's wrong? I heard the car start."

"You'd better sit." He shot a look at Deuce. "Both of you."

"Gary's waiting for me in the car. I'm going, Uncle Alex. I'll see you tomorrow."

"What? What's wrong with the guest room? It's all brand new up there. I built it myself."

Fucking shit, all he'd wanted was for Rig to have a good Thanksgiving. "I didn't say anything against Gary. Go get him and stay in the fucking guest room. We can talk in the morning."

Deuce looked at him, then Rig, then nodded. "Okay. Sure, Uncle Jimmy. Sure. I'll get him to come on."

Was he ever that young?

"I'm taking your Uncle Alex back to bed before he falls over." That way he wouldn't be tempted to say anything when he saw Gary.

"Okay. Night, y'all. I... We'll see you in the morning, yeah?" Deuce just looked dazed.

"Deuce? You okay?" Rig was catching on, starting to worry. He could tell.

Goddamn it. "He's just fine. Gary took offense at something I said is all. It doesn't matter right now." He looped his arm around Rig's waist and headed them back down the hall, stopping at the kitchen long enough to tell Dick they were going to bed.

Rig leaned hard, almost asleep on his feet. "It was a good Thanksgiving, huh? I ate a ton."

"Yeah, it was a good day. And you've got leftovers for the next... year?" He grinned and kissed the top of Rig's head.

"Maybe two. What's up with Deuce and his guy?"

"It can wait until morning." He stripped Rig back down, and then took off his own clothes, sliding them both under the covers.

Rig hummed softly, cuddling right in, snuggling. The hospital bed was gone, Rig's movements easier against him. He closed his eyes, running his fingers along Rig's spine. It might have been his imagination, but he thought maybe Rig had found a few pounds. "Mmm. Thank you for everything, Blue. It was all good."

"Yeah, it was."

He could hear Dick talking to Deuce and Gary, the sound of footsteps on the stairs and the guest bedroom door closing. Then the kid was there, closing the door and stripping down. "Hey."

Rig murmured a welcome, lips on his shoulder.

"Man, we're all bedding down early. All that cooking tire you out, Rock?"

"You know it."

Chuckling, Dick leaned over to give him a kiss, then Rig. Dick met his eyes, the look knowing, a little worried, a little sad. He tried not to sigh, not to stiffen, not to give Rig any reason to do anything but just fall asleep again.

"Y'all okay?" Rig leaned to look, searching his eyes, Dick's. "What's wrong, y'all? What's got everybody all riled?"

Rock shook his head. "Just go to sleep, Rig." He nibbled at Rig's neck, stroked the skinny belly.

"My boys are all tense." Rig arched a little, hummed sweet and slow.

"We just need a little loving." Dick chuckled, but he helped, mouth finding Rig's nipple.

"Well, that's my pleasure." Rig lifted his face, mouth meeting his in a long, serious kiss. Groaning, he sank into it, everything else disappearing but him and Rig and Dick. This was what they needed, this place that was all theirs. The rest of the world could go to hell. Dick's leg slid over Rig's, tangled with his, and their hands met over Rig's prick.

"Mmm. Y'all." Rig wasn't hard, but there was the promise of it there, that fine cock beginning to swell. Fuck, he'd never take that for granted again. At least not for the next few months.

Dick was slowly making his way down Rig's body, so Rock concentrated on that sweet mouth, working it. Rig moaned, eyes closing. Yeah, that was fine.

Just fine.

He didn't expect Dick's tongue on his prick and it had him jerking, crying out in surprise. Rig smiled, hand sliding down to tangle in Dick's hair. Dick's chuckle was sweet, tongue lapping at him and then lapping at Rig, one and then the other. It was maddening.

"I... I should be doing that..." Rig arched, spread, started bucking against him.

"Tomorrow."

"Yeah, tonight just enjoy being done to." Dick grinned up at them and then swallowed Rig's prick whole.

"To..." Rig gasped and jerked, grey eyes going wide, horny.

"Mmm... Yeah, that's it, Dick. You've got him hooked now."

Dick's head bobbed over Rig's prick. Rig fed him one horny little moan after another, just driving him out of his mind. Rig's skin was hot, belly rubbing against him. Fuck, he wanted to fuck Rig, wanted to feel that he could, that Rig was well enough to take it. Moaning hard, he rubbed against Rig's hip.

"Rock..." Rig groaned, wiggled, wanting him.

Rock moved Rig gently, pushed him onto his side so that sweet ass rubbed against his prick. Oh, fuck. Yes. He wanted.

"I can. I need it." Oh, that was his Rabbit.

"Need lube."

Dick pulled off long enough to mutter, "Under my pillow."

"Oh... Oh, Blue. Come on. Need it." Rig sounded damn near desperate.

He reached up for the slick, finding the tube right where Dick said it would be. His fingers were damned near trembling as he slicked them up -- shit, it had been too fucking long. "Slow down, Dick. I want him coming on my cock."

"Touch me. Y'all. Please." That was his fucking Rabbit, begging for him.

"Yeah. Yeah." He nodded as he saw Dick's suction ease. Rock slid his finger along Rig's crack, rubbed it back and forth over that sweet little hole. He teased them both a moment, but it was too fucking much, and without further ado, he pushed his finger into Rig's body.

Tight.

Jesus fuck.

He damn near shot all over Rig's ass. He buried his face in Rig's next, groaning, trying to fucking keep it together. Working Rig's ass with his finger, he just kept pushing it in over and over until he could breathe again. Then he slid a second finger in alongside the first.

"Blue..." Rig moaned for him, muscles fluttering madly around his finger.

"Yeah. Fuck." It felt like the first fucking time and that had him groaning again.

He shoved a third finger in, spreading and stretching Rig out for his cock -- he couldn't wait much longer to take Rig's ass, he needed in. Rig started pushing back, riding his fingers good and hard, deep, hungry sounds filling the air.

"Okay. Okay, now. Fuck." He yanked his fingers out and lined up his prick, letting Rig's movements draw him in. Oh, hell yes. Rig just moved like it was supposed to be, taking his prick and holding it in that perfect fucking heat.

"Fuck." He whispered the word over and over, hips moving, fucking Rig's ass in tiny increments because he didn't want to pull out, not for a second. Dick's head still bobbed, moving with Rig's body.

"Yeah. Yeah, y'all. Just like that."

"You fucking know it." He moved a little faster, a little harder, pushing Rig's prick into Dick's mouth with every thrust.

It was fucking heaven right here on earth. Rig's hand reached back, wrapped around his nape and squeezed.

Yeah.

Heaven.

They moved together, the three of them sucking and fucking and loving on each other. He licked at Rig's neck, and then sucked up a mark.

"Rock." He could feel it, Rig's need, Rig's ass fluttering and rippling around him.

"Yeah, give it to me, Rig. Come on my cock."

That happy fucking cry? That was all he fucking needed - to know that Rig was shooting in Dick's mouth, coming around him, needing them both. He let go, thrusting hard a couple more times before he filled Rig with his spunk, the pleasure fucking huge.

The scent of Dick's come filled the air, and he nodded, panting against Rig's neck.

"Good." Rig sighed once, then just seemed to go boneless, sound asleep. Just like that.

Dick cleaned Rig's legs and then cock and wriggled back up, smiling at him. "Wow."

Rock nodded. Yeah. That had been just what they'd all needed.

He shared a slow kiss with the kid, and then they all settled in to sleep.

Chapter Forty Five

He got up early, heading to make coffee and getting stuck when he remembered there wasn't any.

Again.

Damn it.

Rig grinned and shook his head, looking through the Thanksgiving leftovers for a bite of something and a drink.

Gary came down, wearing little more than his boxers, pushing his hair back. "Oh. I. I didn't realize anyone was up. I was. Just looking for some coffee."

"If you can find some, I'll be your best friend, man. The guys are holding out on my skinny ass."

"That's cruel, man." Gary scratched his belly, blinking a little.

"Uh-huh. They're vicious on this point." He started searching, knowing there had to be some. "You sleep okay?"

"Um... yeah. I guess so. I'll. You want some help there?"

"Sure, Gary." He tilted his head, trying to remember what Rock had said happened last night. "You okay? Sounded like things got a little weird with the guys..."

Gary's chin went up. "I'm surprised they didn't tell you."

"I was tired, man, and they err on the side of sleep for me these days. What's up?" Whatever it was, Deuce was family, they'd work it out.

Gary sighed. "I've got AIDS, man."

"Yeah? That sucks. You on NNRTIs or PIs?" Good thing the guy was ex-military. Those meds were deadly expensive.

"PIs. You aren't going to read me the riot act? Tell me how I can't love Rob if I've got AIDS and still went out with him?"

"What does loving Deuce have to do with being sick? I mean, you're practicing safe sex, yes?"

"Yeah. Yeah, we are." Gary started looking through cupboards with him. "I wouldn't do anything to hurt him. I love him, man."

"Good. He loves you, I can tell." Rig frowned, tried to figure out where Dick would hide the coffee. If Rock had done it, he'd have found it already.

"I know he does. He's a real good guy." Gary grinned. "Quite the stud, too. Are you sure there's coffee here?"

"Well, I just can't seem them throwing it all away..." Goddamn it. It was chilly outside. He needed coffee.

"So what's the deal with hiding the coffee?"

"I'm not supposed to have it. It leaches protein and I have a hard time getting enough as it is. One cup, though. I really just need one cup."

"I don't know, then. I think the big guy would throw it out." Gary shook his head and checked the freezer.

"You think? He likes his morning cup."

"Yeah, but I imagine he likes you better." Gary blushed. "I mean. God, I'm sorry, I'm usually better at keeping my mouth shut."

"Hell, we're family, ain't we? Why worry?" He sighed, leaned against the fridge. "I don't suppose you and me could go get a cup of coffee?"

"Yeah, sure. Rob's got nothing but good to say about you, be nice to get to know you a bit, man." Gary waved at his boxers. "I just need to get some clothes on, man."

"You're a good, good man." He grabbed a t-shirt and a sweater from the clean clothes basket and started hunting socks.

Gary was back before he was done, car keys in hand.

Dick was right behind him, wearing his sweats and yawning. "I thought you'd decided to stay, Gary?"

"I was going take him for a cup of..." Well, fuck.

Dick chuckled. "Oh man, you are so busted. And so lucky Rock's still asleep."

"Busted? I'm just trying to show our guest some hospitality..."

"Uh-huh."

"It's true, man." Gary tucked his keys into his pants pockets and mouthed 'sorry' at him.

He winked, shrugged. "You go back on to bed, Pretty. I'll take Gary to the IHOP."

Coffee. Pancakes.

"No coffee, Rig. And we've got a fridge so full of food it's going to explode. Not to mention, I'll make you a shake." Dick went over and opened the fridge door. "What do you feel like?"

"A cup of coffee?"

Gary started chuckling.

Dick shook his head. "You're just torturing yourself, Rig."

He sighed, gave Dick a long, puppy-dog look. "I'm pretty much recovered, you know..."

Coming over, Dick gave him a quick kiss first, and then picked him up like he was light as a feather. "Nope. You're still way underweight."

"Can I have coffee when I'm back to fighting weight?" He really didn't mind the shakes, but he wanted something warm.

"I think you're going to have negotiate that one with Rock yourself."

"He kind of rules the roost, huh?" Gary asked, watching them together.

"Who? Rock?" He gave that some thought. "He has opinions and my rule is, if he makes sense, I'm not arguing with him."

"Yeah, but if he doesn't, Rig argues." Dick laughed and gave him a quick kiss. "I picked you up some herbal tea when we went grocery shopping -- you want to give it a try?"

"Herbal tea? I don't know, Pretty. That sounds real prissy..." Still, it might taste good...

"I got peppermint. I figured it might be nice to have something hot in the mornings. I think I miss that more than the taste of the coffee itself..."

"Lots of herbal teas have good medicinal qualities," Gary pointed out.

"Don't be a traitor now, Gary." He winked, clapped Gary on the arm. "Okay, Dick. I'll try it. Y'all want eggs for breakfast?"

"I don't know. Pancakes was sounding pretty good." Gary grinned wryly.

Dick laughed. "That's Rock's balliwick. But Rig makes a mean French Toast."

"Mmm. I do. Or we could all go out before the game starts."

"Oh, no dishes -- I approve. Besides, that way we can go wake up Rock instead of having to cook." Dick gave him a wink.

He grinned, belly heating up. "Sounds good. Gary, go get my nephew. We'll meet you in half an hour out here."

"A half hour? Really? That long?" Gary looked confused and then the penny must have dropped because he went red, nodded, and fled.

"Lord, he's a nervous nelly. Rock must've growled." He grinned, headed over for a kiss.

"Yeah, I kind of think he did." Dick's arms looped around him, his Pretty taking himself a nice, long kiss. "We should go wake the bear up."

"We should." He nodded and slid his arm through Dick's.

They headed down the hall, soft noises coming from the guest room upstairs.

"No listening. Just walking. Deuce is a baby."

Dick giggled and then covered his ears for him as they went the rest of the way down the hall. They were laughing hard as they hit the bedroom, hard enough that bright blue eyes opened, staring at them. Dick pushed him toward the bed, rubbing up against him from behind, even as his Pretty's fingers worked open the jeans he'd thrown on.

"What were you two up to?" Rock asked suspiciously.

"We want IHOP. You want?" He tugged the covers off, leaned down carefully to nuzzle Rock's prick.

Rock made a soft sound that was almost a whimper. "I'm getting a morning wake-up call?"

Dick grinned. "You've gotten one from me every day the last little bit."

Rock stuck out his tongue and Dick leaned in to suck on it. Rig hummed, lips sliding over Rock's shaft. Yeah, Dick was good, but no one loved this prick like he did.

No one could.

Rock made another almost pained noise, fingers wrapping in his hair, legs spreading for him.

"Mmhmm." That's right. Mine. All fucking mine. Rig wrapped his lips around Rock's prick and started sucking.

"Fuck." Rock groaned, encouraging his head to bob as Dick worked Rock's nipples.

He gave it all he could, sighing happily as Dick rolled them carefully so he wasn't holding himself up. Rock's balls drew up tight, and the hands in his hair held him still, Rock's hips jerking, pushing the fat prick deep into his throat.

Yeah, yeah. Just like that. He opened up, took Rock down to the root, swallowing hard. Rock's roar nearly shook the windows; it was a sound of pure pleasure, ringing in his ears long after the spunk had stopped flowing. Rig cleaned and licked, sliding over Rock's skin with his tongue.

Dick groaned. "Oh, man, there's no sight prettier than that."

"Feels better than it looks," muttered Rock, fingers moving through his hair.

"Mmm. Missed this. So bad."

Rock patted his head. "I missed it worse than you."

"You think?" He rested his head on Rock's belly. "Mmm. You're warm."

"Yep. Your personal hot water bottle."

Dick laughed softly and kissed them both, heading for the dresser and bending to tug out clothes.

"Mmm. Look at that fine ass. We're lucky men, Rocketman."

"You know it." Rock's fingers tightened on him for a moment. "Fucking lucky."

He nodded and snuggled in. They were. All of them.

Chapter Forty Six

Dick finished up his milk and sat back with a happy sigh. He was stuffed and he hadn't had to cook it himself and he wasn't going to have to do dishes. You couldn't ask for much more than that from breakfast. Rig had even managed to make a good-sized dent in his plate under Rock's watchful eye. He was looking forward to a time where they could care less what Rig ate and how much protein he got into himself. But for now... for now he felt better watching and making sure Rig was eating right, and he knew Rock felt the same way.

"I don't think I should have had that last pancake," groaned Gary. "I'm going to explode."

Dick wasn't surprised. For a little guy, Gary could pack away the food.

Rig nodded, stretched. "The omelet was good - not as good as Dick's, but good."

Hell, Rig hadn't even bitched about the coffee, asking for milk. He beamed at Rig, reaching under the table to squeeze his thigh. "Thanks."

"Just the truth." Rig grinned at Deuce. "The pancakes as good as Rock's?"

"Nah. Not even as good as Aunt Julie's."

Rock grinned. "You know it."

"Rock's pancakes are world-famous. At least they are with anyone he's ever cooked them for." Dick explained for Gary's benefit.

"I've heard about them. Rob talks about you guys a lot."

"Yeah?" Rock asked. "On the other hand, he hasn't told us much about you."

"I'm an artist. I'm queer. I've got AIDS. You all have the story."

Deuce arched an eyebrow, shook his head. "Gary's from Kansas City. He's got three sisters. He can't cook worth a shit."

Rock nodded. "Did you hear that, Rig?"

Dick sighed, glad it was all in the open and he didn't have to keep anything from Rig anymore, but Gary'd stiffened up and Rock was looking stern.

"Hear what? Shit, man. Deuce knows how to cook. Momma taught him."

Rock rolled his eyes. "Gary's got AIDS. Knew he had it when he took up with Deuce."

"With all due respect, sir, it isn't any of your business." Gary's mouth had gone tight, as had his shoulders.

"Yeah... but, Deuce, you knew, right? I mean, y'all were honest with each other, right?" Rig looked confused.

"Yes, Uncle Alex. He told me the day we met."

"Well, then. That works."

Rock just stared. "It doesn't bother you?"

Rig shrugged. "I mean, it sucks for Gary, but he's on some good drugs. They'll be careful."

Rock shook his head. "I just don't understand how someone could say they loved someone and take up with them, knowing."

Deuce growled. "You saying that you wouldn't love Uncle Alex if he had AIDS?"

Rock growled right back. "No, that's not what I'm saying at all. I'm saying I love him enough that if I had AIDS, I wouldn't risk him."

"Rock." Rig's hand landed on Rock's arm. "Easy. And Robert, breathe. He's just worried."

"When you love someone you protect them." Rock bit the words out.

"I am. I do." Deuce pulled out his wallet, threw two twenties on the table. "Come on, Gary. You were right. It's time to go home."

Dick reached out and touched Deuce's arm. "No, come on. Deuce, Gary, sit down. Don't go away mad. We can talk about this."

"What's there to talk about? He thinks I don't love Robert. He thinks I'd deliberately do something to hurt him. What's there to talk about?"

"It's not the end of the world, Rock. There are new drugs coming out all the time." Rig squeezed Rock's hand.

"I just think you're opening yourselves up for a world of hurt." Rock said quietly.

"That's their choice though, Rock, isn't it?" Dick looked at Rock. "Our job is just to be here when they need us, yeah?"

"I love him, Uncle Jim, and he loves me. That's what matters."

Rock shook his head. "Fuck, you both are so damned young. We're we ever that young, Rig?"

"Yeah. Yeah, Rock. If you remember, I headed across country to follow a man that could kick my ass, didn't know I was coming and hadn't shown any interest in a long-term fuckbuddy."

"Crazy fucker," murmured Rock, eyes on Rig. Dick breathed a sigh of relief. He could tell Rock still didn't think it was right, but he was doing to let it be.

"You know it. You can't help who you love, yeah? And the good Lord gives us what time we have." Rig just held Rock's eyes.

Rock grunted, nodded.

"The important thing is to appreciate the time you do have," Gary said quietly. "Love the people you love the best you can."

"You know it. Now, enough fucking drama, yeah? Let's go watch football." Jesus, Deuce was becoming Rock in his old age.

Rock grinned suddenly. "Yeah, you got the right idea, Deuce."

It felt good to laugh, and then to argue over who was going to pay the bill and who was going to win the game.

Normal shit.

Dick approved.

Chapter Forty Seven

Rock still wasn't entirely happy with the situation, but for the sake of peace, he put it away. Rig seemed satisfied enough. He just couldn't help it -- sooner or later this was going to bite Deuce in the ass, hard. If Gary died because of the AIDS, it was going to devastate Deuce.

They'd just nearly lost Rig, and he didn't fucking wish that feeling on anyone.

Especially someone he cared about.

Aside from that, he had no problems with Gary. The kid had been in the Navy, but Rock wouldn't hold that against him.

Half-time rolled around and he looked over to Dick. "You got munchies to bring out?"

Dick looked back. "You going to give me a hand?"

"I'll help, Dick." Rig stood, heading for the kitchen. The man's jeans were still too loose, damn it.

Rock started to growl about Rig helping out, but Dick put a hand on his arm. "There's not a whole lot left to do and I think he's starting to go a bit nuts with us not letting him do anything."

Kid was probably right. "Call if you need help."

"Yeah, okay." Dick chuckled and leaned in to whisper. "Don't hassle the kids."

Deuce rolled his eyes. "We're big boys, Uncle Richard. We can take him."

Dick looked a little sheepish. "You weren't supposed to hear that."

"Go help Uncle Alex make snacks. We're cool. I swear."

"Okay, okay, I'm going." Grinning, Dick headed out into the kitchen.

He turned to Deuce and Gary as Dick disappeared, with his best eat the grunts for breakfast expression.

Deuce just grinned at him. "Man, do they teach all the old guys that look? My DI was all about it."

He arched an eyebrow. "I bet you didn't give your DI that kind of lip, though. And you'd better watch who you're calling old, kid. I could still take you." Little shit. He reminded Rock of himself.

"You know full well I didn't. I'm still alive, yeah?" Deuce chuckled, swatted him playfully. "And I still hump mud for a living, not weights."

Rock laughed. "There's a lot less paperwork in mud humping."

"I bet. Christ, they're talking about sending me to PLDC, making me an NCO, man."

"No shit? Do I say congratulations or offer my condolences?" He held out his hand, though; all teasing aside, he was damned proud of Deuce.

Deuce's hand slapped into it. "Just say congrats, I think. Whether or not I re-up, it'll be good for me."

He shook Deuce's hand hard. "Well done, Deuce."

"Thanks, Uncle Jimmy. You know it's all because of you, yeah?"

And didn't that make him proud, too. Rig's brother was such a poor excuse for a man, he was glad that his attempt to be an example for Deuce had had such great results. "I may have showed you the way, but it's down to you, Robert. You made your own choices."

"Yeah. Yeah, I did." Deuce nodded, cheeks pink. "I wish Ma-Maw was here, man."

Rock nodded. "Yeah, she and Jeremy would have been so proud of you. Rig's gonna be -- have you told him?"

"Not yet. I figured you would be the first one to tell."

He patted Deuce on the back and then stood. "This deserves a toast. We've got something decent here somewhere. Rig! Where's that champagne at?"

"Champagne? In the fridge? We celebrating?"

"We are." He went for the fridge, poking around behind a million leftovers. He grinned. "Grab some glasses and come on out."

"Sure. Can you grab them, Pretty? My hands are full with queso and chips."

"Leave that for now, come on. This is good news."

"Yeah? Okay..." Of course, Rig brought the food along, Dick following behind with glasses. "What's up?"

Deuce grinned. "I'm fixin' to be an NCO."

"That's awesome!" Dick grinned and nodded at him. "Open the champagne, Rock."

"What do you think I'm doing over here?"

"Woohoo!" Rig hooted, Gary clapped and Deuce just beamed.

He finally got the cork to pop and he filled their glasses. "All right, all right. A little quiet now. Here's to you, Deuce. We're all really proud."

"You know it, kiddo. Momma'd be busting her buttons."

Deuce looked up at Rig, lips tight. "You think?"

"I know. She'd be so proud."

"That's what I told him. Jeremy, too. Drink up, this is the good stuff."

They all drank, even Rig - which he wasn't sure was a good idea, but it'd already happened. Besides, it was a celebration. He didn't refill Rig's glass, though, when he topped everyone else up. Still smiling wide, he sat, helped himself to a chip and the queso.

Rig sat next to him, just leaning. "Hey, Blue."

"Hey." He put his arm around his Rabbit, tugged him close. "You doing okay?"

"Yeah. The bubbly went to my head faster than usual."

"You're turning into a cheap date," he teased. It was that or fuss.

"Yep." Rig leaned, whispered into his ear. "Blowjob. Glass of bubbly. Quick midnight fuck. Any of those and I'm all yours." Groaning softly at Rig's words, he shifted, his prick filling. It reminded him that half time usually meant any one of those things. Well, not the bubbly. "Want you, you know. Want to spend a whole fucking day touching and sucking and being together."

Rig was going to drive him out of his fucking mind.

"If you're not careful I'll put you over my shoulder and drag you off to the bedroom, guests be damned."

"You won't. You have to watch football with your nephew." Rig's tongue flicked in his ear, teasing him.

"A man can only hold out from that mouth for so long, Rig." He was growling a little now, getting looks from Gary.

"Be good, Blue. The babies are watching." Fuck, tipsy Rigger was cute as fuck.

"I'll try my best, but you know you make me hotter than hell."

"'s what I was made for."

"You know it." He didn't care who was watching, Rock pressed his lips to Rig's, the kiss soft and slow.

The room was quiet when the kiss ended, Gary and Deuce gone, Dick standing and watching with a dazed, horny look on his face. He figured he should feel bad for driving them away, but between Rig and Dick's expressions, he just couldn't.

"They went for a 'nap'," murmured Dick.

"Naps are good." Rig slid into his lap, straddling him.

He chuckled, hands sliding to Rig's ass. "Something tells me sleep's not what you're after."

"Hmm?" Rig started kissing him, one long, slow kiss after another.

"Nothing," he muttered, opening up and letting Rig in deep.

"We gonna do this here?" murmured Dick, already pulling Rig's t-shirt up over his head.

"You think we should take it to the bedroom, Blue?"

"Yeah, yeah we should." Rock grabbed Rig's ass and stood, carrying Rig as they headed to the bedroom. "Don't want Deuce to feel like he can't come down out of his rooms when he's visiting."

"Yeah. And then we can nap after you fuck me." He did enjoy the bonus naps, now.

"Gonna suck me while Rock does you?" Dick asked, closing the door behind him.

"What if I want to get sucked while you do Rig?"

"I do love it when you fight over me, boys."

He chuckled. "There's my slut."

Rig grinned against his lips, grey eyes laughing. "Yours."

"You fucking know it." He licked his way into Rig's mouth, the kiss quickly going hard and deep. Dick worked his magic, getting them all naked nice and quickly. "So you want my cock in your mouth or your ass, Rig? You take us how you want us."

"I owe Dick a blow, man. I haven't had that pretty prick in my mouth."

A low moan filled the air, and Dick nodded hard. "Yeah. Yeah, I want."

Oh yeah, he could sympathize. He'd felt that way just the other day. "On your back or all fours, Rig?"

"On my back." Rig flushed a little. "It still pulls my incision when I'm bent over."

His hand went automatically to Rig's scar, barely touching. "Are you up to this?"

"Hell, yes. Yeah. We just... well, we have to work around the healing parts, yeah?"

"Yeah. We'll be careful." He met Dick's eyes, the kid just barely nodding. No more bending for Rig. Rig pushed into his arms, dragging him down into another kiss. He was careful not to press down onto Rig, but he dove into that kiss with as much enthusiasm as ever. Rig moaned, one leg wrapping around his hip. Rig's cock was filling, swelling against him. It felt amazing, having that reaction back.

Dick slicked up his fingers for him, and when he went to slide one in, he found Dick already there. He pushed a finger in alongside Dick's, the two of them working together to stretch Rig out. Rig smiled against his lips, tongue sliding and rubbing against his. He smiled back, rubbing their noses together, laughing softly.

Dick slid a second finger into Rig, fingers circling, making Rig buck up.

"Mmm. My men. Fuck, yes." That look did it for him, made him feel a thousand feet tall.

"You ready for us, Rig? Ready to feel my cock inside you, fucking stretching you wide?"

"I was born ready, Rocketman."

He chuckled and settled on his knees between Rig's legs. Dick was hard as nails, the long prick curling up and leaking.

"Oh... Look at that." Rig moaned, licked his lips.

"All for you." Dick palmed his erection, jacked it.

"Uh-huh. All for me." Those grey eyes were fucking focused. Cockhound.

"Don't you want a little foreplay first, man?" Rock chuckled as they both gave him a look that said "no fucking way."

"Foreplay. Who are you and what did you do with my marine?"

"Since when is 'I haven't had that pretty prick in my mouth' not foreplay?" Dick asked.

He just grinned at them both. "Sluts."

"Yep." Rig just beamed. "Y'all's."

"Puts me in pretty good company." Dick slid his thumb across his slit, spreading the liquid there. "How do you want me, Rig?"

"Come here and fuck my mouth, Pretty." Rig stretched, reached for Dick. Dick made a sweet noise, and straddled Rig's head, facing him so he could watch as that long prick was slowly fed into Rig's mouth. Rig took Dick, so easy, so eager. That was the hottest fucking thing. Dick's eyes shut, a look of bliss on his face. He started making those porno noises, groaning and moaning.

That was Rock's signal to slide into that fine, tight ass. Eyes on Rig's mouth and Dick's cock, he pushed in all the way, that ass holding him so tight. Both his men groaned, Rig squeezing around him, sucking hard at the kid's long prick.

He moved slowly, waiting until Dick's eyes opened. "Together," he murmured, and Dick nodded, hips starting to move to his rhythm.

Rig rocked, sliding on the bed, pushing between their cocks. There were only two things missing, and he took care of one by grabbing Dick's head and tugging him forward until their mouths met in a long, wet kiss. His other hand wrapped around Rig's prick, letting Rig's own movements drive that heat along his palm.

Fucking perfect.

Dick was damn near sobbing into his lips and he knew what the kid was feeling, knew how good that mouth was around his cock. He didn't figure Dick was going to last much longer and he sped his thrusts, urging Rig on. Sure enough, Dick cried out into his mouth, body shuddering. Rig swallowed hard, a dull flush climbing up the flat belly. Dick's movements became shallow, just the tip of his prick continuing to slide in and out of Rig's mouth. Rock took another kiss, tongue tangling with Dick's.

He could feel Rig getting close, feel the way that long body shook. He let his thumb rub across the tip, pressing against Rig's slit as he slammed into Rig's body. "Come on, Rabbit. Give it to me."

Just like it was meant to be, Rig gave it up, bucking and moaning underneath him, sweet as you please. He rode it out, and when Rig's body loosened, he started moving again, thrusting hard toward his own climax. It came over him in a rush and he roared as he came, filling Rig in long pulses.

Fuck, yes.

"Mmm. My men." Rig looked purely happy.

He and Dick settled where they belonged, on either side of Rig.

He stroked Rig's belly and then Dick's, and then closed his eyes and napped.

Chapter Forty Eight

Rock couldn't believe it was fucking December, already.

December and turning chilly out there, making it nice to be inside with the fire going and everyone relaxing and him napping a little, like a man should on a Sunday afternoon.

Rig was cozy under a blanket, head on his thighs. He was a lucky fucking man that he still had this, that things had turned out as they had and the skinny asshole lying on him was still alive. He grunted, punctuating the thought.

Dick cleared his throat, and Rock cracked one eye open to see the kid bouncing on his heels, looking like the cat that got the cream.

"Look what I have." Dick held something small up, the thing catching the light.

"What is that?" He frowned, stared over. Fuck him. That was Rig's nipple ring. The sorry son of a bitch had had to take it out and they just... Well, they hadn't worried about it.

"Nurse gave it to me at the hospital. I've been keeping it for the right time." Dick came over, squeezing in next to him, one hand going to stroke Rig's curls. "Do you think it's the right time yet?"

"Fuck yes. It's time we had our Rabbit back." The words just pushed out of him, his cock growing hard in his sweats and bumping Rig's cheek.

Rig was waking up, nice and slow, cheek rubbing against his prick. "Mmm. Hey."

He spread his legs some, hips moving to press his cock more firmly against Rig. "Hey, yourself."

Rig hummed and stretched for him, a warm smile on that face. It still made his heart beat too fast, thinking that they might have lost this, lost Rig. Dick pressed against him and he banished the thought. They were all here, all three of them and they had a job to do.

He growled a little. "Something's missing, you know."

"Mmm? What? Dick's right here." Rig reached out, patted the kid's leg.

"Thanks for noticing." Dick's eyes danced, his hand stroking over Rig's shoulders.

Rock rolled his eyes. "Not someone -- *something.*"

"Oh." He could tell Rig was confused, but too busy touching to care.

"How many rings do we have?" he asked.

"Oh, wait, we need to be shirtless to count." He couldn't always count on the kid to be right there in the naked department.

"Count what? Are y'all speaking English?" Rig chuckled, licking his abs as they came into view. Rig was cute all sleep-addled like that. Not to mention the ab-licking was pretty fucking nice.

Dick got them all topless, and then leaned to whisper into Rig's ear. "Try his nipple ring."

Rig's hum vibrated against his belly, mouth moving up, just like that, heading for his nipple. Oh, fuck that felt good.

Groaning, he slid his hand through Rig's curls, not guiding so much as holding, stroking Rig's scalp. That hot little tongue slipped in between the ring and his flesh, the tip teasing his nipple, driving him crazy.

"Fuck!" He held Rig in place, legs spreading as his cock pushed hard against his sweats. Rock felt Rig's chuckle, electricity shooting up his spine as Rig sucked.

"That's one," murmured Dick. "You should count the next one now."

"Count all you want, kid. Rig's just fine right where he is."

Rig nodded, hand sliding up Dick's belly, mouth still working as those long fingers headed toward Dick's nipple.

The kid started making noises before Rig had even touched that little ring. He knew how Dick felt. Fuck, every time Rig blinked, those long eyelashes tickled his skin. Dick's fingers crept over and rubbed at his prick, so he returned the favor. Shit, how had things gotten so hot so fast?

"That's... that's t-two," stuttered Dick.

"Mine's gone. I can't find it." Rig tugged his ring, just a little.

"I told you something was missing." He grinned smugly down at Rig. He knew his Rabbit would eventually get it.

Rig's head tilted, grey eyes glittering. "Do y'all have it?"

Dick held open his hand, the little ring sitting in his palm.

"Oh. Oh, fucking cool. You think it'll go back in?"

"It will."

Dick nodded. "Hopefully."

He elbowed Dick. "It will."

Rig leaned back, tugging his shirt off. "I want it back."

"You fucking know it."

Dick moved to the other side of the couch, sitting back and opening his arms. "Lean against me while Rock puts it back in."

Mmm... yeah, that would work. Rig damn near whimpered, cock straining against those jeans.

"Naked." He cleared his throat, fingers rubbing along the bulge in Rig's jeans. "I want you naked."

"Uh-huh. Anything." Rig tugged his jeans off, wiggling, bouncing for him. Dick's fingers slid around to play over that skinny stomach, rub over Rig's hips. Fuck. Look how hard Rig was, how that cock was full and red-tipped, throbbing against Rig's belly. Bending, he kissed the tip, flicked his tongue across it.

"Rock." Rig's hips rolled, bucking up as his Rabbit tried to get more.

"Oh, I think we need to take care of a little something first." Dick's fingers slid up to flick at Rig's bare nipples.

Rig reached down, grabbed Dick's wrist. "Oh, man. Sensitive."

"Just wait 'til Rock puts that ring back in. I'm going to drive you crazy."

"We both are." Rock rubbed the ring against Rig's right nipple. That little bit of flesh went tight, hard, just begging for it. He looked up, met those grey eyes. "You remember when we got these?"

"Fuck, yes. I creamed my jeans."

"I should have left them on you so you could cream them this time, too." Bending, he flicked his tongue across the hard little bit of flesh.

"Blue." Rig jerked, almost sitting up. "Fuck. Blue."

"You ready, Rabbit?"

"Fuck, yes. Make me y'all's again."

He met Dick's eyes, then Rig's again, and nodded. "Ours."

His fingers pinched Rig's nipple, and he set the ring against the little hole on the side. Out of the corner of his eye he saw Dick grab Rig's cock, and he pushed the ring into Rig's flesh. Rig's cry rang out, sharp and sweet, spunk spraying over Rig's belly. Dick bucked, pushing Rig up against him, and he closed the ring, pressed a kiss to the nipple before running his fingers through Rig's come.

Rock knew, without even looking, that his Rabbit's cock was still hard, that Rig was right there, needing so bad. He pressed his wet fingers into Rig's body, spreading that perfect ass open.

"I need. I need, y'all. Fuck. Please." Oh, fuck yeah. He hadn't seen Rig wild like this in months.

He made short work of spreading Rig, pulling his fingers away and settling between Rig's legs.

"Blue. Fuck me. Come on." Dick was tugging, sucking that pierced tit. Rig's eyes were just wide.

He pushed in, just like that, sliding into the best fucking heat.

"Yes!" Rig grunted, hands tangling in Dick's hair.

He nodded, holding those grey eyes. "Yes." With a grunt, he started thrusting.

"Y'all's. Fuck, I can feel it. It's tingling. Harder, Rock."

"Whatever you want." As he thrust harder, Dick twisted that nipple ring, tugged on it. Fuck, look at that. Look at his fine motherfucking man. Rig bucked, ass clenching around his cock, milking him.

"Rig! Yes!" He pounded away, fucking flying.

"Jim." More spunk sprayed between them, Rig's eyes rolling back into his head.

He could smell the kid go off, too, Dick coming without either of them touching him. So fucking sexy.

He roared as he came.

Rig was moaning for him still, flying as he came down. He stayed buried, leaning forward enough to give Rig's nipple a kiss, and then to take Rig's mouth. Rig moaned, arm wrapping around his neck, holding him tight. Dick's lips slid against theirs, and they let the kid in, the kiss becoming a three-way. Rig groaned, pushed in and hummed, rocking nice and slow.

Oh, yeah, this wasn't over yet. Still hard, he moved with Rig, the kid shifting, cock pushing between their bellies. Rig's ass rippled around his cock, milking and massaging it. They could stay right here and do this all night.

Hell, for fucking ever.

His finger reached for Rig's nipple ring, touching the metal.

Yeah.

Chapter Forty Nine

Man, the kitchen needed reorganizing. Rig pulled down the cans from the pantry, humming "Silent Night" with Garth. The front door opened and closed -- his marines had gotten in the habit of taking turns coming home to have lunch with him.

"Hey, Rig." Dick smiled at him and took the cans out of his hands, putting them on the counter. "Should you be doing that?"

"Hey, Pretty." He leaned in for a kiss. "The kitchen needs reorganizing. Your nose is cold."

Dick grinned. "I could help if you wanted. It's a slow day at the gym."

"Yeah? That sounds good to me." He went to grab another set of cans, idly planning Christmas dinner in his head. Ham, he thought. They'd have steaks to celebrate Dick's finals.

Finals.

When were finals?

Dick took the cans down from the top shelf. "So why exactly are we taking all the cans out of the pantry? Is there something you can't find?"

"Huh? No. No, they're out of order. I haven't looked into them." He was bored. Needed something to do. "When do you have finals?"

"Finals? Oh, I don't. Out of order -- I guess me and Rock didn't do a great job keeping things the way you like 'em, huh?" Dick grabbed more cans and took them to the table.

"You don't what?"

"Huh? Oh, the cans. Not being in order. I didn't even realize there was a right order. I mean they're just cans, right? You stack 'em the best way they fit." Dick demonstrated his stacking, playing with the cans.

He arched an eyebrow. "Dick, what's up?"

Like cute, tall and guilty could lie to him.

He sure was trying though, eyes wide as they glanced his way. "What do you mean?"

"Don't. What's wrong? Is school kicking your ass?" He just pushed right up to Dick, hugged tight.

Dick's arms wrapped around him. "No. No not at all. I got my classes deferred. So I don't have exams this term."

"Oh." Oh. Oh, Goddamn. He. Shit. "I'm sorry, man."

Fuck.

He fucking sucked.

Dick's arms tightened around him. "You don't have to apologize, Rig. It was just easier to defer them than to deal with everything that was coming down. The course load was too heavy anyway; I probably would have failed at least Stats if nothing else. So it worked out for the best."

"I'm sorry. Shit. I didn't... you worked so hard..."

"It's okay. I didn't fail, you know? It was early enough to defer them. I'm signed up for a class next term. I'll do better then. Make you and Rock proud." Dick's fingers stroked along his back. Christ.

"I wish I'd've waited. Just a couple more months and you'd've been on break..."

"Rig... you can't choose when you're sick. Shit, you should have done it six months sooner."

"I could've waited for the test." He would've waited to tell them, had it been cancer.

Dick pulled away. "Stop it. It's bad enough you were throwing up blood and shit for nine months before you went in for the test. This isn't your fault, okay? And nothing's screwed up, so it's fine."

"It's not fine. I'm tired of being sick and ready to go back to how I was. I'm tired of fucking things up."

"I want you to be better, too, Rig. And I want things to go back to normal, too. But not at your expense! Shit. It's bad enough you were that sick for that long and didn't tell me. And that I didn't realize."

"I did tell you." He shook his head. "You and I talked about it and I went to the doctor, just like I promised."

"But you let me think that everything was fine!"

Of course he did. He loved them. He loved them both. "I didn't lie."

Dick rolled his eyes. "No, I suppose technically you didn't."

"Don't you roll your eyes at me. I was doing my best." He'd been fucking scared and did either of them say a word? No.

"Damn it, Rig. You were doing your best alone, and that's not right."

"What was I supposed to do? What were you going to do?"

"I don't know! Worry. Hold you. Tell you everything was going to be all right." Dick grabbed him and pulled him in for a tight hug. "It kills me you were scared and all alone for most of this."

"I..." He didn't want to lie, say he hadn't been scared, so he just leaned.

Hard.

Dick held onto him, rocking slightly from side to side. "You gotta promise me you won't do that again."

"Do what? Get sick?"

"No. Well yes, except I know you can't promise that. But the going it alone thing. Promise me you won't do that again." Dick pulled back to look into his eyes. "Please."

"I told you I wasn't feeling good, Dick. I went to the doctor." He just hadn't whined.

"And you never said you were still sick! Come on, Rig, you know what I mean."

"I do. I couldn't come home and look at y'all and just... I didn't know, Dick."

"Well you figure out a way how. Because God knows I don't want it to happen again, or something else to happen, but if it does, you tell me. I don't care how hard it is, I don't care, okay? I just. You need to tell." Dick's voice broke, pretty eyes blinking, and then Dick jerked him back in close.

"Hey. Hey, I got you. I got you, man. You know I wouldn't leave y'all." Not ever.

"Better not," whispered Dick, just holding on.

"I won't. I can't." He kissed Dick's shoulder, dancing them in lazy circles to the song on the radio. Lord have mercy. Dick fucking thought too much for his own good.

"But you'll tell, right? If?"

"I'll do my best. You know I will." He wouldn't lie; he hadn't been trying to hide it from the guys. He couldn't tell them.

"Okay. Okay." Dick nodded into his neck, and they kept moving, kept dancing as Dick held him tight.

He just hummed, letting himself enjoy this - just this, right this second, with Dick so close.

"We haven't been dancing in forever," whispered Dick.

"I know. It's a shame. I'm just starting to feel up to it again."

"We could go somewhere before Christmas. Who knows, maybe Rock'll even come along."

"Works for me. I'm sorry about school, Pretty. You were doing so good." He grinned, nuzzled a little. "I promise, no dramatic surgeries next semester."

"I'm going to hold you to that." Dick pulled back enough to smile at him, and then bring their lips together. The kiss was soft, a low moan pressing into his mouth.

He took that kiss, then offered another and another, fucking Dick's lips nice and easy. Dick grew hard against his lower belly, hands sliding over his back, one going down to grab his belly, the other wandering. His own body was slower to respond, but he was willing to take some time, just feel.

Their dancing slid into just moving against each other, rubbing together like they had all day.

"You need to call Rock or are you good?" He didn't really need to finish the kitchen right now.

"I'm good. Was gonna go Christmas shopping after lunch."

"Mmm. That sounds fun. Can I come too?" They could play.

"Only if we get to finish this first." Grinning, Dick rubbed against him, made sure he knew exactly what 'this' was.

"I might could manage a bit of that..." He chuckled and then, suddenly, they were both laughing together. Fuck, that felt good. Honest. Real.

Dick squeezed him tight, half supporting him, half leaning against him as they caught their breath again. "Glad it was my day to come home for lunch."

"Yeah? I'm pretty fucking tickled myself." He nodded, gave half of his world a grin.

Dick grinned right back. "Wanna do it on the couch? We haven't done it on the couch in ages."

"Mmm. Poor couch." He started walking Dick back into the front room, hands exploring all that hard, fine body.

"Yeah, all those asses and none of them naked." Dick laughed, and then moaned a little at his touch.

"How depressing..." He got Dick's shirt pulled up and off, lips on one collarbone.

"For the couch." Dick's voice faded away, sweet moans filling the air.

His own t-shirt was tugged up and off, Dick's fingers spreading across his chest. He shook his head as Dick avoided his scar. He grabbed Dick's wrist, slid it up to the ridge. "It's part of me, too. Touch me."

"I don't want to hurt you." Still, Dick's fingers slid over it, traced it.

"If it hurts, I'll tell you. It means I'm alive."

"Yeah, I guess it does." Dick's fingers slid back over it as his pretty pressed their mouths together.

He brought them down to the sofa, encouraging Dick to land on him, press him down. Dick hesitated for a moment, and then leaned into him, let him have his Pretty's weight. His scar was touched again, and then Dick's fingers found his unadorned nipple, teasing it. "Mmm. Dick. Come on. Love on me." Touch me like you mean it.

Nodding, Dick moved in to lick at the sweet spot on his neck, clever hands tugging open his jeans. He got busy working those sensitive nerves at the base of Dick's spine, scratching and rubbing and dragging his fingers over them. Dick jerked and cried out, fingers working faster, tugging his jeans down with little finesse or care.

"Fuck, yeah. Come on." That was it. He wanted needy and wild.

Rolling away for just long enough to get his own jeans off, Dick rolled back, pressing their bodies together, skin on skin. Those sweet porno noises started up, Dick moving against him, fingers grabbing hold of his nipple and twisting. That made his balls draw up, his cock hard, full, starting to leak.

The lube was still under the couch cushion and Dick searched for it, holding it up triumphantly when he found it. "Want you."

"I'm yours." His and Rock's - through and through.

"Yeah, mine." Dick leaned in and started sucking up a mark on his neck, fingers slick and sliding along his crease.

"Yeah." Rig panted, one leg falling to the floor so he could spread. "More."

One of Dick's fingers pushed into him, his pretty groaning. "Oh, fuck. Tight. Rig."

"Uh-huh. More." No thinking. Just fucking. Lots of fucking.

Another finger pushed in, Dick spreading him, hitting his gland.

"Oh." He went still, gasping as he shifted, trying to get that again.

"Here?" Dick asked, fingers searching, pushing, sliding over that spot again.

"There. There. Again. Fuck. Dick. Please." Hell, yeah.

"Uh-huh." Dick went back to sucking that mark up on his neck, fingers pushing into his gland time and time again, sending him flying.

"Pretty!" He was fixin' to shake apart, just shatter. "Oh, sweet fuck. Please."

The fingers inside him disappeared, Dick's panting loud in his ear as it seemed to take forever before the long cock pushed against him, slowly spread him open.

"Dick. Oh, sweet fuck." His hips rolled and he took every fucking inch.

Moaning, Dick rolled his ass just a little, pushing in that last bit. A soft whimper sounded, and then Dick started to move, eyes meeting his as Dick pushed back in.

"That's it." He grinned, so fucking happy it wasn't funny.

Dick grinned right back, skin starting to shine with sweat, thrusts coming harder and harder, his pretty so deep inside him.

"Need this." He needed both of them. All of them.

"Anything." One of Dick's hands wrapped around his prick, tugging and pulling.

"Uh-uh. Everything." Oh, shit, that felt good.

Bending, Dick bit at his earlobe. "Gimme."

"Yes." Rig nodded, arched and shot, pleasure galloping along his spine.

"Oh, fuck!" Dick cried out, jerking inside him, coming deep.

"Mmm..." Rig nodded, satisfied to the core.

Hell yes.

Forehead resting against his shoulder, Dick stayed buried deep for long moments, making happy little noises as his breath slowed. "Shit, that was sweet."

"Mmhmm. Should do it more often."

"Okay." Dick pulled out slowly with a soft "oh" and settled next to him.

"Mmm. You good, Pretty?" He kissed Dick's jaw.

"Oh yeah. Yeah, I'm good." Dick chuckled and snuggled closer. "I really good."

He grinned, nodded. "Yeah. Yeah, I hear you."

"You wanna nap before we go shopping?" Dick's head was already on his shoulder.

"Uh-huh." He was becoming an incredible fan of naps.

"Cool. Then we can go have lunch somewhere nice and decide what to get for Rock."

"Sounds perfect." He settled with a happy sigh. He could worry about the kitchen later.

Much, much later.

Chapter Fifty

They had hotdogs at a stand near the beach and then went to the mall to go shopping, wandering through the stores and picking up socks and underwear and other stocking stuffers for Rock and Deuce and Gary.

It was fun, and it felt like normal. Dick hadn't realized how much he'd been wanting for things to be normal until now, enjoying the shopping far more than anyone should. "So what are we going to get for Rock this year?"

"I don't know, man. You spend more time with him than I do these days. What does he want?"

Dick grinned. "You. Healthy and whole." It was what they both wanted.

"Well, that y'all got." Rig winked. It was true. Rig was looking better and better. He still had thirty five pounds to gain - another twenty before he could go back to work - but he looked better.

"Then we're good. Although I saw this sand dune buggy thing that he might like..."

"Oh, yeah? Oh, Dick, that would rock! We could go four-wheelin'!"

He grinned and nodded, loving that excitement. "Yeah. I think it's a bit pricey, but if we went into it together, and didn't get each other anything big..."

"I could probably finance it. I'm a little cash-poor from not working."

"Yeah? I don't want you to have to go into debt for a Christmas gift, you know?"

"Rock's worth it." Rig squeezed his fingers, gave him a wan grin. "Hell, my part of the surgery and hospital stay is damn near eighty thousand dollars."

He stopped still and just shared. "Shit, Rig. That's a lot of dough."

"Yeah. You think we ought to send Julie's kids gift cards?"

"Gift cards? Um, sure. What happened to your insurance?"

"That was after coverage. I'm fighting it some. You don't have to worry on it." Jesus. Eighty thousand dollars. Did Rock know?

"After coverage? I hope you're fighting it a lot -- that's crazy." He'd just assumed Rig's coverage had taken care of it. Just like he'd assumed Rig was just fine. Man, he needed to start paying better attention.

"I bet we could come up with something else Rock would really like."

"Don't worry, huh? This ain't your problem."

"You're wrong, you know." He could see the food court up ahead and he angled them that way. He needed ice cream.

"You hungry again?"

"Just want an ice cream or something sweet." He chewed on his lip, telling himself to drop it, to leave it be, but it just kept nagging at him.

"'kay. What's up?" Rig was right at his elbow, staring.

"This whole 'it ain't your problem' thing."

"It's not. You have enough to worry about."

"It is, too, Rig." He knew Rig didn't mean to shut him out, but that's exactly what he was doing. "I'm your partner. Yours and Rock's. So your problems are my problems. You can tell me not to worry about it -- but don't tell me it's not my problem, too."

Rig stood there, lips opening and closing for a second. "I."

"I know you're trying to protect me, but I'm not a baby green anymore and I want to shoulder my share of the responsibility in this family."

"You do, don't you? I don't treat you like a child, Dick."

"No, you don't, but stuff like this. Well." Dick pursed his lips trying to figure out how to say what he meant. "When you've got problems, then I've got problems, whether it's being sick, or owing money, or whatever, you know? Good and bad should be shared."

"I don't want to fuck up your life, Dick. I really don't." No. No, Rig wanted him to have nothing but peace and easy going. He knew that.

"I know. Rig... having you in my life -- you and Rock -- that's the most amazing thing in the world. I have the best life ever. And that includes when things aren't going great."

He put his arm around Rig's shoulders and guided him to the ice cream line. "Long as you're in it, you can't fuck up my life."

"Oh, I don't know. I might be able to..." Rig leaned for a second. "I want a scoop of strawberry."

"I'm gonna have the cookie dough. You want it in a cone or a cup?" He rummaged through his jeans' pockets, sure he had a five in one of them.

"Cup. See if they have a kiddie size, huh? I just want a couple bites." Man, it was still harder than hell to get food into Rig. Although he had picked most of the meat out of his hot dog at lunch.

Dick ordered and paid, giving Rig his kiddie cup. "Let's go sit in the corner there, it looks pretty quiet."

"'kay." Rig was fretting, he could tell. It was like he'd lost something, some peace in the last year, maybe even since Rig's momma'd died.

He waited until they were sitting and he'd had a few licks of his cone, Rig a bite or two. "You okay?" he asked softly.

"Yeah, Pretty. I'm good." Jesus, he'd heard that. Over and over. And over.

He waited until Rig met his eyes. "You sure nothing's wrong?"

"What's supposed to be wrong?"

"I don't know, Rig. But something's bothering you -- that much I do know." And he was so done letting Rig fob him off. Look where that had gotten Rig last time.

"I'm just tired, Dick. Tired and a little worried, that's all."

He reached over and took Rig's hand, stilling the fingers that had been fiddling with the edge of the cup. "What are you worrying on?"

"Money. Whether I'm ever gonna feel right again. Whether I'm ever going to make it through a day without napping."

"I don't know about that last one. Napping's highly underrated." He winked and squeezed Rig's hand.

"Yeah, but... I used to be able to do more."

"Yeah, well this thing's been kicking your ass for months, Rig. Hell, probably for a couple of years."

He thought about it a bit. "It's only been what, just over a month since you had the surgery? It's going to take time, Rig. You have to be patient, let your body heal. You know that -- it's what you'd tell any of your patients, isn't it?"

"It is, but you know what they say, we're our own worst patients. I need to start being useful."

He grinned suddenly. "You never have been good at just relaxing."

"I don't like it. I like being busy."

He let go of Rig's hand, moved back a little. "You could always take up knitting."

"Fuck you." He got a wadded up napkin tossed at him.

Laughing, he caught it and lobbed it back.

"I know, I'll get back in the woodshop, start working on stuff, at least for a week or two before I get to work half-days."

"Hey, maybe we could make something for Rock for Christmas. I'm getting better."

"You want to? I like working with you... Maybe I could work some at the gym for y'all, too..." Uh-huh. Right. Like Rock would go for that.

"I'd love to do some woodworking with you. We'll have to wait until tomorrow to pick up the wood as Rock's got the truck, but we could decide what to make, figure out what all we need for it." A project was exactly what Rig needed. Something to keep him occupied where he could take as many breaks as he needed.

"I like that. What do you think he'd like?" Rig started chattering, awake and eager and excited, honestly excited.

He'd put that look on Rig's face -- he'd helped make Rig feel better. That felt damned good. They tossed ideas back and forth, eventually wandering back through the mall and picking up gift cards to send back to Rig's family along with some more bits and pieces.

When he could tell Rig was starting to fade again, he suggested they head home. "We could pick up some take-out on the way. Save anyone having to cook."

"Yeah? Works for me. I'm wore." Rig sighed, rubbed the back of his neck.

"I could give you a massage when we get home. Oh, hey! Do you think we could make a massage table for Rock? Do you think he'd like that?"

He put their stuff in the trunk and made sure Rig got settled okay in the passenger seat.

"Maybe, yeah. There's lots of moving parts with that, but we're smart dogs."

"Well, you are anyway." He grinned and got them going. "I can look stuff up on the internet, though."

"Mmhmm. What do you want for Christmas?" Rig stretched, eyes closing.

"You mean besides all three of us healthy and happy? Hmm... I don't know."

"Well, think about it." Rig's hand landed on his thigh, solid and warm.

"Yeah. Yeah, I will." As soon as they were out of the parking lot, he let his hand drop down to cover Rig's.

He figured maybe had everything he really wanted already, which was good because you couldn't buy men like Rig and Rock at the mall.

Chapter Fifty One

Saturdays were still one of Rock's favorite days. He liked to sleep late and then be woken up in the best way possible. For as long as they'd been together, Rig still tended to indulge him, too. He was one lucky S.O.B.

Even if he had a bone to pick with his favorite cowboy.

It would wait, though, because he had another bone that needed attention and if Rig didn't show up soon, he was going to have to make some noise to catch Rig's attention. He grunted, refusing to open his eyes. He heard Rig's chuckle, so soft, just against his belly.

"Mmm..." He slid his hand through Rig's curls, his prick jerking just from know Rig was right there.

Lips trailed from his navel to his pubes, just avoiding his cock. He grunted again, the sound almost a chuckle. Teasing slut.

"Mornin', Blue." That tongue tickled, right where balls met prick.

Leg jerking, he laughed softly. "Morning." His hand stroked through Rig's hair again, catching in the soft curls.

Rock could feel Rig's smile, feel one hand sliding up his thigh. Spreading, he opened up, a low rumble coming from somewhere deep in his chest. The long, slow licks started, Rig making happy, horny little sounds over his cock, taking time to enjoy.

He fucking loved that, loved when they could make it stretch out for as long as they fucking wanted. Opening his eyes, he looked down, enjoying the sight of that pink tongue on his swollen prick. Rig smiled at him, lapping just around the tip, nudging the crown of his cock over and over. His eyes dropped half closed at that, the sensations beginning to lick up along his spine like flames of fire, fucking hot.

It got hotter, sharper when Rig slid up, tongue pressing into the slit of his prick.

"Fuck. Fuck, Rig." Groaning, he tightened his grip on Rig's hair, the sensation making his balls draw up tight.

"Mmhmm." Those long fingers slid behind his balls, brushing over his hole. A shiver went through him and he spread for Rig, letting his Rabbit touch. Rig started pulling harder, that finger rubbing around and around, pushing inside to touch him every few circles.

He started moving with Rig, hips rolling, rocking. Fuck. Fuck, that was perfect. Rig's finger slipped deep, nudging his gland as his cock pushed into Rig's throat.

"Fuck!" His whole body jerked, his hands grabbing the sheets and holding tight.

"Mmm." Rig just kept it up, pushing and pulling harder and harder.

He muttered and groaned, his rocking getting stronger. "Close," he murmured. "Fucking close."

One finger became two and the pressure just went wild, squeezing tight. He bucked and shouted, hands digging into the mattress as he came hard. Rig, cockhound that he was, swallowed every drop, sucking and licking and moaning around Rock's cock.

Moaning happily, he relaxed back against his pillow, hands petting whatever part of Rig he could reach. Rig leaned in, cheek on his belly. "Hey, Blue. Mornin'."

"Mmmm. Morning. Best fucking way to wake up." He smiled down at Rig. stroking one cheek.

"You know it." Rig gave him a grin, a wink.

Grinning, he took hold of Rig's arm and tugged a little, getting himself a kiss. "You needing, Rabbit?"

"I might be." Rig was hard, hot against his hip.

"This feels like a lot more than 'might'." He wrapped his hand around Rig's prick.

"Mmm. Your hands." Rig's head fell back, throat just working.

"They know you." He leaned in to run his lips along Rig's neck, sucking that Adam's apple.

"Fuck, yeah." Rig moaned, hips pushing the cock into his hand over and over. He squeezed and stroked, thumb sliding across the tip like he knew his Rabbit liked, turning it so that his nail scraped lightly across it. That earned him a cry, a jerk, Rig stretching against him. Yeah. Yeah.

His lips slid over to that spot on Rig's neck, tongue flicking across the nerves there. Rig started humping his fist, moaning and bucking against him. "Yeah, that's it. Take what you need."

His free hand slid around to Rig's ass, squeezing it.

"Need you." Rig groaned, spunk pouring over his fingers.

"Mmm... right here." He squeezed a moment longer, and then brought his hand to his mouth, licking it clean.

"So fine, Blue."

Grinning, he pressed a kiss to Rig's forehead and then put his arm around the man, tugged him in nice and close.

"Mmm. Hey." Rig kissed him, nice and slow, tongue fucking his lips. He sucked on Rig's tongue, his hand squeezing that perfect little ass. He hated to break the fucking good mood. Rig's hand slid down his belly, fingers combing through his curls. "Trying to make me hard again?"

Rig could do it, too. Just like that.

"Mmm. You want to go another round, you fine bastard?"

"Always." He took Rig's mouth, tongue pressing in, his cock rising. He got an armful of warm, relaxed cowboy, hands on his scalp, holding him close. His tongue played with Rig's. The man tasted good. Fucking good. Rig's cock started to fill up, cuddled right against the curve of his belly.

Hand sliding, he stroked Rig's spine. Man was still too skinny, but better.

"Mmm. Hey. So good." Rig licked the corner of his mouth, humming sweet and low.

Fuck, it had been too long since sex had led to more sex and he just went with it, turning to capture Rig's tongue in his mouth. His fingers slid over the skinny body, finding the scar on Rig's side. He touched it, felt it, moved on to those little titties he knew were so fucking sensitive.

They perked right up, needing his touch, wanting him.

"What have we got here?" He tugged the naked one, finger flicking across the tip.

"Rock, if you can't remember, we've got a... Oh. Oh, good."

Laughing, at Rig's tease and the predictable reaction to his touch, he slid his hand over to find the other one, tugging on the ring as soon as he caught it between his fingers.

"Rock." Rig groaned, gasping a little against his lips. "Again."

"This?" He tugged again, twisting the ring this time, pulling pretty hard as he watched those grey eyes.

"Yes!" Rig arched, cock starting to leak against his belly. Fuck yes. He kept tugging, kept twisting, making Rig writhe against him.

"I... Fuck me." Rig's eyes were huge, fucking needy.

"All I need to know is how you want it. You want to ride me? You want me to fuck you hard? Soft? Long?" He could fucking go for all of it, one after the other. They had a lot of fucking time to make up for.

"Yes. I want it all."

He rolled onto his back, bringing Rig with him. "Ride then. Fingers first." He offered them up to Rig, looking to have that fucking amazing mouth wet them.

He got this grin - a million watt, at least - then Rig's lips wrapped around his finger. Oh, fuck. What that mouth could do to just a finger. His breath caught in his throat and he groaned, hips moving restlessly.

Rig looked like he was perfectly happy, sucking and moaning, working his finger like it was all the man ever wanted to do. Sexy fucker. He watched, his cock jerking as he pushed a second finger into Rig's mouth. His sexy fucker. Rig sucked hard, head bobbing, pulling at his fingers.

"Enough," he finally growled, yanking them out and sliding them down behind Rig's balls, searching for that sweet hole. "Want you."

"I'm all yours. Come on." Rig arched his hips, begging for him, for his touch.

He rubbed his fingers against Rig's hole, and then slipped them in, letting Rig's movements take them right in. So fucking hot and tight. Rig moaned, rocking and fucking himself straightaway, riding his fingers like he was a pony. Reaching up with his free hand, he tugged on the little ring, knowing it would make Rig crazy.

"Blue!" Rig's ass squeezed his fingers, muscles rippling around him.

"Yeah." He grinned and tugged again, fingers pushing, searching and pegging his gland.

"Fuck. Fuck me. Don't stop." Rig gasped, bucked underneath him.

"Want my cock, Rabbit? Gonna ride me?" He could hardly fucking wait.

"Uh-huh. Need. Need you." Rig nodded, climbed up and spread across his cock. He put the head of his cock against Rig's hole and pushed up, slowly spreading Rig open. Rig's moan just started soft, filling the air as he sank in deep.

"Fuck. Oh, fuck." So fucking tight around him.

"Just like that."

"Yeah. Yeah, Blue. Yours." Shit, yes. His.

He wrapped his hands around Rig's hips, helping him rise up, bringing him back down nice and hard.

"Yes!" Rig jerked, squeezed hard. Oh, hell yes. Someone liked that. He did it again, hips bucking this time, pushing his prick even deeper. Rig's head fell back, hands landing on the mattress by his knees. "Again."

He did it again, and then again, giving everything he had to Rig.

"Love this. Made for it." Rig squeezed, bucking on his cock.

"You fucking know it." They came together over and over, that sweet hole squeezing him tight.

"Help me lean forward, Blue." Rig needed to get into the fucking gym, just to get himself back.

He slid his hands up to Rig's shoulders, and tugged him forward, his cock changing angle inside that hot hole.

"Oh!" Rig leaned down, eyes wide, lips almost against his. "Again."

He chuckled and pushed in again. Oh yeah, that was the spot. Rig panted and squeezed, gripping his cock tight. There wasn't anything else fucking like it.

"Don't stop, man. 'm close." Rig looked shocked. As if he'd stop. He pushed harder, working Rig. Rig started jacking himself off, each pull rocketing through the long, fine body.

Digging his heels into the mattress, he kept bringing them together, fucking flying on the feeling of that ass squeezing around his prick. Heat sprayed over his belly, over Rig's fingers. The walls around his cock squeezed hard, milking his own orgasm from him. He gave it up for Rig, roaring as he came.

Rig slumped down against him, melted, grinning, heart pounding.

"Mmm..." He rumbled some, hands sliding on Rig's back, enjoying the sweaty, almost sticky feel of Rig's skin against him.

"Mmhmm." Rig nodded, wrapping close. "Good, good fucking morning."

"It sure as hell is." He kissed the top of Rig's head, listening to Rig breathing, to the sound of the waves on the beach.

Rig sighed, the sound happy as fuck, just letting him hold on.

He grunted and did just that; he didn't see any reason to ruin a perfectly good morning by bitching.

Chapter Fifty Two

"Trouble, put that down!" Gross, dead crab. Rig wandered down the beach, whistling and shivering. He'd been cooped up in the house too damn long. He needed out. The clouds were rolling in, the wind almost icy.

His jacket slipped around his shoulders, Rock's arm coming around his waist.

"Mmm. Hey." So fucking good to him.

"Hey." Rock tugged him close and kissed his forehead. "Bit cold for wandering without a coat."

"Yeah, I came out for some air and found myself walking. Been in the house too long."

"You have been pretty cooped up since the surgery. You don't want to go too far though, and run out of steam before you get back home." With that said, Rock actually turned them around, headed back up the beach.

"Hey. I'll know when to turn around, Rock. I'm not tired yet." And he wasn't six.

Rock stopped and looked at him, grunted unhappily and turned them back around again. "Fine."

He sighed, closed his eyes a second. Jesus, he hated this. He hated being the weak one, the sick one, the one that wasn't enough. He just hated it.

"Wanted to talk to you anyway. Suppose this is as good a place as any."

"That sounds ominous..." He looked over, just a little worried.

"Oh, now, you know I don't understand when you start throwing those five dollar words around." Rock winked at him, gave him another half squeeze.

Oh. Oh, okay. Not a heavy, heavy conversation. "You know me, Blue Eyes. I'm all about the vocabulary."

"Well you do like to use that mouth." Rock grinned a moment, and then sobered some. "I was talking with Dick."

"Yeah? He told me about school and stuff, Rock. I'm real sorry his semester got messed up." He'd do damn near anything to have not caused that.

"He made that choice himself, Rig. I told him we'd make it work if kept going, but you're more important to him, yeah? Anyway. That's not what we were talking about. He said you had some hospital bills that were a little out of hand." Those blue eyes looked over at him, just like lasers.

He looked back, shrugged. "You know that shit isn't free, man."

Not free at all. Hell, it was going to take him twenty years to pay it off.

"What the hell happened to your coverage? The fucking insurance sure as hell isn't free either -- but everyone justifies it because when something like this happens, you're good and aren't left with a crippling fucking debt."

"It paid eighty percent of a lot of it, but they're saying they won't pay the hospital bill. That I shouldn't have gone to San Diego. That I was only covered in ICU for one day. You know how they are." Every dime they didn't have to pay, they wouldn't.

Rock growled. "I thought San Diego was where the experts were?"

"It is. They don't care."

"Bastards." Rock was quiet for a bit, but he wasn't relaxed yet, wasn't finished. "You fighting it?"

"As much as I can, yeah. I'm trying to figure out if it'll cost less to get a lawyer to help. It's way over my head." He'd talked to Helen at the clinic; she'd suggested a couple names and offered her help.

"How much?"

"Huh?"

"How much do you owe?"

"Almost ninety thousand dollars."

"Jesus fucking Christ!" Rock stopped and stared at him. "Why the fuck didn't you tell me?"

"Because it'd stress you out and I've done that enough." Because if he didn't know what the fuck to do about it, how could Rock?

That earned him a snort. "You don't have to handle that kind of shit alone, Rig. Just like you didn't have to fucking keep being sick to yourself."

"I didn't know how to fucking tell you, Jim. You don't think I wanted to? Shit, I was fucking losing my mind and..." And shit. The guys were busy and working and he just couldn't.

"You gotta start telling me things, Rig. Especially things that are making you lose your fucking mind."

"I don't... Shit, Blue. I don't want to be your problem. I want to be the fucking good in your life." He'd used up the worry years ago, used it up by damn near getting beat to death. Rock didn't need this shit.

"Jesus fuck, do you think I won't want you if you've got problems? What the fuck would that make me?"

"You'd always want me." He never doubted that. Never. "I'm yours. I just want to be your good, Jim."

They'd stopped walking, Rock facing him now. "Christ, Rig. You don't think you're my good? You and the kid? Everything else is just details, yeah?"

"Yeah. Yeah, just details." He twined their fingers together, squeezed hard. "I wanted you there in San Diego. It was all I could think."

"Coulda had me, Rig. For every fucking second of it. I would have been there if you'd just asked." Rock shook his head. "Hell, I would have been there if I'd known, invited or not."

"I know. I'm sorry. I thought I was doing what was best for you, and I was too fucking scared to make good sense." There it was.

Reaching out, Rock touched his cheek. "Hey. I'm good at scaring away monsters. Don't be forgetting that."

He leaned, nodded. "You are. You make things better."

"Fucking remember that, Rig. You got anything else you been keeping to yourself?"

"I'm tired of being in the house. I'm tired of being sick, of being tired. I want my coffee back. I want a cigarette."

"All right, why don't you come to the gym with us? And you can have the occasional coffee once you've gained another twenty pounds and you can just forget about the fucking cigarettes -- sick or not, I will kick your ass from here to Texas and back if I find you smoking."

"Twenty pounds?" He wrapped his hand around Rock's arm, pushed close. It was fucking cold. "Slave driver."

Rock chuckled and wrapped both arms around him, pulling him up against that hot body. "Yeah, making you eat. I'm a fucking monster."

"I thought that was a fucking machine..."

"You fucking know it!" Grabbing his ass, Rock squeezed, rubbing them together.

Rig laughed, took himself a hard, deep kiss. His fucking machine. Rock's strong arms tightened around him, like he was going anywhere, and their mouths fused together. He pushed up into the kiss, moaning low. Hips rubbing against him, Rock sucked on his tongue. One hand pushed into the back of his jeans, Rock's palm cool, but warming rapidly against his skin.

Oh.

Oh, now.

Yeah.

Rig groaned, pressed closer and started rubbing. Rock worked his other hand between them, popping open his button and shoving that hand down into his pants, giving him skin to rub against.

"Rock..." He met Rock's eyes, that hand feeling so hot compared to the cold wind blowing in.

"I won't let you fall." The words were growled softly against his lips.

"No." No, not his Rocketman. It wasn't fucking going to happen.

The hand on his ass squeezed and pushed, and then the hand on his cock did the same, Rock working him back and forth as they stood there in the middle of all that sand. Rig moaned, rocking nice and steady, just as caught up now as he'd ever been. Those blue eyes held his, Rock's low moans joining his as Rock's tongue pushed into his mouth. Back and forth, Rock pushed him, sent him flying. Oh, shit. He was fixin' to come, right here, just like that.

Lord, he'd never make it back to the house all boneless.

"Give it to me," growled Rock. "Fucking give it to me."

"Rock!" He shot, his knees buckling with the rush of heat, of pleasure. He didn't fall, Rock holding him up, keeping him pressed tight against that hard, muscled body.

"Just like fucking that."

"Uh... Uh-huh." Fuck, the world was spinning.

Rock kept him steady with that hand on his ass, while pulling the other hand up, covered in his own come and offered over to him.

"Fuck..." He moaned, licking and sucking Rock's hand clean. "Not as good as you."

"You needing a taste of the Rocketman?"

"Fuck, yes." Rig eased down to his knees, still shaking a little from his orgasm.

Rock opened his leather jacket, wrapping it around his head, covering him from sight and protecting him from the cold wind. Rig took a deep breath, the scents of leather and male and need addictive as hell. He slid his lips up the shaft, lips open and hungry as they reached the tip. The noises Rock made were muffled by the jacket, but he could hear them, could feel Rock's pleasure in the way the man's thigh muscles tightened, hips pushed. He closed his eyes, sucking hard, head bobbing as he pulled the salt into him. Drop after drop slipped on his tongue and went down his throat, Rock's hips pushing harder, that thick prick swelling further.

His Blue. Fuck, yeah. He hummed and let himself enjoy it, let himself need. Rock's hand landed on the back of his head, guiding him. As if he didn't know what his Blue wanted. He opened his throat, let Rock in to the root, throat working the tip.

"Fuck!" He had no problem hearing Rock's shout.

Two thrusts later and spunk poured down his throat, Rock's fingers digging into his scalp. He cleaned Rock's cock, licking and sucking until he had every drop. He'd barely done when Rock pulled him up, taking a kiss, one hand putting away that heavy prick.

"Come on, home."

He nodded, leaning hard. "Yeah. Yeah, Rock. It's getting chilly and I think we should make chili."

That had Rock chuckling, arm going around him again, pulling him close as they headed into the wind to go home. "Is chili on the good for you list?"

"It's meat, veggies. I'll drink a shake first, like a good boy." He goosed Rock hard, enjoying the hell out of that laugh.

They were almost home when Rock spoke again. "I think we should go to a lawyer. Just to find out what he thinks about this insurance situation."

"Yeah?" He leaned harder, nodded. If Rock thought it was a good idea, it couldn't hurt.

"Just to talk to someone who knows, yeah? You think anyone at your office would know someone who's battled the insurance companies before?"

"Helen gave me some names, yeah. We just have to pick one."

"Well then, you pick one and make the appointment. You just tell me when and we'll go see him. Or her, I guess. We'll take it from there."

They climbed the stairs to the deck, Rock turning him to the ocean and wrapping warmly around him, the beginnings of a beautiful sunset lighting the sky.

Chapter Fifty Three

Dick made sure the tree was properly set up and then brought out the boxes of decorations, informing Mutt and Trouble in no uncertain terms that they were to stay away from the boxes on pain of death. Of course that meant they sent in Ms. Susie to investigate and he had to shoo all three of them out onto the deck. Silly mutts.

He poked through the boxes again and tried to avoid checking his watch. Rock and Rig had gone to the lawyer to see if it was worth fighting the insurance company on the bills. They'd all decided it was simpler if just Rock and Rig went -- Rock knew all his financial business and they'd tell him all about it when they got back.

The dogs set up barking and he strode to the door just as Rock and Rig were climbing out of Rig's sports car. The dogs came in along with his lovers, and he pointed a finger at them. "You can stay -- but only if you stay away from the boxes."

Then he turned back and got kisses from his men. He was really good. He waited until the front door was closed behind them before asking. "So? What did the lawyer say?"

Rig looked a little dazed. "Well, it'll take time and money, but he'll be able to help some. He thought he'd be able to get more than half taken off, maybe more, if we're lucky."

"Well as long as his fees aren't worth that half, that's a good thing, right?"

Rock nodded. "Yeah. Nothing's guaranteed of course -- cagey bastard wouldn't commit to anything -- but yeah. If things go well we should have brought the total owed down to less than fifty thousand."

"Yeah." Rig nodded, swallowed hard, looking a little green around the gills. "Yeah, it'll work out."

"It will," growled Rock. "And tomorrow we've got an appointment at the accountant. We'll all need to go to that so we can sign on stuff. The lawyer made it clear what bills were going to stand so we know what needs to get paid off."

"I don't... This isn't y'all's debt..."

"Sure it is."

Dick nodded in agreement with Rock's words.

"I." Rig looked just sick.

Not like 'oh, this is a bad idea' sick, but like 'I'm going to puke up a lung' sick.

"Rig?" Dick grabbed one of the boxes and upended it, then passed it over, just in case Rig did puke. "Are you okay?"

"I..." Rig bolted, the door to the bathroom slamming shut.

"Well, shit." Rock growled and headed for the bathroom, and he was hot on the big guy's heels.

He grabbed a washcloth to cool Rig's neck with and Rock rubbed those thin shoulders.

"Sorry. Sorry, I just. Damn." Rig's shirt was plastered to him, the man having cold shakes.

Shit, he didn't want Rig to have to do this again. "Do you think we need to go to the hospital?"

"I don't know," growled Rock.

"I don't... I don't think so. No blood. No pain. Just nausea." Rig looked over, at him, panting. "Call Helen, huh?"

"Yeah, okay." He touched Rig's head and went for the phone, dialing quickly.

"Doc Rig?" He could hear the baby jabbering in the background. "You ready for Christmas yet, honey?"

"It's not, Rig, it's Dick. He's sick. He's throwing up, he's got the cold shakes."

"Okay. Okay, Dick. Relax. Is there blood - red or black?"

"No, no blood. No pain. He says it's just the nausea." He looked over at Rig, please let it just be good old-fashioned flu.

"Oh." He could hear Helen relax. "Ask him when he ate last."

Oh, for... "Rig? When did you last eat?"

"Uh. Breakfast. I had breakfast." Right. Two sips of milkshake and half an egg. The man had been all nerves.

And it was nearly four. "Shit, that's it Helen. He hasn't eaten since this morning. Sorry to bother you."

"No bother. It's better to be safe than sorry. He's not going to want to eat, but that's what he needs. His blood sugar is probably low as anything."

"We'll get something down him. Thanks. Bye."

He hung up and leaned against the bathroom wall with a huge sigh of relief.

"You need to eat more than once a day."

"I do." Rig heaved again. "The meeting ran long."

"Yeah. Yeah, okay. We need to make sure you always have snacks with you. Powerbars or something."

Rock grunted. "You're saying he's sick because he didn't eat."

"Yep."

Rock growled.

"Come on, let's get you food."

"Uh-uh. I can't. I can't, y'all."

"Yeah, Helen said you weren't going to want to, but it's what's going to make you feel better. So you have to."

Rock wrapped an arm around Rig's waist and got him up, got him moving.

"You think you could manage a shake, Rig?"

"I want a shower." Rig followed, though, let Rock help him.

"Yeah, in a bit. Helen said your blood sugar was low. Come on." He pulled out the milk and found the protein powder.

Rig leaned down, head on his hands. "I don't want to ruin y'all's credit. I don't want to be sick any fucking more."

"You're not going to ruin our credit," growled Rock.

"You'll feel better once you've got some protein in you." Dick mixed up the shake and put a straw in it, sitting next to Rig as he passed over.

Rig gagged, but brought the straw to his mouth, sipping slowly. It took a couple of sips, but Rig lost that green look.

"Yeah, that's it. Keep going." He was almost shaking he was so relieved.

"I. Can I have an egg, Dick? I could eat an egg. Hell, Rock's probably starving."

"I'm fine."

Dick grinned. "An egg is good. I could make some sausages, too."

Rig leaned into Rock, head on the broad shoulder. "Sorry, y'all."

Rock patted Rig's head. "Just don't do it again. The kid was right -- you need to carry protein bars with you."

"I just didn't think. I... I hate this shit. When the fuck does life back off and be easy?"

Rock snorted. "Who promised you easy?"

"Fuck off." Rig looked like he was going to snarl, but started chuckling instead. "Asshole."

"Yeah, but I'm your asshole." Rock winked. "Tell you what. Instead of making us a big meal, why don't I take us out to the IHOP?"

"You up to that, Rig? I don't mind making you an egg. Honest."

"Oh, IHOP works. We could even think about catching a movie or playing a bit of pool. Let me change shirts."

Rock's eyebrow rose. "It really was just a low-blood sugar thing, huh?"

Rig shrugged. "It's called dumping. The surgeon said that I need to worry about pain and blood, losing weight."

"Well let's not do it again." Dick gave Rig's arm a squeeze. Truth was it had scared the shit out of him. He had a hunch it might take a while before that wasn't his first reaction.

"'kay." Rig nodded, sighed. "I just was all nervy today."

"Little bites often, huh?" He leaned in and kissed the side of Rig's mouth. "You want that shower before we head off?"

"Yeah. Yeah, Blue? You want too?"

"Getting wet with the two of you? I'm there." Rock grinned and stood, held out his hand to Rig. Rig took it, gave Rock a smile, the tension in the thin shoulders fading. Rock's other hand was held out to him and Dick took it, letting Rock lead him, lead them.

Hell, it looked like the day was looking up.

Chapter Fifty Four

Rock looked around at the crowds and growled a little.

Christmas made people fucking nuts. And the closer they got to Christmas, the nutser they got. One of these years he'd get his fucking shopping done in November. This was not that year. He checked his watched. Quarter past three. They were supposed to be meeting back up at three and so far, he was the only one in front of the food court.

He told himself it was just because the place was so busy, and Rig and Dick would be along any second now. Rig showed up first, looking fucking exhausted, but happy. He needed to get Rig into the gym. It would help.

"Hey. You got everything you needed?" He asked. If Dick didn't show up soon, he was commandeering the bench a group of teenagers were hanging around on.

"If I didn't, I'll have to get it later." Rig grinned, winked.

Dick came rushing up. "Sorry! I got caught in line behind this lady who was trying to return a shitload of stuff. She didn't have the right receipts, half the stuff had no tags. Who does stuff like that?"

"Who cares? Let's go get some coffee..." Rig looked at them both, eyes laughing.

He shook his head, but smiled. "I want more than coffee. We deserve a treat after braving this shit."

"You taking us out?" Dick asked. "We haven't been to the steakhouse since... before Thanksgiving."

"Oh. That sounds good." Rig nodded, grinned. "I could just share with y'all, even."

"You're assuming I'd be willing to share. I'm starving." He gave Rig a look. "When was the last time you had something to eat?" Lunch had been several hours ago.

"I had a smoothie with protein powder about one thirty. I could have another bite now."

"That's okay, then. I'll get the big steak so you can share."

"You can have some of mine, too." Dick grabbed Rig's bags for him, and they weaved their way through the fucking crowds.

"God, people are getting pushy." Rig ducked a flying shopping bag, shook his head.

Rock growled and put his arm around Rig's shoulders, tugging him close where he wouldn't get bumped. "Clear a path, Dick."

The kid nodded and stepped up ahead of them. Nice. Getting a clear path and a view of that fine ass.

"Man, he's really good at that." Rig was admiring too.

"It's all those muscles." Rock grinned, licked his lips. He had him a fine pair of men.

"It's the whole package."

He chuckled; he couldn't disagree. They finally made it out the door and he grimaced. It was a fucking cold December. Not cold the way he used to know it, but they'd been here long enough he was getting soft. It made him keep his arm around Rig, looking to share body heat as they headed across the parking lot for Dick's car.

"You think we might actually get snow this year?" Dick asked, eyes on the clouds.

"That'd be something." Rig shook his head. "No, I think it'll just be wet and miserable and require hours of couch snuggling."

"Better make sure we've got movies stocked." He could handle couch snuggling; it usually led to couch fucking. Of which there had not been enough lately. His prick tried to get interested and he ignored it -- steak first, fucking after.

"Oh, yeah. That works. We could get a bunch and fuck through them all." Dick giggled and unlocked the car.

Rock nodded, opened the front door for Rig. He didn't like the back, but for now he preferred having Rig up front.

"You don't want it, Rock? Stretch your legs out?" Rig slid in as he shook his head, hand patting his cock through his jeans.

"We could share the back..." He wouldn't say no to a little more attention from that hand...

"Oh..." Rig almost hopped out of the front, scooting in the back with a wicked fucking grin.

Dick pouted at him from the driver's seat. "You can drive on the way home from the restaurant."

"You got it. Just make sure you take the long way around." Rock winked and got in.

Rig's arms were open, reaching for him. "C'mere."

He settled in the back seat and instead of going to Rig, tugged the man into his. "No, you come here."

Fuck, Rig's laugh tasted good, that heat slapping against his chest. He sucked on the man's tongue, taking that flavor into him, his hand sliding along Rig's back, headed right for that bubble butt.

Rig was chuckling for him, cowboy hat flying off as Rig's hands slid around his neck. Dick started the car up and they started moving. He hoped the kid took the really long way to the restaurant. Grinning, he goosed Rig. Hard.

"Bitch!" Rig's laughter got louder, filling the car in a way he hadn't heard in forever.

He just grinned, that sound making him happy deep down. His hand slid, cupping one ass cheek, squeezing gently.

"Hey." Rig slid more fully into his lap, nose rubbing against his own.

"Hey, there." He took a kiss. Fuck, that mouth tasted good.

"Mmm. You had chocolate at the mall."

"Would I do that?"

"You would. Kiss me again."

He chuckled. "Yeah, I would." And that kiss? He had no problem giving that. Rig groaned, pushing into his arms and rubbing.

"Mmm... you're wanting." He rolled Rig against him.

"Yeah. Yeah, feeling good, Blue. Feeling like me again."

He slid his hands over Rig, nodded, winked. "You do feel good."

"Yeah? My ass back to form?"

"Getting there." He slid his hands down to grab it again. "Yeah, getting there."

He rolled their hips together, their pricks rubbing together through two pairs of jeans.

"Mmm. Beautiful son of a bitch." Rig tilted his head, kissed him so hard his breath caught.

"Haven't done anything like this in too fucking long."

Dick grinned at him and Rig through the rear-view mirror.

"I know it." Rig licked his lips, nice and slow. "We're going to have us a sweet, slow, private Christmas, Blue. No kids. No drama."

"Mmm... sounds good." He humped up with his hips, hands keeping Rig close.

"It does. Fuck, I want you. Do we have to eat?"

"Yes. I'm hungry and you have to." He slid a hand between them, not even bothering with belt and button, just pulling down Rig's zipper.

"Touch me." Rig laughed again, cock sliding on his palm, hot and slick.

"You fucking know it." He wrapped his hand around that heat, sliding it slowly up and down, looking into those grey eyes. Rig moaned, moving with him, staring at him like he was pure magic.

"Get me out." Two pricks were always better than one.

"Uh-huh." Fuck, those fingers were smart, working his jeans open, fingers protecting him from the zipper. Groaning, he wrapped them both together as soon as Rig had him out, hot silk on hot fucking silk.

"Fuck, yeah. Promise me we can play for awhile tonight. Fuck and suck and touch..."

Dick piped up from the front of the car. "Oh, yeah. I wanna."

"Yeah, me too." He tugged at their pricks. "Take all the time in the world, yeah?"

"Yeah. Fuck in the hot tub with the rain falling. In the shower. On the sofa under the quilts..."

"With the Christmas lights on, making everything shine. Making all that skin bright."

"Don't drive us off the road, Dick."

"I won't. You've got another few minutes."

"Better hurry now then." He tightened his hand, jacking them faster.

"Uh. Uh-huh. Rock. Blue..." Look at those motherfucking eyes shine.

"Right fucking here, Rig. Right fucking here." His voice was husky, need making his balls draw up.

"Yeah." Rig nodded and shot, just like that, fucking sweet as could be.

"Fuck." He bucked up, his hand working hard, and then came, too, coating his hand.

Rig groaned, brought his hand up, licked it clean.

"Sexy fucker." Fuck, he loved that mouth.

"Mmhmm." Rig nibbled and licked and sucked, threatening to get him up again.

"You need food," he reminded Rig, refusing to ask his Rabbit to stop.

"Uh-huh."

"I'm turning onto Storm Street, guys. We'll be there in a second."

He just growled, holding Rig's gaze. Rig smiled, kissed the center of his palm, mouthing words against his skin.

"Fuck. Dick. You think we can hit a drive through window instead?"

He met Dick's eyes in the rearview mirror, and the kid nodded. "Yeah. Yeah, I think so."

Fucking A.

"Mmm. Cool. We have steak in the freezer. We'll make 'em tomorrow." Rig's lips wrapped around his thumb, sucking good and hard.

"Uh-huh." It was like there was a connection between his thumb and his cock, the later filling easily. Rig's teeth scraped all up along his thumb, making him jerk. They pulled into the drive-through, Dick ordering for them.

Rock didn't even give a shit what Dick got them. It didn't fucking matter. He had horny, happy, sex-kitten Rig in his lap, asking for him.

And that made it fucking perfect, all on its own.

Chapter Fifty Five

Dick managed to get them home without having an accident. No mean feat given the way Rock and Rig were steaming up the windows.

"Come on, horn dogs. Let's go in." He grinned, horny as hell himself. "We've got plans."

He grabbed their food and all the bags, being good and not peeking, though he was sorely tempted.

"Mmm. Food. Couch. Movies. Coffee?" Jesus, Rig never stopped pushing.

Rock snorted. "I thought you wanted to fuck all night long?"

Dick got the door open and their bags in the closet where the dogs couldn't get to them. "I think that's a no on the coffee, Rig. We haven't got any in the house, anyway."

"Fucking works. I could fuck faster with coffee."

He looked over at Rock, who looked back at him and the two of them just started laughing. Rig gave them a shit-eating grin, a wink, their cowboy just tickled. Dick set up their supper, and grabbed some cokes from the fridge, while Rock set up a movie.

It wasn't long before they were all settled together, Vin Diesel jumping off a bridge as they ate their burgers. Rig leaned against Rock, socked feet on his lap. Rock jollied Rig into eating more of his burger. "Come, Rig. I'll give you a kiss for another bite."

Rig played along, too, and it made him feel good - to see Rig try, to see Rig fighting to get better.

Once they were done eating, he pulled Rig's socks off and started to massage the man's feet. "You've cute toes, you know."

"Toes aren't cute." Rig stretched out, alternately watching the movie and nuzzling Rock's package.

"No?" He took one and wriggled it. "This little piggy went to market..."

Rig snorted, nudged his belly with one heel. "Shit, no. We've marketed. We're home."

Rock shook his head. "You're nuts, kid."

Chuckling, he started rubbing Rig's sole hard enough not to tickle. "Nah. I'm just having fun."

"It's been a while since that was all we had to worry on, huh? Just us and goofing off?" Rig grinned at Rock, kissed the big guy's stomach. Rock grunted, and stroked Rig's head..

"Yeah. Yeah, it's been too long." He brought Rig's foot to his mouth and kissed the ankle. Rig smelled good. He smiled, kissed again as it hit him, in his gut. Rig smelled like Rig again. He licked up Rig's ankle as far as the denim would let him.

He hadn't even realized how much he'd missed that smell, that taste, the rightness of it.

"Mmm. That's warm, Pretty." Rig reached up, started unbuttoning Rock's shirt.

"You taste good," he said softly, nuzzling, licking some more. He reached up, undoing Rig's belt so he could get the jeans undone and off. Rock stretched out, arms along the couch -- offering himself up to Rig. It was easy, warm. Like coming home. Rig was exploring Rock's belly and chest, humming happily. Rock helped him a little with the jeans, and he took the man's tightie whities off at the same time. He didn't hurry, just tasted, the hair under his lips making him chuckle now and then.

It was surprisingly hot, Rig wearing nothing but one of Rock's sweaters, the edge just at the bottom of that sweet ass. Rock's hand came down to pat at Rig's hip, the big guy making a low, happy sound. Rock's eyes met his, satisfied as fuck. Settled.

Dick grinned against Rig's skin, licking over one calf muscle. He nibbled, too, teeth rubbing gently. Rig leaned up a little, worked Rock's jeans open. That heavy cock was filling, peeking out from under the edge of the sweater.

Oh, he had a goal now.

Still smiling, he slowly continued licking upward.

Rock's legs spread, and there was another heavy cock coming into view as Rig got Rock's jeans open. They all made these great noises - happy and male and rough and together. Rig's cheek slid up along Rock's shaft; Dick kissed the inside of Rig's thigh.

He nosed Rig's balls, tongue licking over them, the strong flavor of Rig matching his scent. He couldn't keep the slow pace up any longer; he went down on Rig's cock sucking that taste right in.

"Dick!" Rig sat up a little, eyes wide. Rock chuckled, hand sliding briefly over his head. He just hummed around Rig's prick, looking up into those grey eyes, his tongue playing with the slit of Rig's prick.

"That... that's not slow. Oh... Good." Rig blinked a little owlishly, slowly leaning back into Rock's arms.

He pulled off and licked a circle around the head of Rig's prick. "If you want slow you shouldn't taste so good."

"Dick..." Please.

"Tease," Rock accused softly.

Laughing, Dick took Rig back into his mouth, going slowly all the way down, lashing at the silky flesh with his tongue. Rig leaned all the way back, Rock's arms wrapping around the lean body and holding on. Rock's fingers tugged the sweatshirt up, big fingers playing with those sensitive little titties. Dick kept his head bobbing slowly, sucking strongly around the hard skin.

Rig started moaning, groaning low as he pulled and swallowed around Rig. He slid his fingers over the Rig's balls, rolling and stroking them. Fuck, he loved this.

His men didn't look like they were arguing either, two sets of eyes on him, laughing, needing. His cock throbbed in his jeans and he just ignored it, knowing that he'd have his turn. Those eyes were making promises. Dick let his teeth threaten, not hurt, never hurt, but just gave Rig a little extra strength.

"Mmm. Yeah, Pretty. The tip, huh? You know that does it for me." Oh yeah, he knew. He flicked his tongue across Rig's slit again, and then pushed into it, holding Rig's balls in his hand. Rig gasped, hips bucking up a little. "Hey. Yeah. Yeah, Dick. More."

He used his teeth next, letting Rig feel it across the top of his prick.

"Oh." Rig arched, all that long, lean body offered up and both him and Rock moaned to see it. Moaning himself, he did it again, and then took Rig in down to the root, burying his nose in the blond pubes. He swallowed hard.

Rig's hands landed on his head, holding him down as that pretty cock throbbed. He swallowed, taking everything Rig had to give him. Rig tasted almost sweet, now that he was well, tasted rich and male and right. He hummed happily, hips humping the couch lightly as he cleaned Rig's prick with his tongue, slowly letting it drop from between his lips.

"Prettiest fucking sight," muttered Rock, one finger wiping a drop of come from the corner of his mouth.

"So good. So fucking sweet." Rig gave him this smile that just warmed him up.

He beamed up at them both, and then sat up so he could pull off his t-shirt. Rock got with the naked program right away, tugging Rig's sweatshirt the rest of the way off. Rig sat up, worked Rock's jeans off, nuzzling and touching the whole time.

It wasn't long at all before they were all naked, him and Rock kissing while Rig licked at Rock's fat prick. Rig shifted him over, lined them up, the hot, wet cock loving on him too. He made a soft noise, his belly going tight as his prick jerked at the attention. Grunting, he took another kiss, and he fed more noises into Rock's mouth.

It was like Rig was fucking worshipping his prick, Rock's. Those lips gave him long, wet kisses, tongue sliding over their skin.

"Oh, God." He moaned, holding onto Rock.

Rig's hum answered him, the vibrations making them both gasp.

"Fucking sweet." Rock's hand slid through Rig's curls and reached down, too, touching one cheek, the side of Rig's mouth.

Rig was smiling. Sucking, humming and smiling, like he was the happiest man on Earth. This, right here this was all he needed to have the best fucking Christmas ever.

Rock's hand slid down his spine and found his crease, found his hole, pressing against it. Okay, so it could get even better.

Half laughing, half groaning, he moved his hips, pushing back against Rock's finger and forward to slide his cock along Rock's, into Rig's mouth. Rig took them both in, pulling and sucking, squeezing them together.

Rock's eyes closed, a low, throaty moan sounding. Fucking manly compared to his own whimper, but fuck, that felt unbelievably good. Rig's fingers worked his balls, rolling so gently, rubbing. It was more than any one guy could take and he lost it, hips jerking as he sawed between Rock and Rig.

They all moved together, Rig pulling and sucking and damn near feeding off them both.

"Oh, fuck. Oh, fuck!" He cried out, coming into Rig's mouth, his ass going tight around Rock's finger.

"Shit, feel that," muttered Rock.

Rig groaned, swallowing hard, driving him crazy. If it kept up, he wasn't going to go soft.

Of course, the way Rock was moaning, he might just keep it up regardless of Rig.

"Wanna fuck you." Rock's words hung in the air.

Rig licked the tip of Rock's prick. "Which you?"

Those blue eyes met his, and then Rig's. "Both of you."

Dick felt a shiver go down his spine at Rock's tone.

Rig grinned, the look lazy and wicked. Dick almost chuckled as the game of 'tease the bear' started. "You haven't even gotten off yet. You'll never outlast both of us."

Rock's eyes just shone, the man knowing exactly what Rig was doing, but going along with it anyway. "That a challenge?"

"You think you're up to it?" Look at those two, vibrating, happy, staring each other down.

"Is this up enough for you?" Rock slapped his prick against Rig's cheek. "I'm not so old I can't keep up with the two of you -- show you both how it's done."

Shit, watching them was better than television and movies anyway. Rig moaned, face turning toward Rock's cock.

"Can I go first?" He wasn't being greedy, but he did love being lazy and melted, still feeling Rock inside him while he watched the big guy do Rig.

"Mmhmm. I'll get Rock wet for you..." Rig's tongue dragged up Rock's prick.

"Like he's not already." Chuckling, he looked for the lube.

"Hush. Wetting." Rig gave him a wicked, shit-eating smile.

His chuckles turned into laughter, and Rock just sat there, spread like the biggest, macho-est, studliest slut in the world, blissful look on his face as Rig worked that gorgeous cock.

"Who's gonna get me ready?" he asked, spreading wide himself.

Rig chuckled, eyes cutting over to him, wanting both of them. He jacked himself lazily, knee going up over the back of the couch, so Rig could see exactly what was on offer.

"You're cheating." Rock was grinning, though.

"Right -- like having that bad boy out isn't cheating."

They grinned at each other.

"Hrm..." Rig frowned a little, then grinned and slid to the floor, upper body leaning on the sofa. "Okay, lean over me, Dick, and Rock? Get in position behind him. I'll get you both ready."

Rock burst out laughing, and he wasn't far behind.

"Slut," Rock accused fondly, fingers stroking over Rig's face.

"Y'all's." The air got serious for a second, Rig meeting Rock's eyes.

"You fucking know it." Rock's voice was all growly and those blue eyes flicked in his direction for a moment. "You both are. And nobody'd better fucking forget it. Not for a Goddamned second."

Rig nodded and pushed back up into Rock's lap, pulling him over so they could share a kiss, all three of them together. It was long and slow and was all three of them just being there in that moment, living in that kiss.

Rock grinned when their mouths finally parted. "Didn't someone mention fucking?"

"Uh-huh. Couple of us." Rig grinned, rubbing against them both.

"You still wanna get us both ready at the same time?" The idea of it was fucking hot. But then so was pretty much everything they did together. He lived in a wet dream.

"You know it." Rig slid back down, arms open for him.

He gave Rig a kiss before kneeling on the couch, spreading to bring his ass down to where Rig could reach him. His belly was tight with anticipation of that tongue. Rig moaned, nose bumping his balls as heat brushed behind them, heading for his hole. Groaning, he held onto the couch, going tight with need. He could feel the heat of Rock's body come up behind him.

Oh.

Oh, fuck.

Rig started licking, tongue flicking between the tip of Rock's cock and his hole. He whimpered, holding himself tight so he didn't start rocking. The tip of Rock's prick bumped against his hole, making him cry out.

"Yeah." Rig was licking, touching, helping, driving him out of his mind.

He started moving, sliding back and forth so that Rock's prick rubbed along his crack. Finally Rig slid away, hand lining Rock up.

"Oh, fuck, yes." Rock's prick pushed in, spreading him wide. Moaning, he pushed back. Rock chuckled, bit the back of his neck. "Impatient."

Rig chuckled, nuzzled his arm. "He's young."

"I'm horny." He grinned over at Rig, and then cried out as Rock sank deep enough to hit his gland.

"You're fucking beautiful." Rig's words were whispered into his ears.

He grabbed Rig and took a kiss, putting everything he felt into it, putting how they made him feel into it. One hand slid up his spine, another headed down and Dick could feel when Rig and Rock's fingers twined together. Rock's thrusts got a little harder, pushing him against Rig, nailing his gland -- making him fly.

The kiss got deeper, wilder, Rig fucking his lips in time with Rock's thrusts. His cock slid along Rig's belly, caught, just like he was. Caught between Rock and Rig and there was no where else he'd rather have been. Rig's hand slid down his back, teasing the bundles of nerves at the small of his back.

Oh, fuck.

Moving faster, he sawed between them, his balls drawing up. Then Rig's fingers scooted down more, touching his hole, Rock's prick.

"Fuck!" He shouted it this time, body jerking as he came, come splashing over Rig's belly.

"Oh, fuck yeah. Just like that." Rig looked like the cat that had eaten the canary.

"Uh-huh." He was panting and boneless, his arms wanting to give way, and finally they did and he settled on Rig, Rock heavy and hot at his back.

"Mmm. Better?" Rig was petting Rock; he could feel the big guy hum.

"Fucking perfect." He gave Rig a kiss, whimpering into that hot mouth as Rock's cock slid out of him.

"Your turn, now."

"Mmmhmm. My turn." Rock got another grin. "If you're still wanting?"

"Gimme that ass," growled Rock.

"Want me to get you ready?"

It was Rock who answered. "Just switch places, I've got it covered."

Rig whimpered - actually whimpered - and, fuck, it was hot. Then they shifted, sliding over each other. He lay on the couch, Rig's knees on either side of his hips, giving him plenty of access to touch and slide his hands over Rig's skin. Those warm grey eyes were staring at him, just as happy as they'd ever been. They went wide as Rock bent, tonguing Rig's hole if Rig's reaction was anything to go by.

"Blue. Blue, sweet fuck." Oh, yeah. Somebody liked that.

He reached down, fingers sliding along Rig's crack, tickled by Rock's tongue when he hit Rig's hole. Rig tensed and groaned, ass cheeks squeezing his fingers and Rock's tongue. He groaned as well, his prick jerking and trying to fill. He wrapped his other hand around Rig's head and tugged him down for a kiss, tongue sliding in, mimicking the way Rock's tongue fucked Rig's ass. Those eyes were wide, needing, happy down deep.

"Ready for the Rocketman?"

Dick let the kiss end and grinned, and answered for Rig. "Always."

"You know it." Rig's lips brushed his shoulder. "Fuck me, Blue."

"Mmm... Yeah, Rock. Fuck him." He met those blue eyes, Rock looking as happy as Rig did, as happy as he felt.

Jesus, it was good to be home.

Rock pushed in and Rig pushed back and they all moaned with it. He wrapped his hand around Rig's prick, letting their movements slide it along his palm. Reaching up with his other hand, he tugged at Rig's nipple ring, watching the grey eyes closely. They went wide, then heavy-lidded, Rig's lips parting like magic. Grinning, he did it again, reaching with his other hand to feel where Rock's cock pushed into Rig's body, the hard, velvet covered flesh going in over and over again.

"Isn't he fine?" Rig gave him a goofy grin, leaning more fully over the back of the sofa.

He laughed, feeling happy and melted and just right. He stroked Rig's hole and Rock's prick both. "You are, too. I have the best life."

"We do. Harder, Blue Eyes. You can't break me."

Rock rumbled, hands dropping to Rig's hips, wrapping around them and tugging him back into each thrust. Dick could smell them both, could smell the way their need got hotter, deeper. Rig started panting, skin warming up to a sweet, deep rose. He tightened his hand around Rig's prick, watching them move together, moving against him.

"Come on, Rig. Gimme." Rock groaned, and moved faster.

"Uh-huh. Uh-huh. Rock..." Rig jerked, eyes rolling back in his head.

"Come on," he whispered, free hand moving to tug on that little nipple ring. That earned him a cry and a jerk, Rig spending right into his hand. Rock roared, jerking a few times and then stilling.

"S...stud." Rig slumped down, panting hard.

"You know it." Rock collapsed down against Rig and Dick grunted, laughing at the weight of them on him.

"You good, Pretty?" Rig hummed and blinked, slow.

"No -- I'm way better than good." He stroked Rig's arm, Rock's back. "Way better."

"Mmm. Good." Rig grabbed the blanket, covered them up a little.

Dick shifted a little, settling more comfortably, and let his eyes close.

He'd never take this for granted again.

Chapter Fifty Six

The place smelled fucking amazing.

Pine and food and chocolate underlying it all. There were cookies and squares everywhere. He considered growling at Rig about how hard Rig was pushing himself, but in the end Rock couldn't bring himself to. He didn't want to. Rig looked better than he had in a year, and he was happy, and Dick was happy and hell, Rock himself was fucking happy.

He'd just heard from the bank -- their consolidation had gone through. The business and the house were mortgaged to the hilt, but there was a check on its way to the insurance company.

Christmas shopping was fucking done. Hell, he'd even wrapped everything.

Rock felt fucking fine.

Except the chocolate smell had gotten stronger and his stomach was telling him there was a chocolate sized hole in it, right there. Grunting, he headed to the kitchen.

Rig was fucking singing, ass shaking as he stirred something. The dogs were circling, hoping for a drop. Dick was sitting on the counter, eating fudge, and laughing.

He stood in the doorway a moment, just fucking enjoying it.

They looked like a fucking Christmas card.

"You didn't tell me there was fudge," he growled.

"There's three kinds of fudge and a chocolate pie in the fridge. I'm making the pecan now." Rig was wearing his sweater, the huge thing hanging on his skinny redneck. It was fucking sexy.

"I want the chocolate fudge." Everyone knew that.

Dick pointed to the table and there it was. He grabbed the plate and moved to stand next to Dick, the kid leaning in and kissing the side of his mouth.

"I made lace cookies, too." Rig pointed with his chin, the cookies in a pile, waiting on him.

Oh, somebody loved him.

He took a few pieces of fudge and put them on the edge of the plate of cookies and then picked that up. "Mine," he said around a mouthful.

Rig grinned, looking fond and pleased as hell. "Yeah. I made rum balls for Dick. Those are yours."

Dick waggled his eyebrows. "I get balls."

Rock snorted and ate another lace cookie.

He got beamed at, then Rig filled a pie crust with goo. Gross. "Open the oven, Blue?"

"Sure." He managed to do it without letting go of his plate of cookies, too.

"Thank you." The pie was slid in, Rig setting the timer and stretching.

He reached out and touched Rig's belly as the man stretched. "Mmm... you've been cooking up a storm. It's beginning to feel like Christmas."

"Mmhmm. You did a good job on the tree and lights. I approve." Rig's stomach growled loud enough for him to hear it.

"We did. And the dogs haven't pulled it down yet." He shoved a lace cookie at Rig. "Here. Have one."

He saw Dick grin out of the corner of his eye, the kid sliding off the counter and starting to pull down the makings of a shake.

"They're yours. I made them for you." Rig shook his head, took a kiss instead.

"Dick's making you a shake."

"Fruit shake -- I think you'll like this, Rig."

"Yeah? What kind?" Rock knew Rig was getting tired of the constant chocolate-vanilla thing, but it was the best, easiest way to get protein into the man and it was working. Rig's last blood tests were well on the way to right.

"This one's mango-guava flavored. I even picked up some mangos so I could mix it in." Dick dropped the fruit and some ice cubes in, blending the whole thing together noisily.

"Mango-guava." Rig looked dubious. "It smells okay..."

"Hey, I taste tested it - it's not bad." Dick poured the shake into a glass and handed it over with a flourish.

Rock wrinkled his nose.

Rig took a sip, then nodded, taking a long drink. "I like it."

Dick beamed and Rock shook his head. "Mango and guava. It's got nothing on chocolate." He wouldn't believe it did for a minute.

"I'm just tired of them, Blue. I've eaten a zillion of them."

"You don't say that about another liquid I know you drink every fucking day." He winked, slid his hand over Rig's ass.

"Fuck you." Rig chuckled, leaned a little harder.

"I think the words you're looking for are 'suck you'." He wrapped his arm around Rig and held him where he was.

"Mmm. These are a few of my favorite things." They all chuckled, Rig leaning into him. "Man, that weather is wicked cold, huh?"

"Yeah, but I got a fire started in the other room. And it's nice and cozy here." Maybe moreso because they could hear the wind just howling.

"It is. Makes it great for cooking." Rig grinned and stretched.

"Makes it great for other things, too."

Dick laughed. "You would think that."

"Like you're not thinking the same thing."

The kid didn't deny it for a second.

"Y'all are something. I was going to make sugar cookies for the clinic."

Uh-huh. No clinic visits for Dr. Rig. Helen and the rug-rat? Sure. Work? No.

"You've made enough cookies for today." Grumbling, he grabbed Rig's hands and tugged him out of the kitchen. Rig followed along, just tugging back a little bit. There was a fire in the front room, the tree -- it was nice, homey and special. He sat on the couch and tugged Rig down into his lap, careful not to upset his plate of cookies.

"Mmm. Hey." Rig was the fucking master of snuggling, arm over his shoulders like it belonged there.

"Hey." He took himself a nice slow kiss.

"You having a good holiday so far?"

"You know it." Rig nodded, settled closer. "I always have Momma in the back of my mind, this time of year."

"She did love Christmas."

"She did. So did Daddy. You remember the first year you came home with me?"

"I do. Didn't know what to expect." He grinned. "I should have, though. I knew you."

"Daddy thought you were something else." Rig's fingers traced his lips.

He smiled, licked at Rig's fingertip and then nibbled on it before answering. "He was a good man. Good as any I knew."

Rig nodded and pushed into his arms. "He was. I have a lot of 'em in my life."

Smiling again, he stroked Rig's hair back, then bent to take another soft kiss, tongue sliding into Rig's mouth. Rig opened right up, sweet and hot, knowing just how he liked being kissed.

Dick came in with three steaming cups. "Hot chocolate with marshmallows on top."

Oh, nice. Almost as nice as the taste of Rig in his mouth. Rig's legs wrapped around his hips, tugging them closer together.

"Want a taste?" Dick asked, sitting next to them and licking where their lips met.

"Uh-huh." Rig shifted, let Dick in. Oh. Chocolate.

Their tongues all tangled together, lazy and slow, male and chocolate flavors mixing together. Rig's cock started filling; he could feel it between all the layers of denim and sweater and sweatshirt. It was so fucking good, having Rig back, eager and ready. He could feel Dick's cock, too, sweet and long, pressing against his side.

"Mmm. Our drinks are gonna get cold."

"They'll microwave," Dick offered helpfully.

Grinning, he brought their mouths back together again. They had this down, tongues sliding and slipping, soft moans and chuckles and shit. Rock fucking approved. It became more than just kisses by slow increments, Dick's hand rubbing his belly, Rig's.

"Did... Did I set the timer on the pie, y'all?" Rig was all pink, flushed, panting.

"Uh-huh." He and Dick answered at the same time, and the kid laughed. Laughed and started stripping them down, starting with Rig's layers.

"Oh, good." Rig lifted his arms, the sweater sliding right off.

"Take this one, too." He pulled the sweatshirt up and off as well. He and Dick went for those little nipples right away.

"Y'all!" Rig arched for them. His finger caught the ringed one, that tender little nipple going hard and dark. He just had to taste and he bent his head, tongue flicking that ring up and down before he wrapped his lips around the hard little nub and sucked.

"Blue. Rock. Fuck. Please. Rock..." Rig's hands wrapped around his head, hips bucking and rolling. He fucking loved that, loved being able to make Rig so crazy on so little. Dick was working that other nipple, tugging and twisting; he could see it out of the corner of his eye.

Fucking A. They could bring Rig off, just with this.

He took that little ring between his teeth and tugged on it, tugged hard.

"Rock." Rig's belly went tight. "Fuck."

No, no they weren't fucking. Not yet. He could feel Dick's breath as the kid's tongue flicked across Rig's other nipple. He could fucking feel Rig's heart pounding under his lips, hear the sweet, raw cries. He sucked harder, tongue playing the tip over and over. They were going to do it, they were going to make Rig come and come hard.

Rig started gasping, hands opening and closing. He could smell Rig's need, the passion. He nodded. That was it, just let go.

"Y'all's." Rig shot, shaking hard, just the finest fucking thing he'd ever seen.

He kept sucking, gently now, making Rig shiver, his hand stroking down over the thin back. Rig whimpered softly, head rolling on his shoulders. So fucking fine. He and Dick stopped at the same time, both giving Rig's nipples one last lick.

"Mmm..." he just rumbled, letting Rig hear it, feel it.

"Uh-huh," agreed Dick.

Rig just gasped and nodded. They moved back to kissing, him and Dick sliding their hands over Rig's body, keeping his rabbit warm. Rig hummed, relaxed and lazy between them, giving them both long kisses.

Dick reached for one of the mugs of hot chocolate, offering it to him and Rig. He grabbed it, taking a large mouthful and moving to kiss Rig, to share the drink. Mmm. Chocolate-flavored Rig. That was something special.

"Lemme taste." Dick's tongue slipped into their mouths and now they were all chocolate-flavored.

Fuck. He might have to request this more often. Shifting, Dick straddled the two of them, taking the kisses deeper, moaning into their mouths. Rig's fingers slid down his belly, up over Dick's arm, just holding them together. Dick's fingers slid through Rig's hair, and over his own scalp.

"Man, I want to this for Christmas. Spend the whole holidays just touching, fucking."

"Sounds perfect. Food. Fucking. No troubles." Rig nodded.

"Sounds fucking perfect. Long as we have chocolate pie for energy and presents." He gave them a wink.

"Chocolate pie and fudge, man." Rig leaned, reached for the hot chocolate.

"Picky, picky."

Dick laughed. "Chocolate pie, fudge and rum balls."

"And lace cookies and pecan pie." Look at Rig laugh.

"If we're making wishes here, we might as well have steaks as well." He fucking loved chocolate pie, but man needed a steak now and then. Kind of like loving blowjobs and wanting to fuck as well.

"Hell, yes. Steaks, then ham and turkey for Christmas proper." Rig nodded, smiled at him. "Lots of protein."

"Good man." He chuckled. The irony of Rig suddenly having to eat a high protein diet wasn't lost on him. "We'll have you bulked up in no time."

"Yeah, right. Muscle-bound redneck." Rig's words got them all laughing, good and hard.

"Reach me a cookie, Dick."

"What do I get if I do?"

He raised an eyebrow. "My undying fucking gratitude."

"Mmm. Gratitude. Yummy." Rig chuckled, bent and reached, snagging him a cookie.

"Thank you." He ate the cookie from Rig's hand, nibbling fingers.

"Anytime." Rig winked at Dick. "See? Gratitude."

He stuck his tongue out at Dick, who leaned in and started sucking on it.

"Oh, pretty pretty." Rig's lips found his throat.

He rumbled, the sound getting louder as Dick's hands slid over his pecs, thumbs brushing his nipples.

"Happy holidays, y'all." Rig licked his way down, heading toward Dick's fingers.

"Yeah. Fuck. Happy." He nodded, prick going from half hard to all the way interested, just like that.

Rig laughed, kept heading south, tongue sliding on his belly. Groaning, he spread his legs, and puffed out his chest, trying to get Rig to notice his cock, and Dick to keep playing with his nipples.

"He's really good at that, huh, Pretty?" Rig started rubbing his prick.

"Uh-huh. Really good. Tastes good, too."

Dick played with his nipple ring, flicking it up and down with that tongue.

He grunted. "Less talk, more doing."

"Mmm. Got you." Rig's hand moved, just like he needed it, strong, firm pulls that curled his toes. He could do this, right fucking here for just about ever. With more sucking. Like his Rabbit was reading his mind, Rig got right in the game, lips circling the tip of his cock.

"Fuck, yes." He leaned back into the couch, legs and arms spread like he was the biggest slut in the room.

Dick's tongue teased and played with the ring in his nipple, and Rig's mouth... Shit.

Rig fucking worshipped his cock - focused and hungry, lips sliding up and down his prick like he was a Goddamn lollipop.

"Mmm... yeah, Rig. Like that. Just like fucking that."

Those long, long fingers slid around his balls, pushing and nudging them in their sacs. Oh, fuck him. Combined with the way Rig sucked him in, swallowing and groaning around his cock, it was going to send him to the motherfucking moon.

"Don't fucking stop." He knew Rig wouldn't, knew Dick wouldn't either, but he still said it, letting them know how fucking good it was. No, no. Rig didn't stop. In fact, those lips went all the way to the base of his cock, pulling good and hard. His hips jerked, his hands finding Rig's head, fingers curling into the white curls. Rig moaned, deep-throating him, head bobbing up and down on his prick.

"Fuck." Groaning, he started humping into Rig's mouth, pushing, thrusting. Dick's hand dropped to join his, petting Rig's head. The kid's mouth slid up to glide across his jaw, slowly bringing their lips together. He groaned into Dick's mouth, moving with the two of them. Dick found Rig's rhythm, both of those fine bastards trying to drive him crazy. There was nothing finer. His balls tightened and he fought it, not ready to be done yet. Just like they heard him, both of them slowing down, making it last.

He rumbled for them, petting Rig's head, then Dick's, eyes closed as they made him feel fucking fine. Dick's fingers slipped into Rig's mouth, brushing against his cock. He jerked, crying out, his balls drawing up. Rig stroked the strip of skin behind his balls, hummed around his cock.

"Fuck!" He shouted it out, hips pumping as he came, pouring himself down Rig's throat.

And, just like it was supposed to be, Rig drank him right down, pulling at his cock. He let Rig suck and lick him, and then he tugged his Rabbit up, bringing their mouths together so he could taste himself on Rig's lips. His Rabbit wrapped around him, dragging the kid close. Oh, fucking perfect. A threeway kiss.

Their tongues all tangled together, kisses morphing one into another, gentle and lazy and perfect.

Rig pulled the blanket around them, settling in. "Mmm. Good, huh?"

"You know it."

The kid added an "uh-huh," too.

"Nap. And then more cookies."

He liked it when a plan came together.

Chapter Fifty Seven

They hadn't been so lazy in forever. Cookies. Spiced cider. Stew. Movies. Long lazy naps.

Rig laughed as Dick hurried back to the hot tub, hot chocolate in hand, shaking in the chill. "Come on! Hurry!"

He got half-way out, grabbed the big old mugs. Fuck, this was decadent.

Rock tugged him back in as Dick climbed in and sank down to his neck, coming close. "Shit, it's cold!"

"Not in here." He grabbed Dick and wrapped around him. "Fuck, this is fun."

Dick's arms went around his waist, his Pretty smiling and happy.

"Hey." The wind was bitter coming off the ocean, but the hot tub was perfect, the three of them just floating and watching the waves and the moon.

"It's fun, though, isn't it?"

"Sure is." Rock's arm wrapped around both of them, tugging them against his solid bulk.

Tomorrow was Christmas Eve and they were ready. Settled and cooked out and just solid. "Man, I know I'm supposed to be missing Texas, but this has been fine."

"This is home," murmured Dick, smiling just for him.

"Yeah. Yeah, Pretty." He rubbed Dick's back a little, fingers sliding in the water.

His Pretty arched, moaning a little.

"Mmm... look at that," murmured Rock.

"He's fucking beautiful." He meant it too. His men were the finest bastards anywhere.

Dick blushed and sank below the water, Rock laughing in his ear. Rock's hands were on his hips, his belly, moving and touching him, always making sure he was good. Something tickled his prick, and then surrounded the tip, suction hard for just a moment. Then Dick burst up from the water, grinning.

"Good Lord." He hooted, dragging Dick in for a kiss.

Sloppy and happy, Dick's kiss had plenty of tongue, and there was lots of rubbing, Dick's prick nudging and rubbing his.

"Somebody's warmed back up, Rocketman." Christ, had he ever been that young?

"Did he ever cool off?"

"Yep. He was all shivery and shit."

"*He* is right here," groused Dick, pressed close, nudging that long prick against him.

"Is he sure?" He wrapped his legs around Dick's waist, holding on tight.

Dick popped his arm, laughing. "He is. And he likes that, the way his cock... yeah..." Dick moaned as their pricks slid together, licked his lips. Rock rumbled happily behind him, chest vibrating with the sound.

"Mmm. This is perverse, y'all. So decadent."

"Could be even more perverse." Rock moved against him, thick prick sliding on his ass.

"Y'all are leading me down the garden path." Uh-huh. Right. 'Cause he was virginal, pure as the driven snow."

Rock started to laugh, Dick, too, both of them pressing him between them. "It's not a garden, Rig, it's a beach." Dick managed to get the words out before he started laughing all over again.

"It's a... Y'all. Y'all look." There were snow flurries in the air. Not many, just enough to barely notice in the porch light.

"I'm looking; it's still a beach." Dick grinned at him, Rock still chuckling behind him.

"Buttheads. Momma told me not to take up with Yankees..."

Rock snorted. "She didn't see the size of our..." Rock slid against him, cock hard and sure on his ass as Dick's eyes went wide.

"What? I was going to say muscles."

Rig laughed, leaning his head back against Rock's shoulder. "She would've just made some crack and made you blush."

Christ, he still missed her. He thought he might always would.

"Yeah, she would have. Only woman on the planet who could, " Rock said, fingers stroking his belly and Dick gave him a soft kiss.

"Mmm. Y'all." He leaned harder, let them love on him.

"Tell me one of you brought lube," muttered Rock.

"Are you kidding? Dick is the most organized man on earth. He'll have lube."

Dick chuckled. "I better have because I am not going back out there. It's too damn cold."

Reaching over the edge, Dick came back with lube, eyes suddenly going wide. "It's snowing!"

"I told you!" He chuckled, popped Dick's ass.

"You did not!"

Dick looked at Rock. "Did he say it was snowing?"

"Nope."

"I did too. I told y'all to look."

Bastards.

Beautiful bastards.

"You didn't say at what! I thought you were talking about the beach." Dick laughed, eyes dancing as he watched the flakes.

"Fucking cold enough to snow." Rock shook his head. "Why the fuck are we outside in it again?"

"Because it won't keep up and the hot tub rocks?"

"It does. Fucking in the hot tub rocks even more." That fat prick kept moving against him. "Hand over the fucking lube, kid. And it had better not be water soluble."

"It isn't. I made sure I brought the right one."

Rig reached out, pulled Dick back into his arms. "What a good boy you are."

"Good enough to get fucked I hope." Dick batted his eyelashes, making Rock snort.

"Oh, man. You don't have the innocent gene anymore..." Rig got tickled, started laughing but hard.

"Shit. Well, as long as I still get fucked." Dick bit his chin, laughing along.

"Don't worry, Dick. I'm doing Rig, and he's doing you. A nice little chain."

"Mmhmm. Come ride my cock, Pretty. I'll warm you up..."

Dick nodded eagerly, floating close. Rock handed him the lube with one hand, the other busy pushing two fingers into him, stretching him open for that fat cock that was currently pressing against his lower back.

"Oh." He groaned, leaned forward to let Rock in, fingers fumbling with the lube.

"So fucking hot," muttered Rock, mouth finding that spot on his neck, teeth worrying it. Dick's fingers slid over his, helped him get the tube open.

"Th...thank you. Oh, Blue. Right there."

"What here?" Rock pegged his gland again.

"God, I'll never get tired of watching the two of you." Dick pressed close, kissing him hard. He moaned out his agreement, nodding, bucking on Rock's fingers. Dick grabbed his hand and pulled it under the water, guiding him to Dick's hole.

"Pretty. Pretty, so fucking hot. So fine." He pushed in deep, whimpering into Dick's lips.

Dick swallowed his noises, fed him those sweet porno sounds in return. The three of them moved together, pleasure passing back and forth and they finger-fucked and rubbed. It was hot, sure it was, but it was easy as breathing, too. Something solid and just about perfect.

Rig moaned, shifted a little to get more of his Rocketman. Three fingers pushed into him, spreading him wider. "Ready for my cock, Rig?"

"Uh... Rock." Oh. Good. So fucking fine.

Rock's low chuckle slid over his skin. "I thought so."

The big fingers disappeared, and Rock shifted him, got him right where he could feel that hot, hard prick push at him, start to spread him wide.

"Yeah..." His fingers curled stroking Dick's gland as Rock filled him up. His Pretty cried out, arms looping over his shoulders as Dick rode his fingers. Rock kept nibbling on his neck, cock pushing deeper and deeper.

"Y'all. Fuck. Dick, I..." Rock was driving him crazy.

"Mmm... incoherent. Good." Rock nipped and nibbled at that spot.

"Rock..." He blinked at Dick, just fucking soaring.

Rock rumbled, Dick's body squeezing tight around his fingers. Then Dick tugged his hand away from that tight little hole, and lowered himself down against Rig's prick.

"Fuck, yeah." His eyes closed, the pleasure just fucking huge.

Rock waited until Dick had settled, and the he began to push, sending Rig back and forth. He couldn't breathe, couldn't do anything but rock, his men just surrounding him. Groaning, Rock pushed a little harder, a little faster, Dick's eyes rolling up in his head as his noises filled the air.

"Yeah. Yeah, Pretty." He moaned low, asshole squeezing as his balls drew up.

Dick rolled and bounced on him, gasping. "Touch me."

"Uh-huh." He managed to get his hand wrapped around that long, thin cock, started stroking it. "Oh, fuck! Yes!" Dick nodded, breath coming faster, bouncing coming faster. Rock matched the speed, pushing into Rig, pushing him deeper into Dick. "Soon. Gonna. Come on, Pretty."

Before he lost it.

"Rig!" Dick arched, body going stiff and tight around his prick as his Pretty came.

"Yeah." He held on long enough to watch the whole thing, to watch Dick's eyes just get all heavy-lidded and sated.

Rock hit his gland hard. "Come on, Rabbit. You next."

"Blue!" His eyes rolled back in his head, body clenching tight. "Again."

"Uh-huh." Rock nailed it again and again, moving him and Dick, both, his Pretty heavy in his arms.

"Fuck." He grabbed Dick's hips, fucking into the tight ass over and over as Rock sent him to the moon.

"Now," growled Rock. "Now. Now."

"N...now." He shot so hard his muscles drew up tight, his cry just ringing out into the night.

"Mmm..." Both his marines murmured against his skin, soft, happy sounds of pleasure.

"Promise me we get this every Christmas from now on."

"Promise," growled Rock, hands sliding on his skin under the water, cock twitching inside him.

Dick's head rested on his shoulder. "It sounds great. I'll back you up with Sissy and everyone if they get pushy."

"You leave pushy relatives to me. I know how to make it stick."

"That he does." Rig nodded, leaning into Rock. "Rock's got Julie's number."

Rock always had.

"You know it." One hand came to rest on his hip, like Rock was laying his claim.

He could feel Dick's grin against his shoulder. Rig winked down at his pretty. Fact was? That hand belonged right there. Dick straightened up long enough to give him a soft kiss, and then settled back against him again.

"We shouldn't stay in too much longer," Rock warned, though he made no move to get out.

"Mmm. We could watch a movie or something." He was getting lazy in his old age.

Dick sat back up, ass squeezing his prick. "I picked up the Die Hard box set -- we could have a marathon."

"Oh, I like those." Rock nodded his approval.

"Cool, I can reheat the hot chocolates, make some popcorn..."

"Sounds good. I'll grab quilts." He smiled up into those amazing blue eyes. "Unless we want to marathon in the bed?"

Rock grinned. "Hell, yes."

"Well, then. Explosions and popcorn naked in bed, Pretty."

Because that was how it was supposed to be.

Chapter Fifty Eight

Dick was working in the kitchen again, working on a great big ham this time. He'd talked Rig into a pre-stuffed breast for the die-hards who insisted on having turkey, so that was cooking nicely on its own. The ham needed lots of basting, though, if it was going to be really yummy. So far Rig was out visiting with Deuce and Gary, Rock dishing out drinks and munchies. Dick was pretty sure he had everything else under control. Still, there was something nagging at the back of his head, like he'd forgotten something.

Rig came in, hand sliding up his spine, loving on him. "What can I do to help, Pretty?"

He glanced at the clock, nearly one -- that wasn't bad at all. He leaned into the touch. "I don't know. I keep thinking I've forgotten something."

"Well, the pies are done. The salad got in the fridge last night. The potatoes? The rolls?"

"Done and done." He turned and looped his arms around Rig's waist, leaning in for a kiss.

"Good deal." Rig gave him what he needed, the kiss long and lazy and slow.

"Mmm... maybe this was what I forgot." He grinned and took another kiss, and then another.

"Could be. Let's do it some more..." Rig's arms slid around his shoulders, holding tight. Rig was looking amazing - healthy and tanned, solid and happy. Better than Dick had seen in a few years.

"Okay." He tugged their lower bodies together, hands sliding to Rig's ass as they shared more kisses. He had a handful of melty, lazy cowboy, that ass sliding and pushing into his hand. It would be so easy to forget all about Christmas dinner and their guests and just make out for the rest of the day.

"Thank you for all this, Dick. You work too hard." Rig's fingers found the small of his back, petting nice and easy.

"I'm only doing what you always do every year. Hell, less than you usually do." Not that he didn't appreciate the rubbing.

"Mmm. It smells perfect." Rig kept rubbing. "The guys are all chowing down on odds and ends and watching football."

"The cheese ball! I knew I'd forgotten something."

"Oh, I'll help." Rig kissed him again. "Bacon and ranch dressing or olives?"

"Rock likes the bacon and ranch best." And he and Rig could steal bites of bacon while they were making it.

"He does." Rig grabbed a skillet and set it on the stovetop. "I like them both, but the bacon rocks."

"It does. Hey, make enough to slip a slice or two to the mutts." He got out the ingredients and set them on the counter, nudging hips with Rig.

"And enough to slip a slice or two to the cooks." Rig nodded. "Did I tell you Helen called this morning? She's pregnant again."

"Again? She does know what's causing it, right?"

"Apparently. They're tickled. They want a boy this time."

Dick laughed. "Cool." He started mixing up the cheese.

They worked quietly for a few minutes and then he nudged Rig's hip again. "Hey. You think Gary's looking a little thin?"

"A bit. He's been fighting pneumonia, Deuce says. They've had a rough few weeks." He reached out and took hold of Rig's hand. That all sounded a little too familiar for comfort. Rig squeezed. "Deuce picked a hard row to hoe. We just have to support him."

"Yeah. It's just... I know he's not technically my nephew, but I still want him to have good things in his life, you know?"

"He does. He loves Gary, Pretty. That's good."

Dick nodded slowly. "And Gary loves him." He sighed, and held onto Rig's hand a moment longer.

"Well, then. They'll have as long as they have, just like we do." Rig was so... Southern about all that.

"Yeah..."

"What's going on out here?" Rock wandered in, empty beer bottles in hand.

"We're making cheese balls." Rig lifted his face for a kiss. "Oh, do I get beer yet? Or coffee?"

Rock snorted. "How about some tongue?"

Dick leaned against the counter, watching as their lips met, mouths opening for each other. Rig still kissed Rock like it was the whole fucking world, like nothing else mattered. And it still made him horny as hell to watch them make out together.

He reached out, lazily tracing where their lips met. Two tongues slid against his fingers, hot and sweet. It went straight to his cock. He groaned and stepped closer. Rig's arm wrapped around him and the kiss went three-way, went nice and hot. He just melted into it, their tongues all tangling together. There was nothing like it.

Rig jerked suddenly, eyes laughing at them. "Save the bacon!"

"Shit!" He pulled the pan off the heat, turning the bacon so the top side would get done. "Oh, I think we caught it in time."

He laughed and shook his head. It wouldn't have been the first time they'd ruined food by getting wrapped up in each other.

"No burning down the house, y'all." Deuce came lumbering in, grinning. "What's that going in? Pre-meal sammiches?"

"Cheese ball. I swear you eat more than Rock does."

"I'm bigger than Rock is." Deuce grabbed another beer. "Cheese balls are good. Is it the same as Aunt Julie's?"

Rig nodded. "You know it."

"Not that much bigger." Rock flexed.

Rig moaned a little and Deuce rolled his eyes. "Show-off."

"I still got it." Rock looked smug.

"You sure do." Dick let his fingers slide over Rock's bicep. The man was built, sexy.

"Mmhmm. Deuce - either chop green onions or go amuse your man."

Deuce gave them a shit eating grin. "How come I don't believe you want me to chop onions, Uncle Alex?"

Rock cuffed Deuce's back. "Brat. Go."

Deuce saluted sharply. "Yes, Gunny. Whatever you say, Gunny."

Rig started laughing, eyes just dancing. "He's going to kick your young ass, boy."

Rock's eyes narrowed. "I'm giving it some serious thought."

"Ah, but I'm young and quick, Gunny."

"But I've got experience and cunning on my side." Rock just growled, he even looked like he was getting ready to go for it.

"You've also got Uncle Alex and Richard there to distract you."

"Oh, now, you're begging for it." Rock could *move* when he wanted to and Deuce never had a chance. Rock pounced, grabbing Deuce around the shoulders and giving him one hell of a noogie.

"Don't injure him! I need him!" Gary was leaning against the doorframe, grinning and shaking his head.

"He started it." Rock was grinning to beat the band, trying hard to keep his hold on Deuce.

"Of course he did. He's a marine." Gary winked and Deuce wrenched out of Rock's grip, pouncing Gary.

"Was that a crack?" Rock asked, looming.

Rig reached out, fingers sliding down the seam of Rock's jeans. "No, Rock. That's a crack."

Dick started laughing as Rock's face showed his battle over whether to be ticked or turned on. Rig touched again, stroking just a little. Turned on won, just like that and Dick's laughter changed, because husky. Rock looked right at Rig. "I dare you to do that again."

"I like dares." Rig hummed, stroked Rock's ass again, even as Gary and Deuce scooted away

Rock groaned, pushing back into touch.

"I dare you to do it to me, too." Dick grinned, unrepentant.

"Mmhmm." Damn, Rig had fine hands.

Rock wrapped an arm around each of them, tugging them both up against that amazing body.

"Mmm. I was supposed to make a cheese ball..." Rig rubbed against them both.

"There's cheese," Dick pointed out. It wasn't in cheese ball form, but still...

"And there's bacon."

"Uh-huh..." Rig was staring at Rock, watching those lips. "We're cooking supper..."

"Cooking..." Rock licked his lips and leaned in.

"Uh..." Rig moaned, stretching up for the kiss.

"I'll show you cooking." Rock closed the last inches, bringing their mouths together in a kiss that was probably as hot to feel as it was to watch.

Dick watched Rig arch and moan, entire body responding to Rock's kiss. He bit his bottom lip. They had too many people in the house to do all the things he suddenly wanted to do. He settled for grabbing both asses. Squeezed them tight. Rig flushed a little, moaned into Rock's lips, focused and happy.

"We got guests," he whispered, chin resting on Rock's shoulder as he watched them kiss.

"Yeah. We have time." Rig licked at Rock's lips, humming soft. "You still rock my fucking world, Blue."

And Deuce and Gary knew enough to stay away. Hell, maybe they were having a little time out of their own. Rock rumbled, arms going around Rig and tugging him in close. "Of course I do. How do you want me to rock it right now?"

"Another kiss, Blue. We don't have to get creative."

"The chandelier's broken anyway." Rock winked and took Rig's mouth.

Fuck, he loved the way they loved each other. The way they needed. It almost took his knees out, and he locked them in place, bit his lip as his breath caught in his throat.

"More," Dick whispered.

Rig nodded, pushing into the kisses, one after another, eyes holding Rock's. They put on a show for him, tongue sliding together, licking at each other's mouths, teeth clashing at one point as Rock suddenly deepened their kisses. Dick groaned and rubbed against them. Rig's hand slid down his back, rubbing lazy circles against his spine. It made him moan and rub harder, finding Rock's thigh with his cock. Rig was humping Rock, moving slow and easy, just like they were fucking. A part of him wanted to reach in there and get them all naked at least from the waist down, but there was something sexy about doing this fully dressed, so he didn't.

"We should..." Rig moaned, tongue pushing into Rock's lips.

Rock's mouth closed over it, Rock sucking on it, making Dick groan and rub harder. Rock could set Rig on fire. Hell, so could he. They had their own personal cockhound back - healthier and happy, wanting them.

The oven timer beeped and he groaned, breaking away to go check the ham.

Rock lifted Rig up onto the counter, pushing right in between those long thighs, Rig wrapping close. He copped a feel of Rock's ass as he went by, giving it a squeeze. Rock flexed his gluts. Sexy fucking man.

Opening the oven, he checked the ham, basting it and checking the sweet potatoes before he shut the oven door.

"All he needs is a flowery apron and he'd be Mr. Domesticity."

Dick stuck his tongue out at Rock.

"He's amazing. I'd fuck him - in an apron or out." Rig's look made him feel ten fucking feet tall.

"If it's a kink I'd bet he'll put the apron on just for you."

Dick punched Rock in the arm, but he was laughing, too. Rock had his number -- he'd do just about anything for the two of them. He leaned against Rock, hand reaching out to run through Rig's curls. "I would, but Rig wouldn't ask me to."

"Nope. I'll take y'all however I can get you."

"Yeah, feeling's mutual."

"You know it." Rock nodded, wrapping an arm around his neck and turning his head for a kiss that scorched him right through.

Rig moaned, lips tickling his ear. "So fucking good, Pretty."

He nodded, breathless and horny, cock trying to push right out of his jeans.

"The baby-marine and his man are going to be good and wait out there until we give them the all clear," muttered Rock, hands poking under his t-shirt and stroking over his belly.

"Mmm. I could suck y'all. Real quick. No mess."

"And I could do you after." It wouldn't be fair if Rig didn't get off, too.

"I love it when a plan comes together. Do the kid first."

"Why, when I can have both of you at the same time?" Rig slid off the counter, kneeling on the floor.

"Oh. Oh, fuck." He loved it when Rig sucked them together.

Rock chuckled, working his own jeans off for Rig, and Dick was quick to do the same. Their pricks popped out at the same time, hard and eager for Rig's mouth.

"Mine." Rig moaned, drew them together with a moan, tongue sliding over both their cockheads. The heat of Rock's cock was amazing pressed up against his own; Rig's tongue felt even better. He slid his arm around Rock's waist, Rock holding his shoulders. Their free hands slid through Rig's curls as that tongue worked them like only Rig could.

Their cocks were licked and laved, Rig looking about as blissful as could be. Rock's mouth found his and they kissed.

He sucked on Rock's tongue, hips jerking as Rig pushed against his slit. Rig's fingers found his balls, and by Rock's groan, was doing the same with the big guy's. He bit down on Rock's lower lip, earning himself a rumble and a bite of his own. Then Rock slid up under his t-shirt and twisted his nipple ring. He gasped, hips jerking.

"Bet you'll go off first," muttered Rock.

"You're on."

Rig's chuckle vibrated his cock. Goddamn. Rock twisted his ring again and he reacted just like he had before, gasping and jerking and if he wasn't careful, he'd be giving it up without even fighting back. Moaning, he slid his own hand beneath Rock's t-shirt, going for the nipple without the ring first. He was going to build up to the other one. Rig wasn't helping - fortunately he wasn't helping either of them.

Asshole.

Beautiful, hungry asshole.

He tugged Rock's T-shirt right off, mouth moving over Rock's shoulder as his fingers danced their way to the ringed nipple, taking his time. Rock knew it was coming, but not when, and the anticipation was going to make the tug more intense once it happened. Of course before he had a chance to get there, Rock's hand was down the back of his jeans, one finger pushing into him, making lose his train of thought...

Then Rig's finger starting petting his balls, stroking him over and over.

Oh, fuck, he was going to lose it any minute.

He grabbed hold of Rock's nipple ring and tugged, and then twisted, his mouth coming off Rock's skin with a pop. He licked at Rock's earlobe. "You want to fuck me, Rock? You want to fuck Rig? Sink into that sweet cowboy ass?"

Rig and Rock both moaned, the suction getting harder, sweeter. Shit, he was going to come any second. He was going down fighting, though. He slid his hand over Rock's belly, stroking that beautiful six-pack, and then sliding his hand around to find the buddle of nerves just above that rock-hard ass.

"He's so tight and he knows just how to work your cock."
His voice was soft and husky, betraying how close he was.

Rig groaned, pulling hard, taking them both to the root. He
cried out, hips snapping as he lost it and fucked Rig's mouth.
Rock was right there with him, moving counter to him, their
cocks sliding against each other as well as in and out of Rig's
mouth. Rig, like the horndog that he was, just took them in
and demanded more.

By the end, he was just holding onto Rock, not even trying
to hold back anymore, his hips flying. His cry came just
before Rock's, the two of them going off almost at the same
time. Heat flooded around his cock, even as his own spilled
down Rig's throat. Rig took them both, cleaning their cocks
with his tongue.

"Fucking love that mouth." Rock stroked Rig's head,
petted him. "Who won?"

Dick started giggling.

"Me." Rig grinned and reached up, letting them help him
up, the bulge in Rig's jeans obvious.

"That's not an answer," grumbled Rock.

Dick whapped him in the shoulder. "Of course it is. Now
come on, let's return the favor. He dropped to his knees,
mouth Rig through his jeans. Rock joined him a moment
later, fingers working on the button and zipper.

"Oh. Oh, Marines. I need, huh? I do."

"We've got your back."

Dick grinned and shook his head. "No, we've got his front,
Rock."

Rock rolled his eyes and Dick crowed as Rig's prick
pushed out of his jeans and right into his mouth.

"So long as y'all got me. I'm real easy, now."

"Mmm..." He hummed around the prick in his mouth,
sucking gently, wanting to build Rig up slowly. Rock's
fingers dug into Rig's underwear, tugging out the man's sacs,
playing with them.

Rig spread, whimpering just a little. "Fuck, I'm a lucky son
of a bitch."

Dick nodded, moving Rig's prick up and down -- they all were.

"Merry fucking Christmas." Rock licked at one ball, and then other.

"Yeah. Yeah, Blue."

"Share," Rock growled and Dick grinned, pulling of Rig's cock. He'd wondered how long it would be before the big guy demanded a taste.

"Please..." Rig was staring down, grey eyes just shining.

Dick licked the tip, and then mouthed his way down the side of the shaft, giving Rock room to play with the head. As little as Rock gave blowjobs, the man knew exactly - exactly - what Rig needed, working the tip hard, making their cowboy cry out.

Keeping to the base, Dick hummed and licked, stimulating the flesh there. They reached around Rig at the same time, squeezing that cowboy ass. Rig shot hard, going up on tiptoe and bucking, pouring himself into Rock's mouth.

He pushed his tongue into Rock's mouth, teasing the tip of Rig's prick and getting a taste at the same time.

Rig's knees almost buckled, a soft moan leaving him. "Oh, damn. Y'all."

Dick leaned against one thigh, Rock against the other.

"Merry Christmas, y'all. Merry fucking Christmas."

Yeah. It truly was.

Chapter Fifty Nine

Jesus fucking Christ.

Rig had to be the most stubborn, annoying, stubborn, impossible, *stubborn* man in the entire world.

Rock stood at the deck rail, looking out over the ocean, watching the waves come in, his fingers curled around the railing.

Dick came out and handed him a beer. "You two were at it again."

"He's being a stubborn ass."

Dick snorted, like he was the pot calling the kettle black.

"There's a difference. I'm being stubborn to keep him alive -- he's the one who wants to work himself back into the hospital."

"He needs to go back to work, Rock. He's bored, he doesn't feel like he's pulling his weight, he *likes* helping people."

"I've heard it all, Dick. Over and over again. He is not going back to work full time, even if it means I have to go down to the office and drag his sorry ass home every afternoon."

"Shit, the two of you are as stubborn as each other. It's damn near January and you've been at it since Christmas. Give it a rest already."

Dick headed back inside, still grumbling away.

He refused to feel guilty. He just didn't want Rig to get sick again -- it was as simple as that.

It wasn't long before Rig came out - beer in one hand, glass of something clear and bubbly in the other. "Beer?"

"Kid brought me one." He raised the bottle for Rig to see. "You warm enough in that sweater?"

"I'm fine, yeah." Rig set the glass down, grabbed the beer and headed down to the water, gimme cap pulled down low. Rock stood there for another couple minutes. Just on principle. Then he sighed and went after Rig, legs eating up the space between them.

Rig wasn't hurrying, the man was just wandering, head down, beer swinging. It meant something that his redneck hadn't opened it yet. He grunted as he fell into step next to Rig, hands shoved into his pockets.

Rig didn't say anything, but he kept right up with him, the tension in the skinny shoulders easing.

"Nice night," he finally murmured, breaking the silence.

"Yeah. I love it here, you know. I really do."

Rock nodded. "It was a good call. It's a good place. Ours."

"Yeah." Rig sighed, then reached out one hand to him.

He took it with his own, twining their fingers together. Squeezed.

Rig squeezed back, shoulder bumping his. "How can I make this right between us, Blue?"

"Stop being so stubborn about going back full time." He held up his free hand -- he wasn't done yet. "I'm not saying don't go back. Just... you know, ease in."

"The problem with that, Jim, is that you and I both know I'll promise it, but then I'll get in there and have patients and I'll be there full time."

"Then only go in a couple of days a week. I'm not losing you, Rig. I lived with you going off coffee and I didn't put up with that for nothing."

Rig stopped short, staring at him and he braced for the screaming meanies. What he got was a laugh - loud and happy and long.

He stared, a little stunned, one eyebrow going up. Then he shrugged and grinned. He'd take that.

"You know, you drive me crazy sometimes, you big asshole." Rig's arm slid around his and they started walking again.

"Me? What did I do?"

"Same thing I do, when I fuss about you taking your vitamins and your blood pressure meds."

"That's different."

"No, it's not."

"It is. You were in the hospital, Rig." The man had nearly died.

"I didn't have a choice, Jim. This wasn't something I could prevent."

"But you can prevent it from happening again. You can be careful."

Rig needed to learn how to fucking relax and take it easy.

"If it happens again - and it can - I'll just go get the surgery again." Uh-huh. Right. Twenty percent of stomach gone now. Then a little more and a little more and...

And all of whatever savings they'd managed to build back up by then. He stopped walked and turned Rig to face him. "There's already risk with surgery. You need to make sure it doesn't get to that. Kid and I'll help."

"Help what?" Rig looked a little grey. "Hell, I've mortgaged our house, your business. Taken your savings."

"That's not what I was talking about. I was talking about keeping you healthy by helping you keep to the diet, encouraging you to fucking stay home a couple days a week so you don't work yourself into exhaustion!" His Rig was the most stubborn man on the fucking planet.

"I'm so fucking TIRED of this shit!" The beer bottle went flying, smashing against the rocks.

"Well excuse the fuck me for giving a shit whether you live or fucking die."

Rig spun around, eyes flashing. "Don't be a shithead, Goddamn it. I know you give a shit. I know. I'm fucking allowed to hate being sick! I'm fucking allowed to miss chili!

Coffee! Having Goddamn motherfucking ENERGY!" He hadn't seen Rig this furious in years.

"I'm not the fucking bad guy here!"

Rig opened his mouth, staring a second, then just shut it with a snap, deflating. "No. No, you're not. Go on home, Blue. I'm going to take a walk, clean up my mess."

"No, I will not. You pushed me away when you were sick, tried to pretend like everything was fucking normal, and I'm done pretending. You might fucking hate it, but you are not going back to work full time, and you are not staying out here freezing your ass off all by yourself."

"Are you telling me what to do?" He couldn't tell whether Rig was pissed or fucking relieved.

So he just went with the truth. "Yes. I am." He stood there, feet slightly apart in the sand, bracing himself.

"I." Rig swallowed hard, cheeks flushed pink, just vibrating.

"You aren't alone; you don't get to act like you are." He grabbed Rig's shirt and tugged him close.

Rig stepped closer, heart pounding against him. "I'm all fucking stressed out."

"You've been thinking too fucking much." He closed his lips over Rig's, taking that mouth like he always did.

Rig fed him this hollow little noise, skinny body shaking hard. Stubborn fucking cowboy. He spread Rig's lips wider, tongue sweeping through Rig's mouth. The kiss took a second to catch fire, but when it did - Jesus Christ, yeah. Yeah.

He grabbed Rig's ass with one hand, pulling Rig's long, lean body in close. Rig shook against him, cuddling in close, clinging to him. He wrapped his arms around Rig's waist and lifted him up off the sand, heading back toward the house.

"Where're we going?" He got a kiss after each word, Rig slowly fucking relaxing.

"Home." He wasn't fucking Rig in the sand in this cold.

"I like our home." Yeah. Yeah, he knew that.

"Uh-huh." He climbed the deck, Rig not heavy at all.

"You're going to hurt yourself one day." Rig's lips wer
his, too damn cold.

"The day I can't carry you is the day they can put me in the
ground." He growled a little, hurrying up and getting Rig
inside. The house was warm, cozy, a fire in the tiny fireplace,
blankets on the big, heavy sectional. He lay Rig out on the
couch. "Now this is a place to get something started."

Rig nodded, arms reaching up for him. "I need you."

Rock knew that too. He just needed Rig to remember it.
"I've got what you need, Rig. Got it right here."

Those dove grey eyes stared up into him, watching.
Agreeing. He straddled Rig, rolling his cock against Rig's
package.

"H...hey. Hey, Blue." Rig moaned, hips shifting.

A low, rumbly sound came out of him, and he leaned
forward, lips pressing against Rig's mouth as he rubbed them
together. Rig's fingers wrapped around his head, tugged him
in close and held him tight.

"Mmm..." There wasn't anywhere else he wanted to be.

The blankets were pulled down and over him, Rig
cuddling up against him.

"I'll warm you up," he promised. Inside and out.

"Good." Rig nodded, tongue fucking his lips, almost
desperately.

Growling, he sucked on that tongue, fingers tugging Rig's
t-shirt out of his jeans. Rig's belly was hot, skin soft to his
fingers. The man was filling out, the edge of the scar ridged.
He traced that scar, fingers sliding over it again and again.
He'd almost lost his rabbit. Suddenly he needed so fucking
badly, his fingers clawing at the button and zipper on Rig's
jeans.

Rig helped, pulling at his belt, pulling at his shirt. "Jim.
Rock."

"I've got you." He rose up enough to get his own jeans
undone, his prick pushing out, hard and eager.

"Swear it."

"I fucking swear it, Rig." He growled, tearing Rig's jeans along the seam, from the bottom of the zipper up around the ass.

"Rock. Damn, you..." Rig spread for him, just like that.

"Yeah, yeah. Your favorite fucking pair." He slid his fingers behind Rig's balls, finding that little hole and pressing against it.

Rig shook his head, one knee bending. "Nah. They're old. You're so fucking strong."

He chuckled, fingers rolling Rig's balls, and rubbing the smooth, hot patch of skin behind them. "You usually grumble at me when I rip your clothes." He couldn't help flexing a little, too, showing off for his cowboy.

"I'm tired of grumbling."

That had him chuckling again and he slid one finger into Rig's body, up to the first knuckle. "Long as you're not tired of this."

"Never. Need you like air."

Rock nodded. He knew that. Knew it was a mutual feeling, too. He wriggled his finger inside Rig, and then pushed deeper, searching for Rig's gland. Those lips parted when he found it, Rig gasping and jerking, bucking on his touch.

"Yeah. Just like that." He pegged it again, his other hand rubbing across Rig's belly.

"Uh. Uh-huh. Rock." Rig's shoulders raised up off the couch.

He kept moving that one finger, watching the flush travel up Rig's neck and over his cheeks. "Could do this all night long."

"That'd drive me out of my Goddamn mind." Like that was supposed to stop him.

"Oh, I'd mix it up now and then." He danced his fingers across Rig's belly again, circling Rig's navel.

Fuck, he loved those needy little cries. He alternated between pushing against Rig's gland and sliding his fingers over the skinny chest, and almost touching Rig's hard prick. His Rabbit was his - one hundred percent, no question. His.

Bending, he brought their mouths together, taking that mouth as he worked a second finger into Rig's body, stretching that tight hole. Rig fucked his lips, that tongue pushing in and in, needing him. He spread his fingers wide, his cock nudging against Rig's as he rocked his hips. This rough, raw little sound pushed into his mouth, Rig grunting for him.

"I want this forever, Rig. I want to fuck you until the end of fucking time." He wasn't going to lose Rig. He was not.

"Okay." Rig's hand cupped his cheek, staring at him. "I promise."

Nuzzling into Rig's palm, he slid his fingers out of that tight heat and started rubbing the tip of his cock over Rig's hole, wetting it with the come already leaking out of him.

"Yeah. Yeah, Blue. In me." Demanding cowboy.

He didn't say anything, just pushed, letting Rig's need do the work, that hungry body swallowing him up just like that. Fuck. It was sheer fucking heaven. Rig's fingers dug into his shoulders, pushing hard enough to leave bruises. He grunted and began to move, coming nearly all the way out inch by inch, and then pushing back in just as slowly. Rock swore he could feel Rig's body clutching at him, every single fucking inch.

"More. More, Blue." Rig licked his lips, just giving it up for him.

"I'll give you more." He pushed harder, faster, mouth sliding on Rig's.

"You give me what I fucking need." Yeah, he knew that too. He crushed their lips together. No more talking. Not right now. Good thing Rig was all over that, kissing him like there was no fucking tomorrow, tongue fighting with his. His hips moved faster, ass pumping as he went for it. Rig's body rippled around his cock, milking it, milking him. With a shout, he came, his fingers wrapping around Rig's prick and tugging hard.

Rig jerked, shuddered. "Again. Close."

He pushed into Rig again, hand squeezing Rig's hot flesh tight. His Rabbit just gave it up for him, seed pouring over his fingers. He hummed into Rig's mouth, hand moving easily over slick skin, his weight settling slowly, pushing Rig into the cushions.

Rig hummed, relaxing under him, holding on tight. He pushed his face against Rig's neck, breathing in. He fucking loved that smell.

"Mmm." Rig's breath was slowing, hands not letting him go even a little.

Shifting just enough so he wasn't crushing Rig, he let his eyes close. They could nap before ringing in the New Year.

Just as he drifted off he felt Dick's kiss to his forehead, heard one given to Rig, too.

Chapter Sixty

"Okay, Linda. You look like you're healing up good, ma'am. I don't think you'll need to come see me again." Rig bandaged up the single mom's hand. "Unless you decide to tangle with repairing that washing machine again."

"I'm glad you're back, Doc. The others are okay, but they don't get me like you do."

No.

No, Rig didn't expect so. Linda was an accident waiting to happen and had a fascination with power tools that he could understand and appreciate.

"I'm glad to be back. I was just supposed to do paperwork this week, but I heard you were coming in." He hugged her and pointed her out. "Stop by and check with Mary Alice, please, but you should be good."

Helen wandered by, just beaming, so happy about being pregnant again it hurt. "Are you supposed to be working? It's not the new year yet, honey."

"Hmm?" He went for innocent. "That wasn't working. That was being friendly and taking out stitches. Is there anything else I need to do?"

"You need to come on home." Rock stood behind Helen, Dick right there next to his Blue.

"We came to rescue you." Dick's eyes were twinkling. "You know, from tiring yourself out on your first day."

"I wouldn't do that, would I?" He rolled his eyes, but grinned. "How's the gym?"

"Memberships' up." Rock gave Helen a smile, a nod of the head, but he was the focus of that gaze.

"Everyone's getting ready for those new year's resolutions. I was thinking we could do a late lunch -- I want something Mexican."

"Oh, yum." He nodded, stomach growling. "I could handle that. I'm starving."

"You didn't eat the lunch the kid packed for you?" Rock shook his head and came in. "Did it even make it into your bag?"

"Huh?" He blinked up, a little confused. He made lunches. Usually. Or he had.

Dick just smiled at him. "We'll all have to get used to the new routine, yeah? It was nice having you home all the time."

"You'd get bored having me home all the time. Just let me make sure nobody needs anything..."

Helen laughed, shook her head. "Go. Have. Lunch. Doc."

"Listen to the woman, Rig." Rock actually took his arm, encouraged him up out of his chair.

He grabbed his paperwork up, let Dick pack up his laptop. "I'll be back in tomorrow, Helen."

"No, Doc. Come back on the third. Take your holiday." Helen kissed his cheek. "We'll both drink sparkling grape juice."

Rock just beamed at her. "She might need a raise, Rig."

"Might? Pshaw. I definitely need a raise." Helen went up on tiptoe, kissed Rock's cheek.

"Quit seducing my marines, lady. You got a sailor of your own."

Rock put his arm around Helen and gave Rig a wink. "Sorry, ma'am. Tempting, but wrong equipment."

They all laughed, Rig shrugging his coat on. "Come on, you hooligans. You promised enchiladas."

"You want one of us to drive your car for you?" Dick asked as they made their way out into the chilly day.

"Nah. I'm good." Things were a little sparkly, but not bad.

"Cool. I'll ride with you." Dick's arm went around his shoulders.

"Hey." Rock glowered.

Dick laughed. "Hey, we brought your truck. I get to ride in the little white sportscar."

"We could all go in the car." Rig's hand was shaking a little - man, it was time to eat.

Rock looked him over and nodded. "Yeah. But I'm driving." His Blue grabbed the keys from him.

"Hey!" He blinked over. "I'm okay to drive, man."

"Yeah, but I'm the Rocketman, and I'm driving."

Dick took his briefcase and laptop bag, headed over to put them in the trunk of the car. Jesus, they just hovered. All the time.

"You can ride shotgun," Rock told him, opening the passenger door for him, leaning close to give him a peck.

"Only if you give me a better kiss." There ought to be a benefit to being hovered over.

A smile bloomed over Rock's face. "Oh, I can do that."

Rock pulled him close, eyes looking into his as their mouths closed together. Oh, fuck him, that was so much better than bitching. Tongue pushing into his mouth, Rock rumbled, hand sliding down to his ass. Heat pressed up against his back, Dick's tongue sliding across the sweet spot on his neck.

"Mmm." Okay. Okay. Focus. This was work.

Work.

Not necking time.

"Lunch. Queso. Beer." Right, like Rock'd go for that.

Rock chuckled. "Get in the car. We'll get you something real for lunch."

Dick's fingers slid across his ass as his Pretty climbed into the back seat.

"Mmm. It was good, to be back." He could feel it, though, feel all these little aches and pains. "I think I need to come work out a few days a week, though. I don't have any stamina."

Dick's fingers slid over his shoulders as he sat back, rubbing as Rock drove. "I bet they were happy to see you."

"They were. Helen's just tickled to be expecting again and the other guys have been sharing my patients." Not that he had guilt...

Rock glanced over at him. "Well I bet you've taken on your share of their patients for them over time."

"Yeah, but not for six weeks, as a rule." He stretched a little, toes curling.

"They wouldn't have done it if they didn't think you were worth it," murmured Dick, fingers digging in a little harder.

"Oh..." Oh, God. That felt so Goddamn good. "Uh... What?"

"We're here." Rock pulled into the parking lot of their favorite Mexican restaurant and Dick gave him shoulders one last squeeze.

"Man, that was fast." He grinned, hopped out. Lord have mercy, he felt like he could eat a zebra.

"Nah, you just fell asleep there for a bit," Rock deadpanned.

"Bitch." Naps were healthy. Rock said so all the time.

Rock's arm went around his shoulders. "Calling me names. Cranky. You must be hungry."

"I am. I'm starving half to death."

"Let's get you fed."

Rosa greeted them at the door, all smiles. "Dr. Alex! We haven't seen you in so long."

"Hey, beautiful! I've missed you!" He grabbed her in a hug, kissed her cheek, chuckling as she poked his belly.

"You're skin and bones! Why haven't you been in? I can fix this."

"He needs lots of meat, Rosa."

Dick nodded in agreement with Rock. "Yeah, we need to fatten him up."

"I can. I have a good special today - pollo Mexicano."

"I'm wanting an enchilada, honey. Just one, please."

"Just one? No. No, at least two. Maybe three."

Rock spoke up before he had a chance to reply. "Yeah, get him three, Rosa. And I want the beef carnitas."

Dick didn't bother looking at the menu. "Can I have some tacos, please?"

"Three cervezas, too?" Rosa gathered the menus up.

"No." Rock shook his head. "A milk and two Cokes."

Oh, now. That was going too far. "You drinking milk, man?"

"Hey -- I'm not having a beer."

"I'll take a milk, too -- so make it two milks and a Coke," interrupted Dick.

"Make it three Cokes. Please." Rig wasn't going to play this game. Not in front of Rosa.

Rock glared at him.

Rosa clucked. "I'll get you water to start with and you can give your drink orders when I come back, yes?"

"Sure, honey. Thanks." He could feel the fury, climbing up his back.

As soon as she was out of earshot, Rock spoke up. "You need the fucking protein that's in the milk, Rig."

"I'm not a child, Rock. I'm a fucking PA. I know what I need."

"Yeah? Then how come you're not ordering the milk yourself?"

"Because I don't *want* milk. I'm not five. Okay?"

Rock crossed his arms. "You need the fucking protein."

Okay. Okay, fine. He stood up, nodded. "Order whatever. I'm going to hit the head."

He was going to hit the head, then walk back to the fucking clinic and get Helen to take his ass in. He wasn't a kid, Goddamn it.

Chapter Sixty One

Dick stared at Rig's ass as it disappeared down the hall into the back of the restaurant, and then he turned to glare at Rock.

"Nice one."

"What?"

"He isn't five." Dick shook his head. "You can't treat him like he is."

"He needs the fucking protein!"

"He's having chicken enchilladas! Give him a break, Rock."

"This shit could come back you know."

"For fuck's sake, Rock, I know that. Rig knows that." He leaned forward, looking into Rock's fucking stunning blue eyes. Rig needed those eyes to look at him with nothing but want.

"He doesn't want to get sick again either, Rock, but you're not letting him live. Shit, you need to learn to compromise, to let it go now and then. So he doesn't have the milk today -- he's not having beer, either, so just let him have the Coke or a ginger ale or something."

Rock rolled his eyes. "Fine. Why don't I go buy him a pack of cigarettes while I'm at it?"

"Fuck off, Rock." He glared over. "Are you going after him or do I have to?"

"You're the fucking peacemaker."

"And you're the one he's pissed off at." He'd give Rock a ten count and then he'd kick the big jerk and go find Rig himself.

"Jesus fucking Christ." Rock's chair scrapped across the floor as he stood.

Dick watched Rock's ass as it disappeared down the hall to the back of the restaurant, and then sat back with a sigh.

He still hated it when they argued.

***

Rock grumbled to himself all the way to the men's room.

He wanted everything back to normal, God damn it.

And maybe Dick was right, maybe he was still treating Rig like he was fragile. Better that than lose the asshole.

He tried the door, cursing when it proved to be locked. He knocked. "Rig? Let me in."

"Rock, I can piss by myself."

"I fucking know that." Christ, he wasn't going to fucking talk through the fucking door.

The door unlocked and Rig stepped back. "I'm done. You can have it."

"I came back to talk to you."

"Why?"

He opened his mouth and closed it again. Somehow he didn't think saying 'because Dick said I should' was going to go over well. "Because..." He growled. "Because you're pissed off."

"I am. I don't want you hounding my ass. I am not a kid, Goddamn it, stop treating me like one."

He leaned against the doorway, arms across his chest. "I'm not trying to treat you like a kid." He was being supportive for fuck's sake.

"Then what, Rock? I'm doing what the surgeons said. Mentrier's doesn't happen because of something I did."

"I'm trying, Rig. I'm trying to be fucking supportive."

"I know, but you're pushing too fucking hard, man. I'm not self-destructive. I'm not a kid."

"I should just stick to what I'm good at."

"Yeah." Rig nodded, grey eyes fastened onto him. "I like what you're good at. You kick my ass when things go too far."

"So. Fucking and ass-kicking. I can do that." He jerked his head back toward their table. "We should go back. Eat our fucking lunch before anyone keels over from hunger."

"Yeah. Did we order queso for our chips?" Oh, hell yeah. He felt himself relaxing some, just knowing Rig was going to let it go for a bit, just knowing his Rabbit was fucking trying.

"I don't think so, but you know Rosa is going to bring it and salsa for them." He put his hand in the small of Rig's back, and Rig didn't bristle, relaxing him further.

Dick looked up as they came back to the table, smiling wide when he saw them. "All right. We're going to eat."

"Yeah, it smells good in here." Rig sat, grabbed a glass of water and drank half of it. "Y'all decide whether we're going partying on New Year's or staying home?"

"I want to stay home." Dick grinned as Rosa came by with three cokes and chips, queso and salsa.

"Just the three of us, food, movies, a little champagne at midnight."

Rock opened his mouth and Dick shot him a glare. He finally nodded as he sat. "All right. A little champagne never hurt anyone." He looked over at Rig; he could be reasonable and compromise.

"Sounds good to me." Rig dug in to the queso, humming softly. "We can fire up the hot tub."

Dick grabbed some chips, too, dipping eagerly into the queso. Rock stuck to the salsa, trying not to grumble as Rig picked up his Coke. Rig didn't drink much of it, though, going back to the water. They munched through the chips, Rig groaning as the enchiladas arrived. "Man, I shouldn't have ordered those too."

Rock snorted. "Like the kid and I won't eat anything you have left over."

But he was going to make sure there wasn't that much for him and Dick to eat. He might be compromising, but that didn't mean he wasn't going to try to stuff Rig as full as possible.

"Y'all have at. I'm full." Rig leaned back, stretched. "Smells good, though."

"So have a bite. Rosa'll be insulted if you don't eat anything at all." He just barely kept himself from leaning over and cutting a chunk off for Rig.

"Yeah, okay. One bite." Rig nodded, took a bite, humming happily. "Oh, that's good."

"Why not finish the one you started, and then Rock and I can finish the other two without fighting over who gets more?" Dick took a bite of his enchilada, looking innocent as pie.

"I don't think I've got room, kid." Still, Rig took another bite.

"How're the tacos?" Rock asked, getting ready to dig into his own meal. It was fucking good food, always had been.

Dick just nodded around a mouthful, passing one of the tacos over to him. "Give it a try and let Rig had a taste, too."

Oh, man, the kid was slick.

Rock took a bite and passed the taco over. Rig took a bite of it, humming a little. "Oh, that's nice. We should make tacos more often. Momma used to make them once a week."

"You can have the rest of that one if you want, I've got plenty here."

"Yeah? Thanks, Pretty." Rig nibbled at it, actually finishing the damned thing.

Shit, the kid had the touch.

Dick shot him a smug look.

Well, he could do it, too. "Want some of my carnitas?"

"Are they good? I'm really full..." Still, Rig looked over, smelled them. "One bite."

"Here, I'll trade plates with you." He grabbed Rig's plate with the left over enchiladas. There were about half the carnitas left.

Dick just grinned and stole one of the enchiladas. Rig ate a handful of bites of the pork, all of them relaxing, easy chatter starting. Goddamn, this worked for him.

When Rosa came by again, Dick asked for a deep fried ice cream and he wanted the sopapillas. "And decaf coffees all around."

He raised an eyebrow and checked for Rig's reaction.

"Mmm. Lots of cream for me, please. I'm still easing in."

Dick's foot rubbed up along his calf and he rolled his eyes.

"What's wrong, Rock? You good?" Rig was always fucking watching.

"I'm fine. Kid's trying to start something under the table." That'd serve Dick for 'rewarding' him for being 'good'.

Dick grinned unrepentantly. "Call me impatient. I can't wait 'til we get home."

"Horndog." Rig chuckled, leaned back and winked. "Y'all going into the gym tomorrow?"

"You gonna come with us if we do?" Rock slid his foot up Dick's calf, and then Rig's. The kid had the right idea. Dessert and then home to fuck.

"Sure. I have all the paperwork I need to finish. I could come and distract you."

"We could set a routine up for you, too. Get some muscles on those bones."

"Yeah? I probably ought to, huh? Get my stamina back, get to feeling better."

Shit, if Dick beamed any harder, Rock was going to beat him. Then Dick's foot was back, rubbing along his thigh. Kid had a one track mind. He liked that. At least until their desserts showed, and then Dick was all about the food.

They couldn't get Rig to eat that, but the man oohed and aahed over the coffee, drinking it down. He and Dick shared theirs between them, the kid feeding him spoonfuls of ice cream.

It was sexy as hell.

Rig was watching, eyes heavy-lidded, just hot as fuck. "Y'all are something else."

Dick fed him another spoonful of ice cream.

"We try." The kid winked at Rig, and Rock nearly choked from laughing.

"Lord have mercy." Rig chuckled, empty coffee cup hitting the table. "Y'all finish up and we'll have ourselves a long, slow afternoon."

Dick put down his spoon. "We're done."

Rock laughed and pulled his wallet out of his pocket. "We are."

"Good deal. I am too. Take me home, huh?" Rig stood, hard on obvious in those loose jeans.

He threw some bills on the table and got up, following that ass like he was attached to it by a string, Dick right there with him.

Rig moved like the man knew they were watching, hips swinging, swaying nice and easy. He grinned over at Dick. "You think we can break the land speed records to get to home?"

"We can try."

"Quit yammering, Marines. Home." Demanding cowboy.

Rock twirled the keys. "Get in the car. We need to get home and take care of a few things."

"Just a few?" Rig shook it any more and Rock was going to hump the sexy fucker right here.

"Yep." He pointed at himself. "One." Then at Dick. "Two." And then Rig. "Three. That would be a few."

"Point taken." Rig slid in the car, looking smug as hell.

"Oh, no, I haven't taken that point yet. Just you wait 'til we get home."

He and Dick climbed in and he started up the engine, headed them home. Rig settled, eyes closing before they got three blocks. He met Dick's eyes in the rearview mirror, shook his head and grinned. Dick grinned back, shrugged.

"We've got to convince him to actually eat a lot of little meals instead of picking at one or two meals a day."

"I'm fresh out of ideas," he told the kid, and Dick nodded.

It wasn't far to home, and Dick's fingers squeezed Rig's shoulders as they got there, waking him up gently.

"Mmm. Home?" Rig got out of the car, moving like a zombie, still mostly asleep.

Rock shook his head again. "And he wanted to work a full day."

The kid opened the front door and he made sure the car was locked up and then followed them in.

"I vote for bed," Dick suggested as he closed the front door. "That way if we want to get busy, we can get busy, if we want to nap, we can nap."

"I vote for busy, then nap, then busy again." Rig grabbed his hand, petting one of the dogs along the way. "Then I'll make you supper."

He squeezed Rig's hand. "You think you're up for that?"

"I'm really good at busy." Rig leaned up, kissed him hard enough that he shorted out a little, eyes rolling back in his head.

Rock didn't think that was the part he'd been wondering about, but frankly, he didn't exactly care right now. He grabbed Rig's ass and took another kiss, groaning as he felt it to his toes.

Rig climbed right up his body, clinging to him, tongue fucking his lips and just driving him crazy. He automatically shifted his hold to carry Rig and he walked down the hall toward their bedroom, cock rubbing against Rig with every fucking step. His. Fuck, yeah. His hungry, horny cockhound. Rock's fingers squeezed, belly tight as Rig humped him.

He could feel Dick's hands on him, guiding him to the bed, pushing when they got there. He fell back onto it, laughing into Rig's mouth, the air whooshing out of his lungs. Rig grinned for him, then pushed back into the kisses, moaning for him. He lost himself in it, in the feeling of Rig over him, Dick's fingers sliding on them, working their clothes off, the kid telling them to move this way or that.

Rig's skin was warm as hell, that full cock sliding on his abs, leaving hot, wet kisses.

"Want you, Rabbit."

"Yours, Blue. Balls to bones." And that was the fucking truth.

"You know it." He grabbed Rig's ass and squeezed, rubbing them together.

Dick straddled them, on his hands and knees over them. Rig reached up, fingers sliding over his shoulders, then up the kid's arms. Dick's sweet sounds filled the air, the kid giving it all up for the simple touches.

"Y'all's." That smile just rocked his socks.

"You fucking know it." He slid his prick against Rig's, Dick's hot like a brand against the small of his back.

Rig nodded, pushing up to kiss him. "I do, you beautiful bastard."

Shit, Rig could still make him feel ten fucking feet tall. Rig's hand wrapped around the back of his head, holding him right there so Rig could kiss him stupid. Dick reached around him, fingers slick, working toward Rig's hole. He could tell when the kid got there, too, Rig's moan vibrating his tongue, making him growl a little.

"Gonna make him ready for you." Dick's murmur made Rig jerk beneath him. "Two fingers now."

"More." Rig's hips rolled, eyes heavy-lidded.

Rock grinned. "Such a slut."

"Yours." Rig's smile was fucking hot.

"Yep."

Laughing, Dick muttered three, making Rig jerk again.

Rig was starting to pant, to shift and breathe into his mouth in rhythm with those hips. Fuck, he got off on this, on the way they all fucking worked together.

His fingers found Rig's nipple ring and tweaked it. Those eyes went wide, teeth sinking in his bottom lip.

"Shit, hurry, Dick."

The kid just laughed and did something that made Rig jerk hard.

"Need. Need, fuck. More. Come on."

"You wanna fuck him together, Rock? We haven't done that in so long." Oh, fuck. Dick had the dirtiest fucking mouth.

Rig whimpered, licked his lips. "Pretty."

"Yeah. Yeah, kid. Lots of lube."

Dick chuckled and bit his shoulder. Rig surged up, lips crashing against Dick's, their tongues teasing his skin. Fuck, they were sexy motherfuckers. Lucky for him, they were his.

"Dick on the bottom, Rig. You need to ride him for this."

"You... you just want to watch. See your cock next to his inside me."

Well, no shit. "Uh-huh." He gave Rig a hard kiss, and then rolled off as Dick moved, settled on the mattress next to them. He whispered into Rig's ear. "Give the kid a little lick to slick him up."

Rig shuddered, rocked against him. "Yeah. Yeah, Blue. 'mere, Pretty, gimme that cock."

Dick's hand wrapped around Rig's head, and Rock watched, jacking himself slowly as that amazing mouth worked Dick's cock. Dick started whispering to Rig, a dull flush climbing up his Rabbit's back. Oh, fuck. That was fine. He had to stop them, though, when Dick's hips started jerking, humping up into Rig's mouth.

"Okay, slow it down there. We've got a plan here." Dick stared over at him, swallowing hard, eyes just dazed as Rig's tongue slid over the long cock. He slid his hands up Rig's back and squeezed his shoulders, tugging him back a little. "Don't make the kid come, Rig."

The kid whimpered.

"No. No, I want y'all both." Rig's lips trailed over Dick's belly. "Need it."

Groaning, Dick pushed up into Rig's touches, hand wrapping around his own cock. "Come on and take me, Rig."

Rig swooped down, kissed the tip of the kid's cock before shifting up and pushing down, sinking onto Dick's cock.

"Oh fuck..." Dick's hips jerked up and then settled, the kids hands wrapping around Rig's hips.

"Mmm... " Rock watched for a minute, admiring the fuck out of his men, and then he encouraged Rig to lean forward, exposing that filled hole for him.

Rig moved, nice and easy, riding that long, skinny cock, up and down.

"Sexy motherfuckers."

He shifted, moving between Dick's legs as they spread to give him room. Slicking up his cock, he got himself ready, the smell of the three of them something special. Rig leaned down, gave Dick a kiss as the kid's hands landed on Rig's ass, spreading his Rabbit wide. Bending, he kissing the top of Rig's crack, his fingers sliding down to rub where Rig and Dick met.

Then he settled in, guiding his prick to that little hole and pressing in.

Rig's motions slowed, that tiny ring of muscles spreading for him. He watched, the sight of his cock pushing in next to Dick's making his balls ache. The feel of it nearly blew the top of his head off.

"Y'all..." Rig moaned for them, shivering, letting them in.

He stroked his hand along Rig's spine, his fingers going right down to where he and Dick were squeezed tightly together, to where they were both pushed into Rig. Groaning, he rubbed Rig's stretched flesh.

"Oh. Oh, fuck. Rock. Blue..." Oh, he felt that. His hips jerked, pushing in all the way. Rig's body was so fucking hot and tight, squeezing him and Dick together.

"Yeah, fuck." He nuzzled Rig's back, mouth sliding, taking in the salty flavor of Rig's skin.

"Full. Full of y'all." Rig shuddered, moaning for him.

"Uh-huh." He kissed Rig's spine. "Okay, Dick, let's move. Nice and slow."

The kid pulled out as he pushed in, the two of them finding just the right rhythm. Rig didn't move, just relaxed and let them move and take that tight little ass. It was fucking amazing, feeling Dick's cock inside Rig with his own.

"We could do this for fucking forever."

"Okay. Hard... hard to work out like this, Rocketman." Oh, if Rig could make jokes, he wasn't doing this right.

He pushed in a little harder, Dick picking up the pace right along with him. He reached around with one hand, finding Dick's hand on Rig's cock, so he slid up to tweak that little ring in Rig's nipple.

"Blue." Rig's ass clenched, body rippling around him. Them. Squeezing him and Dick together.

"Yeah, that's better." He pushed harder, knowing one of them was hitting Rig's gland, maybe both of them. He twisted Rig's nipple ring harder, mouth finding Rig's spine.

Fuck. He could feel each tug inside Rig, feel the heat pouring off the fine bastard. Dick's noises were getting louder and louder, the kid's free hand coming around to grab hold of his hip.

"I... Touch me. Y'all. Please."

That had Dick jacking Rig faster, and Rock reached around to cup Rig's balls, rolling them with his fingers. Hell, yeah. Rig bucked, hips rolling, that skinny body clenching around him.

He bit at the back of Rig's neck, fucking harder, fingers sliding on the smooth skin. He smelled Rig's orgasm - fucking smelled it. Dick was next, the long cock squeezed against his own throbbing, heat spreading out from the tip. He couldn't fucking hold back with the two of them shooting, and he roared, coming hard.

Rig slumped down, panting against Dick. "Fuck. Fuck. Good."

"You fucking know it." He and Dick stayed buried deep inside Rig, all three of them panting together.

Rig nodded, licked the kid's shoulder, just relaxing. He touched them both, their skin good under his fingertips, damp and warm. Rig's lips teased his fingers, nudging them gently. With a groan of disappointment, he slid from Rig's body. He didn't move, though, staying close.

"You good?" he asked.

"Happy. Nap?" Rig was almost asleep already.

"Uh-huh." He might even move over so they didn't crush the kid.

"'kay." Rig shivered, then sighed, falling right to sleep.

It made him rumble a little and Dick's hand patted his arm. "He's fine, Rock. Just napping. Like I'm going to, too."

That made him snort. "Sure, sure, you two just roll over and go to sleep and I'm the one without any romance?"

Not that he wasn't half asleep himself.

He patted Dick and Rig and let it all go.

Chapter Sixty Two

"Rock! Rock, help!" Oh, fuck him. He'd gotten bent down to lift the ham out of the oven and the fucking thing was too heavy, Rig's arms just like jelly. He must've overdone at the gym yesterday and, if he wasn't in danger of boiling his nuts, he wouldn't holler, but...

"Help, y'all!!"

"Rig! What the fuck!" Rock and Dick nearly collided in the door way as they hurried into the kitchen.

"I can't lift it. It's hot. Grab hot pads." He couldn't decide whether to laugh or get fucking pissed off.

"I've got it." Rock grabbed the hot pads and picked the pan out of his hands, setting it up on the counter.

Dick came around to close the oven and rub his arms. "You okay?"

"Yeah, that's what I want to know." Rock was practically growling.

"Yeah. I just... I'm fine. I just couldn't lift it."

Rock folded his arms across his chest. "Since when can't you lift a fucking ham out of the oven?"

Okay, pissed off won. "Since I got fucking old and sick, I guess. I'll be back. Don't touch the Goddamn ham."

Rig turned on his heel and headed out the back door, keys in hand. The stores'd be open for a while yet. He'd just get some stuff and get home before the fucking Happy New Year drunk assholes.

Rock was right on his heels, catching him before he got off the deck. "Where the hell are you going?"

"To the store. I'll be back." Don't. Don't push. This was hard enough.

"You sure you're up to the fucking store?"

"I'm sure. I don't have to pick anything up or think too hard. I can manage. Hell, if I get tired, I can use one of those fucking electric carts." Jesus. Somebody just fucking shoot him.

"Make a list of what you're missing and the kid can go for you."

"No. No one's fucking going to the store for me. You go inside and I'll be back." If he was any more reasonable, his head would explode.

"You should maybe reconsider the offer as you're obviously already wrung out. Christ, Rig. It's called taking it easy."

"I'm not wrung out. Jesus fucking Christ. My muscles are sore. I'm recovering from motherfucking surgery and it HURTS to pick shit up and that fucking ham weighs thirty pounds! I'm not a fucking invalid! I'm sorry that I'm not perfect specimens of manhood like the two of you, but God DAMN it, Rock, I'm trying!" Man, he hadn't had a good, loud beller in a while.

"I know you're fucking recovering from that Goddamned surgery. That's my fucking point! You think you can just go out and work full-time and do everything you used to be able to and you fucking can't. Not yet. And anytime I try and help make things easier you get all holier than fucking thou and act like I'm an asshole treating you like a baby."

"I DO NOT! Jesus Christ, you asshole, you think this is easy? You think any of this is easy? I ASKED for help, didn't I?"

"No. No, easy is not the fucking word I would use. Not for fucking any of it."

"Hey." Dick came out with jackets for both of them. "Come on, let's all go -- we'll grab some cinnamon buns or something while we're out. Make it fun."

They both stopped, stared at Dick. "Dick, we're having a fight. Me and Rock. Screaming, hollering. I might even throw a rock. Not *at* him, just throw one."

Dick's mouth fell open. "I know... but... I hate it when you guys fight."

"You could throw a rock, too." Cinnamon buns actually sounded pretty good. Cinnamon buns and hot chocolate...

Rock snorted. "Neither of you could throw me."

"Oh. Oh, that was funny." He looked at Rock, started chuckling. The chuckles turned to honest, happy laughter just like that. His Blue was so fucking *funny*.

"What?" Rock looked slightly put out, which had Dick laughing, and then Rock pounced his Pretty, giving Dick a noogie.

Rig rescued his coat, shrugging it on and watching. Jesus, they just couldn't let him stay in a snit. He settled on the steps, Trouble and Lucy coming over for scritches. His marines scuffled for a bit, tussling and wrastling and laughing, Dick trying his best to throw Rock, or at least push him around. His Blue prevailed, though, the man still the strongest son of a bitch he knew. They were both chuckling and flushed when they were done, Dick calling "uncle".

"So, y'all. Did you want hot chocolate and cinnamon rolls?" He leaned, not able to fight his grin.

They answered "Yes!" together, Rock punching Dick's arm, and Dick punching back.

"You really need stuff at the store?" Dick asked.

"No. I was just needing out, more than anything."

"So are we going out to the mall to get the hot chocolate and rolls, or are we gonna make 'em here?"

"We make 'em at home we can do blow jobs waiting for the rolls to cook," Rock pointed out.

"We have some in the freezer that just need an hour in the oven. Do we have stuff for cocoa?"

Dick nodded. "Yeah, we've got some left. I vote for blow jobs at home."

"Yeah, me, too," added Rock, holding his hand out for Rig.

He reached out, fingers twining with Rock's. "Sounds like a plan, Marines." He was getting soft in his old age.

Rock pulled him up and against all those muscles, amazing blue eyes smiling down at him. "Sounds like a fucking good plan, I'd say."

"You know, we used to fight longer." He pushed close, face lifting for a kiss.

"Yeah, we did." Rock's lips moved against his. "We just know we got better things to do now."

"We do." And fuck knew they didn't have time to waste.

"Mmm..." Rock deepened the kiss.

"Hey, let's get back inside before we start anything." Dick grabbed their arms and started tugging.

Rock grabbed him, lifting him up and heading into the house. "Don't you drop me."

"Please. I have never dropped you."

No. No, Rock never had. "There's always a first time." He kissed the corner of Rock's mouth, licking a little.

Rock snorted. "Not for that. This ass is worth more than gold."

His cheeks heated, making his skin feel tight. Jesus, he didn't know how Rock did that - managed to make him all fluttery like a girl - but the man was still fucking good at it.

Those blue eyes grinned at him. "I bet if you asked real nice, Dick would get the cinnamon buns going while you blow me."

"What? You're not going to suck me off? Man..." He couldn't fight the grin, so he didn't try too hard.

"And deprive you of the taste of my cock? I don't think so."

"Man..." They plopped onto the sofa, Rig landing in Rock's lap, both chuckling. "You're a thoughtful bastard, aren't you?"

"I am. Always thinking of you and Dick."

"Yep. A gem of a guy."

Rock started tickling and he started laughing, the big hands knowing just where to touch him. Blue's lips met his, sucking his laugh right into that hot mouth. He pushed against Rock's belly, cock seriously considering getting hard. Rock's fingers slid through his hair, tilting his head back to deepen the kiss.

Oh.

Oh, hello.

He let Rock blow his mind, tongue fucking his lips and stealing his breath.

"You've got the best fucking mouth."

He hummed in response, diving into the kiss, focusing on driving Rock nuts. Groans and moans came out, pushing into his mouth as Rock arched beneath him. They should fight more often.

Rig tilted Rock's head, fingers rubbing the man's temples. The kiss got deeper, a little harder, those blue eyes shining into his own. Fucking loved that son of a bitch. All of him.

The kiss broke slowly, Rock's smile all for him.

"Hey." He leaned in, just staring. "Need you."

"You fucking have me -- head to fucking toe."

"Thank God." He reached down and worked Rock's belt open, started unbuttoning Rock's shirt.

Rock's hands wandered over him, the thick thighs spreading for him. He could smell Rock, cock pushing against the zipper. His groan slid from him, his mouth starting to water. Oh, damn. He wanted.

Rock's eyes lit up; his Blue knew.

Fucker.

Beautiful. Fine. Stunning fucker.

He fished that heavy, full cock out, fingers sliding along the shaft. Rock's low groan vibrated right down his spine. He slid down, shrugging out of his coat, lips open as he headed for that cock.

"Yeah, that's it, Rig. You know you want it."

"You do, huh?" He wanted.

"Uh-huh." Rock bucked up a little, prick bumping his chin.

"I'm not the only one who wants it." He rubbed, letting Rock feel his stubble.

"Fuck no." Rock jerked, and his hands slid through Rig's hair. "Fucking love this mouth."

Yeah. Yeah, he knew. Rig took Rock in, humming low as that heavy cock split his lips. Rock's fingers wandered restlessly, sliding over his scalp, tracing the curves of his cheeks. He sighed, settled in his bones and right where he wanted to be. His mouth moved on that fat cock, tongue knowing just where to push and touch and caress.

"Fuck... there is nothing on earth like your mouth, Rig." Rock's voice was husky, need clear as a fucking bell. His fingers stroked the heavy balls, rolling them just a little in thanks. Groaning, Rock spread his legs wider, the hands in his hair opening and closing. It was the fucking easiest thing on earth, touching and sucking, fucking making love to that cock and letting everything else go.

Low groans and happy sighs came from Rock, the sounds turning into a moan whenever he went for the sweet spots.

"Oh, fuck, just like that." Rock's hands petted and touched, making him hum around the flesh in his mouth.

He felt more than heard Dick coming into the room, his Pretty curling up in the armchair, eyes like touch. His thighs parted, hips moving restlessly while he sucked.

Groaning, Dick shifted, and then stood. "Wanna suck you while you do Rock."

He groaned, ass tilting, offered over to his Pretty. Anything. Everything.

Dick made a soft noise and warm hands slid down his back, cupped his ass. Rock's cock jumped as he hummed, vibrating the shaft and making his Blue jerk a little. Dick lay down behind him, and wriggled in between his legs, head squished up against the bottom of the couch, fingers tugging at his jeans.

Pulling off Rock's cock, he looked down. "You comfortable down there? We can move."

Rock grunted. "Move?"

Dick laughed and stroked Rig's belly. "I'm good."

"Mmm. 'kay." He got back to what he was doing, sucking and licking his Blue into total insanity.

Judging by the noises Rock made, he was moving well toward his goal. Meanwhile, his Pretty had a goal of his own, Rig's jeans soon open and pushing down his hips. He wiggled to help the denim fall, then moaned as his cock bobbed, trying to get Dick's attention.

"Mmm... look at this. All for me." Dick's fingers slid over his prick, tracing the shape lightly.

His balls drew up tight, aching a little. Oh. Fine. Dick's tongue dragged up along his cock, from base to tip. Rock's prick muffled his cry and he pulled harder.

"Fuck!" Rock grunted, hips jerking, pushing that fat prick deep into his throat.

Making a happy noise, Dick took the head of his prick in, sucking on just the tip, tongue playing with his slit.

Oh, fuck.

Oh, fuck.

That felt.

He.

Damn.

Dick's fingers rolled his balls, the suction becoming stronger. Rock grunted, hands tugging in his hair as Dick made him forget what he was doing. He groaned in apology, trying to focus, taking Rock down to the root.

Hips jerking, Rock moaned, fingers tracing his lips where they were stretched around that amazing prick. He pulled harder, swallowing, taking each and every salty drop that slid down his throat. Dick seemed to know exactly what he was doing, his Pretty almost mimicking the way he was sucking, the speed and intensity of it. His hips moved restlessly, frantically. Rock was the only thing keeping him in rhythm. Dick's hands slid around to grab his ass, squeezing it, fingertips teasing his hole.

Rock's hold grew tighter, keeping him in place as that fine prick fucked his lips. Rig just shorted out, sucking and moving and caught between his men. Dick sucked harder, while Rock fucked harder, the two of them sending him to the moon. He buried his nose in Rock's pubes, pulling hard as he came, just pouring himself into Dick's mouth.

"Fuck!" Rock's fingers tugged at his hair, the fat prick in his mouth growing harder and then shooting spunk down the back of his throat. He drank Rock down, swallowing and humming, taking his Blue in. Dick's mouth gentled on his cock, hands sliding over his ass, his balls, the touches sure and easy.

His cheek rested on Rock's thigh, breath just coming in pants. So fucking good. Humming around his cock, Dick kept licking for a moment longer, before slowly pulling off him. His Pretty kissed the tip, hands massaging his ass, the backs of his thighs.

"You want me, Dick? I'm right here for you."

"Yeah, I want you. I want to fuck you." Dick's fingers slid over his hole.

"Yeah." He nuzzled Rock's balls, just loving on his Blue as he offered himself to Dick.

Rock dug around under the cushions and held up a battered tube of lube. "Come on. Wanna watch."

He crawled up on the edge of their big couch, draping himself over Rock so that Dick could settle behind him, saving both of their knees.

"Fuck, you two are still the sexiest thing I have ever seen. Ever." Dick's fingers rubbed his ass, prick hot against the back of his thigh.

He leaned in, lips soft and careful against Rock's nipple, sucking gently. "Mmm. Pretty."

"Fuck, Rig." Rock groaned, shifting a little.

Dick chuckled, and pushed a slick finger into his ass, nice and slowly. He pushed right back, riding the touch, moaning against Rock's chest.

"So sexy," murmured Dick, mouth landing on his spine, breath hot, tongue hotter.

"Mmm." What was he supposed to say to that? This was fucking perfect.

One finger became two, Dick taking his time, slowly spreading him open. "So hot inside. So tight even after all these years. I can't wait to be inside you." His whimper just slipped from his throat, those soft, perverse words making him fly. Rock rumbled, hand sliding over his scalp while Dick pushed a third finger in. "Yeah, so tight. I'm gonna fill you all the way up, Rig. Push in so deep."

"Pretty." Don't stop. Fuck. So hot.

"Just a few more seconds, Rig. And then I'm going to be inside you." Dick's fingers pushed hard, hitting his gland.

He cried out, surprised, his cock trying to fill back up. He looked at Rock, lips tugging at the man's nipple ring.

Those blue eyes shone down at him, Rock smiling. "You gonna get me up again?"

"I am." He was fucking good at that.

"Good man." Rock gave him a wink and Dick's fingers pegged his gland again.

"Oh." His thighs went tight, knees digging into the upholstery.

"You ready for my cock now?" Dick asked, mouth at the top of his spine, body hot against his back. "Ready for me to fill you?"

"Just fucking do it already," grumbled Rock.

"Romantic." He pinched Rock's hip.

Rock bucked and stuck his tongue out, Dick's laughter sweet against his spine. He surged up, caught Rock's tongue and sucked on it, pulling good and hard. Groaning, Rock's arms went around him, hands sliding to grab his ass cheeks and hold him open for that long, hot cock as Dick pushed inside.

That was fine.

Just fine.

Goddamn.

He pushed back, riding Dick easily.

"Oh, fuck, you feel so good around me, Rig. Like magic." Dick pushed a little harder, noises soft and sexy.

Magic. Him. Right. Oh... There. He stared into those blue eyes, just caught.

"So good..." muttered Dick,the sound fading away as his Pretty's thrusts grew stronger.

Rock kissed him harder, tongue tangling with his, just driving him out of his fucking mind. Then one of Rock's big hands wrapped around his cock, started tugging on him. Oh. Oh, fuck. He hadn't even remembered getting hard.

"Shit, I can feel that, Rock." Dick groaned, moving faster, Rock matching the rhythm, hand moving easily over his cock.

Rig's eyes dropped closed, breath huffing out of him, muscles shaking as he got closer. Dick's hands grabbed his hips, tugging him back into each thrust, his Pretty finding his gland and working it. "Oh. Oh, fuck. Y'all. Right there."

His words had Dick working him faster, harder, low noises becoming louder. He was fixin' to come again, just like he was twenty and a loose fucking cannon. Rock's thumb pressed against his slit as Dick pounded into him, both of them panting, groaning. Seed poured out of him, spreading over Rock's hand and belly, ass squeezing tight around Dick's prick.

"Rig!" Dick cried out, jerking into him a couple more times before an answering spray filled him deep.

He blinked a little, arms shaking as he lowered himself on Rock's chest. "Damn."

Dick pressed down against him, sandwiching him between his two favorite hard bodies.

"Mmm. Warm." He hummed, kissed Rock's shoulder.

"You know it."

Dick nodded his agreement. "And we'll have cinnamon buns and hot chocolate ready in about twenty minutes."

"Oh, yum." He approved.

"Yeah. And Rock 'n I can help with the rest of New Year's Eve dinner after."

"Works for me. It'll be simple." The black eyed peas were soaking for tomorrow. The ham was done. They'd mostly eat finger foods, feed each other. Goof off.

"Yeah, but simple is nice."

"Uh-huh. Nap now." Rock sounded half asleep already, hand petting him and then Dick.

"Mmhmm." His eyes dropped closed, dozing right off.

Chapter Sixty Three

Dick finished up the last of the dishes and checked his watch. Eleven thirty p.m. Perfect.

He could go wake Rig and Rock and the three of them could ring in the New Year together.

It had been a good day. Lots of food, lots of loving, a bit of fighting that had ended with the three of them making out on the couch and then eating cinnamon buns and drinking hot cocoa like they didn't' have a care in the world.

Dinner, hot tubbing, more making out.

It was no wonder that Rig had fallen asleep with his head in Rock's lap during the Die Hard DVD marathon.

Now the place was tidied up, the dishes done, and he had champagne chilling in the freezer, three glasses with strawberries at the bottom on a tray along with a plate of Rig's brownies, still a little bit warm.

Sweet and simple and the perfect celebration.

Grabbing the bottle of bubbly, he took up his tray and headed for the living room where Rock was snoring to beat the band as John McClane called out his last "yippy ky-ay, motherfuckers".

Dick set the stuff down on the coffee table and turned off the movie, making Rock snort and grumble, the bluest eyes on earth blinking open.

"Hey, I was watching that."

"You were not -- you were snoring," he accused.

"I was not. I was watching shit get blown up."

Dick just grinned and leaned in for a kiss, shutting Rock up the best way there was. Rock's arm landed on his shoulder, tugging him in closer, the kiss going wild and deep, tongue pushing into his lips.

Moaning, careful not to get a knee in Rig's face, he leaned against the couch, the kiss blowing his mind. Fuck, Rock could make him breathless and fucking needy in no time flat. Rig moaned and he felt a soft kiss to his belly.

Smiling into the kiss with Rock, he dropped his hand down to slide his fingers through Rig's curls. They were both warm and cozy and sexy and he couldn't think of a better way to spend the last minutes of the year. Rock obviously concurred, because the hand on his shoulder wrapped around his neck, tilting his head to take the kiss even deeper.

Rig wriggled up, pushing into the kiss, making it a three-way, hands sliding around his waist. He hummed happily, one hand on Rock's shoulder, the other finding Rig's back and stroking along his spine. It tasted good, all three of them together. It tasted right.

"Mmm. Hey. Hey, y'all." Rig was smiling, licking and lapping at their lips.

He settled in next to Rock, Rig soft of straddling the two of them, both him and Rock touching Rig, each other. It was nice and easy and felt really great.

"I brought champagne with strawberries and fresh brownies to toast the new year in."

"Perfect." Rig grinned and leaned in, taking another kiss.

Smiling himself, he licked at the inside of Rig's mouth, loving the taste of happiness shared between them. Rock's tongue traced their lips where they met, pushing into the kiss. Rig's groan tasted like fucking heaven. The kiss went on and on and eventually they had to break for breath, their noses rubbing together.

"You guys making any new year's resolutions this year?"

"I'm considering giving up surgery."

Both he and Rock stared at Rig, blinking at the man.

"What? I had enough this year, yeah? Enough to last my lifetime."

"I just didn't expect to hear you say something like that," Rock admitted.

"Well, I could resolve to work out more, I guess. Get all buff like my men."

"You could use a little meat on your bones," murmured Rock, rubbing Rig's belly. "Like you how you are, though."

Dick grinned, and nodded. "Yeah, you're pretty fucking awesome just as you are."

"Yeah, yeah, yeah." Rig's fingers slipped underneath the edge of his shirt, tracing his muscles.

"Mmm...yeah, just like you are." His belly muscles flexed under Rig's touch.

"What... what about you, Rock?"

Rock grunted. "I don't know. I suppose if Rig is giving up surgery, I could be less of an asshole about the vitamins."

Dick looked over at Rock, just as surprised. Rig hummed, nose sliding over Rock's cheek on the way to give the big guy a long, breathless kiss. Dick moaned a little as he watched. It never got old, watching them together, knowing he was a part of them.

Rig eased back, leaning into him harder. "What about you, Dick?"

"I'm making a resolution not to miss moments like this. We get so busy sometimes and I forget just how good I've got it. I'm not going to forget that this year."

"Sap," accused Rock, but the jibe had no heat behind it.

"No missing. No missing anything." Rig kissed him, and there was heat behind that.

He wrapped his arm around Rig, his other hand touching Rock.

No, he wasn't going to miss a second of this.

None of them were.

End